Indecent Encounter
By M.S. Parker

This book is a work of fiction. The names, characters, places and incidents are products of the writer's imagination or have been used fictitiously and are not to be construed as real. Any resemblance to persons, living or dead, actual events, locales or organizations is entirely coincidental.

Copyright © 2016 Belmonte Publishing

Published by Belmonte Publishing.

All rights reserved. Without limiting the rights under copyright reserved above, no part of this publication may be reproduced, stored in or introduced into a retrieval system, or transmitted, in any form, or by any means (electronic, mechanical, photocopying, recording, or otherwise) without the prior written permission of the copyright owner.

The author acknowledges the trademarked status and trademark owners of various products referenced in this work of fiction, which have been used without permission. The publication/use of these trademarks is not authorized, associated with, or sponsored by the trademark owners.

ISBN-13: 978-1530439959
ISBN-10: 1530439957

Table of Contents

Chapter 1 1
Chapter 2 7
Chapter 3 13
Chapter 4 17
Chapter 5 25
Chapter 6 29
Chapter 7 33
Chapter 8 41
Chapter 9 49
Chapter 10 61
Chapter 11 71
Chapter 12 77
Chapter 13 81
Chapter 14 91
Chapter 15 101
Chapter 16 105
Chapter 17 109
Chapter 18 115

Chapter 19...123
Chapter 20...127
Chapter 21...131
Chapter 22...141
Chapter 23...153
Chapter 24...163
Chapter 25...169
Chapter 26...181
Chapter 27...189
Chapter 28...199
Chapter 29...211
Chapter 30...217
Chapter 31...225
Chapter 32...231
Chapter 33...239
Chapter 34...249
Chapter 35...261
Chapter 36...269
Chapter 37...281
Chapter 38...291
Chapter 39...299
Chapter 40...305
Chapter 41...315
Chapter 42...323
Chapter 43...333

Chapter 44 341
Chapter 45 349
Acknowledgement 359
About The Author 360

Chapter 1

Chelsea

He was out on a date and there was nothing I could do about it. She was a friend of his from the office and he talked about her often. He said it was just dinner, but he put on a tie, and I smelled the aftershave he only wore on fancy occasions. After he left, whistling his way down the front steps of the house, I lay on the couch with a blanket over me like a shroud. I'd begged him not to go, I even cried, but that hadn't stopped him. I was only eight years old.

Karl, my younger brother, sat on the floor in front of the television with a plastic Frisbee precariously balanced on the edge of the coffee table. It was his latest obsession and when he had it, nothing else mattered, not even his sister playing dead on the couch. Oblivious to its instability, he spun it anyway and happily flapped his hands like a bird as it went around and around, faster as it started to fall. As soon as it clattered to the bare wood floor and was still, Karl picked it up and spun it again. The repetitive action soothed him, and he could spend hours doing nothing else. Later that week, he would go in for testing and be diagnosed with autism, but that night it was something I hardly noticed, much less worried about. Cindy, our babysitter, worried about it, but she'd learned not to take the Frisbee away from Karl if she had any hope for a quiet evening.

"Ah, I see the princess is laid to rest. How tragic was her passing!" Cindy mourned, as she came into the living room. Although I couldn't see it from under my death veil, I knew she carried a large bowl of popcorn. Cindy always made popcorn when she watched us. "If only she was still alive, she could make a proclamation about what show to watch."

I lay still and squeezed my eyes shut. All I wanted to do was cry, but I was starting to learn that tears were useless. My father had still gone out on his date, kissing me lightly on the head before he went out the door.

Earlier that morning I'd fallen off my scooter and scraped my knees; crying hadn't stopped the stinging pain then, either. All it'd done was give me an added headache. Crying hadn't helped my goldfish swim again, and crying hadn't brought back my mother.

The wonderful, comforting, smell of the popcorn wafted out to tickle my nose and coax me into a better mood. I peeled back enough blanket to peek my head out, and said, "How about the one where the mom is a secret agent and saves the world."

"Sure, sweetie, I'll see if it's on."

More of the blanket fell away as I sat up. Cindy grabbed the remote and sat down next to me. She scooped me up with one arm and hugged me tight. I squeezed my eyes shut and let myself snuggle in closer to her. I knew she was only there because my father paid her to watch us, but I lived for those hugs.

As Cindy flipped through the television channels, I pretended she was my mother like the ones in the television sitcoms, perfect and always caring. Before I could believe it was true, my mind fired up the growling sound of a motorcycle, and my eyes flew open.

When I was six, my mother left us. She sent Karl and me to bed one night, then jumped on the back of her new boyfriend's motorcycle and took off for New York. Just like that. As if she hadn't even given it a second thought. It was like a knife to my heart. The shattering memory roared through every happy daydream I'd had since.

"I don't think your show's on tonight. Wanna watch a movie instead?" Cindy asked.

She looked concerned when she noticed my hand tight on her arm. I pried my fingers loose and slid off the couch. I found what I was looking for hidden on the bottom of a small stack of our movies. I was sure Cindy hoped we could watch something else, anything else, but she was also the only person I knew who would sit through the entire movie for the eight-hundredth time.

"*Alice in Wonderland*," I said, as I held it up triumphantly.

I popped the tape into our VHS player, and the movie started where we'd left it the last time Cindy babysat. My father had gone out to a party that night, and I'd made myself throw up so he had to come home early.

"Don't you think this is a little scary?" Cindy asked.

My ponytail swished as I shook my head. I loved this part. Alice had to drink the potion on the table in order to shrink herself down and fit through the tiny door to Wonderland.

As I turned to launch myself back on the couch, Olympic swimmer style, the front door thundered with an urgent knocking. I froze. The knock was louder the second time, so loud I thought it might shake the foundation lose on the entire house. Karl slapped his spinning Frisbee flat on the ground and listened without moving. Cindy jumped to her feet, a finger on her lips telling me to stay quiet.

"Cindy?" A muffled male voice came through the thin wood of the front door. "Cindy, it's Deputy Benson. I'm here with Sharon Wilberger from Child Protective Services. You've got Chelsea and Karl with you. We need to talk to you."

"How'd you know I was here?" Cindy asked, leaning an ear closer to the door.

"Your mother's the hostess at the restaurant where Mr. Randall…er…their father was tonight. She's the one who told me you were babysitting."

I could hear the man's words as I hovered in Cindy's shadow, but my child's mind couldn't comprehend what was happening. All I knew was that a peculiar sick feeling began to creep into the pit of my stomach.

On tiptoes, Cindy stretched toward the peephole, keeping her body as far from the door as possible. "Show me your badge, Deputy."

"Yes, of course. Here it is. And this is Sharon Wilberger from Child Services."

"You already said that," Cindy said, opening the door to reveal a huge man and a smaller woman. Neither one of them was smiling. "What's going on?"

I wanted to run and hide. Something bad had happened. I glanced back at the television and saw Alice drink the potion. She grew smaller and smaller. Karl picked up his toy and spun it again, fixated on the motion, though I could see a deep frown on his face.

"Chelsea?" The lady asked as she stepped around Deputy Benson. Her voice was gentle and soft as she held out her hand and motioned for me to come close. "Come here, dear."

"There was a car accident. Your father died," the deputy blurted out. He stood just inside our living room door with a wide stance and one hand on his hip, his words coming out with a hint of a wheezing sound as if the massive stomach that protruded over his uniform belt caused him difficulty breathing.

"Jesus, Bob, that's not how you do it!" Sharon gasped.

I looked back at the television and saw Alice eat the cracker that made her grow. She was too large for the little door that led to Wonderland. Now she was crying giant tears, and I was confused about what was happening in my living room. Why did this strange lady want me to go with her? Why had the deputy said something so mean?

Cindy dropped to her knees next to me, her own sobs crashing against me as she wrapped me in another hug. On the television, Alice swam in an ocean of her own tears, but I was the one drowning as the shock of the Deputy's words turned to reality.

Chapter 2

Chelsea

"I still can't believe you're going to Holland. You know that's insane, right?" Clara asked as she flopped down on our sagging denim couch to watch me pack.

I looked around our small dorm room and tried not to think about how much I would miss it. Portland State University had snazzy, modern campus housing, but Clara and I liked our double studio in the historic Blackstone Residence Hall just fine. Parked between the couch, the over stuffed armchair, and wide window seat was a coffee table made from one of my foster brother's old surfboards. It wasn't a lot, but it was ours.

Clara and I had spent many nights on that couch talking about everything from my business classes, to which of the hunky, body-builder twins from the floor above we wanted to date. And sometimes we talked about our brothers.

"I didn't have the heart to tell Karl I'm going to Holland," I said. "I wanted him to focus on going to Rainbow Roads. I'm so glad you told me about it. Now I can get him out of that state run program and get him the help he needs."

Clara's older brother was autistic like Karl, and he was flourishing in the program. It helped him learn how to interact with society, no easy feat for the profoundly autistic, but it offered more hope than most people had given our brothers.

"I know it's expensive, Chelsea. Do you really think this job will pay enough?" Clara asked as she flung her legs over the fat arm of the overstuffed chair.

"Twenty thousand for the summer. Enough for now, anyway. My classes will be lighter next year, and I should be able to work enough to make the monthly tuition payments."

I bit the inside of my cheek. The truth was, I didn't really know how I would afford it. I had one more year of college, and then I could work full-time after graduation. I was the new college statistic. Unlike years ago when a student could make it through in four years, I was doing a fifth year, thanks to the budget cuts at state universities. I couldn't get the classes I needed in order to finish my degree in four years.

"Twenty thousand dollars in three months and you don't think this job is a little shady?"

"Geez. Stop being so suspicious," I said and rolled my eyes. I'd already explained it a million times. "I left the website up on my laptop. Check it out for yourself." I held up a t-shirt I was about to fold and waved it in the direction of the desk.

"I did and that's why I'm worried," Clara said. She got up from the chair and wound her long blonde hair into a tight bun before she sat down at my desk.

I frowned and started over, folding the shirt again. "I told you, it's simple. Homeowners looking for in-home help put up postings, and after you make a profile you can apply for jobs."

I longed to have the summer to myself to write – my secret passion – but I had to face reality. I had to earn money. I turned and held up a white summer sundress with a short flared skirt. There was no need for a bra since the top part of the dress was a bustier, with a built-in bra. When I'd tried it on in the fitting room at the store, I was pleasantly surprised at how fashionable I looked in comparison to my usual jeans and faded t-shirt. "What do you think? Should I pack this?"

"I get it," she said, ignoring my question. "My problem is, all the 'homeowners' seem to be old men and all the 'in-home help' are young hotties. What kind of duties do these guys expect?" Finally, she tore her eyes from the computer screen and turned to scrutinize the sundress in question. "And absolutely not. You won't need any clothes like that. You'll have a hard enough time keeping the old guys' hands off your perky breasts."

"Clara, you have the dirtiest mind! I'm going to spend the summer scrubbing toilets and dusting cabinets, probably laundry and grocery-shopping too. All the things bachelors don't like to do for themselves. Seriously, that's all it is," I said.

"Chelsea, you know I love you, but you're being so naive. Who pays a maid that much money? These are a bunch of sugar daddies looking for a little…hot ass," Clara said and turned back for one more look at the screen. "I mean, at least your guy is a silver fox. I hope this isn't a fake picture. What if he just found this picture on the Internet and used it because in real life he has no teeth…or a big hook nose…or no morals for doing such a thing?"

"Who cares what he looks like?" I asked. "The website verified his identity and the money is already in an escrow account. It's all legitimate, and all I need to do is housework for a whole summer and I'll get paid."

Clara left the computer screen and came over to dig through my clothing choices. "And what if he wants to give you *bonuses*?" she asked as she began tossing out my lacy, flirty underwear from the pile of clothes to be packed.

I laughed. "Ew. Don't be gross." I snatched a pair of white panties from her hand and stuffed it into the suitcase. "I think it'll be the other way around, and the bonus for him will be to simply see me cleaning his house every day because that's all it's going to be. No compromising my morals for money."

"Who's compromising your morals?" a voice from the doorway asked.

Clara and I jumped, and then laughed as Zach sauntered into the room ready to drive me to the airport. I saw Clara's cheeks turn pink as my foster brother flashed his bright white smile. She'd recently confessed to finding him attractive, and I had to admit, she wasn't wrong. Zach was tall and lean, his muscles built mainly from rock-climbing and surfing. His long, wavy brown hair, streaked by the sun, was pushed back carelessly. In all our years of living together with our adopted family, I didn't think I'd ever seen him use a comb.

When I'd been sixteen, the foster care program had sent me to live with the Carerra family. They were the type of foster family every child in the system dreamed of. At the peak of my teen years, there'd been fourteen children living under their roof, and every single one of us called them 'mom' and 'dad.' Zach had joined us about a month after I arrived, and we'd lived there together until we left for college.

He produced a fist full of tulips from behind his back and offered them to me with a flourish. I thanked him and handed them directly to Clara. I wished Zach would change his mind about me and notice the way my roommate looked at him. Somehow Zach had gotten the idea that we were the stars in a romantic comedy. Someday we'd overcome the awkwardness of our shared last name and foster sibling background and fall in love.

The night before I'd left for college we had 'the chat.' I'd told Zach that he was a great guy, but I was more interested in my college studies and preparing for a solid career than I was in romance. He told me he would wait until I was interested.

"Thanks for the flowers, Zach. Clara will have to enjoy them for me. I don't think they'll allow tulips on the plane."

He looked crushed for a heartbeat, and then brightened. "At least you'll see a bunch more once you get to Holland. They'll make you think of me."

I smiled and turned back to my packing. I really hoped my time away would make him reconsider his crush. I jammed the last few items I thought I needed into the old suitcase, which was just about everything but the kitchen sink. I was the type of traveler who never knew what mood might strike my fancy, so I had a tendency to over pack. But now, I couldn't get the zipper to close, so I had to reevaluate. When I opened the suitcase again, I discovered a wad of lacy underwear shoved into a corner.

"What's this, Clara? A minute ago you were throwing this kind of thing out of my packing pile." I held up a pink satin bra covered in sheer black lace.

"I changed my mind. Just in case you want to do a little side work while you're there," Clara said with a wink.

"I told you, it's not like that," I said, drawing out the last words, and wagging my head in her face, like, "duh."

"Yeah, Chelsea isn't like that."

I turned and looked at Zach. He was eyeing the pink bra with a strange mixture of longing and a frown on his face. I shoved the racy lingerie back into the suitcase and forced the zipper closed, hoping neither of them noticed, but they did. Clara laughed. Zach just glowered.

"Go, have fun, we'll be here when you get back," Clara said.

I clamped shut the lid of my laptop and shoved it inside my carry-on tote bag. Clara crushed me with a big hug as Zach grabbed my bulging suitcase. I followed Zach out the door with the picture of my new employer, the "silver fox," burning an image in my mind. As I crossed the threshold, a twinge of doubt stung my gut. Clara had better not be right about all of this.

Chapter 3

Alex

"Just resend the pages from the last three scenes."

I leaned back in the leather chair, crossing one leg over my knee. "We've got a team here ready to fix the ending. We'll let you know when we're ready to move forward," I said as I tapped a finger on the dark, mahogany wood of the conference table.

There was a pause on the other end of the line. I swore I heard the director grind his teeth before he snapped, "You expect us to reshoot the entire ending? That's months of scheduling, not to mention all the special effects editing. I have another commitment coming up."

"Sorry. You'll have to give it up. We can't have the franchise die because of one film."

I raised my eyebrows and turned my palms up to the team around the conference table. They all nodded in agreement as my father spoke up, "I'm sorry, Jim, but Alex is right. It's just the way it has to be."

"Henry, we go back a long way," Jim said to my father. "You know how it is. If I'm not available for the start of the other project, then I'm out."

"You heard him, Jim," I said. "It's just the way it has to be. The rocket has to miss, no matter how many storylines that unravels. Wait for our decisions, then get it done."

I leaned forward, and pressed the button that ended the call. The small team around the conference table let out a collective sigh, everyone that was except for my father. He stood, straightened his perpetually perfect tie, and buttoned his suit jacket. I knew he was tallying the costs in his head.

"The story needs integrity in order for it to have a sequel," I insisted. "The ending has to be changed, otherwise anything that comes after won't make a bit of sense."

"What doesn't make sense to me is all this fuss over the ending. Don't be so idealistic, Alex. The ending isn't what people come to see. Our viewers are in it for the experience, and *that's* what'll keep them coming back for more. I know what I'm talking about. In case you've forgotten, I've been making hits for years."

My father, Henry James Silverhaus, was the head of Silver House Productions, and he prided himself on his business acuity. The films he made were about the money. An emigrant from Holland with nothing in his pocket, my father had taught himself exactly what audiences wanted, and he delivered it without apology. Lack of content, character, or cohesiveness never bothered him, because Silver House Productions created blockbusters. Details didn't stack up next to the 'wow' factor he always put first. It was what made him such a wild success.

I stood as the other team members gathered up the various laptops, tablets and smartphones they used in business meetings. My father used nothing to take notes except an occasional small calendar/planner he kept in his inside suit jacket pocket. He believed in keeping his creative mind unencumbered with too much organization, lest it put a damper on his next big idea.

"Look, we can have the ending turned around within the week. If Jim can stick to a schedule, instead of his usual circus, the film can be done on time." I was adamant. I wasn't going to back down this time, like I always had before.

Staring at me with my crossed arms, my father didn't look

convinced. His eyes narrowed slightly and he lowered his voice a notch. "I backed you. See it through."

My arms dropped to my sides. There it was. He'd put me in my place just like he always did, but today I wasn't going to let it stop me. I had a project of my own. It burned with my own creative ideas, and gave me the gumption to be bold enough to ask, "Before you go, can we talk about the Indie project?"

The team had slipped out the conference room door and it was just the two of us left. Henry gave me a placating smile as if to avert any serious discussion of my ideas and steer the conversation back to his genius conceptions. "Did I tell you we secured April?"

"The blond from the sunken ship movies?"

"Exactly," he said, smoothing down his suit coat. "People recognize her and your little project needs all the help it can get guaranteeing an audience."

"She's a terrible actress," I protested, holding back from slamming my hands down on the conference table.

"She's hot right now."

"Oh, I get it. You think she's hot."

Henry laughed. "And what if I do? Just because you've been working too hard lately to notice the fairer sex doesn't mean all of us have to live like monks."

I furrowed my brows. *Damn him.* He was pushing all my buttons. "I'm not living like a monk."

"Come on, Alex," he scoffed, "you're obsessed with work. You need an outlet."

I'd predicted this conversation, and it was impossible not to smile to myself as I said, "Funny you should mention that. I went ahead and took a piece of advice I overheard from one of your other executive friends."

My father had pulled his small calendar from his pocket. He examined it as if there were something very important on its pages. With his eyes on the calendar and an air of unconcern in his voice he inquired, "What advice would that be?"

The intercom buzzed and my secretary's voice said, "Mr. Alex, your new employee has arrived at the airport. Your driver will take her to the house within the hour."

"Thank you," I said and gathered up my laptop.

"What new employee? What advice?" Henry asked again.

"You know, one of those websites that set up sugar daddies with a little summer treat. You'll be happy to know your profile picture landed me a really tasty new live-in maid."

Henry's mouth gaped open as I sauntered to the door, glad my back was to him so he couldn't see my wicked smile. I tossed over my shoulder, "Your friend, Albert, said he was really pleased with what the little college girl he got did for him until his wife came back from Europe…early."

Working for my father wasn't exactly a piece of cake. He always got what he wanted and flaunted what he had; everything from suits to cars to mansions and mistresses. Now, my little ruse would make it appear to everyone that he had to hire a woman. That he couldn't get one on his own. For once I had the upper hand, the last laugh.

I shut the door behind me before I actually laughed though. The look on his face had been a priceless mix of embarrassment and anger. I definitely felt better.

Chapter 4

Chelsea

A tall man in a dark chauffeur's uniform stood at the baggage claim area holding a sign that read 'Chelsea Carerra.' I rubbed my eyes. The flight had been long, more than eleven hours, and I was sure jet lag was getting the best of me. I'd just come through customs and my eyelids felt like bricks. If I didn't know better I would've thought someone snuck sticky glue in them while I'd slept on the plane.

"I'm Chelsea Carerra," I said to the man. He nodded and gave me a sharp dip of his matching uniform cap. "Do you need to see my passport or I.D.?"

"No, miss. Please, let me take your bag. This way," he replied politely, his English heavily accented. He picked up my suitcase and strode through the busy airport without looking back to see if I was following.

Once outside, I was taken aback. I hadn't been prepared for the busy metropolis that met my eyes. I shook my head. I'd researched Holland and the city of Rotterdam on the Internet, but somehow, I'd still expected nothing but tulip fields and windmills.

When the man in the dark uniform stopped in front of a sleek black BMW. I looked around in disbelief. "I'm sorry, there must be some mistake. I'm here to work for Alex Silverhaus."

"No mistake," the driver said. "Mr. Alex sent me to pick you up. I'm his chauffeur. He will be waiting at the house when we arrive."

He loaded my suitcase into the trunk and opened the back door for me. Still confused, I slipped into the luxurious leather interior and let him close the door behind me.

Once he was in the driver's seat, I said, "This really isn't necessary. I'm supposed to be working as a maid."

"I was given the understanding you will have a variety of duties." He flashed a quick look at me in the rear view mirror.

I wondered what he meant by that comment, but soon we started driving, and the sights of Rotterdam enveloped me. We passed countless museums housed in stunning architecture from the time when dukes and viscounts had lived as near the city center as they could. The streets were studded with monumental old buildings testifying to eight centuries of governance in this historic city. The fairytale-like splendor was romantic and mesmerizing. Nothing like back home.

The driver roared past the seat of the Netherlands' parliament without even a glance. "I'm sure you'll find Mr. Alex's estate to your liking."

"I'm sorry, did you say *estate*?" There had to be some sort of translation error.

"Yes. The manor and grounds were a gift from his father. Mr. Alex comes every summer."

As the tires ate up the road, the modern and medieval mix of The Hague flashed by the car windows. My mind reeled with cityscape impressions. Graceful skyscrapers glowed in the afternoon sun, rising above regal courtyards and statuesque fountains. On either side, people sat enjoying the sunshine in sidewalk cafes. It was all so picturesque. It made me want to join them, and take my time to sip coffee while taking everything in.

Instead, I relaxed back into the lush leather and took a moment to clear my senses. As tempting as it was to close my eyes, I knew that would only lead to sleep, and I didn't want to miss a moment of the scenery. Not to mention the impression it would make.

I felt the smooth acceleration of the car, and soon we sped into more open countryside. The driver told me it wouldn't be much farther, and I allowed myself to enjoy the view. Long driveways led to palatial mansions tucked in between ribbons of immaculate lawns that unfurled like endless green carpets to the edge of the road or to grand wrought iron gates.

Zach had been right. As soon as I saw tulip beds I thought of him. A smile crossed my face as I remembered his warm gesture with the flowers, but in the next moment it faded. Looking at these mansions made me realize how different I was from the people who owned them, but no matter how out of place I felt, I knew the distance from my life back home would do me good.

"Is Mr. Alex a good employer?" I asked, focusing on the job and the money I needed to earn to help my brother.

"Yes. Very fair. And your workload should be light. The house is run single-handedly by Mr. Jamison," the driver said.

"Mr. Jamison?" I asked as we turned down a long gravel driveway. That sounded so formal and stuffy. Would I be expected to bow or curtsey to the master of the house? A nervous flutter arose in my stomach as I wondered if I would be competent enough, have the correct manners and etiquette needed for such high standards. After all, I was just an American college student, and both of those labels equaled casual.

"The butler. There he is on the front steps."

The front steps–more like an entire stage, I thought as my vision went hazy. I finally remembered to breathe and sucked in giant gulps of air. It was hard to reconcile the elegant mansion with my place of employment.

Behind the sweeping expanse of the front steps rose a stone facade dominated by a turret. Bright windows framed with ivy stretched out on either side, and I quickly estimated a crazy number of rooms. The posting had said the owner was a bachelor, and yet the mansion was massive.

"No wonder the pay is so good," I muttered and threw

open the car door. That place was going to take forever to clean.

The butler waited, eyebrows raised, until I finally tore my eyes away from the fairytale-like setting and smiled at him. He scowled in return, and said in a clipped British accent, "Welcome, Miss Carerra. You may call me Jamison."

"Nice to meet you, Jamison. This place is amazing."

"Yes, this place is *amazing*," he sniffed. "You will be staying in the servants' quarters. I will take you there now."

He led me across the highly polished white marble floor of the two-story foyer and through a doorway half-hidden under the stairs. It opened into the servants' hallway, and from its narrow confines I only caught glimpses of the other grand rooms. I was anxious to see more of the house, but we veered into what looked like a large storage room. Floor to ceiling cupboards were built in to the walls in between hutches to store china.

"This is the butler's pantry," Jamison said. "I know Americans are not familiar with such things, but this is where we keep all the silver, china, serving dishes and the like. It's also where we stage the meals for the dining room."

"Got it." I gave a nod. "I'm a fast learner, Jamison, and I'm ready to work." I wanted to show him that I was eager to do a good job, but I quickly got the impression that I was being a little too exuberant.

He looked me up and down from above the bridge of his pinched nose. "I'm sure you are. However, I think you'll find your duties more menial than you were expecting."

"Oh, well, I was only expecting to be a maid."

"Good. The master of the house is a very busy man and does not associate with the help," Jamison said. He opened the bottom drawer and selected a white skirt and a white button down uniform blouse. "I assume you purchased the proper shoes as indicated on the paperwork you signed, white, similar to the ones worn by nurses and waitresses."

The reference to a waitress stung more than "nurse," but I brushed it off.

"Whatever enticements the website posting may have promised, they're not welcome here. The household staff wear uniforms," he said as he tossed me the uniform and added a bright white apron to go with it. "The apron is to be worn when you are preparing and serving food. We must make a good impression."

I checked the labels and saw he'd given me a tiny shirt and oversized skirt. I tucked the shirt under one arm and held the skirt up to my body. Geez, did my hips look that big? Not only would I have to cinch the waist with a safety pin, but also the length of the skirt made me look like some kind of a nun. Maybe that was the intention. I looked up from scrutinizing the skirt to say something, but before I could protest, Jamison had swept out of the room.

I followed him out of the narrow hallway and into an arched ceiling kitchen. It was like coming out of a crawl space and into a church. I gawked again. A center island as large as a king-sized bed gleamed under a domed skylight. The tiled backsplash formed a beautiful mosaic, and I smiled as I saw my first windmill.

An enormous restaurant-quality cooktop dominated the back wall and prompted me to ask Jamison, "Who else is part of the household staff?"

"I run Mr. Alex's household," he sniffed.

"All by yourself? This huge place? I bet you're glad he finally hired a maid."

Jamison said nothing and led me through the kitchen door to the outside of the house. We walked across a short cobblestone courtyard to the servants' quarters. It was more a cottage than an extension of the house, with clean, white stucco walls and exposed pine beams inside. A tiny staircase led from the front sitting room up to the kitchen. It was small, but after the whirlwind of the airport, The Hague, and the huge, unexpected mansion, I finally felt comfortable.

"I love it," I said.

Jamison frowned. "My rooms are through there. You will be staying in the attic room."

Delighted despite his obvious disapproval, I trotted up the narrow corner staircase. My room was tucked under the eaves with slanted ceilings. A soft white bed covered in a white eyelet duvet, a white wicker armchair, and a narrow writing desk were the only pieces of furniture in the dreamy attic room.

"You passed the built-in wardrobe and drawers on the stairs. You'll find a bathroom through there, however, the shower is broken. You'll have to use the shower in the pool house."

"Thank you, Jamison, this is perfect," I said with a smile.

He scowled. Before leaving, he said, "I just got word Mr. Alex expects to see you in half an hour. Be dressed in uniform."

I noticed my carry-on bag sitting on the bed, and I dove into its large pocket to find my laptop. My fingers itched to hit the keyboard and write down all the scenes and characters I'd experienced so far. I studied business for practicality sake, but creative writing was my passion. An ocean away from all my responsibilities, I gave myself the luxury to think about what I truly wanted to do. If time could stand still for a moment, I would sit at the table and start the screenplay that was burning inside me.

After I ceremoniously placed my laptop on the writing desk, I pulled out a notebook and my collection of various pens, fine point Sharpies and pencils that I used when creating characters and scenes. I used different colors of ink, or writing utensils for each purpose. It was just one of the things I did to put myself in the creative zone. Dumping my ideas onto paper first was part of my process. I'd let anything and everything come out. Then I'd transcribe the ideas onto the computer, giving the raw material more shape as I worked.

I placed the notebook to the side on the tiny writing desk and opened the laptop instead. When my social media page popped up, I realized I only had enough time to send a quick message to check on Karl before I had to be dressed in uniform. With long distance phone calls costing twenty cents a minute and Karl's slow communication skills, I'd promised to keep in touch through emails and private chat messages.

Chapter 5

Alex

"The new maid will stop by in a few minutes, sir," Jamison said.

"Sir?" I asked. "You're still not speaking to me?"

"I refreshed your drink. Will that be all, Mr. Alex?" Jamison sniffed.

"Come on, Jamison. I thought you'd like the help this summer." The sound of ice cubes tinkled against the fine crystal of my glass. It was absorbed by the walls' wooden panels, designed to give the room a warm coziness despite the large size. I raised a Scotch on the rocks to my lips in the hopes that the stiff drink would help me relax.

I'd been around women. Assloads of women. Hell, there was no shortage of eager, large-breasted and long-legged females waiting in the wings for me. Yet, somehow, the prospect of meeting Miss Carerra had me a little unsettled. I'd chosen her specifically because she hadn't been like the other women on the website. No scantily clad pictures, or blatantly revealing bikini shots on her profile, and she didn't yammer on about jet-setting, drinking Cristal, or dancing at the clubs all night. I'd combed over her profile with an eagle eye, but she hadn't once mention a burgeoning acting career or the desire to marry rich so she could dedicate her life to volunteer work and saving the hungry little children of the world.

No. Chelsea Carerra's profile seemed to miss the point of the website, and that intrigued me.

"You met her. What's she like?" I asked Jamison. I swiveled in my desk chair, and peered over the rim of my monogrammed rocks glass.

"American," he said.

I laughed. "So am I, but that never seemed to bother you before. Is she the gold-digging, morally-loose nightmare you'd imagined?"

Jamison pursed his lips and tidied up the chic whiskey decanter and tumbler set on the side shelf that doubled as a bar for my office. "Apologies, Mr. Alex, but I have dinner to prepare."

"Fine, Jamison. You're dismissed. I'll meet the maid alone. Gee, I hope she doesn't throw herself at me first thing. How will I ever control the urge to shower her with money if you're not here," I teased.

Jamison opened his mouth to retort, but was interrupted by a soft knock on the door. He answered it and stood with his hand on the doorknob as Miss Carerra entered.

She stepped over the threshold and her ocean blue eyes met mine. My jaw dropped to the floor, or so I imagined, and I forgot to introduce myself. Jamison cleared his throat and said, "Miss Carerra, this is Mr. Alex Silverhaus."

"Please, call me Chelsea," she said with a timid smile.

With a little devil on one shoulder, I raked her body with my eyes. Then something strange happened. It felt like a zing of electricity shot through me, igniting every single cell. She tucked a wayward strand of soft black hair behind one ear, exposing her smooth pale neck. That just made it worse. I imagined my lips tasting her skin while I breathed in her scent, and ran my fingers through that hair. I felt a tug between my legs. My father had been right. I'd been concentrating on work for way too long.

I rushed a gulp of Scotch to my lips, not knowing what else to do to give myself a moment to regroup. I dismissed Jamison, and from the corner of my eye, I caught his worried look, but I couldn't tear my eyes from Chelsea.

The white uniform shirt with the Silverhaus family crest emblazoned across her chest was much too small for her. The fabric strained, and the top buttons had to be left open, leaving the lapels to lay out wide, enticing me with more of the same smooth skin I'd lusted for a moment earlier. To make matters worse, as she came closer I saw the round swell of her breasts.

I stood and she approached with her hand outstretched. As we shook hands I assessed that she was small, about five-foot-four. She had a slender frame, but there was something delicious about the way she filled that too tight of a uniform top that sent my juices flowing and I wondered what it would be like to press her body against mine.

Her eyes flicked to our hands, still touching, and I quickly let go, not realizing I'd been holding the handshake. I smiled and tried to casually shove my hand in my pocket, but my jeans made it too tight. Instead, I crossed my arms and tucked my hands under my biceps. Best to keep my hands where they can't get me in trouble. After all, I'd just met the poor girl.

"I'm sorry, I'm confused," Chelsea said with a rosy blush. "You don't look anything like your profile picture."

I laughed. "Disappointed?"

Her deep blue eyes swept over me, and I felt the tug again. I wanted those eyes all over my body and those tantalizing lips…they were pale petals, the bottom one ripening as she chewed it nervously. *Damn*. If I didn't know better, I'd swear she was teasing me with it. How long would it take for my happy cock to find its way into that mouth? *Shit*. I needed to stop that train of thought right now.

"No. It's just I was expecting someone else," she said.

"Someone older? I didn't want to use my own photograph, because the website has a…well…a certain reputation," I said.

Chelsea's eyes widened. "I'm here to work, Mr. Alex. My intention is to earn my salary and nothing more."

She straightened and threw back her shoulders, standing tall. Her head only reached my chest, and she had to lift her chin to look me in the eyes.

My hands, having a mind of their own, sprang out from the safety of their crossed position and landed on her shoulders. "Don't worry. There are no hidden agendas here, Chelsea. As Jamison always points out, we Americans can be very direct."

My hands trailed down to the bare skin of her arms, and she felt like silk. I lingered all the way to her delicate hands and wondered again what it would be like to pull her close and kiss those sweet petal lips.

Chelsea tugged her hands free and stepped back so she didn't have to crane her neck as high. "Thank you for this opportunity, Mr. Alex. I plan to work hard and earn my pay."

Her words broke through the haze of my fantasy, and I asked, "You have big plans for the money?"

She frowned then said, "This job will help secure my future, ah, career."

Chelsea's blue eyes were clouded, and I instantly cooled. She wasn't the typical overt nymph featured on the website, however, her last remark set my suspicions on alert. I figured she knew my name was associated with the movie industry when she found me on the website. Career, eh? She was probably here on a roundabout path into Hollywood. My father wondered why I didn't date much anymore. Well, this was the exact reason why. I didn't like the feeling of being used.

"Nice to meet you, Miss Carerra. I hope you enjoy your summer job," I said and dismissed her.

Too bad, I thought as I watched her leave. She was the first woman to pique my interest in a long time.

Chapter 6

Chelsea

As I knelt over the swimming pool filter basket, I looked up and caught a glimpse of Jamison's face in the kitchen window. The stuffy, British butler almost looked happy. I shifted my attention back to the leaf basket and realized I had no choice but to use my bare hands to remove the decaying dead leaves and…oh, god…was that a dead frog in there? It was hard to tell for sure. Maybe it was just my mind playing tricks on me, but there was something green and slimy mixed with lots of brownish black gunk. I guessed Jamison didn't do pool duty. No wonder he looked so happy.

I closed my eyes and tried to get up the nerve to plunge my hand into the blockage. After a morning of scrubbing toilets and floors, I was happy to be outside. The summer sun beat on the back of my uniform shirt and it felt wonderful. It helped to avert the sting of the rough cement that grated against my bare knees as I worked. I hoped the fresh air would quell my gag-reflex as I dug into the slime-filled catch.

This was just one of the disgusting duties Jamison had for me on his list. It appeared he was determined to test my resolve. So I took a deep breath and dunked my hand in. As I pulled out the first fistful of greenish slime, I held my breath long enough to see stars.

"Rainbow Roads," I gasped as I flung the mass of

decomposed leaves into a bucket and my thoughts turned to Karl. I'd get my brother into that program if I had to spend the entire three months up to my elbow in slime.

I missed my brother. He had Zach coming to visit him while I was away. I knew that because Zach had been sending me emails *every day*. He'd even found an apartment near the program's campus. He said we could live there together, and assured me it was an easy commute to Portland State University. Each email ended with a flurry of romantic sentiments I couldn't bear to read. He just didn't get it. I didn't feel the same way, and I doubted I ever would.

I shook my head as I worked. Besides, romance was the last thing on my mind, had been the last thing for a while. I'd had a short fling once with a fellow Economics major, but between classes, work, and Karl, the relationship had fizzled. That had been a year ago and I hadn't bothered since. Zach thought that meant we were supposed to be together, but I didn't even want to think about love right now. How can a person be open to love when they had so many other responsibilities?

Like digging out slime. I looked down at the open hole looming in front of me and plunged my hand back in one last time.

I stifled a gag and tried to think about something else, like why had Alex Silverhaus used a false profile picture? It was kind of a dirty move, but as much as I wanted to be righteously angry at his deception I could understand why he did it. If he'd used his real photograph, the posting would have generated millions of responses. As it was, I wondered how he chose me out of the fifty-three other prospects.

Alex was six-foot-four and built like a Norse god, all golden hair that swept across his face with a few longer locks that fell in his eyes. I'd had to stifle the insane urge to lean forward and feel how smooth his hair was between my fingers. His white dress shirt hadn't concealed the tight flex of his muscles and his powerful shoulders. When I imagined what he'd look like shirtless, it got harder to breath. Alex's square jaw was clean-shaven and even from across the room I'd caught the cedar and cinnamon scent of his aftershave. It was intoxicating. The effect he'd had on me concerned me. We'd barely exchanged a few pleasant words of introduction, and I was already a hot mess.

I remembered the weight of his large hands as they'd rested on my shoulders. A wave of heat had rushed through my body and settled deep in my belly. The intense gaze that had gone with it had made my stomach twist. As his hands had trailed down my arms, the molten feeling had slipped lower, and just the memory was enough to make me wet again. I wanted to rub against that hard body, feel the contour of his muscles with my taut nipples. Reach around him and feel the solid slope of his back down to the slope of his tight ass. I'd pull his hips against mine and feel…

I shook my head. I could almost hear Clara's laughter. If she could see Mr. Alex Silverhaus, no doubt she'd already have eight plans for me to seduce him. The situation was perfect for an easy affair, and would be a good way to thwart Zach's affections. The more I thought about Alex, the more my pulse picked up. It could happen. Alone in a big mansion, except for one surly butler. I could easily come across Alex in one of the many rooms and simply shut the door behind me. My mind filled with naughty thoughts, and I didn't even care.

After all, I reasoned, that was the reputation of the website. Other women responded to postings fully expecting to get paid while having hot sex with their employers. Why couldn't I? Something about Holland, being out of my normal surroundings, gave me the liberty to admit my desires in a way I never would've done back home.

I imagined finding Alex in his office, and what would happen next. He'd call me over to where he sat behind his desk, and then pull me into his lap. Those big hands would cup my breasts, rubbing and squeezing until my nipples were hard. Then he'd swoop down and suck them through the thin material of my uniform shirt. He'd pick me up, his strong hands gripping my ass and pressing me against his hard cock.

Dear God, I thought with a hot blush. Holland or no Holland, it'd been way too long.

I laughed at myself and got back to clearing the leaf basket. Alex Silverhaus was undeniably attractive, but I had to shove that realization aside. He was my boss, and as much as I was already fantasizing about him, I knew they were just silly, sexy daydreams. I was here to work, and Alex had made it clear that he expected that, too.

Just as I pulled another huge clump of slime from the pool basket, I saw Alex striding out of the house. He smiled brightly and waved. I reached up to wave back and forgot the handful of rotted leaves. A dark brown sludge dripped onto my white uniform shirt. I was mortified.

Worse than the stain on my shirt, however, was the fact that Alex wasn't waving at me at all. A beautiful woman with thick, white, blond hair appeared outside the pool house and Alex strode up to her, whirled her into the air before giving her a tight hug.

She was exactly the perfect woman I pictured him dating. It made much more sense than a man like him waving at a slime-covered maid. I looked down and hoped he wouldn't notice how red my face was. I was here to work, nothing more.

Chapter 7

Alex

It seemed like I ran into Chelsea everywhere, despite living in a mansion. Jamison was torturing the poor girl with a variety of menial tasks, and I found her doing things like scrubbing grout with a toothbrush and sweeping out a crawl space under the stairs I'd never even known existed.

I stood in the foyer with a smile, ogling her like some kind of perv, unable to look away as she shimmied back and forth on her hands and knees. Jamison had finally given her a work uniform that fit, and the shorter skirt was deliciously teasing as the hem swayed with her movements just enough to give my cock some ideas, but not enough to get a peek at that gorgeous round ass. She had no idea what a fine young woman down on her hands and knees with her ass in the air did to me. I could easily have grabbed a handful of that long hair and take her from behind, her tits dipping into the water on the floor and peaking hard through that white top. *Fuck*. I needed to get my libido under control.

Or jack off more often.

"Funny, I never knew that was there," I said and Chelsea jumped. "Now I'm glad it is."

Still on her hands and knees she turned her head to speak, but continued wiping the floor with a wet sponge. "Sorry, Mr. Alex, I didn't know you were still home. I can work somewhere else if you prefer."

"No, don't mind me. I'm enjoying the view." I said, stroking a hand across my jaw. I should've been more of a gentleman and left the poor girl to work, but then again, in the words of the famous actress Lana Turner, "A gentleman is simply a patient wolf."

Chelsea popped up and tugged down the back of her skirt as she sat back on her heels. She threw me a shuttered look with her deep blue eyes, and went back to cleaning the last layer of dust from the crawl space. She was impossible to read. Most women I knew giggled and flirted, even when I didn't want them to. Chelsea just worked.

"If you're home today you probably don't want me making such a mess here." She sat up again, and tossed the sponge into the mop bucket. "I'll go finish airing out the upstairs closets."

"No, don't worry. I often work from home, and I know better than to interrupt Jamison's plans," I said.

She smiled at that and stood up. "A home office must be nice," She said, a little out of breath.

I watched her delicate hands as she wiped the last bit of wetness on the front of her uniform shirt. It was more of a nervous gesture as she'd already dried them on a small white towel lying next to the bucket, but it made her ample breasts move and jiggle just enough to afford me another delightful visual.

I bit my lip to hide my smile, and tried to engage in a serious conversation so as not to give away my lustful thoughts. "It is. Much better for getting things done than the chaos of the set or the mess of the production office."

Chelsea blinked a few times and asked, "The set?"

"Yeah," I said, "movie sets are a bitch. Creative people tend to make for crazy workdays. I swear, they act like once they get an idea, they have to take action or else it might fly right out of their head."

"Oh," she said and crinkled her nose. "I thought you were a hedge fund manager or something. I didn't know you worked in movies."

I caught myself smiling at her adorable expression of confusion before I realized what she'd said. "Ah, yeah. I run Silver House Productions. My father is Henry James Silverhaus. Maybe you've heard of him?"

Chelsea blinked again and shook her head. "Sorry, no. Though I think I've heard of Silver House Productions. Is your logo something like a very ornate lion holding a sword?"

"Yes, a crest with a lion on a shield and a crown on top. It's a symbol of The Netherlands also."

"But you're American," she said, crinkling her adorable nose again.

"My father is originally from here, but he made his fortune in America, and I was raised there," I explained. "You've seen a Silver House Production movie, right?"

"Of course. Hasn't everybody? I used to go to them all the time," she said and then quickly added, "but I mean, they're great. I love them."

Her cheeks turned a light pink, and I knew she was lying.

"Ha. No you don't," I said. "But that's okay. Everyone's entitled to an opinion. I won't hold it against you even though you're working for me." I gave a little laugh, and I could see her shoulders relax. "Anyway, they make more money than films with meaning…as my father always reminds me."

"Do you love them? The films you make?" Chelsea asked.

I scrubbed the back of my neck, struggling to find the right words. She had no idea what I did for a living until a minute ago, and now I felt like she saw right through me. Her eyes were on me, but the glow of a starlet's ambition that I was used to seeing was absent, and I had to admit, it caught me off guard. I wasn't used to having to work for women's attention or to prove myself to anybody. It was disconcerting, to say the least.

"Uh…well…I spend most of my time making my father's films," I said with a shrug. "They're big commercial successes."

"So you have one of your own you want to make?"

Again, I felt as if she was looking inside me, and it made my chest ache for a reason I couldn't quite figure out.

I cleared my throat and said, "Well, yes, actually. I'm just taking over our first independent film, and I think it really has a chance to be something special."

She smiled and nodded. "If a movie has heart, the audience will find it. Sometimes it's through word of mouth, like on my college campus. If we go to see a really great movie that speaks to us, we talk about it, tell all our friends to go see it, and you know, it's like a snowball rolling downhill, it builds and eventually everyone has to go see it and then, before you know it, it goes viral, and you have a huge success."

"You know, that's exactly how I should pitch it to my father…a long-term investment." The gears were spinning in my mind. She was right and I was just feeling the excitement again, talking about my project when I heard my cell phone ring.

I'd been expecting a call. I fished my phone out of my pocket and saw the name on the screen. I said, "Speak of the devil." I rolled my eyes. My father had the worst timing. I was just getting to know a little about Chelsea. "Sorry, I have to take this."

Chelsea smiled again, and turned back to her work under the stairs. I went across the foyer and cut through the library to my office.

"Good news, Henry, I know how to make the indie film a success," I said, and headed to my office.

"Alex, please, get your priorities straight. Have you looked over the specs for the alien series? I think the fourth script is our best bet. The climax should be a real seat-shaker," he said.

I closed my eyes and shook my head. My father based his script opinions on whether or not the action sequences would be loud enough to shake the movie theater seats. He was old-fashioned, egotistical and stubborn as a mule. He prided himself on pulling himself up by his bootstraps and making mountains of money in a cutthroat industry, but he had no affinity with the artistic side of films. To him, it was all about the profit margin, the cha-ching he heard in his head at the thought of each ticket sale.

"Look, I was thinking, if we make the indie film a priority it'll pay off in the long run."

Before I could finish, he cut me off with a gruff tone. "That's not what I called about. Your little joke with the mail-order whore paid off. All of my friends and work associates heard about it and I've been the butt of endless jokes. Everybody got a good laugh. Is this what having children brings?"

Henry was on the verge of ripping me a new one. He couldn't bear that his friends might view him as over-the-hill, no longer able to get a woman on his own. I'd walked as far as my office door, each step and each of his words, bringing more tension, until my hand curled into a fist.

"And now I hear she's still there. What on earth are you doing, Alex? Get rid of her."

I stopped short outside the threshold of the door and clamped my teeth, gritting them to keep from snapping back at him. I relaxed my jaw and finally spoke, "For your information, I chose the only woman on the website who didn't have ulterior motives, so Jamison put her to work. She's cleaning out the crawl space under the front stairs right now."

"Ridiculous. You're letting yourself be taken in by this girl? She's after your money or a part in a movie," he barked.

"You're wrong," I threw back.

"Fine, Alex. Find out the hard way. I don't have time for this right now."

I opened my mouth to defend myself, but the silence of the disconnected call said it all.

Fuck. The old bastard did it again. I wanted to throw my phone at the wall. Why did my father always have to do this? Or better yet, why did I always let him push my buttons?

I marched over to my desk chair and flopped into its soft, leather comfort. I raked a hand through my hair. I swore, my old man was going to drive me to drink. I blew out a breath and let my hand fall from my head onto the stack of movie scripts he'd been nagging me to review. I grabbed the script off the top of the pile, and rolled my chair back to settle in for some reading.

Alien movies. Yeah, like that's what the audiences really wanted. The brain-dead young people who made up the largest demographics of moviegoers weren't into aliens anymore. He was so out of touch. It was zombies, walking dead, ghouls with rotted flesh falling from their carcasses, *that's* what was popular now, not freaking aliens. And yet, the more I thought about the moviegoers, the more I began to think maybe Chelsea was right. Not all young people were artistically defunct. Maybe audiences were tired of meaningless fluff movies, and they wanted something with a message, something with a philosophy about life that they could talk about after the movie, not just treat a movie like a ride at an amusement park.

I thumbed through the pages, intending to read it, but my father's words still echoed in my head. What bothered me more than his dismissal of my passion project, the indie film, was his condemnation of Chelsea. That had been totally uncalled for. He hadn't met her. He didn't know anything about her. *Give the poor girl a break, for Christ's sake.*

Without reading a single word, I closed the script and tossed it on the desk. Leaning back, I closed my eyes, and steepled my fingers under my chin in thought.

Chelsea came into my mind in a flash. That soft black hair, that lithe body, the round softness I glimpsed through the gap in her shirt.

Oh, Jesus.

Knowing I wouldn't be able to focus until I cleared my head, I decided to go for a swim. The pool house was a quick walk across the courtyard from my office, and I slipped in the back door less than two minutes later.

The small building consisted of an airy sun porch, a changing room, and a large bathroom centered around an open shower with a rain shower head. I was just ducking into the bathroom to find the goggles I'd left there when I saw her.

A wave of white shampoo suds glided down her long, wet, hair. I followed the bubbles as they slipped down her back and onto her round ass. Chelsea lifted her arms to rinse her hair again, and the slight turn revealed one perfect breast, the nipple dark and tight under the showering water.

The thought of raking my teeth over that hard nub and pinching it between my fingers made my cock jerk in response. I wanted to run my fingers over her porcelain skin and push them into her tight slit. I'd bet she was wet from more than the shower.

Her waist was tiny, and curved out to her smooth round hips, just visible over the wall of the shower. I could almost feel my arms slipping around her, palming a handful of ass and pulling her onto my hard cock. I inched forward to see more before I stopped myself.

She was supposed to be a harmless joke on my father. I'd intended to meet her, pay her, and send her home. Once she was here, I'd thought she would be an easy fling, a quick summer affair, or at least a one-time stress relief, but seeing Chelsea that first time had changed everything.

Maybe I needed to make my intentions known. My blood roared at the idea of consummating whatever connection we had right now. I could easily slip into the shower and fuck that tight pussy. Except, I knew that if I did it, it'd all be over, and I didn't want that. I wanted more. I wanted to run into her around the house. I wanted to be surprised by what she said. I wanted those eyes on mine as we finally wrapped our bodies around each other and came together. Drawing out the sexual tension between us would make it even more deliciously hot, I decided.

I made it back out to the sun porch where I had to sit down and catch my breath. I felt like I'd been kicked in the chest. She was gorgeous, but I didn't understand the effect Chelsea had on me. It wasn't like anything I'd experienced before. All I knew was, joke or no joke, I wanted her to stay.

Chapter 8

Chelsea

Brushing my hair up into a ponytail made me wince. My arms ached, my back was stiff, and I could even feel the pull of tired muscles in my butt and thighs. Still, I was beginning to like my job, and I could even see the possibility of getting along with Jamison despite his stiff British exterior. I smiled at myself in the tiny mirror of my attic bathroom. I didn't even mind that the shower was broken up here, because I'd discovered that the pool house bathroom was like a private luxury spa with one of those fancy rain type shower-heads.

It was still early even by Jamison's standards, and I smiled again. I had been up for an hour, sitting at the small writing table in my room. It felt good to see the scribbled pages of my screenplay stacking up next to my laptop. I could've easily typed it all, but something about this room and being in a mansion that was built before modern technology was invented inspired me to write the old-fashioned way, with paper and pen. After talking with Alex about the independent film he wanted to make, my imagination felt like it'd been set on fire. I started writing in the evenings or whenever I could manage to catch a few spare moments while on a work break.

Not that Jamison gave me many breaks. The butler was still testing me, though he was running out of disgusting tasks. After I'd finished sweeping out the crawl space under the stairs, I'd organized everything in it and labeled all the boxes. Jamison had no choice but to tell me I'd done a good job.

I smiled and tapped my pen on my notepad. It appeared I was finally winning the stuffy old Brit's approval, and the work routine was falling into a rhythm. I imagined the rest of the summer would go even more smoothly. By the time I returned home, I'd have enough money for Karl, and at least a partially finished screenplay.

I closed the lid of my laptop and set my notebook with the finished pages on top. A sharp pang of guilt pulsed in my stomach. There on the desk was the pamphlet for Rainbow Roads. I should've emailed Zach that morning for an update. I hadn't been checking in on my brother as often as I'd planned, partially because of the complications with Zach, but also because, as each day passed, I found myself more and more absorbed into my job and my life here. I carefully tacked the pamphlet on the wall and reminded myself why I was here.

The thought of my brother in a program that would help him flourish was enough to banish all my aches and pains. I couldn't help but look around with a buoyant smile. The sweet attic room was light and airy, the perfect retreat from the not so bad job after all. Maybe Lady Luck was starting to smile on me for once.

I descended the tight staircase and discovered I had the small servants' cottage kitchen to myself. I savored my extra time, making my morning coffee with the extravagant espresso machine that ground imported Italian beans. Despite my menial position, all of my food and such was provided for, and Jamison didn't skimp on the staff provisions either. I felt like I was surrounded by all the small luxuries I could ever want.

When the buzzing of the coffee grinder was done, the morning settled back into blessed stillness. After the constant clatter of living in a college dormitory, the servants' cottage was a peaceful sanctuary. I sat back and listened to the ivy rustling outside the window. Although the fancy coffee machine made espresso and café Americano, this morning I'd pushed the button for a frothy cappuccino. I heard the sound of the steam foaming the milk. I stepped over to the machine near the kitchen window to watch as the milk-foam billowed up in the cup. This time I heard a new sound in the still morning. Somewhere outside, water was lapping.

I wondered about it as I waited for my special cappuccino cup to fill to the wide, round rim. It brewed fresh, and straight into my coffee cup. As soon as it finished, I grabbed the cup and headed outside. The sound of the water had reminded me that I could sit by the swimming pool. One of the wicker lounge chairs along the sun deck would be the perfect place to finish my heavenly morning.

I floated out the front door of the servants' cottage, and instead of heading across the courtyard to the main house, I turned right toward the pool. My coffee sloshed, and I lost a dollop of the lovely foam down the side of the cup as I ducked under the leafy, vine-covered pergola.

I blinked. *Did I just see a naked man?*

I peered through the morning glories and caught another glimpse of golden skin. It was Alex. He strode along the sun deck and dove into the pool in one graceful arc. His naked body sliced into the water with only a small splash, and I watched as his powerful arms cut strong, steady strokes. He swam back and forth with ease, and I was mesmerized. Unable to help myself, I crept along the length of the pergola scouting out a better vantage point. *Wow. Talk about "perks" of the job.*

The early morning sun was just touching the water when I found a gap between the morning glories and the climbing roses. Alex's body moved through the clear water with the clean strokes of a practiced swimmer, and now, I could see all of him.

Wide shoulders tapered to a tightly muscled back, and his even tan suggested this was a daily practice. If that was true, I was setting my alarm clock early every day. He kicked, barely causing a splash, and I traced the defined muscles of his calves up to his flexing thighs and to the round crest of his tanned ass. It jutted out of the water and rolled with each long stroke. Instinctively, my fingers flexed around my coffee cup as I imagined what it would feel like to have my hands on that firm set of muscles.

He flipped at the edge of the pool, his feet slapping the surface as he somersaulted under water and then pushed off the wall. It was all easy, the smoothness of his actions hinting at the power he left in check. *Hot damn!* The competitive swimmers I knew at college would look like sticks next to Alex. He was an oak, not just tall, but solid and strong.

My cappuccino was getting cold, but I was unable to tear my eyes away. I teased myself, wishing he'd turn over and practice the backstroke, when he stopped at the wall right in front of me and stood waist deep in the water. I froze. Could he see me through the climbing roses? He shook the water out of his gold-streaked hair and smiled to himself, clearly enjoying the morning exercise. He rolled his shoulders, shook out his arms, and stretched. I savored each reach and pull, as the morning sun dried his body and I practically whimpered. All I could think about was pressing my cheek against his solid chest and feeling its warmth.

My fantasy slipped into visions of me brushing my lips across every dip and curve of his sculpted abs, me naked in front of him in the water and…*oh, my*. He pulled himself up onto the pool deck, and I gasped out loud. I cringed and prayed he wouldn't come to investigate the sound. Alex cocked one eyebrow and stood facing the climbing roses. Thank god I was completely hidden in the shadows of the vines, because I couldn't breathe, much less move.

My eyes widened as I took another look. *Good Lord*.

He was huge.

I'd never seen a man so well-endowed. It hung thickly against his thigh, another muscle waiting to be flexed. If this was what he looked like just out of the cool water, my mind buzzed with the thought of Alex aroused. I remembered the first time I tried giving a hand job and glanced down at my hand gripping the coffee mug. I wondered if I could even close my fingers around him.

My stomach twisted at the thought of having Alex in my

hands and my gaze was pulled back to his magnificence. My boyfriend experience in college had consisted of a few fun encounters and two short-lived relationships. All I knew for certain was that they were all boys. Alex was all man.

I wanted him in a different way than the boys at college. There was no silly flutter of flirtation, or giggling rites of passage. More than curiosity or fun, my body ached to be touched by his, entered by him. I wanted his hands and mouth running over every inch of my body, leaving me burning. I imagined my fingers exploring his velvet soft skin as I lowered my head to taste him for the first time.

I felt a throb run through the center of me, and the deep desire to have him inside me was unlike anything I'd experienced. I realized I wanted him purely because he was a man and I was a woman. Primal. Primitive. And not as surprising as I'd have thought. Something about his presence, the mere look in his eyes and–well, *damn*, that sculpted body– pulled pure carnal lust from every cell in my body. It was metaphysical, beyond logic.

Suddenly, my clothes were too tight, too restrictive, I wanted to shed them and feel the cool morning air on my skin. I knew I could call out and Alex would find me hiding here. The thought electrified every nerve and I opened my mouth, but no sound came out.

Alex, not hearing anything else from my direction, shrugged his shoulders and snatched up a towel from a nearby lounge chair. I blinked as if coming out of a trance, and remembered those lounge chairs were the reason I'd come outside in the first place. I was going to drink my coffee in one of those chairs, except now my coffee was cold.

He wrapped the towel around his waist and turned away from me. I let out a breath. My shoulders relaxed. If just looking at him left me breathless, what else could he do to me? Right now, hiding in the flowers, I didn't want to know. I saw the statuesque blonde woman reappear from the pool house, waving to Alex with a big smile. Alex's head snapped up in a short nod, and he went around the pool to walk arm in arm with her toward the main house.

"Lucky," I muttered.

"Yes, lucky I found you, otherwise, you'd be late for work."

Oh crap. I jumped. Jamison stood behind me with his arms crossed. When I turned, I sloshed more of my drink. By now it looked as if a volcano of frothy milk had erupted over the sides, and foam dripped to the ground. "I was just enjoying the roses, the pergola, it's so…um…beautiful back here. I'm so lucky to work here."

"You enjoyed the view, eh?" the butler asked, and I saw him almost smile. He swallowed it quickly and cleared his throat. "The staff is only allowed to use the pool on special occasions."

"Except for the pool house shower, right? I was on my way back from the pool house," I stammered.

Jamison looked from my complete lack of towel or toiletries to the bright red blush I could feel on my cheeks. "Lying is much worse than spying. Mr. Alex does not approve of either."

"There's no reason to tell him, is there?" My voice came out with a bit of a squeak.

"Tell him what?" Jamison gave me a smug smile. "Pull yourself together, Chelsea. Breakfast will be served in the main house in ten minutes. You should've been inside helping me prepare it."

Jamison left me under the pergola licking the sweet foam off my hand where it'd run over my knuckles. I thought I heard him chuckle as he walked away. I tried to cool my flame-red cheeks, but it was no use. As I hurried off, another burst of laughter drifted out the open windows from the main house, and I considered hiding in my attic room for the rest of the day. Instead, I continued to the kitchen of the main house.

I was in such a rush to get inside and get to work that I plowed through the kitchen door, my sticky coffee cup leading the way. Once inside, I stopped short. I looked up to see Alex standing behind the immense kitchen island, his powerful bare chest still sprinkled with water droplets.

"Good morning, Chelsea," he chirped with a mischievous smile.

From where I stood, the countertop was just the right height to conceal his towel and it looked as if he were completely naked. My cheeks turned red again. I figured I'd better stop staring and get to work, or I might not have a job at all, just a flight back to the States.

"Nothing you haven't seen before, right?" he asked with a laugh and sauntered off through the kitchen, munching a strawberry he'd picked off a plate of fruit for the table.

I was pretty sure he enjoyed watching me fluster. He must've hung back, waited in the kitchen until I came in, purposely, to tease me. He could have waited in the breakfast nook at the table. *Sneaky bastard*.

I shoved my hair behind my ear, rinsed the coffee off my hands at the sink and set to work preparing the plates for breakfast as Jamison had instructed me. I hoped Alex would put on some clothes before sitting down to breakfast, or else I wouldn't be able to focus on my work duties. A part of me wondered if his type flirted with the help just to break up the monotony of the day.

I picked up the serving platter of cut fruit and pushed my back against the door to the breakfast nook to open it, prepared to see more bare skin at the table. I supposed the rich could be as eccentric as they wanted.

Chapter 9

Chelsea

"The least you could do is wear something nice for dinner," Jamison snapped.

I glanced down at the white skirt and apron of my work uniform and then back up at the butler. I was confused. "I wasn't sure if I was done working for the night or not."

"Yes, I told you this morning we would be done with work at six o'clock, and, contrary to what Americans believe, it is a polite custom to change for dinner. Please tell me you at least brought a sundress or a skirt," Jamison said.

I'd been here for two weeks now, and things were fine, but today was my birthday and I was fighting off the blues as it was, missing Clara and Zach on my special day. I had to bite my lip to keep from snapping back at the old staunch as I spun on my heels to go back upstairs to my attic room. Grumbling to myself, I dug through the wardrobe cupboard on the stairs, finally pulling out my white bustier sundress with the thin spaghetti straps and a short, flared skirt. I'd show him. *I do have something nice to wear for dinner, you old...*

Luckily, I'd packed one nice dress on the off chance that I might have a reason to wear it sometime this summer despite my plans to spend all of my time working. I liked the way the built-in bra accentuated my figure. The fabric was white eyelet embroidered with a few delicate blue flowers across the top, and it was one of my favorites. I took down my ponytail and brushed out my hair so it fell over my bare shoulders, so long that it practically hid the thin straps of the dress. At least I'd feel good about how I looked on my birthday.

In the daytime for work, I went light on the make-up, but since I'd essentially been ordered to dress better for dinner, I decided to use this opportunity to show Jamison just how well this *American* could clean up. I tossed my hair out of my face and leaned into the mirror.

And maybe after dinner I'd run into Alex and give him a taste of his own medicine. I'd pretty much decided Alex Silverhaus was a player, a handsome, wealthy show-off who just liked to mess with people. Well, two could play his little game. I could be a tease, and then wave bye-bye just like he'd done earlier. I was almost positive he knew I'd been watching him in the pool, and he'd pulled the whole kitchen stunt intentionally. Sure, I'd gone all weak in the knees earlier when I'd seen his gorgeous body turning somersaults in the sparkling, blue pool, with water glistening on his golden skin...*dammit*...I needed to stop thinking about it. He was an arrogant ass.

I chose a sultry smoky eye shadow, and just the right amount of mascara to frame my eyes. A quick brush across my lips with a light pink gloss, and I was ready. I winked at myself in the mirror.

I cleaned up pretty damn good if I didn't say so myself, and besides, it was my birthday. I was allowed to have a little fun.

Dinner in the main kitchen was a regular thing. Usually, Jamison and I sat on the high stools at the kitchen island and tried to pretend that we were both civilized people. Tonight was different. When I entered the kitchen I was surprised to see the breakfast nook table set for three.

As I assessed the food preparations to see if I could help, I heard a voice come from the doorway.

"I hope you don't mind if I crash your party," Alex said.

He looked deliciously handsome in a crisp white, collared shirt, rolled up at the sleeves. The shirt contrasted perfectly with his tanned skin and golden hair. The glint of his expensive watch reflected off the kitchen lights when he pushed back a stray lock of hair that had fallen out of place.

Jamison sniffed, and said, "Mr. Alex is welcome whenever he wants."

Out of habit, and mostly to avoid fawning over Alex, I went to the stove to help Jamison serve, but he swatted my hand away. He turned back to his work with barely a nod, but I knew it was his way of saying he approved of my dinner clothes. When I turned around, Alex was right in front of me opening a bottle of champagne, and there was nothing for me to do but stand between the two of them, feeling awkward. Jamison with his back to me, and Alex close enough in front that I had to slightly tip my head to look at him.

Well this was uncomfortable.

"My, my. You look very lovely, Chelsea." Alex's eyes raked me up and down with approval.

I wished I were immune to his charm, but it felt like his hands had followed his gaze, and I couldn't stop my smile. I pulled my long hair to cover the bare skin at the top of my dress, and tried not to let him see how much he affected me. Now I knew the meaning of "undressing me with his eyes."

"What do you say we have a little of the bubbly?" Alex gave me one of his heart-stopping smiles as he twisted the cork, and his eyes blazed into mine, daring me not to look away. The bottle exploded with the signature *pop*, but his eyes remained on me. Something inside my stomach twisted, and a jolt of electricity went zinging through my veins. He cocked an eyebrow as if to say, "Was it as good for you as it was for me?"

His charm was working, and it *had* gotten to me, though I didn't want it to. Damn, I was so easy. I'd been gone the minute I'd laid eyes on him. I spun around and tried to sound casual as I talked to Jamison's back. "Dinner smells wonderful, Jamison." I rattled on, running sentences together out of sheer nerves. "What is it? Salmon? It looks like salmon. I love salmon." I craned my neck and peered over his shoulder hoping the heat I felt was from the stove and not Alex.

"I know," the butler said, "I also made those sweet potato French fries you raved about."

"Oh, that was really kind of you. Thank you." I calmed myself, and then turned back to find Alex handing me a glass of champagne.

"Is work going well?" Alex asked.

I just stared at him with my mouth open and blinked. What was going on? Why was he here, making small talk with me and drinking champagne while Jamison made my favorite foods?

Alex looked past me at Jamison and laughed. "I told you we should've gotten balloons."

He picked up the bottle of champagne from the counter, and followed Jamison to the table in the breakfast nook while I stood there, gaping like an idiot.

"And I suppose I should've invited the neighbors and arranged for a circle of chairs in the living room too," Jamison huffed as he pulled out a chair for me.

"A circle of chairs?" I asked as I sat down. "What are you talking about?

"Your birthday, of course. You really are oblivious, Chelsea," Jamison said, pushing in my chair.

"He means 'happy birthday,' " Alex said, sitting down across from me.

"This is all for my birthday?" I asked, surprised. "You shouldn't have. But how did you know?"

"It was on your paperwork when you applied for the job," Jamison chimed in.

"Oh, of course," I said. "But usually I don't make a big

deal out of it."

"I'm assuming that means 'thank you?'" Jamison asked Alex, eyebrow raised.

"I'm sorry, Jamison. Thank you! It's just been a long time since I had a birthday party," I said.

I felt a little more at ease now with the distance of a table between us, but Alex had chosen the seat directly across from me. That meant he had the perfect vantage point to punish me with his outrageously good looks. Maybe I could master the art of undressing him with my eyes too, but then again, I didn't need to have much imagination to do that. I'd ready seen his incredibly hot body in all its naked glory. And that was the problem. The image of him standing by the pool easily popped into my head no matter how many times I tried to push it away. Even the thought of it now turned my cheeks pink.

Alex stared at me curiously. I touched my fingertips to my cheek, hoping my face wasn't flushed enough to give away my thoughts.

"You probably don't know how birthdays are celebrated in Holland, do you?" Alex turned to Jamison and said, "Jamison, we should've celebrated the way my father used to, in the tradition of Holland, and invite the family and neighbors over for coffee and cake."

"Please, I'd rather not." Jamison addressed me and explained, "In Holland the tradition is to put a circle of chairs in the living room, in which no one is allowed to leave their seat to mingle while they have coffee and cake. Quite boring, I'm afraid." He gave me a placating smile. "I spared you the drudgery. It's the old way. I prefer my way."

"Oh, I see. That doesn't sound so bad, the cake and coffee part."

"Well, I made lemon meringue pie instead of a cake. I hope that will be acceptable," Jamison said. He served all three of us before taking his own seat.

"We didn't know your favorite dessert so Jamison made mine," Alex said. "Now that I think about it, this is exactly what most of my childhood birthday parties were like."

Jamison raised his champagne flute and said, "Happy birthday, Chelsea. I'm sorry, but I don't sing."

I laughed and raised my glass. "Thank you. I sing. I just don't sing well. Believe me, you wouldn't want to hear it. It sounds something like a dying cat. But this is wonderful."

I sipped the dry champagne, and the bubbles tickled my nose. I wasn't an expert on wines or champagne, but I could tell this was an expensive one. As I looked around the table at my two bosses, I realized for the first time that Alex treated Jamison more like family than a butler.

Just as I was thinking this, Alex leaned in and elbowed the older British man in the ribs. "Remember when David refused to eat the salmon because he could see all those green bones?"

The usual sternness faded from Jamison's face when he turned to Alex, and something like fondness filled his eyes. "I kept trying to tell him it was just rosemary, but he wouldn't listen."

"Henry made him sit at the table until he ate it all. He was still sitting there when I woke up the next morning," Alex said.

"Alex was always an early riser, but you discovered that for yourself the other day, didn't you, Chelsea?" Jamison asked as if holding a smile in check.

My breath seemed to solidify in my throat and I nearly choked. "Um…" was all I could get out so I took another sip of champagne to cover and just nodded. A knowing glance bounced between the two men, and I could tell by Alex's wicked smile that Jamison had told him all about my spying, although I had a suspicion that Alex had already known. Shit.

"So, Chelsea, are you an early riser too?" Alex asked. His glance slid to my bustier top and his mouth softened.

"Yes, ever since I started college," I said, hoping to turn the subject to something less embarrassing. "Seems like I always got stuck with the early classes."

"What about swimming?" Alex said.

Damn him.

His steady gaze bore into me and something intense flared

between us. *Oh crap.* I knew I shouldn't be feeling this way about Alex. He was my boss. This kind of attraction could be dangerous, and the worse thing was, each time it happened, the pull became a little stronger. I knew he wouldn't stop. I was sure he charmed the pants off every woman he met, and I was no different, even if I was the hired help. I supposed I should've been grateful that he saw me the same as every other woman he flirted with. I was nothing special.

I pushed the thought from my mind and answered his question, "I love swimming. Actually, I competed on my high school team."

"Ah, finally a worthy opponent," Alex said.

I thought I detected a flicker in his blue eyes. My pulse quickened at an implication I was sure I hadn't imagined.

"Perhaps you should join me," he said. "I'll let you train a bit before I challenge you to a race."

The thought of joining him for a morning swim stopped my fork halfway to my mouth. I forced myself to take the bite and chew slowly, trying to keep the images of his glorious wet body out of my head.

"I didn't bring a swimsuit." I put my head down and chewed vigorously, glancing up only to see Jamison roll his eyes and then scowl at Alex. A warning of some kind?

Apparently, it had no affect on Alex. "No problem, just swim naked like me."

I took another sip of champagne, but the bubbly did little to cool my burning cheeks. Alex's light blue eyes were tracing their way down the spaghetti straps of my dress and across the creamy rise of my breasts. Suddenly, I regretted wearing such a seductive outfit. I'd planned on teasing him, and then brushing him off, but he was so compelling and his magnetism so potent, my plan was blowing up in my face. I kept reminding myself not to fall for it. He was a flirt, and I was here. That was all.

"I think you'd find it refreshing, and a little company would help kick start my workout. You know, get the blood pumping," Alex said.

Much to my relief, a timer dinged in the kitchen. I didn't need swimming to get my blood pumping; Alex was doing a fine job of that all by himself.

Jamison popped up from his chair and said, "Excuse me. I don't want to burn the meringue."

Once Jamison was out of the room, Alex said, "Yum."

I watched, mesmerized, as he licked his lips. It was a purely sensual gesture, and I knew it had nothing to do with the pie. I imagined skipping dessert and letting him taste me instead. My nipples hardened at the thought, standing out against the thin fabric of my sundress. When Alex's eyes grazed them, I felt the same sizzle of electricity that'd pulsed through me before.

If he could do that with only a look...

I pushed my sweaty palms down the skirt of my dress under the table and swallowed. "I…I wouldn't want to intrude on your mornings," I stammered, desperately thinking of something to say to change the subject. "Doesn't your…ah…friend like to swim?"

"My friend?" Alex asked, puzzlement written on his face.

"Yes," I said. "I've seen her before. The tall woman with the blonde hair?"

Jamison returned to the table and gave Alex a look I couldn't read. Suddenly, the hot, flirtatious mood disappeared, and Alex's expression turned sullen. He leaned back in his chair in silence and pushed a green bean around on his plate with the fork.

"She's very beautiful," I ventured.

"Yes," Alex said, his eyes still trained on the plate. "Carrie is very beautiful."

Jamison caught my eye and gave a small, negative shake of his head. Disapproval rolled off of him in waves.

"I'm sorry," I said to Alex, leaning forward. "I didn't mean to pry."

"I understand," he answered, "I'm just not used to other people being here watching me. It's not easy to get used to."

That was an odd remark for someone who lives with a

servant. First, he swam in the nude as if he didn't mind who saw him, and then all the blatant flirting. But he wasn't used to people watching, and I wasn't supposed to comment on anything he didn't initiate? I didn't get it. What did he want from me?

"Chelsea is not practiced in the art of service. She'll get used to working more and observing less," Jamison said with a sniff.

"I wasn't spying on you," I said, mortified. Technically, I had been, but that hadn't been my intention. "I'm sorry if you feel I've invaded your privacy."

My stomach turned cold as Alex nodded. Our dinner fell silent. I didn't understand what had happened, but I knew one thing for sure. For all his money and privilege, Alex seemed rather lonely. And the thought bothered me more than I cared to admit.

I glanced at the elegant silverware sitting on the table and imagined how many childhood birthdays must've been celebrated with Jamison at this very kitchen table. Had it just been the two of them when Alex made his birthday wishes? Yet Alex had said he grew up in America. It was clear that Jamison was more than a butler to Alex, no matter where Alex had grown up. He treated Alex like a son more than an employer. I'd only been working a few weeks here in Holland, but I was definitely still the outsider. *Dammit!* Not only was I failing to be professional in my work, but also I wasn't even being a gracious guest in their home.

Jamison finally broke the silence. "Since you didn't notice this celebration dinner was for your birthday, I'm assuming you missed the wrapped present in the middle of the table."

"Is it a swimsuit?" I asked, hoping to lighten the mood.

Alex laughed, and I felt the ice in my stomach melt. He said, "No way. If you want to swim with me, you've got to be brave. Au natural."

"Sounds chilly. Doesn't that shrink your, ah, muscles?" I asked, surprised at my own bold flirting. Maybe it was just the relief of having sidestepped the awkwardness, but it worked.

He perked up, and his face brightened.

"Not me. I'm used to it. But don't take my word for it. I'm officially issuing you a challenge, birthday girl. Meet me in the pool tomorrow morning." His eyes flashed electric blue as he once again swept his gaze over my body.

I heated at the look, but stuck out my chin and said, "Why? I'm not so old that I have to exercise everyday to keep in shape."

"I have no problem with your shape," he said as his eyes blazed brighter. "An open invitation to the pool whenever you want. How's that for a birthday present? The only catch is you have to swim with me tomorrow morning. You know, so I can familiarize you with the pool rules and everything."

Oh crap.

Jamison sighed dramatically, as if he was used to Alex's antics, and said, "I think she may like the wrapped present better."

I shook off the warmth of Alex's flirting and turned to Jamison. "A special birthday dinner was enough of a treat for me. You really didn't have to, Jamison. Thank you."

I reached for the present and tugged loose the bright silver bow. The heavy wrapping paper was bright pink and shiny, and I carefully slit open the pieces of tape. Inside was a long cardboard box. I was surprised to see that it was postmarked from Oregon. I looked up with a questioning eye.

"Jamison special-ordered it," Alex said, "He thought you might like a little bit of home."

I opened up the cardboard box, and found a plastic-sealed package inside. A live Redwood seedling from Oregon was wrapped in damp moss. I carefully took the baby tree from the box and reverently held it up for everyone to see.

"Oh, Jamison, this is the sweetest present anyone has ever given me," I breathed. A lump formed in my throat.

"There's a pot with dirt waiting for you near the servants' quarters," Jamison said, his words brisk, but I knew now just how much of that was posturing.

Blinking back tears, I said, "Thank you so much."

"Maybe you can set it under the pergola, near the climbing roses?" Alex teased, completely subverting the moment.

"I think I want it on the windowsill in my room," I said, grateful for Alex not making me even more emotional. "If that's okay?"

"Of course. Happy birthday, Chelsea," Jamison said as he stood up and cleared our dinner dishes. I moved to help him, but he told me there was no need to work on my birthday. Alex smiled at me and carried the empty champagne bottle and glasses into the kitchen following behind Jamison.

Again, at a loss for what to do, I gathered up the box with my Redwood seedling, and headed to the kitchen door to look for the pot to plant it in. I found it near the front steps of the servants' cottage and sat down next to it, taking care not to dirty my nice sundress.

"He's gruff, but he's the most thoughtful man I know." My head popped up at the sound of Alex's voice. I set the box to the side as he dropped down to sit beside me.

I turned to my right and gave him a sidelong glance. "Really? I thought he didn't like me," I said and raised a brow.

I'd meant for my remark to be funny and sarcastic, but suddenly all I could think about was how close Alex was to me. Our shoulders were nearly touching. I tried to glance away, but all I wanted to do was get lost in his beautiful blue eyes. Trying to keep my composure I snapped my attention back to the seedling laying on top of the box near my feet.

"And this…" I motioned with my hand. "This is great. Honestly, it's the best present I've ever gotten."

"Really, Miss Oregon?" His voice had changed. It was low and velvety, luring me in.

Dammit, I was caving, submitting to that deliciously warm feeling tingling inside of me. Even his voice had a magical effect on me. Helpless to his charm, I turned to meet his gaze again.

"Yes," I whispered, not sure if we were still talking about gifts and seedlings...or if he was asking some sort of permission.

Alex ducked his head and pressed his lips gently to mine. I gasped in surprise, inhaling the cedar-cinnamon scent of his aftershave. He held the soft kiss until I relaxed, his lips still and warm against mine. When I pressed back, he slipped one hand through my hair to the back of my neck. He tipped my head back, and touched his tongue to mine for one deep, lingering taste as I completely melted under his touch.

"I'm glad you're here. Happy birthday, Chelsea," Alex whispered against my lips.

Well, damn. My whole body was electrified, and a low level buzzing made my brain feel all fuzzy. After the kiss faded I still felt the energy vibrating in me, and then, just like that, he stood, gave me a soft smile and turned to leave.

I sat all dreamy-eyed on the steps, blissfully lost in the intensity of that kiss, watching Alex as he walked back to the main house. Right before he disappeared through the kitchen door, he paused, pushed a hand through his golden hair and gave a tug on his stylish shirt.

Then it hit me, full force.

Alex Silverhaus had just kissed me. A gorgeously handsome man who I work for had kissed me, and to make things even more complicated, I'd promised to meet him for a naked swim in the morning. One simple birthday kiss, and he'd knocked me to my knees. I'd never felt anything like this before, and I was at a complete loss in how to deal with it. I squeezed my eyes shut with a grimace as I plopped my chin into my hands.

I was so screwed.

Chapter 10

Alex

When I stepped outside, the pre-dawn sky was gray, with only the barest hint of sunrise. The air was cool, but I knew the water would be warm. The quick punch of anticipation in my stomach reminded me of the challenge I'd issued to Chelsea the night before.

I licked my lips where I could still feel the soft give of her kiss. She'd tasted sweet, and I wanted more. I had to admit, I'd been surprised when she'd walked into the kitchen dressed for dinner. I'd already thought she was beautiful, but, *wow,* that dress had really set off her eyes…and her tits. I couldn't help but notice. They were pushed up, crowning out of the top of it, just begging me to touch them. I groaned. She was killing me, but I still hoped she'd be waiting for me by the pool.

I tossed the towel over my shoulder and purposefully walked the long way around the pool, past the pergola in case she was hiding there again. I paused in front of it, but it was dark and quiet, just the rustling of the leaves up the latticework. I found myself looking for her ocean blue eyes among the morning glories, and I shook my head. She wasn't coming. I didn't know why I'd thought anything different.

I turned and looked at the pool. Empty. The entire place had a deserted feel to it, and I couldn't deny the relief that followed my disappointment. Although there were plenty of perfectly fuckable women here in Rotenberg, my appetite for fast, hard sex had taken a dive since I'd come to Holland. It'd been a while since I'd gotten off, so just the thought of Chelsea, naked in the pool, was enough to make me rock hard despite the morning breeze. I didn't even want to imagine what would happen if I saw her.

I dove into the cool water and started swimming. I pushed hard through the first laps, the image of Chelsea in her sexy sundress vivid in my mind. The lace neckline dipped between those perfect breasts, ripe peaches I wanted so badly to taste. I imagined that she wore nothing underneath the light dress, and that if I'd swept my hands up her long legs, she'd be wet and submissive to my explorations. I liked women like that, willing to please.

After that sweet, soft kiss on the steps I'd wanted to give her a birthday night she would never forget. I'd wanted to spread her legs open and taste the sweet juices flowing from her. I imagined her thighs brushing my cheeks as I drove her to orgasm, feeling her pulsing climax on my tongue and lips.

I turned another lap in the pool with Chelsea still on my mind, wondering if I was going to need to go up to the master suite and take a long cold shower with a hard cock in my hand. Chelsea aroused me almost as much as she confused me.

I'd never met a woman who didn't want a spectacular event made out of her birthday. One past girlfriend had declared that the entire week should be dedicated to her birthday. I'd spent obscene amounts of money to make each day's surprise more elaborate than the previous, and she'd still seemed disappointed when it hadn't ended with a ring. But Chelsea hadn't even realized one simple dinner was meant for her. She would've missed the surprise completely if Jamison hadn't pointed it out.

No sooner had I thought this, than I popped my head above the water for a breath and I saw her stretched out in one of the lounge chairs. I finished the lap to give myself a moment to collect myself, and then swam over to the wall in front of her.

"I'm surprised to see you here," I said as I propped my arms on the edge of the pool.

"I told you I was an early riser." She gripped her coffee with both hands, and held it to her inviting lips as if she were using the thick porcelain mug to hide her shyness. "Besides this is a nice place to drink my coffee."

"The water will wake you up quicker than coffee," I told her. "Come on in, I'm just getting started."

I noticed her cheeks turn a bright red, as she glanced back at the servants' quarters. Her reaction made me wonder how much experience she'd had with men. Her innocence was an appealing thought. I could open her world to all kinds of new sexual experiences if she'd give me the chance. I caught her eyes again, but she shied away from the look and sipped her coffee instead.

Bedroom eyes. On anyone else those would be called bedroom eyes. On Chelsea, however, they were more. They were deep oceans I suspected could shipwreck lovesick boys. She was one of those innocent heartbreakers who probably didn't even realize her own power. One look was enough to elicit fantasies of her draped in nothing but her silky black hair.

Oh what I'd love to do to that delicious, lithe body. It cried out to be touched and caressed…and fucked. *Oh, damn. I needed to stop.* If she knew what I was thinking, she'd probably slap me. Yet, she was completely unaware of her effects, and sat with her shoulders hunched down as if she didn't really want to be noticed. I didn't understand it.

"Are you telling me you just came here to watch?" I asked. "I've heard some people really like that." I wiggled my brows just to razz her more than I already had.

She scowled and said, "You gave me an open invitation to use the pool."

"That's right, you just have to swim with me this morning and then the pool's all yours whenever you want it."

She pursed her lips, inhaled a breath, and deliberately set her coffee mug on the small table next to her lounger. As she moved, my eye caught a slight tremble in her hand. She stood up from the lounge chair and shimmied out of her jeans. It was a good thing I was leaning against the side of the pool. The sight of her long legs stepping out of her jeans was enough to arouse me again.

She left on a pair of black, cotton panties that hugged the curve of her ass, dipping low on her hips and a t-shirt with the faded logo of a popular band across her breasts. I liked it. My breath caught in my throat at the thought of how the t-shirt would look wet. My cock twitched. The fabric was thin. And white. *Damn.* It twitched again. *Jesus, woman, you're killing me.*

I watched in awe as Chelsea took a few quick steps toward the edge and dove over me into the pool. A few seconds later, she popped up out of the water and slicked back her hair.

I stared at her, and she grinned. "What? You never said I *had* to be naked."

Damn. She was right.

"Fair enough, but all of that clothing is just going to create drag. You'll never beat me in a race that way," I said.

To my disappointment, she stayed far enough under the water that I couldn't get a good look at the wet t-shirt. It billowed out with the buoyancy of the water instead of clinging to her skin. *Damn you, buoyancy.*

The disappointment must've been readable on my face, because she laughed and took off across the pool with long, sure strokes. I caught up with her and tugged on her foot but she kicked free and kept swimming. After a few more laps, I grabbed her foot again and worked my hands up her calf. When my fingers brushed the back of her thigh she stopped in the middle of the pool.

"You warmed up?" I asked her as I reluctantly released her leg.

"Warmed up for what?" she asked, treading water and eyeing me suspiciously.

"Enough to race." *And enough to fuck you until you scream, sweetheart,* I added in my head. She had no clue how hard she was making this for me. I blew a breath into the surface of the water and said, "I'm looking for a challenge, and from what I've seen so far, you're the perfect one."

"Fine," she said. "Are you better at sprints or distance swimming?"

"Distance."

"Then I'll race you one length of the pool," Chelsea declared.

There was a wicked flash in her eyes and I wondered if she was flirting with me, or if it was something else.

We slowly swam to the far wall. I stood up in the shallow water and watched her eyes darken as they scanned my chest. I forced my breathing to stay even as her look trailed lower into the water. I usually enjoyed when women looked at my body, but with Chelsea, something about it was different.

I forced myself to focus. "Alright. Here's the deal. I'll agree to your sprint if you grant me one condition."

She dragged her eyes back up to mine, and I could see that she was enjoying the view. It confirmed my suspicion that little Miss Oregon had a wild side she was suppressing, and I found the thought to be a huge turn on. I really wanted to be the person who drew that out of her.

"What condition is that?" she asked warily as she straightened.

Fuck me.

Well that's what I wanted to say because we were in the shallow end of the pool now, so as she stood, the wet t-shirt clung to the ripe curves of her breasts. No bra. At last I could see her nipples, hardened against the cloying fabric. I imagined peeling it off and up over her head, watching her tits pull up with the wet shirt and then drop with a soft bounce. Her hands would come down on top of my shoulders, and I could catch her hard against me, feeling those nipples press into my chest.

"My condition is that you take off that shirt." I had to clear my throat before I could speak again without my voice cracking. "It'll just create drag. I don't want you to accuse me of cheating when I win."

A glint flashed through her eyes again, and I smiled. There was a bright, competitive streak in Chelsea and I liked that, though I wasn't sure what exactly she was competing for at the moment.

"I get to say 'go'?" she asked.

I nodded and held my breath as Chelsea reached for the hem of the shirt just under the surface of the water. She peeled it up slowly and revealed the flat expanse between her panties and her belly button. She rolled her hips back and forth as she worked the shirt up higher, and then paused as the first soft flesh of her breasts was exposed.

I stood rooted to the spot. My jaw relaxed and my lips parted instinctively. I was held in place, mesmerized by the pert curves of the undersides of her breasts, just waiting for what would happen next. Then in the next delicious moment, I felt a hot surge race to my groin. I was standing with my hands on my hips and the water nearly up to my waist, and just as I wondered if a full erection would break the surface of the water, Chelsea ripped the shirt off in one quick move.

"Go!"

She was a quarter of the way across the pool before I realized what had happened. I dove into the water and chased after her. The thunder of our kicking and the splash of our strong strokes echoed across the courtyard as I tried to catch her.

Chelsea was fast, and she hit the wall one stroke ahead of me. I saw the quick flash of her smile, and then she dove straight down into the deep end of the pool. I took a deep breath and went after her. I opened my eyes to watch Chelsea in front of me. She was beautiful and sexy, a nymph, free and easy in the water. I could see her near-naked body, long arms and legs swirling in suspended animation under the water, moving with a natural grace, her silky black hair floating and trailing behind as she swam.

I held my breath as long as I could, then I had to surface. Chelsea rose right in front of me and smiled as she blinked away the water.

"Couldn't catch me? That's too bad," she said.

I reached out to encircle her slick body, but she slipped away with a bubbling laugh. The victory of the race had made her bold. She flipped on her back, flashing her breasts at me, and held one small foot up in the air in front of me, taunting. I dodged after it and pretended to miss until she was almost to the other wall.

When she realized I had her cornered, she stopped with a delighted squeal. Her only defense now was to splash me, so she slapped the water hard and sent waves of white water over me.

"Ha! Think you can stop me with that? Child's play!"

With a wicked grin, I held my breath and pushed forward, her weak splashes not enough to keep me back.

"No fair!" She shrieked with laughter as she dodged my first attempt to grab her. "What're you going to do now?"

"I'm going to toss you back into the deep end, nymph!"

Chelsea dodged again, no longer shy about her nakedness as she splashed me, and looked for an opening to dive past me. Each time she tried, I blocked her, and she shied away before we touched. Her feigned attempts to escape became less energetic as I moved closer, and to my delight, she willingly backed into the corner of the pool.

Her ocean blue eyes met mine, and I was sure the bolt of lightning I felt ran through us both. She tried one last feint, and then laughed as it failed. In an instant, my arm snaked around her waist. I pulled her slick body against mine. She wrapped one arm around my shoulder as the other tried to push me away. I knew the push was in jest. I knew what she wanted, because I wanted it too.

My mouth found hers, and as our wet mouths glided into a deep kiss, her other hand slipped away, and I felt the softness of her naked breasts pressing against my hard chest. A gasp parted her lips, and I slipped my tongue in to taste her.

Her hand reached up, her fingers tangling into the back of my hair. She wanted this as much as I did. I released my arms so I could drag my fingers down the soft, wet skin of her back.

God, she felt good in my arms, better than I'd imagined. My hands caught her tight waist, and I pulled her up and out of the water, closer to me, closer to the kiss. Chelsea arched against me, her nipples hard little points. I plunged farther into the kiss, catching her soft moans deep in my mouth.

I dropped one hand back into the water, tracing my fingers over the soaked fabric of her cotton panties, teasing a finger under the top edge. She moaned again as I cupped her ass. With one hitch, I brought her leg up around my waist. The other followed, and she wrapped her legs around me as I pressed her against the pool wall.

My cock nudged the soft mound between her legs, and I groaned when the cotton panties stopped my exploration. She flexed her thighs and pulled me tighter against her, rocking her hips against me and dragging another deep groan from my throat.

Above my own growling arousal, I heard Chelsea whisper wetly in my ear. My brain failed to process what she'd said.

"What?" I asked against her lips.

"Rip them," she said.

Sweet Chelsea, so shy and tempting. Now, desperate with desire and begging for my cock. It sent my blood rushing and my head spinning. I could have her here. I could fuck her right now, right here in the pool. But I didn't have a condom and…*shit*.

I couldn't even think straight. I just wanted to fuck her. My entire body was primed to drive deep inside her. I hooked one finger in the thin material, and it took every ounce of restraint I had not to tear it right then. I could have plunged my throbbing cock into her right there, against the side of the pool, but something in me said this wasn't what I really wanted. I didn't want a quick, "wham, bam thank you ma'am" in the pool. I wanted to spread her out on my king-sized bed, relish the sight of her entire body as it ached for me. I wanted to take my time to explore every inch of her.

"No," I managed to get out. "Come with me."

I slipped her back down to her feet and led her to the

concrete steps of the pool. We were just heading across the pool deck when I heard the kitchen door slam. *Fuck. Who the hell…?*

The steps that led to my private balcony and the wide expanse of my master suite were just a few feet away, but I dropped Chelsea's hand and quickly grabbed a towel for her instead. Any other woman, I might not have cared, but I didn't like the thought of anyone else seeing her half-naked.

Jamison arrived at the pool three seconds later and cleared his throat before he spoke, "Mr. Alex? You told me to remind you of your morning conference call."

I snatched up another towel and quickly covered my raging erection. It wasn't the first time Jamison had caught me with a naked woman, but that didn't make it any less awkward. I had to take a deep breath and compose myself before answering.

"Yes, Jamison. Thank you. I'll be right there." He turned and walked away as I called out to him, "Has anyone told you, you have bad timing?" But my words fell on deaf ears. He just continued walking.

I shook my head. Chelsea was probably horrified that Jamison may have seen her, but when I turned back to apologize, she was ducking into the pool house. She probably had to shower and get ready for work. I thought about following her, but I knew the moment had passed.

At least for now, I promised myself, and then I headed to up the master suite for another one-handed, cold shower.

Chapter 11

Chelsea

It was easy to go without seeing Jamison all day. I was too mortified by what he might have seen by the pool to face him. And I didn't know which was worse, him seeing me almost naked, or the fact that I'd been practically fucking my boss in the pool. At least, I'd wanted to. Oh, God, how I wanted him. And if we hadn't been interrupted…

It occurred to me that Jamison could've been watching out the kitchen window. With a guy as good-looking and open with nudity as Alex, I imagined this kind of thing had happened before. Maybe even with the tall blonde woman no one wanted to talk about. Jamison had probably known what was happening. His seemingly inconvenient interruption suddenly seemed very convenient now.

The more time passed, the more awkward I realized it would become when I finally saw him. As I debated back and forth between seeking him out to act like nothing had happened, I mopped the kitchen floor with a vengeance. There was also the bigger issue to mull over, and I hoped the physical exertion would keep my mind off the encounter with Alex.

Encounter. *Whew!* Even that word was completely wrong for what had happened in the pool that morning.

When I woke up this morning, Alex was the first thing on my mind. My message inbox on my computer was still full of birthday wishes I hadn't responded to, but all I could think about was his heart-stopping kiss. I reasoned with myself that it was just a polite kiss, a gesture for my birthday, because he thought I was homesick. Although from my end it felt nothing like a "polite" kiss.

Then my mind turned to the challenge Alex had issued. Just the memory of it was enough to send a shot of steel through my spine. I'd never able been to turn down a challenge, the outcome of fighting for attention in a house full of children. Plus, Alex had dangled an open invitation to the pool as the prize. The thought of having access to the cool inviting water whenever I wanted over the entire summer had been too much to pass up.

I paused in my floor mopping to reflect on everything that had happened. I'd gone out to the pool with the innocent intention of winning the use of the pool. At least that's what I was trying to convince myself I'd done.

I shook my head and started mopping again. Who was I fooling? Even I didn't believe that was the truth. The temptation of seeing Alex naked again, the thrill of being invited into the pool where his golden body glistened in the water. *That's* what had drawn me there.

At the time, I thought maybe the water would cool the temptation. I was sure my skinny body had no great allure for a man like him, but I was wrong. Gloriously, electrifyingly wrong. But then I heard Clara's warnings about naivety ringing in my head. Logically, I knew she was right. What guy wouldn't go for a naked girl begging him to rip off her panties and take her? I'd been practically throwing myself at him. Okay, there was no doubt about it. I'd literally thrown myself at him.

The kitchen floor gleamed, and I stopped to fan my hot cheeks. It didn't matter anymore whether Clara was right or not about this job. I'd known what direction things would go the minute I'd gone into that pool. If anything else was going to happen with Alex, or even if it was just a one-time fun game we had, I still had to face the uptight butler for the rest of the summer. I propped the broom against the counter and went in search of Jamison.

Despite the size of the mansion, Jamison was easy to find because he loved his routines. I knew I'd find him dusting the north-facing rooms on the main floor. I walked along and found him in the small parlor dusting the chandelier. The staid butler was wearing his headphones and singing along to a catchy pop song. Not what I'd imagined.

I paused for a second before I entered the room and called out, "Jamison?"

He didn't hear me and burst into the chorus for a second time. To avoid the fallout of his vigorous dusting I stepped around the stool.

"Mother of mercy!" he shrieked and almost toppled off the high stool. "Chelsea?"

"I'm so sorry, Jamison! I didn't mean to frighten you," I said with a giggle. "Or make you shriek like a little girl. I guess I should spend more time at the pool and work on my tan."

I was testing out his reaction with my remark about the pool, watching his face for any sign of disapproval or annoyance. I didn't want to lose my job after all, but he ignored it and stepped down from the stool.

"I'm not used to people sneaking around."

"Um…you sneak up on me all the time," I reminded him.

"So this was retaliation?" he asked, carefully brushing unseen dust off the front of his impeccable white shirt.

"No, not at all," I said. I considered another approach. "I…um, finished mopping faster than I thought and wondered if you could use any help?"

I hadn't really come in here to help him. I came to talk. I'd already made reference to the pool, but he wasn't biting. Either he didn't want to talk about it, or he was willing to let the matter slide. But it mattered to me, and although part of me wanted to drop the subject of the pool incident, I also knew work would be very awkward if we didn't get things out in the open.

Jamison thrust the duster into my hand and pointed to the wide mahogany buffet on the sidewall. I went to it and carefully shifted the delicate vases as he'd instructed me.

"Have you really kept the house up all by yourself until now?" I asked as I dusted.

Jamison unrolled his sleeves and buttoned his cuffs before he said, "As I told you before, we have a cleaning service that comes in twice a week, so really keeping the house up myself is not that difficult."

I decided to try to ease into the conversation with a little casual chitchat while I worked. "How long have you worked for Alex?" I asked. "I mean, Mr. Alex?"

Jamison accepted my casual reference with a dramatic sigh and said, "I've known *Alex* since he was in training pants."

"So it's probably a little awkward when you see him…um…invite women for a swim?" It was painful to ask, but I wanted to clear the air.

The butler laughed with a sharp guffaw that surprised us both. "I'm the one who taught Alex to swim. I'm also the one who taught him how to talk to women, not that I was much of a teacher. Women aren't really my cup of tea."

I smiled; glad for the little bit of personal information Jamison was willing to share. He couldn't be too angry with me if he was willing to talk like this. "What about Alex's mother? What was she like?"

"Absent," Jamison said. "She divorced Henry early on, the settlement was bitter, and Alex was in school by the time it was finally finished. Good-riddance, though I sometimes wonder if that's why Alex is so determined to get his way."

"Well, he certainly doesn't come off as pushy or anything like that," I said. "He knows how to be charming. I bet he gets that from you."

Jamison gave a small smile. "I wish I was able to teach him something more substantial. Without a mother, and a father who cared more about work than his son, the poor boy really had no one else around to look up to except me."

"Well, his charm and determination are exactly what he needs to succeed in the movie business," I said. "I mean, from what I understand, producing movies is mostly about diplomacy and keeping everyone happy enough to get the work done."

I knew I'd lost Jamison when he straightened up and pulled on his dark suit coat. "If you're interested in what Mr. Alex does for a living, I suggest you discuss it with him."

Crap. I stopped dusting and turned to him. "No, please, Jamison. Don't get me wrong. I'm not trying to break into Hollywood or anything." I turned a palm up to the air. "I mean, look at me, do I look like an aspiring actress to you?"

He tilted his head, regarding me and asked, "You don't think you could be an actress?"

"Last time I checked, Hollywood still loved the busty blonds, and I'm a skinny girl with black hair." I turned back to my dusting. "Oh, plus the whole lack of talent thing," I joked.

Jamison sniffed. "You're not like the others. I'll give you that."

"And I'll take that as a compliment," I said with a nod and a smile over my shoulder.

Jamison smiled again. "You know, I ran across a stack of papers someone left in the servants' kitchen the other morning. The makings of a screenplay. Seems to me there was talent in that writing."

I stopped my dusting and faced him again. At first I felt a little embarrassed that he'd read my writing. I wasn't sure I was ready for anyone to read it, especially since I was so new at it, but in the next second I was excited. He'd said I was talented.

"Really?" I raised my brows and tried not to sound to eager. "Do you really think so?" I left my duster on the shelf and took a step toward him, wringing my hands. "It's just for fun. I'm not planning on showing it to anyone. *Ever*," I said.

"Well," Jamison said, gathering up his headphones as he

prepared to leave, "keep working on it. I'd be willing to run across it again one of these days when you have more written."

"You would? You really would?"

In my excitement, I'd inched forward again, apparently too close for his comfort zone, and just when the conversation seemed to be getting friendly he changed the subject. "After you're done in here, I expect you to help prepare lunch."

"Of course," I said, and backed away. "And, Jamison?"

"Yes?"

"Thank you. I mean it. That was the best birthday I ever had." I returned to my duster and the mahogany buffet. As he crossed the threshold of the door, he glanced back. I swore I saw his gray eyes soften, and I felt like he was on my side now.

As I moved to dust the last shelf of the buffet I wasn't any surer about Jamison than before. He definitely was a man of mystery, always hiding behind his stately, British veneer. Yet, at times, like with my birthday dinner, he let his true personality shine through. I smiled and placed the last piece of china in its place on the shelf. He seemed to be okay with seeing me with Alex at the pool. Of course, Jamison was just going to gloss over it, because apparently, it happened quite often.

I bit my lip and walked out of the room with a frown. I hoped that I'd made a new friend today and that Jamison wasn't just pretending to like me, biding his time just to use my indiscretion against me later. Clara was right about one thing. I was pretty naive at times.

Chapter 12

Alex

"I'm not some lap dog that's going to roll over every time you call," I growled into the phone.

Earlier this morning, the regular team conference call had gone well, but my father had purposely withheld the sticky details from the rest of the team. It was his usual tactic to wait for the team call to end, and then drop the bomb on me in a private call.

"We need a big name, and the love interest is the best part," he said.

"That's exactly why I'm not casting April as the love interest," I said from between gritted teeth. "She's a walking disaster…too much of a drama queen. That role carries the weight of the backstory and she'll never be able to pull it off. I don't want her in that part, or any part."

"I told you, the finances are in place. But if I tell them you want to go ahead without a big name actress in the starring role, then you might as well start collecting aluminum cans on the side of the road," Henry said. "Don't be foolish, Alex. You pick a strong director, and we'll make it all work in editing."

My fist clenched tighter around the phone. I wasn't going to let him win this argument. Again. "I have a strong director, one who'd rather go back to making car commercials than work with a diva like April."

"She's not that bad, Alex. She just needs a little extra attention."

"Jesus, Henry. Is that your answer to everything?" I snapped. "Because my idea of 'extra attention' doesn't involve bending a woman over a chair in the casting room. So I don't care what you're willing to give her. If we want this film to have any integrity at all, then we have to find a real actress for that part, not a bottle-blonde starlet who loves tabloid headlines more than real work."

My dad's voice went up a notch. "Honestly, Alex, sometimes I think you want my company to fail. My own son. Are you trying to ruin Silver House?"

"That's a little dramatic, don't you think?" I asked, though I knew from many similar conversations with him those comments were nothing but manipulation tactics.

"Well that's what this decision could mean to the company. How do you think Silver House Productions would fare if this little passion project of yours turned out to be a flop?"

"Just fine," I said, trying to keep my voice even. "With all the royalties from the alien movies, plus the slasher franchise, Silver House will make money well into the next millennium, no matter what happens to my 'little passion project.'"

"That's it, then?" my father asked. "You're willing to just sit back and coast on all my hard work?"

I could feel my pulse quickening. My father was going to raise my blood pressure at too young of an age. He was always like this. Pig-headed and set in his ways with his own ideas of what made a movie a blockbuster. "I'm trying to move the company in a new direction."

"And you think if you deny your financiers their one, reasonable request that they'll return for future projects? There'll be no forward motion if you kill this movie now," he said.

I slammed my fist on the desk, but had to admit my father was right. I couldn't afford to produce the movie on my own. Not because I didn't have the money, but because it would mean losing the trust of the financiers when I wanted to make another film. Accepting April in the starring role was the only diplomatic move that would assure my movie got made, and guarantee funding in the future.

"Alright, fine. I'll talk the director down off a ledge later. Tell April she's on."

"You can congratulate her yourself," he said. "She's arriving at your house early in the morning. Tell that maid of yours to get the guest cottage ready."

"What?" *Fuck*. "You told April she could stay here?" I asked.

"I told her you insisted. She was quite pleased," Henry said. "What else was I supposed to say? Apparently, what you said about her acting skills lacking truthfulness got back to her and she was ready to refuse the part."

"What do you mean? What did I say?"

"You said her acting skills lack realism."

"I did? I don't remember…"

"Let me refresh your memory. She was playing the part of a woman who just broke up with her boyfriend and reacted with hysterical laughter. You said, instead of acting like a human…and I quote, 'she reacted like a space alien behaving in some bizarre, unbelievable way.' Do you remember now?"

I flopped back in my office chair and pinched the bridge of my nose with my thumb and forefinger. I resigned myself to the fact that I'd have to suffer the anguish of humiliation. "So not only do I have to accept April in the starring role, but I have to convince her to take it?"

"Yes, but don't worry. I'm sure you'll figure out a way to woo her. It might be good for you. I still think you've been working too hard, and April is a very attractive woman," Henry said.

I blew out a breath and shook my head, swearing. The older he got, the more embarrassing it was to watch my father chase after young girls half his age. It wasn't unusual in our business, but it didn't make it any less mortifying.

"She's not really my type," I said, flatly.

"Since when?" Henry asked with a snort. As I hung up the phone, I wondered the same thing.

It bothered me that my father acted as if he knew me well, when he didn't. He hadn't been there for my childhood, essentially leaving me to be raised by the butler. Not that I regretted having Jamison in my life for one minute. I loved Jamison to death. My father was the one I had the issue with. Ours was not a warm father-son relationship. I mean, I called him by his first name. He looked at me as a superficial playboy, only interested in the external trappings of the wealthy life he afforded me, like expensive cars, big houses and fast women. At least that was my assessment of our relationship.

I furrowed my brow, reflecting on my past. I couldn't blame him. On the surface I must've appeared that way to him as I was coming up through my twenties. But lately, ever since my film project took hold of me, things had changed. I'd begun to want something more out of life than glittering parties on a yacht off the coast of France. After a while, the fast life became just one more drunken party with one more rapper/wanna-be actor surrounded by an escort of highly-implanted starlets. All just wanting fame. All of them wondering how they could use me to get what they wanted.

And then I met Chelsea. I leaned back in my chair and swiveled it to look out the window. What did my little water nymph want from me?

Chapter 13

Chelsea

Alex was quiet all through lunch. He'd spent the morning on phone calls in his office, and now he wasn't talking. I told myself not to worry. Jamison threw a few concerned glances across the table my way, but I kept my face serene.

The voice of my best friend, Clara, was busy at work in my head. *If other people can handle casual sex, so can you. We are not our mothers' generation. Woman can enjoy sex for what it is. Don't overthink, just enjoy.*

The advice she'd given me at the beginning of our sophomore year still rang true, and for now, I held it as a mantra. *Don't overthink, just enjoy.* Casual sex. In reality, that's all this would ever be – if we ever got to the actual sex part – and to think otherwise was just foolish.

Finally, Alex seemed to brighten and looked up from his plate. "So, Chelsea, besides swimming, what other activities do you enjoy?" he asked. "Hiking?"

I was too relieved by his easy tone to be taken aback by the question, so I said, "Sure, I like hiking. I bet there are amazing places around here to explore."

"Actually there's a nice trail out back, near the guest cottage," Alex said. "And we'll need to take a look at it, Jamison."

"The guest cottage?" Jamison asked.

"Yes," Alex said as he looked out the window. "Henry has a guest coming to stay tomorrow, so we have to get it ready."

I forced my shoulders not to slump and reminded myself I was here to work. If Alex was inviting me to go on a hike after I cleaned out the guest cottage, I had no reason to feel disappointed or slighted that my job came first. One little make-out session in the pool was nothing, no matter how hot it had been.

"A guest?" Jamison asked.

By his tone I knew there was more being said between the two men. Alex avoided Jamison's eyes, but I reminded myself it was none of my concern. If anything happened between Alex and I, it would be casual, and that meant no expectations.

"Let me know when you're ready," Alex said to me. "I'll be in my office."

He left the table and I looked to Jamison for clarification. The butler carefully chewed the rest of his salad before he said, "The trail up by the guest cottage is quite lovely. And I had the cleaning crew turn the whole cottage out just last week, so all you need to do is tidy up a bit, dust, and make the bed."

Jamison assured me all the cleaning supplies I needed were at the guest cottage. Once we were finished with lunch, he handed me the keys from a peg hanging inside the pantry.

I went to my attic room to put on the shoes best suited for hiking. I resisted the urge to change into something more attractive than my work uniform since I needed to clean the cottage before our walk. I did, however, dig through my suitcase to find the set of white lace underwear Clara had given me as a parting gift.

I cautioned myself not to expect anything, but I couldn't stop the giant leaps my heart took when I thought of Alex's arms around me again. It was easy to fantasize about what might take place in the guest cottage bedroom before I put on the clean linens, but I forced the wishful thoughts out of my head. He'd asked me to go on a hike, not to have a torrid sexual encounter.

Alex was waiting in the driveway by the time I was done.

"Sorry, I'm ready. Ready for anything," I said, my voice breathless. "I mean, I didn't know if you wanted me to prepare the guest cottage before we hiked, but I went ahead and did it so we'd have the rest of the day together." Shit. That'd sounded like I was expecting something. "Anyway, I'm ready. I hope it's not too late for our hike."

Alex smiled, his eyes warming as he looked me up and down, "You know you don't have to wear a uniform. I told Jamison that on your first day. He just wanted to torture you."

"Should I change?" I asked as I made a mental note to tell Jamison what I thought of his little 'joke.'

"As much as I like that sundress you wore last night, we should get going. If we go now I can show you a great view for sunset," Alex said.

I smiled and my heart leapt again. I took the arm he offered me. It was hard not to think his thoughts mirrored mine as we walked arm in arm up the small lane to the guest cottage. Just before we reached the cottage a small trailhead appeared on the side of the lane marked by a charming stone arch.

"Oh, Alex. This is so cool. I love the stonework."

"It used to be a wildflower garden," Alex explained. "The woods are the perfect place for them to grow, and most of them still bloom, but I'm afraid it's become overgrown and wild now."

"Sounds heavenly," I said.

The path was narrow and Alex let me walk in front of him. I took off at a nervous pace until I felt his hand catch mine. I turned around as he pulled gently, and I bounced off his chest. He laughed and I looked up into his sapphire-colored eyes just before he leaned down and kissed me lightly.

"I didn't bring you up here just to kiss you," Alex said with a smile. "It's just that you looked so anxious, I thought it might help."

"Maybe," I said coyly. "Do it again."

He flashed another bright smile and bent his head again. This time, however, I lifted up on my tiptoes and kissed him back. I felt his arm circle my waist and his lips seared across mine, sending heat racing through my entire body.

I was just reaching to tangle my fingers in his hair when he pulled back and said, "Wait. There's something I want to show you."

He moved ahead of me and led me by the hand up the winding trail. The woods were speckled with purple violets and bright white flowers different than the ones I'd seen in Oregon. I noticed the trees forming a tighter net overhead and realized the branches were woven to create a natural tunnel. It was like something out of a fairytale.

Alex ducked to fit through the narrow tunnel, yet grapevines and leaves still brushed across his hair. Then he stepped out into a grove and turned to smile at me. As I emerged from the green tunnel, I was dazzled by sunlight. Tall birch trees ringed the clearing, and gave it the feeling of a cathedral. The grass was a thick carpet, and all around the edge of the grove were graceful drooping ferns as far as I could see.

"It's enchanting," I gasped.

"This is where they make love for the first time," Alex said.

My mouth dropped open in shock, and when he saw my expression he laughed and apologized, "I'm so sorry. I meant, there's a secret grove like this in my new movie. It's where the main characters make love for the first time. I took pictures of this place to give to the writers, but the photographs don't do it justice."

"What, no alien landing pad or grisly murder camp?" I teased, hoping to keep things light.

Alex grimaced, "Exactly. I want this new movie to be as far removed from my father's style as possible. I think the audience will like it, don't you?"

"I love it," I said honestly. "And I love that you have a passion project. Audiences will know if there was love put into it."

He frowned and let go of my hand, "Yeah, well, that's why I'm not too happy about the guest who's coming. She's supposed to get one of the starring roles, but I don't think she's right for it."

"Who knows, maybe she'll surprise you. Or you'll surprise her by getting award winning work out of her," I offered.

"Are you always like this?" Alex asked, taking my hand again.

"Like what? I'm a terrible actress. What you see is what you get."

"Exactly." Alex gave me a warm smile, and then pulled me to him.

He brushed my hair out of my face, and then curled his hand around the back of my neck, pulling me forward until our mouths crashed together. The heady rush of the kiss made me dizzy, and I reached up to grip his wide shoulders. Unable to stop myself, I ran my hands down his back and slipped them under the hem of his shirt. I dragged my fingers up his back, digging into the thick muscles there as his tongue ignited a wildfire inside of me.

He steadied me with one hand while his other reached down and caught my knee. He pulled my leg up to his hip, opening my thighs as my skirt rucked up around my thighs. He pressed me closer and I hooked my knee around his hip, rocking against him, both of us groaning at the blaze of friction. He fumbled for the button on my white work skirt and then stopped.

"Not here," he groaned against my lips.

"Why? Then where?" I asked. If this was just some casual fling, why did it matter?

"There's a Four Seasons in Rotterdam. I should take you out," he muttered, his fingers flexing on my hip.

"And miss this?" I asked.

I broke away from him and gestured to the enchanted grove. Sunset glowed against the white birch trees and the grass was cool and inviting. I sat down in the center of the grove and looked up at the dusky blue sky. It was perfect here, and I didn't want to wait.

Alex knelt beside me and reached for the top buttons on my shirt, opening the top three. His eyes stared at the rise of my breasts as they were revealed, one button at a time. He let out a satisfied sound. Then, as if he couldn't wait to finish unbuttoning the shirt, he dipped his head, kissed the swell of skin pushing up and out of my bra and reached for the hem of my shirt. I raised my arms and he slipped it up over my head, kissing me just as the shirt brushed past my face.

Breaking the kiss, he tugged his shirt off, and then spread it on the grass behind me. I leaned back and tried to breathe as he unbuttoned my skirt with one hand. He left my mouth and burned a trail of kisses across my stomach to where he tugged my skirt down. I lifted my hips against the shockwaves his mouth caused, and soon I was in nothing but the white lace underwear I'd changed into.

He slipped out of his own pants and laid down next to me, his eyes intent on mine. We kissed again, long and deliciously slow as he trailed his fingers up from my knee to tease the tops of my thighs. His tongue worked deepening circles across mine, and I moaned into his mouth.

He groaned, his arousal hard against my leg, but he pulled back from the kiss, and caught me in another passionate look. It was as if he shared what I was feeling, and neither of us could quite believe this was real. It felt like more than a casual moment, more than a summer affair. It was more than I'd wanted. More than I could handle probably, but I'd never wanted any man with such a consuming desire.

I knew what I wanted was written on my face, and I knew he saw it. He bent to kiss me again even as he pushed my thighs apart so he could explore. The teasing strokes across the edges of my lace underwear created waves of aching desire, and I tangled both hands in his hair and kissed him until we were both breathless. I hadn't known just a few simple touches could make me feel like this.

Then he slipped one finger past the soft material and between my folds. He didn't even hesitate as he slid it into my pussy, and a burst of sensation shook my whole body. It'd been too long since I'd had anything inside me. He twisted it, his knuckle pressing against my g-spot. I shuddered, pleasure running through me.

He waited, finger buried deep in me until the quaking subsided, then he slowly moved his finger in and out, bringing the dripping wetness to stroke my clit. A low whimper escaped as I begged for more. Two fingers swirled, teased my engorged nub then dipped back inside, leaving a thumb to expertly knead my aching clit. My back arched, and I cried out with pleasure again.

"Oh, god, Chelsea," Alex said, and in my haze, I felt the muscles in his arms shaking from his restraint.

I didn't care anymore about what other people would think. All I knew was I needed him inside me to satisfy the fire burning through my veins. He dropped his mouth to my nipple, kissing and sucking each one in turn. Tongue, then lips, suction that vibrated all the way down between my legs. I threw my head back with another moan as I pushed my hips up against him, hungry for more. He immediately responded, pushing my legs further apart so he could settle between them.

I didn't need any encouragement to open myself to his pleasure. He moved his head to my shoulder, kissing my neck, and I felt his throbbing hardness against my slippery folds. He lifted his head to my ear, breathing my name in a lusty whisper. He paused for just a split second, his eyes locking with mine, asking what I wanted. I held my breath, every nerve in my body vibrating, on the edge and desperate for release. I pleaded with my eyes. *Take me. Fuck me. I'm yours. For however long you want me.*

He rolled to the side and reached for his jeans, swiftly retrieving something from a pocket. When I heard the rip of foil I knew he was putting on a condom. I smiled, relief and appreciation going through me. I was on the pill, but considering the numerous women he must've slept with, it was a good thing.

As he rolled back on top of me, I made an eager sound in the back of my throat. I was burning with desire and the momentary pause in the friction had actually added to the anticipation. As he slid into me with a deep groan, I pushed my hips up to drive him deep. I wanted more of him, all of him. I writhed underneath him as he thrust again and again, winding me up to the top of my orgasm again until it peaked. I gasped as a white-hot explosion raced through my core, and I fell to pieces in his arms. He held me, driving into me over and over, until, finally, I felt him release.

Alex

I could still feel her soft lips on mine, the taste of her in my mouth, the brush of the cool grass against my forehead as I pressed into her tight, warm body.

Dammit. I leaned back in my office chair and gave in to the memory for the third time this morning.

Chelsea in the secret grove, the sunset glowing on her pale skin. The white lace, her long legs, the sweet wetness as I slipped a finger inside her. Her ocean blue eyes on mine as I thrust into her, my orgasm crashing over me until I didn't know which way was up.

"Knock, knock." It was April, barging into my office. "Am I interrupting anything?" she chirped.

There was no point in telling April she was interrupting because her whole plan was to dominate my attention. She sauntered over to the desk, her virtually non-existent hips rolling, and sat on the corner where she could tease a finger through my hair.

"I thought now might be a good time to talk about my part in your movie."

Already primed by thoughts of Chelsea, I felt a slight

bulge in the crotch of my pants. Now was *not* a good time. I cleared my throat and shifted in my chair. Instead of taking the hint that I didn't want to talk, she leaned closer, dropped a hand to my knee, and pushed it up toward my crotch.

"Unless you had something else on your mind, sexy," April purred.

Shit. How the hell was I supposed to handle this?

Chapter 14

Chelsea

"No, Chelsea, I said the linen napkins. These are cotton," Jamison snapped.

I turned around and rushed down the narrow servants' hallways back to the butler's pantry. I threw open the built in drawers and dug around for the right cloth napkins.

"It's just his father," I muttered. "What's the big deal?"

The truth was, I was nervous too. I felt like Henry James Silverhaus was going to take one look at me, and tell me I wasn't good enough for his son. Not that I was anything but a maid, I reminded myself. So it didn't matter.

I grabbed three linen napkins in two different shades of white and raced back to the dining room. Jamison was carefully measuring the distance between the fine china plates and the gleaming silverware. He adjusted pieces here and there until the table was set to his precise guidelines. I was pretty sure he'd gone to school for that.

Before long, we both raised our heads when we heard a commotion at the front door. Henry had arrived. With a domineering presence, he blew in through the front door like a hurricane in June, his voice greeting us before he did.

"What's a man got to do to get a drink around here?"

Jamison straightened his tie for the twentieth time and

hurried out into the entryway. I followed four feet behind him as the butler had instructed, but still almost tripped over him when Jamison stopped to bow.

"Mr. Silverhaus, sir. Nice to see you again," Jamison said. His entire demeanor, tone, had shifted from how he normally behaved.

I glanced up at Alex's father and swallowed a nervous bubble of laughter. So...here was the man from the picture on Alex's website profile.

Henry James Silverhaus was good-looking, but sharp and wiry where his son was wide and strong. His hair was golden like Alex's except it was silver at the temples.

"This must be the new maid everyone's talking about. Not much there if you ask me," Henry said with a derisive glance in my direction.

Wow. That was...something.

He strode past us and pushed open both doors of the library. Once inside, he settled himself in a caramel-colored leather chair and instructed Jamison to bring him a whiskey, neat.

When the doorbell rang, Henry waved a hand at Jamison and said, "Let the girl get it. This ought to be fun."

I forced myself not to let my eyes narrow at his reference to me as "the girl." Something was up, and I suspected I was about to be the brunt of a joke. Other than his good looks, the infamous Mr. Silverhaus was turning out to be nothing like his son at all.

I shot a glance at Jamison. His face was constrained, but he nodded for me to answer the door. I could feel Henry and Jamison watching me through the open library doors, so I smoothed down my crisp white apron before I opened the door. No matter what else was going on, this was my job.

"Who are you?" A blindingly blonde woman pushed past me and strode into the foyer. "I didn't know Alex had a maid. Shouldn't you be in the kitchen or something?"

It took all of my strength to keep from planting a hand on my hip and flinging a smart remark back at her. Or my shoe.

But I had to remember my place here. Employee.

She tossed a gold satin wrap at me revealing a white dress cut so low it had no discernible neckline. It seemed to start at the waist. Despite her obvious attempt to look like a legendary movie star, I recognized her as April Temple. Her name was synonymous with ear-splitting screams, skimpy outfits, and terrible acting.

And being featured in several Silver House productions.

"Good evening, Ms. Temple," I said.

Henry clapped his hands and stood up from the leather chair. "What an entrance, my dear. You look ravishing, as always."

April dashed across the foyer and held out a hand for Henry to kiss. Jamison slipped around the fawning couple and nodded at me to follow him to the kitchen, where I was relieved to escape before my lunch made an appearance all over the floor.

When we were tucked away safely behind the giant kitchen island, the butler heaved a huge sigh, and I turned my attention to him.

"Are you okay?"

"Yes. Yes, I'm fine," he said, and reached into a bottom cupboard for a hidden bottle of whiskey. He poured himself a stiff drink. He raised it in the air and said, "Quality alcohol. The only thing Alex's father and I agree on."

"Speaking of Alex, where is he?" I asked.

Jamison shook his head and knocked back the whiskey shot, "I don't know but, for god's sake, go find him."

With raised brows, I followed Jamison's gesture as he pointed to a narrow door. Behind it, I discovered a small spiral staircase that I hadn't seen before. I followed the stairs and they led me to the narrow servants' corridor on the second floor. When I pushed open the first door, I found myself straight across from the master suite. Alex and I hadn't seen each other since we'd had sex, so I knocked quietly.

"Chelsea?"

Caught by surprise, I jumped two feet in the air and spun

around as Alex came trotting up the main staircase. I pressed a palm to my heart and said, "Sorry, I thought you were in your room."

He laughed. "I didn't mean to scare you. Everything all right? You seem a little jumpy."

I smoothed down my crisp white apron again, and shook my head. "You'll never believe who's downstairs. April Temple is in the library, and your father is drooling all over her. By the way, does Jamison hate your father?" Alex grinned as I clapped my hands over my mouth and squeaked around them, "Sorry, I talk too much when I get nervous."

"No need to apologize. I meant to tell you about April before she arrived…give you a heads up. She's quite a handful, to say the least."

Alex was talking, but I was having a heard time listening. I couldn't take my eyes off of him. He was dressed in a dark Italian suit with a muted silver tie, and his handsomeness hit me all at once. He stood two stairs down from me, and for once we were eye to eye. I could see he was about to tell me something, but my willpower had gone weak along with my knees, and I acted without thinking. I leaned in and stopped him with a kiss.

Alex pressed into the kiss with a soft sigh, and when we broke apart he smiled with his eyes closed. "What was that for?"

I blinked. I wanted to grab him, run away with him before the magic ended. I didn't want to be his maid or a secret fling. I wanted to own him and be his lover. But then I remembered why I was here. And who he was. Why what I was thinking could never be.

I tried to play it off with a casual remark, not wanting him to see any of what I'd been thinking. "I just couldn't stop myself."

To my delight, Alex smiled wider and pulled me in for another, deeper kiss, his tongue teasing at the seam of my mouth. I was just wrapping my arms around his neck when I heard Jamison calling up the hidden staircase.

I pulled my arms off of him and tucked my hair behind my ear in a nervous gesture. "Oh, god, Jamison wants me. Sorry, what were you going to tell me?"

He opened his mouth to speak but before he could answer, Jamison called my name again. I threw my hands in the air and said, "Never mind. I've got to go. Jamison is about to freak out over dinner."

"Wait, Chelsea," Alex called, but I was already through the narrow door and down the spiral staircase.

As I popped into the kitchen, Jamison was muttering as he stood over what looked like another one of his mouth-watering roasts. "Of course he'd request David's favorite meal. Can't miss a chance to poke at old wounds…see if he can get to Alex."

"Who is David?" I asked stepping up next to him.

Jamison turned, efficiently transferring the roast to a spotless serving tray as he spoke, "David was Alex's older brother. Not the best subject for dinner conversation, but I'm sure Henry will find a reason to bring him up."

"*Was?*" I gently emphasized the word, anticipating what the answer would be.

"Drugs. A serious addiction. He died of an overdose about six years ago." He spoke flatly with no emotion as he placed a large serving fork on the tray. "Alex loved him through all of it. Tried to help him. Nothing helped."

I picked up the tray of prepared salads and said, "Oh, Jamison. I had no idea."

"Better that you know. By the way, did Alex tell you anything about April?" Jamison asked.

"No, I think he was going to, but I heard you calling for me."

"God help us all," Jamison said and led the way to the dining room. I followed, wondering what he meant by that, but when I saw April sitting at the table, I had a feeling I was going to find out.

Jamison presented the roast to the table and then placed it on the sideboard to carve. I went carefully to Henry's left side and placed a dinner salad in front of him the way Jamison had taught me.

When I reached April, she looked up with a simpering smile and said, "I'd like one without dressing, please."

I nodded, served Alex who gave me an apologetic look, and then hurried back to the kitchen to make a fresh salad for April. When I returned I went to April's left side to serve her, but she waved the plate away.

"Too late. We're already on to the next course." She tilted her wine glass at Alex. "New girl not working out too well, eh, Alex?"

Henry chuckled and took a sip of his water.

I just stood there, staring at the untouched salad, unsure what to do, afraid to hear Alex's response. Now I understood Jamison's remark about April, and I was also beginning to see why Alex referred to his own father by his first name. Henry was turning out to be an even bigger ass than I'd originally thought.

Without missing a beat, April chimed in with a toss of her curls. "Good help is hard to find. Attractive help, even harder."

I took her caustic remark as my cue to leave, and ducked back into the kitchen, humiliated. Crushed. A few minutes ago, everything had been going so well. A hot, secret kiss on the stairs. I'd felt special, like I actually meant something to Alex, but the minute I stepped into the dining room, when he hadn't defended me, that special feeling faded and everything changed.

Alex

I watched, feeling like a dick, as Chelsea left the dining

room. Her back was stiff from April's insult, and there was nothing I could say before she was gone. The narrow door to the servants' hallway hadn't even closed when I turned to confront April, but she got to me first.

"Is it true?" April asked. "I heard a rumor that you hired her on the Internet. Your father said it was meant as a joke, but if that was true, why is she still here?"

Henry shot me a look. He knew I was pissed, but from the expression on his face, I could tell he didn't give a damn. Not surprising, considering his history. April had heard about Chelsea from him, however, daddy dearest had conveniently neglected to mention anything else I'd told him, preferring to let people think the worst of Chelsea.

"I thought you said this was going to be a working dinner." I glared at my father. "You wanted to discuss the role. Not my hired help."

Considering I still had to sweet talk April into accepting the role, I realized my tone probably came out a little too cool. I got my emotions under control and continued with a little less ice on each word. "So…let's talk business, shall we?"

April tossed her hair again and threw a downward glance over her shoulder. "Absolutely. Your home is so lovely and the guest cottage is absolutely charming. A bit dusty, but charming. I feel like a fairy princess…there's even a secret path through the woods."

I bit my tongue instead of my food as April turned to my father, fanning her false eyelashes at him. "I followed it before I came to the main house. Did you know there's a clearing in the woods? Other people must because the grass was quite trampled. Young lovers meeting in the secret grove maybe?"

"Sounds familiar," Henry said. He glanced at me. "Isn't there a scene like that in the screenplay?"

"Not between the handsome hero and the hired help," April said snidely. "Too cliché. Don't you think?"

"Oh, would you like to discuss the screenplay now?" I asked, trying not to sound too sarcastic. She wasn't a good actress, and now she thought she was some kind of expert screenwriter too?

April gave me a pouty smile, probably annoyed that I hadn't respond to her needling.

"Actually, I have a few ideas for several of the scenes, you know, ways to punch it up a bit," she said.

"Punch it up?" *Oh, this wasn't going to be good.*

"I agree with April," Henry chimed in. "It seems a bit soft in places."

Henry would agree with anything April said, short of marriage. I saw the way his eyes traveled over her skin-tight dress. Once he got into her metaphorical pants, he wouldn't care, but until then, he'd say whatever she wanted to hear.

"You have to think of it more as a romantic comedy than a slasher flick," I told him, "maybe then you'll understand this movie." I knew I was getting in a jab at the old man, but Jesus– it felt like the two of them were tag teaming against me right now.

"As long as you understand the bottom line," he retorted.

"Romantic comedy?" April asked. "Yes, I guess I can see that." She pretended to mull it over as if she would bless us with her expert opinion, though I doubted there were many expert thoughts rolling around in that airhead. She'd completely missed the point that I was making a deleterious remark about my father's taste in movies.

Chelsea would've gotten it.

"I mean the whole secret grove love scene is so sappy…it could be funny."

Henry said, "Alex used to hide in a grove of birch trees when he was little. Pretended it was some secret kingdom or some such nonsense."

"That's sweet," April said. She smirked. "But the whole love scene is only something a silly, naive girl would dream up. Who wrote this screenplay?"

"Does it matter?" Despite my best efforts to remain engaged and enthusiastic, my voice went flat, and I wanted to slump down in my chair. This entire charade was getting to me, sitting in my stomach like sour milk on a warm day. Henry didn't care about my input, or about me. He'd proven that in the past, and I knew he would again in the future.

"Not at all," Henry proclaimed. "We can make all the changes ourselves."

"And what exactly do you think needs to be changed about that scene?" I asked, trying to keep the sharp edge out of my voice.

"Well, for one thing the hero is with the wrong girl," April said. "Instead of some manipulative girl he doesn't know, the love scene in the grove would work better if he was with his old flame."

The strap of April's dress slipped down as if on cue. She giggled and took her time dragging it back into place. She batted her eyelashes at my father who grinned and casually draped an arm over the back of her chair.

I straightened in my seat, feeling the need to come to my own defense one last time. "I think you missed the point of the scene. The main character is finding his footing again after a tragedy," I explained. "To be there with his new love interest is the only way he knows how to bridge the past with the future he wants."

"Snore," Henry said. "See there, Alex. Even April agrees. The screenplay definitely needs some punching up."

He smiled at April, and she scrunched up her shoulder at him and purred, "I'm sure we can spice things up."

I closed my eyes and bit my tongue. April was turning on the charm *and* the bad acting, trying to butter up the old man. And he was leering at her in return, eating it up.

Suddenly, he tore his stare from April's cleavage and raised his voice for Jamison to hear from the kitchen. "Where's Jamison?" he barked and took his arm off of her chair. Then he looked at me. "I know what David liked to have after his favorite dinner, but I'd sure like some sorbet or something."

My father's mention of my older brother stung, but I knew better than to say anything. Henry always brought up David's name on purpose, like a weapon, whenever he thought I was making the wrong decision. My brother had made the wrong choices and paid the highest price for his mistakes. He'd let down a lot of people, including me, but he deserved better than to have his memory used as a convenient cautionary tale whenever my father wanted me to follow his advice.

Jamison burst through the narrow servants' door and refilled our wine glasses. The hard line of his jaw told me he'd been listening at the doorway and hadn't liked it anymore than I had.

I braced myself, knowing Chelsea would be next. When she entered the dining room, her eyes met mine and my heart stumbled over the concern I saw there. Not anger. Concern.

April saw it too and reached out to stroke my arm. She leaned in and presented me with a wide view of her cleavage that would've made my father salivate.

"Don't you think Alex needs to get out, Henry? It can't be healthy cooped up in here alone all summer," she said.

"Thanks for your concern, April, but I like it here and I like the screenplay just the way it is." I leaned away from her as much as I could without being rude enough to draw my father's ire.

"See, April," Henry said. "My boy's a softie. It's up to us to show him how Hollywood works. You up to the challenge?"

"*Moi*? I'd love a challenge," April said, leveling a sharp look at Chelsea as she spoke.

After dismissing both Jamison and Chelsea without a second look, my old man went back to leering, and April went back to sucking up to him. As I watched, the two of them chatted, heads bobbing close together as April punctuated their talk with shrill giggles. She sure knew how to work it, but I knew the minute my father would leave the room, she'd be all over me.

I slumped back in my chair, defeated. I twirled the stem of my wine glass between my fingers while they talked. This wasn't the way I'd wanted things to go. Not with my movie project, and definitely not with Chelsea.

Chapter 15

Chelsea

I couldn't believe it. Alex said nothing when Henry dismissed Jamison and me from the dining room. Again. He sat at the head of the table and stared at an old painting of a hunting dog as if he couldn't see anything else but the bleeding pheasant in its jaws. I was standing right there under that painting, clearing the last of the silverware. I looked straight at him before we left, but he didn't even acknowledge I was there.

The worst part was when Henry stood up and announced he was going to the library. I looked over at April and saw she was holding Alex's hand. She brought it casually to the exposed skin of her plunging neckline while she whispered in his ear, fawning all over him acting like they were old lovers. She broke away only long enough to tell Henry to go on without them.

Later that night, I couldn't get any sleep. I tossed and turned, going over and over it in my mind. I replayed our time together in the grove and every one of Alex's kisses, scrutinizing each move, and every look in his eyes, wondering if what I felt, and what I thought I saw was only wishful thinking. So it was no surprise when my alarm went off and I was still awake. I'd set it early to meet Alex at the pool. Yesterday, my plan had been to jump out of bed and be there, naked in the cool water when he arrived, surprising him for once. Now, I tried to think of any excuse not to go.

As I sat at my desk, I drummed my fingers on the cover of my laptop, debating what to do. I could email Karl's caregivers again, but I'd just sent one the day before. I could check emails and messages. There'd be several from Zach, but I really wasn't up for hearing from him right now. I thought about writing, but after overhearing Henry and April tear apart Alex's movie, I wasn't feeling very inspired.

The fact that they'd convinced Alex to abandon the heart of the first project he felt passionate about was aggravating enough to propel me into action. I yanked a brush through my hair and pulled it into a neat ponytail, peering into the mirror over my desk. I took one last look, trying to ignore the vast differences between me and the blonde starlet. I rubbed a swab of sunblock lip balm across my lips, puckered them once, stood, and headed downstairs to go to the pool.

Alex was already swimming fast laps when I arrived. I watched him swim two more, before he stopped and surfaced slowly at the wall opposite me. I knew he saw me, but he didn't turn around, and I had to walk all the way around the pool to see his face. This was not a good start to the day.

"Feel like racing?" I asked, forcing a smile.

He rolled his wide shoulders and stretched his arms without answering. I inched closer, kicked off my shoes and swung my legs into the cool water. Alex clenched his jaw and glanced up at me.

"Not today," he said. His voice was flat.

I pursed my lips and tried again. "Feel like company?" I asked, skimming a toe through the water to brush his thigh.

Alex jerked back and said, "No."

I dropped my leg along with my cheery attitude and swallowed hard. He was just upset about what'd happened yesterday. "They gave you a hard time about your movie, huh?"

"What would you know about it?" Alex snapped his question. "You're all idealistic. I get it. Well, good for you.

Some of us have to live in the real world."

"I live in the real world." I spat at him, annoyed at his sour mood. The "poor little rich boy" attitude was *so* not endearing. He was behaving like a spoiled brat.

The picture of him at the head of the table floated between us. He'd sat there like a prince in a grand hall, a blonde starlet on his arm. It was silly of me to think that the heir of Silver House Productions would throw all that away to make an independent movie. Indie films didn't buy the suit he wore last night, the caviar they ate, or the crystal chandelier I'd polished especially for their dinner party.

Why had I thought he'd want me when he already had everything a person could want?

"Sure you do," he said, his tone completely patronizing. "Speaking of your world, don't you have work to do?"

I drew back, hurt by his remark. I nodded. "Oh, now I see it."

He looked up at me with hard eyes. "What do you think you see?"

"The family resemblance," I said as I got to my feet. "You like to think you're different, but when it comes right down to it, you'll trash that movie just to make money and…and when you look at me, all you really see is a servant."

He'd used me. Even though everyone warned me, and the website had made it obvious, I'd fallen for it anyway. I was an idiot.

Alex pushed a hand through his hair as he shoved back from the wall. I immediately regretted my angry words. It was childish of me to lash out at him, especially to say something I knew would hurt him so sharply. Another woman, one who knew how to handle casual sex, would've walked away unprovoked. However, I was too inexperienced not to feel the sting of his rejection. I was so sure he'd felt something more when we were together, but I was wrong, and now I couldn't trust myself.

I turned to step away when he said, "Well, since you really only came here looking for one thing, it's kind of hypocritical of you to trash me."

I sucked in my cheeks and spun around. "What did you say?" I asked, shocked by the question.

"Yeah, just like that," Alex said, scorn written on his face. "You widen your eyes and look all innocent. As if you hadn't known exactly who I was when you applied for this job. As if you hadn't come here looking to break into Hollywood. So you're not some actress looking for a break…you're a screenwriter. Jamison told me about the notebook he found."

"That has nothing to do with you," I said. I backed away from the pool, but couldn't make myself turn around and leave. "And I'm not the one who's a liar. I had no idea you worked in movies."

"Oh, you think *I'm* the liar?" His eyes narrowed and his fists clenched.

"You're the one who put your father's picture up on your profile. I heard April ask you about it. I get it now. I was just some joke. I didn't want to believe it, but now I can see I was right. Well, I hope you all had a good laugh at my expense. Thank you very much." I spit out the words.

Remembering the way that beautiful actress had looked at me last night, now, I really felt like a joke. I wouldn't have been surprised if April was watching us now through the mansion windows flipping her curls. Just the thought of it was enough to send ice water through my veins. I knew how I looked, desperate and grasping at any hint of righteous anger to cover my own foolishness.

I needed to leave. I couldn't face Alex anymore. He hauled himself up on the pool deck and reached for me. I dodged out of his grasp and fled to the servants' cottage, desperate to put as much distance between him and me as I could.

Chapter 16

Chelsea

The sight of my little attic room was enough to make the tears overflow. Bright morning sunlight filtered in through the ivy over the window, and the hardwood floor gleamed. It was a simple room, but it was the first room I'd stayed in all by myself since I was eight years-old.

Yet despite all of its homeyness, I knew I didn't belong. It was the same thought I'd had hundreds of times as a foster child. It didn't matter that I'd been happy here. I didn't belong. I never would.

I drifted over to the narrow writing desk, shaking my head at all the pages of pre-writing I'd done. I hadn't even transcribed them onto my computer yet. The writing had felt great, like I'd opened a window and let in fresh air. Now, it was just another embarrassment, a foolish fantasy that I needed to let go. I scooped up the notebook and dropped all the handwritten pages into the small woven wastebasket.

"I wasn't lying," Jamison said from the doorway, "when I told you it was good. I think you have talent."

I turned away from him, but he strode into my small sanctuary and plucked the notebook out of the trash. He straightened and placed it in the center of the writing desk.

"Let me guess…Henry and his starlet got to you, too?" Jamison said quietly.

"More like I woke up from a daydream." My eyes were red, still burning with tears, so I stepped to the window with my back to him so he wouldn't notice. "Time to get back to my real life."

"You mean to your brother?"

I whirled around and asked, "What do you mean? What do you know about my brother?"

Jamison sat on the edge of the white wicker chair and held both his hands open, palms up. "I'm sorry. I didn't mean to pry. I did a background check after you arrived, and it mentioned your brother. He's in a state-run care facility?"

"It's not jail if that's what you're thinking," I snapped, all of those automatic defenses coming from years in a system always on the offensive.

"I was thinking your brother needs assistance, and you're the only one responsible for his care. I was thinking that's why you took this job."

I blinked back tears again, but this time I didn't care that he saw them. I'd been happy here. I'd thought I'd found a friend in Jamison, and with Alex...maybe something more. But now I could see I didn't belong.

"Your younger brother, Karl?" Jamison asked gently.

"He's autistic," I said. "Sometimes they call it 'profoundly autistic. He can't care for himself, has trouble communicating. I found a program for him. It could change his life, so I needed tuition money."

"Needed?" Jamison asked. "That makes it sound like you've had a change of heart. What happened?"

I gave up and sank onto the bed. "I can't stay here, Jamison." I dabbed at the corners of my eyes with my finger. "I made a big mistake. Alex has April, and his new movie. He doesn't even want me around. He thinks I took the job just to break into Hollywood."

The butler's jaw dropped. "Alex has April?"

"Or someone like her." I made a dismissive gesture. "The gorgeous blonde...I've seen her around here a few times. Anyway, it doesn't matter."

"That's why you're leaving? What about the money?" Jamison's voice showed real concern. "Where on earth are you going to find a job that will pay what you need?"

The shackles of my situation rubbed me raw. I straightened and snapped, "I'd rather sell drugs than be treated like a piece of dirt. You saw the way Henry and April looked at me. I thought I wouldn't care but..." I shrugged, as if I wasn't thinking about how it would destroy me to see that same look in Alex's eyes. What'd he said by the pool had been bad enough.

Jamison stood up and tugged his suit coat sleeves down before he cleared his throat and declared, "I've not heard one single reason why you should leave. Your work has been excellent, and despite a few overlaps between your personal and professional lives, I plan to pay you in full for a job well done."

"What about Alex?" I asked. "He doesn't want me around. He made that very clear."

The butler gave a rude snort, "Nothing is clear with that boy right now."

His words surprised me into a smile, but I shook my head and said, "I'm sorry, Jamison, but you don't know the whole story."

"There's nothing in this house nor in Alex's life that I don't know." He gave me a small smile. "In fact, I'd hazard a guess that I know things about his life that even he hasn't realized yet."

I dropped my aching head into my hands. Jamison wasn't making sense. None of it made sense. Except...of course. I could see it now. The Alex I thought I knew had disappeared after we'd made...after we'd *fucked*. After he'd gotten what he wanted, he dropped the act, and being the naive fool that I was, I hadn't noticed until the dinner party.

The logic seemed irrefutable. I opened my eyes and pulled out my suitcase.

"Chelsea, please, you don't understand," Jamison said.

"Oh, no, I think I understand perfectly," I said cooly. "I

made a big mistake, and the only way to fix it is to start all over again. So, I'm going home to do just that."

To my complete shock, Jamison blocked the door. "No, please, Chelsea. You need to understand that Alex is struggling. He has to make a stand, and he thinks he'll have to do it on his own. So, he's begun by pushing away everyone he loves."

"You're right about one thing," I said. "He'll have to do it on his own."

"Please, this new movie of his…you see, it's a complete departure from everything Silver House Productions has done before. His father is hoping it will fail, because if Alex succeeds it'll cast a new light on Henry and all of Henry's work. It'll make him look old and outdated, like his time in the business is over. And you've seen how Henry doesn't like to think of himself as being old, or a 'has been,'" Jamison said.

I'd just flung open my suitcase on the bed and needed to get to the closet in the hall. The butler blocked the door, but more than his tall, bony frame, his words stopped me. Jamison was right. Alex couldn't have lied about his Indie movie. The fact that it was already in pre-production proved that it was good. He'd made others believe in it, and obviously, they thought it would be a success, or it wouldn't have gotten that far.

"You think he's having a crisis of self-doubt?" I asked.

Jamison sighed with relief. "Yes, I couldn't have said it better myself. Alex is having a crisis of belief. But I believe in him. I also believe in you. We need you here, Chelsea, please stay."

I scowled. I wasn't one hundred percent convinced Alex wanted me to stay, but Jamison did, and my ego was boosted by his sincere words. I felt like I was needed. Jamison valued me enough to enlist my help, not just for cleaning cupboards, but for the one thing most important to him, and that made me feel worthy to be here after all. The question was, did Alex feel the same way?

Chapter 17

Alex

By the time I grabbed a towel and wrapped it around my waist, Chelsea had disappeared inside the servants' cottage. I went for the door but froze at the steps to the porch. She was right. I was a liar. I hired her on a whim to annoy my father. It had been a dirty trick, a petty rebellion that had amounted to nothing, and now all I'd done was make a mess of everything.

I forced myself to move forward placing a hand on the doorknob and pushed it open slightly. Inside, I saw Jamison appear from his room and head up the attic stairs. As he passed, he shot me an icy look that hit harder than any spoken rebuke. I knew what Jamison would say. I was a jackass. Too wrapped up in my own anger and frustration to realize how I hurt others. But I was pissed, mostly at myself, and that meant I was blind to pretty much everything around me.

Time to reap the consequences of my decidedly asshole actions.

I started to step inside, ready to do whatever it took to make things right with Chelsea, but before I could do anything, a woman spoke from behind me.

"Going for a swim?"

I pulled the door shut, dropped my hand, and reluctantly turned to see April. There she was, trouble herself, poised at the end of the sidewalk, balanced on tall, gold sandals with one hand on the ripe curve of her hip. She wore a white bikini that looked like nothing more than three triangles of fabric and some string barely covering her purchased tan. For a brief moment, an image of her stepping out of the water with her spray tan puddling around her feet, popped into my head. I would've laughed if I hadn't been so annoyed with her bad timing.

"Just got out," I said, "the pool's all yours." I kept my voice even, trying to give her the hint to go away and leave me the hell alone.

"Too bad, you should change your mind," she said and tossed her carefully arranged curls. Like she even had any intentions of swimming with that perfect hair and all that make-up. Who was she kidding?

There was no way I could talk to Chelsea now, not with April ogling my bare chest, and probably trying to imagine what I looked like without the towel. Even in my wildest days, I'd never fucked April. I had some standards.

"You're up early."

She flipped a hand in the air and said, "I'm not used to fending for myself. Don't get me wrong, your guest cottage is quaint, but it's like Siberia up there. I came through the main house, but couldn't find anyone. Do you think your maid could bring me some tea?"

My mouth tightened. "Everything is set up in the dining room, help yourself."

"Well, you must be hungry after your swim. I'll join you," April said.

I tried to step past her without brushing against her mountainous breasts, but all it did was leave me straight in front of her, face to face. She batted her eyelashes and rolled her hips into another pose. She looked me up and down practically licking her lips, and purred, "Showering first? Like I said, I'll join you."

I darted to the side, stepping over a flowering shrub and hopping on one foot, in an awkward effort to stop her from following me. "Maybe I'll see you in the dining room." I gave her an insincere smile and took off.

I felt April glaring at me as I cut across the pool deck and up the private staircase that led to my master suite. I stopped on the balcony, not to look at April but to glance over at the servants' cottage. Hopefully, Jamison would work his magic and save my sorry ass like he'd always done in the past. Maybe he could talk to Chelsea and smooth things over. She was probably packing her bags right now, but if Chelsea left, I'd be kicking myself for the rest of my life.

A tight knot pinched the pit of my stomach, and I pounded a fist against the balcony railing. I yanked the door closed behind me and headed for the shower. I'd accused Chelsea of being like April, a manipulative climber only interested in using me as a rung on the ladder to her Hollywood success. If anything, Chelsea was the complete opposite of that cloying, calculating...

Fuck! I jumped back.

I'd turned on the shower and stepped under the spray, not realizing the water was scalding. As I adjusted the temperature, I rolled over my past decisions in my head. I'd already made huge mistakes where my movie was concerned before Chelsea even arrived. I should've handled the entire project completely independent of my father and Silver House Productions. The truth was I hadn't thought I could do it alone. I'd been afraid I wasn't good enough and everything would end in failure.

So I'd pitched the idea of Silver House having an independent niche. It had sounded like a great idea, a way to move the company forward, but at its heart, it had just been another way for me to keep living a comfortable life and never really put myself out there. Without the backing of my father's financiers, I would've had to raise the money on my own, make all the choices on my own, and accept full responsibility for the movie's success or failure.

Then Chelsea had come along and made me want to try. For a short while, it'd even worked. It seemed like everything had been going great, and then my father had to come over for dinner and made me feel like a child playing house at my own table. I slapped my hands against the shower wall. *Damn him. And April too*. She'd wormed her way between Chelsea and me, the same way she had wormed her way into a lead role. Except I couldn't completely blame them. I'd seen the way they treated Chelsea, and I'd said nothing. I was failing everything and everyone that was important to me.

As I turned off the shower and paced the long, galley-shaped bathroom, my mind tore over the same terrain I'd tried to map for months. Could I scrap the entire production and start over completely on my own? That would let down hundreds of people already lined up to work. *Damn it.* It was too big, and it was already in motion.

At least I could take care of one issue and fire April. Henry would be pissed, but he couldn't do anything to me, or scrap the movie without losing more money. All he ever cared about was the money. *Thanks Dad, for putting your son first.*

Bitter thoughts conspired against me, and my mind backtracked to cover the same ground again. I was paralyzed by the idea of making the wrong decision. What if my dad was right? What if I was like my brother, David, and no matter what I did, I always made things worse?

The ring of my cell phone on my dresser snapped me out of my dark thoughts, and I went into the bedroom to answer it.

I smiled at the screen, and pressed the phone to my ear. "Carrie…"

"Hey, kiddo, it's me," a sweet voice said.

"Thank god. How'd you know I needed to hear from the voice of reason?" I flopped onto my bed, my shoulders relaxing as I sunk into its softness.

My sister-in-law always had a clear head, a trait she'd honed when David's addiction had grown worse and forced her into unthinkable situations. Even if the world were on fire, Carrie would rise up and find the right perspective.

"I know Henry came for dinner last night, so I figured you might need to hear a friendly voice," she said.

"He asked Jamison to make David's favorite," I said.

"The roast? That figures. He must've had some sort of

sales pitch he wanted to shove down your throat. Let me guess, he made sure to mention David's mistakes," Carrie laughed.

The mention of David still hurt us both, but she refused to let either of us avoid his name. We remembered the good and the bad.

"We had a guest," I continued. "April Temple, so at least Henry tried to be discreet about it."

"That scream-queen?" Carried asked. "Oh, god, please tell me you didn't have to hire her for your movie."

I groaned and sank deeper into the bed. "I wish I had David's confidence. He just went for what he wanted, no matter what it was."

"And you're too worried about making a mistake," she said with a soft voice.

"The irony is that I tried to avoid a mistake, and instead I've just screwed everything up, royally. I'm an ass, Carrie. Why do you even talk to me?"

She laughed, "Well, I was going to stop because you're so boring, but now this sounds juicy. Does this have anything to do with your pretty visitor from Oregon?"

Carrie knew the entire story about Chelsea, but she wasn't like the others. She always treated people with dignity and respect no matter what their station in life. She saw the best in everybody, including me.

"It's too late. I'm afraid my asinine behavior has already sent her packing. If I didn't have my head up my ass half the time, I would've seen this coming," I said.

"What happened?" Carrie asked. "I had such high hopes. You know she's the first woman you've ever talked about that really seemed to matter."

I rubbed my head. "Really? What did I say?"

"Right after she arrived I asked about your new maid and you told me not to call her that. You said she was more like Jamison, like a friend…" Carrie's voice rose in a question. "Now she's more than a friend?"

"Except for the part where I was a dickhead and said awful things to her and now she's leaving." I winced just thinking about my atrocious behavior.

"Oh, I see. Well, you know the one mistake your brother never made?" Carrie didn't have to say. I knew what was coming. "He was never afraid to admit what he wanted, and then go after it."

I smiled and asked, "Is that how he got you?"

"Exactly. Now figure out what you want and go get it, kiddo."

Chapter 18

Chelsea

"Chelsea, you can stop sneaking around. Alex has locked himself in his office and probably won't come out for the rest of the day." Jamison gave me a sideways glance as he looked up from preparing the dinner menu.

"It's not just him I'm avoiding," I said turning to him while holding a package of Negerzoenen cookies. These heavenly cookies were made of a chocolate covered fluffy, white center. No wonder they were also called Angel Kisses.

"April?" Jamison snorted, "She's gone shopping, of course. So, you can stop sorting the pantry and get some fresh air."

"Fine," I said, and plopped the package back on the shelf. I contemplated taking a cookie with me just to sweeten my mood. They really were one of the best chocolate delicacies I'd tasted since I'd been in Holland, but instead I grumbled, "I'll head down the driveway and replant the urns by the gate."

I needed to keep busy. The voice in my head was still telling me to move on, that I was just wasting my time here hanging on to a thread of hope so thin that it had no chance of surviving. It was hard to ignore it without something else to occupy myself.

"Here…" Jamison stretched out his hand holding a pair of heavy, blue gardening gloves. "I bought these for you while I was out the other day."

I took the gloves and noticed the wrists were embroidered with Lilies of the Valley entwined around the letter 'C.'

"My favorite flower," I whispered.

Jamison cleared his throat. "I had them made for you. It's nice to have someone around the house that enjoys gardening as much as I do."

I blinked back tears and kissed Jamison on the cheek before hurrying out the door. Caring for the gardens was a joy to him as was cooking and keeping a neat house. I was beginning to feel the same way about my work. If only Henry and April hadn't cheapened the feeling, I might've truly enjoyed my summer job.

Lost in my thoughts, I flung open the front door and nearly tripped over a little girl standing on the porch. She brushed back her white-blonde hair and smiled up at me.

"I'm sorry, can I help you?" I asked.

"Daddy told me to come by a lot because good memories are here," she said, still smiling.

"Daddy?" I asked as I leaned heavily against the thick doorframe.

"Emily, I told you to wait. Did you even ring the bell?" a sweet voice called out.

I blinked and the stunning blonde woman I'd seen Alex embrace, the one he and Jamison wouldn't talk about, glided up the steps and took the little girl's hand.

"Hello, I'm Carrie," she said and held out an elegant hand.

"Ah, hello, my name's Chelsea," I managed. Suddenly, it felt like my ears were ringing and I fought the urge to shake my head. I'd had a hard time hearing anything after "daddy." The girl resembled her mother, but her father's features were there too.

"Emily wanted to stop by with a letter for Alex. She drew him a picture and everything, didn't you, sweetie?"

Emily nodded, "I liked swimming in the pool. Daddy did the best cannonballs."

She opened the loose envelope and pulled out her drawing. It was a man and a little girl holding hands. Squiggly blue lines at the bottom of the page were clearly the pool, and underneath, in graceful cursive, was written: *You can always talk to me and we'll always be here for you. Love, C.*

"It's nice to meet you, Chelsea. Are you enjoying Holland?" Carrie asked. "I hope our Alex hasn't been too gruff with you. He doesn't let people in very easily."

Before I could make sense of what she was saying, the ringing in my ears was replaced by the sick thump of my heart. This gorgeous woman was exactly who I imagined a man like Alex would marry. Maybe they were separated or divorced, but she was definitely trying to reconcile. Obviously, he wanted Emily to visit and remember the good memories.

I jumped out of the doorway as if it had burned me. Here I was standing in the way, an obstacle to this beautiful family. Guilt flooded through me, and I suddenly felt like throwing up.

"He's locked himself in his office," I blurted out.

Carrie smiled, "Yeah, he does that sometimes. Not to worry, dear. Could you give him Emily's letter?"

"Yes, of course. It was nice to meet you," I said and inched around them. "I told Jamison I would work on the flower pots." I gave a weak smile and nodded in the direction of the urns. "Have a nice day."

I took off down the driveway and had to press the garden gloves to my mouth to keep from screaming. *Oh, my god!* He was married. At least in my mind I was already convincing myself that they were still married. Why hadn't I seen it before? Alex was married to the perfect woman and they had a beautiful daughter. I'd thrown myself at him and almost ruined that little girl's family. No wonder he wanted nothing to do with me. What we'd done could cost him his wife and child.

I felt as if my heart was imploding inside my chest. I stopped dead in the driveway, still gasping for air, hoping no one was watching, when I realized the worst part. I only felt this broken-hearted because I was falling in love with Alex.

The gorgeous Carrie and little Emily stayed for lunch, and I could hear laughter ringing out from the main house as I worked. Even though my arms felt like lead, I managed to replant the flowerpots. I purposely dallied, trying to waste time so as not to have a reason to go back inside. I was aimlessly digging in the dirt and smoothing it down for the tenth time when the wrought-iron gates at the end of the drive swung open.

I barely had time to dive out of the way before the Mercedes barreled through and sped up the driveway. Henry had loaned April the sleek, silver car, which she treated like it was some sort of present she was entitled to. The radio was blaring bright American pop music, and I could smell the clove cigarettes April smoked on the sly.

I tried to hide behind the greenery in the giant planters, but April spotted me. She tore off her over-sized, white sunglasses and the car screeched to a halt.

April leaned over and called through the open car window. "I hope you don't think you're Cinderella."

I looked down at my dirt-encrusted hands and arms. I certainly looked the part.

"Has the butler talked to you yet?" April asked. "I left a complaint with him this morning about the cleanliness of the guest cottage. Definitely not five-star work, and I refuse to stay in it a moment longer."

Although I was tempted to flip her off and sneer, I simply smiled and asked, "Should I run up and gather your things? I could have everything packed for you and down here in twenty minutes."

"Nice try." April glowered at me. "But the butler agreed you should come up to the guest cottage today and set things right, bring it up to my standards."

I stood up and brushed more dirt off my pants. "I'll go

find Jamison." I wasn't going to let her get to me, again. I refused to give her that kind of power. Once this summer was over, I never intended to see her again. It wasn't worth losing my brother's future.

April laughed, "Would he really want you tracking dirt through the main house? I don't think Alex would approve of that. I'll go find him, you just head up to the guest cottage."

She stepped on the gas and roared the few yards up to the front steps of the house. I shot a glare at the back of the Mercedes that could've burned a nuclear hole in it. The car ground to a halt just behind Carrie's black sedan and April jumped out, leaving the car door open. She popped the trunk and left it open, too, as she sauntered up the front steps.

Jamison came to the front door and was already unloading April's shopping when I caught up and joined him.

"Someone's been busy," he mumbled.

We could hear April standing in the foyer calling out Alex's name. No one answered. I thought of the laughter I'd heard minutes before she'd arrived, and I almost smiled. From the sounds of it, somewhere in the house Alex, Carrie, and Emily were obviously having a good time together. I just wished I could be there to see the look on April's face when she saw who her real competition was. No matter what I felt toward Alex, I knew there was no way he'd choose April over Carrie and Emily.

"Jamison, have you seen Alex?" April asked, coming back out onto the front steps. "I need to speak to him."

Jamison hefted an armful of shopping bags up the steps and said, "He may have gone to work."

"Well, someone has to do something about the state of the guest cottage. It's disgusting." April seemed oblivious to the fact that she was blocking Jamison's way.

He balanced the parcels and asked, "Disgusting? How's that possible, Ms. April? You were quite content with it just the other evening."

April snorted, "I was just being polite."

"How may I be of service, Ms. April?" he asked, straining

under the weight of her parcels.

"You can send your girl there up to the guest cottage to spruce it up."

Jamison, struggling to balance his load and close the trunk, said patiently, "I'll bring Chelsea to the guest cottage myself as soon as we've taken care of a few things for Mr. Alex."

He stepped around April and went into the house. I grabbed as many shopping bags as I could carry and followed them inside. When April blocked his way again, Jamison set the packages down in a pile on the floor. He yanked down his suit coat sleeves, and brushed imaginary dust from his jacket.

"Rest assured we will find time to address your concerns, Ms. April," he said.

"Now is fine," April said, "Send the girl up to the guest cottage within the hour."

She turned on her spindly high heels and sauntered back out the front door. We heard the music blare as the Mercedes started up, and April sped out of the driveway.

I glanced at the dirt on my uniform and said, "Let me just change, Jamison and I'll go to the guest cottage."

"Not today," Jamison said, moving to stop me. "I'll go talk to Alex first."

"No, don't bother him. He's with his family," I said.

Jamison laid a hand on my shoulder and peered into my face. "Chelsea, what's the matter?"

I shook off the heavy feeling and said, "Nothing. I don't mind doing the cleaning. I don't even mind cleaning the guest cottage for April. As long as I stay focused and think about how it'll help Karl, then none of it's a bother."

"But you don't need to do those things for April," Jamison said. "She's not your concern."

"It'll keep her out of your way. Consider it a thank you for the gardening gloves." I tried to force a smile.

"Please," Jamison said, "you look as if something else has happened since this morning. Did you talk to Alex?"

"No, I haven't seen him." I looked at Jamison and

couldn't believe he'd kept something as big as Alex's wife and child from me, especially when I knew he'd seen Alex and I together. I couldn't believe that he'd put me in that situation. Finally, I confessed, "Well, I met his family on the front steps."

"His family? You mean Ms. Carrie and little Emily?"

His tone was casual, with just the right amount of confusion. I couldn't blame him for keeping Alex's secrets. No matter how well we got along, Alex was his family and I was the outsider. He'd made a point of having no opinion of Alex and his affairs previously, and there was no reason that habit shouldn't extend to me. Whatever the situation was between Alex and Carrie, no doubt I was the last person Jamison would tell.

The other woman, I thought, disgusted at myself. That was *me*. I'd royally screwed up and I deserved to spend the rest of the day slaving away under April's command.

"Chelsea, please," Jamison said as I sidestepped him, "I don't understand what's wrong."

"There's nothing wrong," I said stiffly. "I know my place now, and I'll stick to it."

Chapter 19

Chelsea

The small kitchen at the guesthouse had remained untouched, nevertheless, April made me scrub it from top to bottom. As I cleaned everything from the inside of the microwave to the baseboards under the cupboards, she sat at the kitchen counter and sipped a glass of white wine. Though she pretended to flip through a fashion magazine, I could feel her eyes on me as I worked.

"You're good, I'll give you that," April said. "I wouldn't know the first place to start. I've never cleaned a thing in my life."

No shit.

Holding up a manicured hand, she inspected it carefully before continuing to brag, "A reporter just did a story on me, and he was disappointed to find out there's no sob story behind my rise to fame."

I was glad I was on my hands and knees scrubbing so she couldn't see me rolling my eyes. The woman was determined to build up her career despite her B-movie credits.

She was ambitious. I'd give her that.

"I grew up in L.A.," April continued, "My father was a sound editor. My scream was famous by the time I was ten years old. I landed my first on-screen role at twelve and the rest…is history."

"Your father must be proud," I said.

April shrugged, "I don't see him much. He's still in that little shack in Venice Beach. I've moved on."

Her poor father, the first man she'd chewed up and spit out as soon as someone richer came along. I scowled as I realized April could turn on the charm when she wanted to hook a new man. She was the exact sort of pretty, calculating woman my eight-year-old self had been horrified to see my father date.

"You look tired," April said, "what's the word? Haggard. Why don't you do something easier for a while? You could put away the clothes upstairs."

She was unbelievable. I wondered if she even knew how to be anything other than petty and insulting. Relieved to get out from under her glaring scrutiny, I left the cleaning supplies strewn across the kitchen floor and escaped upstairs. I only enjoyed ten minutes of peace, hanging skimpy dresses back in the closet, before April found an excuse to join me. I almost felt sorry for her, having no one else to talk to but a captive audience, but then she opened her mouth and ruined it.

"I really should change before dinner. I expect Alex will take me out on the town tonight. He's such a considerate host," she said.

She pulled out half the dresses I'd just put away and flung them on the bed. As I tried to work around her, she flounced and posed in front of the full-length mirror, trying on one outfit after another.

"Alex is a man who likes a little color in his life," she said, eyeing my plain, white uniform. "I'm lucky, because bright colors don't suit everyone, do they?"

I started to gather up the mountain of discarded high heels and sort them into pairs.

"The first time I met Alex I was wearing emerald green. He couldn't take his eyes off me."

Forcing back my inner urge to bolt for the door, I was determined to do my job, despite her clear determination to make every moment of it miserable.

"It must be one of his favorite colors. I suppose green doesn't do much for your complexion, does it. You're quite pale."

"Oh, what? Sorry, I didn't hear you there for a moment. Is there anything else I can help you with, Ms. April?" Jamison often used stilted politeness as a brush-off. I hoped it would work for me.

"Yes, the front windows are smudged. I can't believe you didn't clean them before I arrived. Hosts usually want their guests to have the best view of the main house," April said, narrowing her eyes at me.

To my dismay, she followed me back downstairs and poured herself another glass of white wine. I just couldn't shake her. I gathered up a spray bottle and towels and started to wipe the spotless front windows.

As I began to wipe the glass, I noticed the view down the hill to the main house was stunning. From the guesthouse windows I could see all the way down to the twinkle of the water in the swimming pool. My mind dove into the memory of seeing Alex swimming naked the first time and, despite my best efforts, my heart thudded painfully.

I rubbed harder, as if that would erase the emotions welling up inside of me. My eyes trailed off to the side of the road and found the hidden stone archway that lead to the secret grove. In all honesty, I had to admit, I'd already been smitten with Alex by the time we walked that sweet, winding path through the woods together. He was genuine and approachable, an honest man stuck in a world of pretense. But more than that, it was the look in his eyes when Jamison had first introduced us that struck me. I'd thought I saw something there, a flicker of something I couldn't describe. Not exactly a look of recognition, surprise, yes, but there was something unique that sparked between us. Or at least that's what I'd wanted to think.

Before long, April pulled me out of my reverie with another complaint. "You smudged that last one. Honestly, it's a wonder Alex keeps you on at all."

I shook my head and redid the window. What little bit of sympathy I'd had for April just evaporated with the spray cleaner on the glass. As I stared at the spotless window I tried to convince myself that the Alex I'd come to know was just a fantasy. I was here to work, to make enough money for Karl's care facility, and to go home at the end of the summer. It was simple, and all I had to do was keep my head down and work. Whatever Alex wanted to do with his film or with Princess April was up to him. I just hoped he didn't hurt his daughter when he did it.

"Speaking of Alex," April said, "when you're done with the windows I want you to set up the dining room for two. I think Alex and I will stay in tonight. We have a lot of catching up to do."

I bit my lip to keep from throwing out some snarky remark, but I couldn't help but throw a glance at the haughty woman. She sat curled in an armchair like a contented cat. I furrowed my brow. It sure seemed like she was making an awfully big effort to prove something to me. I wondered how I could let her know that I wasn't competition. She didn't have to worry about me.

"I know, I know," she purred, "I should be more discreet, but can you blame me? You've seen how delicious Alex is, and I can't help but brag a little. Just us girls, right?"

She winked and licked her lips, the expression on her face clear.

So that was it. She and Alex were lovers. I wiped the last window clean and wondered if Carrie knew. My only consolation was that April's false Hollywood appearance didn't compare at all to the natural blonde and elegant grace of the woman I'd met on the front steps. Alex might be sleeping around with other women while he and Carrie sorted out their family difficulties, but April was nothing compared to Carrie and her lovely daughter.

I knew—because I was nothing too.

Chapter 20

Alex

It was late in the afternoon before I caught a glimpse of Chelsea again. I was on the phone with my cinematographer and had to sit through the last reports about the exterior shots and B-roll he'd captured before I could end the call.

"We'll be done with all of it within a week," he said. "Are you telling me there's going to be a break before shooting, or are we sticking to the schedule?"

"I'll let you know. There are a few problems with casting, but I'm trying to clear everything up as quickly as I can," I assured him.

"Look Alex, I already turned down a chance to work with Wes Anderson. I love this movie, but I'm taking a big gamble here."

"I know and I appreciate it," I said, "that's why I'm going to make the changes I need to on my end. I don't want anything to mess with what we've envisioned for this movie."

He laughed. "Yeah, good luck with that. That's the kind of thing that kills off all the good producers. Hang in there, man."

I reveled in the thought of being one of the good producers and hung up the phone. I'd wasted the majority of the day on phone calls and now I needed to talk to Chelsea. Without her and Jamison's support behind me I'd never have the balls to scrap my father's production of the movie and start over. Jamison had given me a copy of the screenplay Chelsea had written. I glanced at it sitting on my desk again. Although it was a different script from mine, I could see that Chelsea's writing had the fresh voice and perspective I needed.

And I needed her to see the real me. Without her, I was just Henry James Silverhaus' son, the heir to the B-movie kingdom. She was the only one aside from Jamison who'd taken me seriously, and I'd failed her.

I'd accused her of being the type of woman I despised, when in truth she was the exact opposite. Chelsea was the kind of woman I wanted.

The thought made me reel, and I leaned against my desk for a moment. Carrie had suspected as much, insinuated that exact thought when we'd chatted, but now it hit me like a ton of bricks. I was falling for Chelsea.

Now that I thought about it, it was obvious right from the start. Only seconds after we'd met, and her eyes had locked onto mine, I'd known I didn't want to send her away. For the next few days, I'd trailed after her like a puppy dog, finding every excuse just to run into her and talk to her. I remembered the sweet warmth of her birthday dinner, her shy smile, the first quick taste of her lips against mine.

"I've never heard you talk about a woman the way you do about Chelsea," Carrie had told me earlier today. "I had to come meet her for myself. She's shy, but I can definitely see you together."

"Momma says she's your puzzle piece," Emily had said. "You just fit together."

My niece's words rang in my head, and I smiled. Chelsea made me feel whole, and my juvenile antics had almost driven her away. I'd been an ass, but, thankfully, Jamison had intervened. He refused to tell me what he'd said to Chelsea that morning, but I knew he'd just barely stopped her from leaving. Now, it was my turn. I needed to convince her to stay.

"You don't want her to work for you," Carrie had pointed out. "Invite her to spend the rest of the summer here as your guest. Then there won't be any confusion."

"And I'll have someone to play with!" Emily squealed, and clapped her hands with joy.

I imagined Chelsea splashing in the pool with my niece, sitting at the dinner table and laughing with Carrie. The thought was so perfect and felt so right. Chelsea was the piece of the puzzle we'd all been looking for, not just me. If I wanted any kind of a real chance with her, I needed to talk to her.

I opened the French doors of my office and strode out toward the pool house. I crossed the sun porch, rehearsing my invitation, when Chelsea came out from the bathroom and we collided.

She was fresh from the shower and her scent washed over me, a heady mix of vanilla and orange blossom. I caught her slight body, felt the strength of her arms as she reached up to steady herself, and my body leapt at the contact. Her black hair swept against my chest, and I brushed it back from her face, feeling the silk slide through my fingers.

I wanted to lean down and kiss her, but something in her eyes stopped me. Right. I'd been an ass.

"Chelsea, please," I said, "I need to apologize…"

"No thanks," she said and pushed away from me.

"What?" I was confused. My heart twisted painfully. I didn't understand what was happening. "I don't regret it, what we did."

"I made a mistake," Chelsea said as she tipped her chin and pierced me with her look. "I set up the guest cottage for your private dinner with Ms. Temple. I wouldn't want to make you late."

"My what? With April? Is that where you've been all afternoon?" I asked, horrified. What in the hell had Jamison been thinking, letting Chelsea anywhere near April?

"Yes," Chelsea said, "I'm sorry your guest thinks I did such a terrible job of preparing the guest cottage, but I spent the day cleaning..."

"Wait, you spent the day working for April in the guest house?" I furrowed my brow. "You shouldn't have to go anywhere near her."

"Why, because you don't like your mistresses to talk?" Chelsea snapped.

What? She tried to step around me, but I blocked her way. When I reached for her she shrank back, and refused to meet my eyes.

"Is that what you think? You think April is my mistress?" I asked.

"She's not as discreet as I'm sure you'd like her to be," Chelsea said. "But don't worry, I am."

"You? You're not my mistress," I floundered.

"I know." She glared. Her beautiful blue eyes now a steel gray. "I'm just the hired help. Now, if you'll excuse me, I have to get back to work."

"No, Chelsea, this is ridiculous. Just let me explain," I said.

She finally looked up at me, her eyes chilled with reserve. "There's nothing to explain. You can have your mistress, your ex-wife, your daughter, all of it. It has nothing to do with me. I'm here to work, earn my money, and get back home. That's it."

I choked, "M-my ex-wife? Daughter? You mean Carrie and Emily?"

Something flashed in her eyes. "How dare you encourage that sweet little girl to come here for the 'good memories' when you've got women stashed all over." She gave me a disgusted look. "What kind of a man are you?"

"What kind of man?" I asked, anger seeping into my voice, "You don't know me at all! I thought you, of all people, could see the real me, but I guess I was wrong. You're not different after all."

Chelsea shrank back and I quickly bit my tongue, but it was too late. She spun around and fled through the side door. By the time I'd stumbled over her ridiculous accusations, she was gone.

Chapter 21

Chelsea

"I'm buying a ticket, I'll be there in a day. I swear, Chelsea, I'm coming."

I regretted the phone call as soon as I heard Zach's voice, but Clara was still sleeping and I had no one else to talk to. I knew Clara was working a late night summer job as a waitress in a local bar, and she often slept until noon. It was night here, but the time difference made it early morning in Oregon. I'd been sitting alone in my attic room, feeling sorry for myself for hours, wanting to hear the warm, friendly voice of someone who understood me. I'd held off as long as I could. Zach had answered my call after the first ring.

All I'd said was I hated it here, and Zach assumed the worst. Sadly, his assumptions weren't too far off the mark. He was ready to kill Alex and bring me home.

"No, please. Just check on Karl. I only have a few more weeks of work, and then the summer will be over. I'll have the tuition money and everything will be fine," I said with a sniffle. It was just good to know that there were good people in the world, people who actually cared about me.

"You're crying; it's not okay. I'm buying a ticket online right now," Zach said.

"No, I can do this," I insisted, "I have to finish the job and get paid."

"I'll make up the difference," Zach said, eager to be my hero. He was being sweet, but I couldn't allow him to bail me out.

"No. I chose to do this, and I'm going to see it through," I said, comforted by my own determination. "Say 'hi' to Karl for me. I'll be home soon."

After all, Karl was more important than any fantasy, no matter how real it had felt.

So much for Alex's protests, I thought as I worked. April had called me to the guesthouse first thing, and after making sure I saw the tumbled state of her bed, started directing me to a slew of new chores. I'd had a fitful night's sleep after my conversation with Zach, and now it was taking its toll on me. That, along with the way April was treating me, even the simplest tasks seemed monumental.

"We agreed the Feng Shui was all wrong here," April said. She sat at the kitchen counter again, drinking white wine despite the early hour. She waved a hand over the guest cottage's living room. "Before Alex left this morning, he agreed we should rearrange."

I threw my weight against the heavy armchair and pushed it across the room to create the 'reading nook' April imagined. She was really throwing it in my face. Yeah, I got it. She and Alex had wild sex all night. Well, good for them. The truth was I had no idea what Alex had done after our confrontation. If he'd chosen to blow off steam with April, well, that was his business.

I swallowed the rising disgust and crossed the room to retrieve the lamp. I couldn't reconcile what April was saying with Alex's apparent surprise when I'd referred to her as his mistress. Why would April fabricate a relationship between

Alex and herself if what Alex had said was true? Why stage the rumpled sheets and all? She didn't need to be with Alex to get what she wanted. Anything she wanted, she could simply ask Henry for and it was hers. She didn't really have a reason to lie. Alex did.

I turned around and realized she was still talking. "He agrees the whole second story should be gutted and turned into a luxury suite. Two bedrooms are nice, but if he's going to have any other stars staying here they'll want the whole space." April was gesturing toward the upper floor as she spoke.

She watched me and waited for a response, but instead of answering her, I hefted the coffee table up and carried it over to the love seat. As Alex's employee, I worked for her, but that didn't mean I had to talk to her.

April pursed her lips and took another sip of wine. "I'm sure you're used to staying in little broom closets and such, but I feel cramped up there. Luckily, Alex is moving me to the main house later. Make sure you're around to help bring my things down."

Yeah, like Jamison would let that happen. I couldn't imagine him allowing April to lounge around the main house, sipping wine and spewing out her sharp-tongued comments while he worked.

I paused, thinking of the butler. How had I misjudged Jamison? His cold veneer of manners was thin, and once it had melted I realized that at the core, he really was an honest man. Jamison lived by a code and served Alex well. Yet, despite his openness and honesty, I didn't understand how he was able to keep Alex's dirty little secrets.

April directed me to move the lamp again. I went to lift it and stopped. I was about to open my mouth and ask why she was bothering to rearrange if she was moving into the main house. When I turned, there was Jamison in the doorway, his face a frozen mask of disapproval. My heart jumped. And then it hit me. I should just ask Jamison directly about the women in Alex's life. He'd known what had been going on that morning at the pool when he'd caught Alex and me naked, and yet he'd begged me to stay when I'd wanted to go. If anyone could clear the air it'd be him.

April slid off her stool, wine glass in hand, and said, "Oh, good, did Alex send you to help too?"

"Mr. Alex has no idea what you're doing," Jamison said, coming into the room and taking the lamp from me.

"Excuse me?" April asked, showing the bright blue of her contact lens as she batted her eyes at Jamison.

Jamison stood in front of me and addressed April, "This is outside of Chelsea's regular duties. She will be returning to the main house directly."

"Oh, Jamison," April said with an exasperated smile. "Don't be silly. Alex and I discussed all of this early this morning. I know it's hard to be left out of the loop, but trust me, it's what your employer wants."

"Ms. Temple, my employer has been on conference calls with the West Coast since four o'clock a.m. If you wish to speak to him, you may come to the main house now."

Jamison gave a haughty bow and caught me by the elbow. We were out the door and onto the path leading to the main house before April stopped gnashing the bright white veneers on her teeth and rushed to the front door of the guest cottage to hurl her last remarks. "You can't take her now. I'll send the girl back when she's done here. The very least I would expect is clean sheets on the bed."

Jamison paused, turned back to her and said, "Good service does not interrupt the guest. Rest assured you'll have clean sheets. As our guest, I expect you not to worry yourself with the duties of the maid."

April huffed, "I don't know what 'duties' she performs for you…or your employer. Maybe she's better in between the sheets than she is at changing them. Does she polish more than the silverware?"

I yanked my arm out of Jamison's, spinning around as my hands balled into fists, but there was nothing I could do. I was an employee and I couldn't just haul off and hit her, no matter how much I wanted to.

I didn't get it. Was she seriously that mean, or was she actually jealous? I wanted to laugh. That April Temple would be jealous of me was ridiculous. Was I felt to Alex was strong enough that other people noticed it too? That was just as crazy. My feelings were only anchored on my side. Alex had too many other strings attached.

"Ignore her, Chelsea, please," Jamison said, ushering me down the stone pavers to the main house before I could do something I regretted.

Again.

I started walking and halfway down the hill I decided to just ask. Jamison wouldn't take it wrong, I knew. "Is she jealous of me?"

"Yes," Jamison snorted. "Though I've known her type before. She'd be jealous of a newborn baby if it stole attention from her. She's not fond of sharing any spotlight."

Oh. So it really didn't have anything to do with Alex. Not really.

We ducked through the garden path, and headed toward the main house. I opened my mouth to ask Jamison about Carrie and Emily when Alex came around the corner and we all stopped. He looked at me, his mouth working silently, as if searching for something to say.

Jamison spoke first, "April was making Chelsea rearrange furniture at the guest cottage. Apparently, you agreed with April's plans this morning after having spent the night there."

Red anger flooded Alex's face and singed the deep blue of his eyes. He reached for my hand, but I pulled it back, and tried to move around him on the narrow garden path. I wasn't convinced that what Jamison said was true at all. For all I knew, he'd only said that Alex was on the phone to cover for him. Jamison was an honest man, but first and foremost, he was on Alex's side, no matter how much he liked me. I didn't have anyone on my side, and I needed to remember that.

"Chelsea, wait, please," Alex, pleaded.

Jamison disappeared down another path as Alex caught

my arm and pulled me back to him.

"There's nothing to say," I said, looking at the ground. "I didn't ask Jamison to intervene. I do the work expected of me."

"Look at me, please, Chelsea," Alex, his tone almost pleading. "I'm not with April. I've never been with her."

I wrenched my arm free and held up a hand. I still couldn't meet his eyes. "Stop. I don't want to hear any of this. I don't need to hear it. Like I told you, I'm here to work and that's it."

"But I want you to know the truth," Alex said.

"The truth has nothing to do with my job here. Whatever kind of playboy problems you have are none of my concern."

I glanced up to see his jaw clench. Alex's face was a picture of misery when he spoke, and I felt my resolve weaken.

"I realized last night how all of this might look, but I want you to listen to the truth." He gently cupped my chin and forced me to meet his eyes.

I tried to stamp out the little sparks of hope that were igniting in my heart, but his look was like an open flame. All I wanted to do was fall into his arms and taste his delicious lips on mine. I wanted to believe him more than I'd wanted anything in my life.

Just as I was about to give in to my emotions and throw my arms around his neck, a crash shattered the quiet of the garden, followed by another smaller smash. Jamison appeared on the side terrace, urgently waving for us to come in. Alex laced his fingers through mine and we went together into the main house.

There in the front foyer was April, her face contorted into an ugly grimace. Before we could say anything, she threw another vase onto the marble floor, and then stomped her high heels through the shards.

The words flew out of Alex's mouth. "What the fuck, April?! What do you think you're doing?"

"This?" April asked, holding up another expensive vase. "This is nothing compared to what *she's* done."

"What have I done?" I asked, wide-eyed. What was

wrong with this woman?

"How dare you talk to me?" April shrieked, "After you've done everything you can to make my stay a nightmare."

"What the hell are you talking about, April?" Alex demanded.

"She's *horrible*, Alex." April's shrill voice echoed off the walls. "I know you're blinded by lust or maybe you just like the 'duties' she performs for you, but she's horrible."

I tugged my hand free of Alex's before he crushed it. His hand curled into a fist. It looked like he was forcing it to stay at his side and remain calm. He asked April again, this time with a firm, steady voice, "April, what are you talking about?"

"All the little things she's done to make my stay hell. I know you think I'm a demanding houseguest, but think about it from my perspective. Every time I turn around she's done something else to make me crazy," April wailed as she dissolved into tears.

"April, stop. This is ridiculous. You can't tell me one bad thing Chelsea has done to you because she hasn't done anything. And this little scene of yours has done nothing except prove what a terrible actress you are," Alex said. He shook his head. "You're fired."

"Fired? She's the one you should be firing," April cried.

"Go ahead." I turned to Alex. I couldn't believe what I was witnessing. This woman was a number one, certifiable nut case, and my life was already complicated enough. I didn't have time to be caught up in the middle of poor little rich boy's craziness. It wasn't worth a couple more weeks. "If it'll put an end to this ridiculousness and save your production, then fire me."

"No," Alex said, his eyes hard. "I'm done putting up with what other people want. April, you're fired. Jamison will take you to the guest house to get your things. I want you off my property."

April lunged for a small porcelain statue, but Jamison blocked her, the expression on his face clearly saying that he wouldn't let her cause any additional damage. She had no choice but to storm out the front door.

"Wait until your father hears about this, Alex," April snarled, her pretty features contorted into something ugly. "Henry won't let you fire me."

She slammed the door behind her as she stormed out.

Jamison looked at Alex and said, "I'll go get the broom." With a tug of his jacket, he turned and left the room, as if this behavior was par for the course in his line of work.

For all I knew, it might've been.

Quiet flooded the foyer, except for the crunch of glass under Alex's shifting feet.

"I didn't ask you to do that," I said quietly, looking down at the mess. "It's probably better if I don't work for you anymore."

Alex turned on me so fast that I jerked my head up automatically. The blaze in his eyes surprised me.

"That's the whole problem, isn't it? You work for me, and that's all you need to know. This is just a job for you, and I'm just the guy who signs your paycheck."

"What do you want me to say?" I asked, trying not to show how much his words cut me. "I like simple things. All of this is way too complicated for me."

"You're the one that complicated everything," Alex said, running both hands through his hair. "My life was simple until you showed up and now everything's a mess."

"You're blaming all of this on me?" I asked, indignantly. I wanted to storm out the door, but my feet were glued to the floor. Anger at his accusation warred with hurt.

"No…yes. I mean it wasn't supposed to be this way. You weren't supposed to be this way," Alex said, throwing his hands up.

"What way?" I asked, confused. He wasn't making any sense.

He crunched across the broken glass and grasped me by both arms. His lips seared mine as he claimed my mouth, his bruising kiss burning away everything around us.

"Like this, Chelsea," Alex whispered as he rested his

forehead on mine. "Why can't it just be like this?"

"Because it can't," I said, pushing him away. I shook my head. "You're my boss."

Alex slipped his hands down to clasp mine before I moved too far away. "Then decide, Chelsea." His voice was soft and gentle now as his eyes searched mine. "We'll make it simple. Either keep the job, work until the end of the summer, and it's nothing but professional…or quit right now and stay as my guest. Stay and get to know the real me."

He made it sound so easy, and for him, I supposed it was. He didn't understand the importance of the money or my reasons for needing it. He didn't even know my brother's name, much less what I was trying to do for him. Plus, he was married – or divorced – or whatever screwed up complicated situation he had going on. He was right that I didn't know him, but he didn't know me either, or he wouldn't have asked me to choose.

"Stay here in the house, not as a maid, but as my guest," he said. "We can spend the rest of the summer getting to know each other with no complications." He shrugged his shoulders, light and carefree as if such a massive decision were that easy. "What's it going to be? The job or me?"

I pulled myself free of him, hurt by how he couldn't see how unfair that question was. Alex could do what he wanted, and it was pretty clear that he always did. He'd never had to make a difficult choice in his life. Not a real one. Not one that could affect the life of someone he loved.

I, however, had spent my life with the weight of that choice on my shoulders. And it wasn't really a choice at all. Karl always came first. I was all he had, and I wouldn't put what I wanted before him.

"It has to be the job," I said and walked away before I could see the look on Alex's face.

Chapter 22

Chelsea

No one turned down a chance to be with Alex Silverhaus. But I had, despite the fact that the bright flash of his smile made my heart pound and my knees go weak. The memory of his kiss burned into my mind.

He'd given me an ultimatum, but had no idea what it really meant. So whatever could have been, now it looked like there would be nothing between us except professional courtesy. Maybe it would be easier that way.

I straightened my shoulders and sat back on my heels to catch my breath. I was down on my knees and up to my elbows in green slime–again–from where leaves had decomposed in the pool filter. I was cleaning and all I could think about was Alex.

As I threw a handful of leaves into the bucket, the glitter of the sun reflecting off the pool caught my eyes, bringing with it a flash of the first time I'd slipped into the cool water with Alex. His tongue tasting me, his wet, hard body against mine with nothing between us but my thin t-shirt.

I shook my head. That was then, and this was now.

"I know you'd probably rather do that than head up to the guest cottage, but Ms. Temple needs help with her packing."

It was Jamison. I stopped my cleaning and squinted up at him hoping that my face didn't reveal what I'd been thinking. I brushed a forearm across my warm cheek and blinked away the steamy memories.

"Please, let me stay with the green slime, it's much nicer."

"With a better personality," Jamison agreed, "but I thought you might like helping her get ready to leave."

I stood up and sighed. I'd been dodging April ever since she'd caused a scene.

"Is Henry coming to pick her up?" I asked. My life would be so much easier once April was out of clawing distance. I could avoid Alex easily. April hadn't really given me that option.

Jamison nodded. "Of course. He's on his way."

I was relieved. "Then I'll make sure her luggage is waiting on the front steps when he arrives."

I finished cleaning the pool filter and stowed the cleaning tools in the gardening shed, then set off for the guest cottage.

A narrow gravel road led up behind the beautiful mansion to the small guest cottage. I walked the familiar tree-lined path and tried not to think about everything she'd said. She all but called me a live-in prostitute. At least Alex'd had the balls to fire her and kick her out.

I sighed as my work shoes crunched into the gravel of the path. I tried again to concentrate on what I'd chosen: the job and the tuition money for Karl. My heart couldn't come into play. My brother came first. Always.

The thought fled as I caught sight of a shirtless Alex out for a jog, running along the side of the gravel road. His sculpted chest was glistening with sweat, and a couple of stray locks of hair fell into his eyes as he moved. My stomach flipped at the sight of him.

I stepped into the road and waved to him with a tentative smile. We could be professionally polite, right? Alex stopped, breathing hard. His eyes darted everywhere, looking at everything but at me. Then they glanced to the opposite side of the road and the stone archway hidden amongst the leaves.

A jolt ran through my body as I recognized the trailhead to the grove where we'd had sex. I remembered the cool caress of that grass against my bare skin, the sinful yet delicious explorations of Alex's fingers, the way I'd opened to him beneath the dappled sunlight.

It had been magical and earth-shattering at the same time, everything I could've ever wanted. The passion had poured out of us like hot molten fire, but however explosive our first time together had been, a crater now existed between us now. I stared down at his worn running shoes as he stood on the gravel road waiting for me to say something.

"You don't swim anymore," I said, trying to break the uneasy silence. "Isn't it too hot to run?"

He shifted from leg to leg as if gearing up to run again, and I half-expected him to leave without answering. "I don't mind," he said.

I glanced up as he frowned and shot a look at the cottage door.

"You're not going up to help April, are you?"

"She needs help packing," I said.

He stopped his pacing and tilted his head. "You don't need to do that. Jamison said my father's on his way. Let him deal with April. He's the one…"

"I can handle April," I snapped.

Alex held up his hands and said, "Whatever you say." A shadow crossed his face as he added, "You've got a *job* to do."

The inflection in his voice made it sound like he was mocking me.

"Yes, I do." I shot back. "Most of the world has to work for what we want."

His stare drilled into me. Then he leaned in and took me by the arm, whispering harshly, "What do you want, Chelsea?"

"You wouldn't understand. It's not about what I want," I said, my voice small.

Alex pulled back with a look of confusion and dropped his hand. "You have a boyfriend? I should've known."

His eyes swept over me, dark with emotion.

"No." My eyes widened. "How could you think that after what we…after what happened?"

His shoulders relaxed and his gaze returned to rove over my body. "Well, I suppose you think I'm a playboy just looking for a piece of sweet ass, don't you? So why should my assumption surprise you?"

He was right. Why shouldn't he think I behaved the same way he did?

And it shouldn't hurt. I had no claim on him. Who was I kidding? Despite everything, I still wanted him, and before I knew it, I took a step toward him. For a moment, my desire buzzed too loudly to hear reason and I reached out to graze my hand along his fingertips. I drew his hand up to my hip and raised my eyes to his face.

His jaw clenched and he shifted away. He cleared his throat and stammered, "I've…I should go. There's, um…a conference call or something…." He raked a hand through his hair and turned to leave.

"Alex, wait, I…"

I couldn't find the words to explain. I needed the job, but I wanted Alex. But I couldn't have both.

Alex

Chelsea looked smoking hot. If I weren't already out of breath from my run, she'd sure as hell take my breath away. She always did. Her thin white work shirt stuck to her skin in the humid summer air. Those long legs finally had a little tan now that she'd been wearing a shorter skirt. All I could do was stand here like a fool, salivating, wanting her more than ever, with hot throbs of desire pounding in my chest. But it seemed that Chelsea didn't want any more from me than the generous salary I was paying her, and that burned.

She stood there trying to tell me something, getting all feisty and agitated at me, but I didn't mind. I kind of liked her when she got that way, fiery and passionate. I was trying to play it off like I didn't care, but in reality, I only wanted to lock my arms around her and taste her sweet kisses. When she touched me, I couldn't think straight, and I knew I needed to get out of here before I did something stupid.

"I know you hired me as a joke, but I need this job."

Obviously. She'd chosen it over me. I tried to keep my voice light. "Oh, sure, I know. Not for you, but for someone else."

She nodded and then my focus all went to shit again when she took my hand. The touch sent a bolt up my arm and through my body, bringing with it the memories of all of our previous touches. The way her body had felt against mine. Underneath me. I tried to shake them off, but then, just as suddenly as she'd taken my hand, she let go.

"Alex?" A lilting voice called. "Alex, up here."

Fucking April.

I tore my eyes from Chelsea and squeezed them shut. Maybe if I subtly ignored her she'd go away? No, *subtle* wasn't in April's vocabulary. I rubbed the tips of my fingers to my temple and took a deep breath. Chelsea and I both looked up to see April leaning over the balcony railing, curving her body into the perfect pose. Her white smile was bright and cheerful. Apparently, she'd forgotten the ugly tantrum scene in the foyer. But then, that was April. She had a way of leaving moments she didn't like on the cutting room floor and editing together her own version of reality.

She called down to me, "You look all hot and sweaty. Why don't you come up here and use the shower?"

In your dreams. I shot a glance to Chelsea, and then turned with a fake smile to April and yelled up to the balcony, "Sorry, April. I need to head back to the main house. Chelsea too, she needs to help Jamison with breakfast."

Chelsea shook her head, refusing to let me step in. I opened my mouth to protest, but I knew my efforts were in vain. She was too damn stubborn. Before I could say anything to convince Chelsea to leave, April's voice cut in again.

"I just talked to Jamison," she smirked. "He's bringing breakfast up here. Why don't you join us?"

At that moment my father's silver Mercedes roared up the gravel road. I hooked Chelsea's slender waist, and pulled her out the path of the speeding car. We bumped against the stone arch of the trailhead, and I held her tight. If only we were alone I'd take her back up to the secret grove and have a taste of her sweetness again, show her that she'd made the wrong choice.

The car slowed as it passed and the window rolled down. "Better use April's shower," my father said. "We need to have a meeting. Hope your girl can make decent coffee because I need a cup."

I clamped my jaw. *Fuck*. That was just fucking dandy. He never missed a chance to take a jab at me for hiring Chelsea. I kept an even tone and said, "She has a name you know. Chelsea. And Jamison is on his way. He can make the coffee."

Henry ignored me and drove up to the guest cottage. April was waiting for him at the door and immediately wrapped herself around him, her expression one of distress. My father ate it up as his hands traveled down over the curve of her backside.

I scowled at them and then realized my arm was still wound tightly around Chelsea's waist. She hadn't tried to pull away, and I hoped that meant something. One delicate hand was pressed to my chest and my heartbeat sped up underneath her gentle touch, sending blood rushing down.

"You're going to get me all excited right here on the side of the road," I murmured.

"Alex, I . . ."

I stopped her and breathed against the black silk of her hair, drawing in her scent. "Chelsea…"

I felt a delighted shiver run through her, but the smile she gave me was sad. "You don't understand."

"Make me. Please," I said. "But whatever you do, don't make me go in there."

I felt her body shake as she giggled against my chest. Damn, I liked that. "Well, I have to," she said, "so are you coming or not?"

I groaned as she spun gently out of my hold. No sooner had she started toward the guest cottage than Jamison buzzed by on the golf cart he used on the property, and I had no choice but to follow both of them.

"If it makes you feel better, this will probably be more fun for you than me," I said as I caught up to Chelsea.

She laughed and I felt better than I had all morning. She didn't hate me. I didn't understand what was going on with her, but she hadn't chosen the job because she didn't want me.

"Last chance to run for the secret grove," I teased.

I thought I heard her mutter 'I wish' under her breath, but that might've been wishful thinking. Our hands accidentally touched as we walked, and I saw the pink blush on Chelsea's cheeks. My heart was suddenly pounding harder than it had during my run. I hadn't imagined it. She still wanted me. I smiled and dug my heels into the gravel. Whatever her reasons for choosing the job instead of me, I didn't know. And I didn't care. Her smile was good enough for now. We'd figure out the rest later.

April's shrill voice rang out louder than normal. As usual she was constructing a scene, dramatically playing out what she wanted me to notice, obviously hoping I'd see her take Henry through the tall gate to the guest cottage garden and…do what? Get jealous? I shook my head as she pulled him by his tie, purring at him while he happily followed with a stupid grin on his face. I'd say the two were meant for each other, but then I wouldn't wish that poisonous eye-candy on anyone, not even my self-serving father. And I sure as hell didn't want April vying to be my stepmother. That would be a whole other kind of nightmare.

The gate latched closed behind them just as Jamison parked the golf cart and carried a large basket with our breakfast into the kitchen. As soon as Chelsea reached the shadow of the balcony where I stood, I grabbed her hand. She looked up at me and I pulled her into the ivy that covered the stone foundation of the guest cottage, hiding us among the leaves and shadows.

My body was pulsing and hot. I needed to taste her kisses. I pressed my lips to hers. They parted on her surprised gasp and the soft rush of air made a throbbing fire race through me. I tangled a hand into her silky hair, feeling its richness as I pulled until her head tipped back. I let my tongue slide along her soft lips and slipped it in deeper for the taste I'd been dreaming of. Damn, I needed this.

"Alex…" she whispered. Her hands came up to push me away, but then her tongue touched mine and the world around us disappeared.

She arched up against me, and I rolled back against the ivy, surprised by the force of her response. My hands glided past her short skirt, and I dragged my fingers up the back of her thighs, pulling her tighter against me. She rose on her tiptoes, and the friction between us on my hardening cock drove me wild. I rolled along the wall, lifting her as I pressed her into the ivy. She brought her hands up to tangle them in my hair.

"Chelsea…" I panted.

"Oh, god, Alex," she said, pulling my head down to her shoulder.

It was always like this with her, both of us needy, breathless and clawing at each other. I breathed in the scent of her, mixed with the fresh smell of the ivy, and it felt like I was in heaven. I had my answer, Chelsea wanted me as much as I wanted her, but a little hot groping in the shadows was only a tease, it wasn't enough to satisfy me.

"We have to go in," she whispered, her hands running softly through my hair.

I held her there against the wall and breathed into the leaves at her neck. "I can't go yet. Just stay for a minute more."

Chelsea shifted and felt my now fully hard cock pressed between her legs. She half-moaned and half giggled, "You better step back or we'll need more than a minute."

The thought of tugging that short skirt up to her hips, those legs opening for me, the sweet honey feel of her, made my knees wobble. It was more than tempting.

I let her down and leaned heavily against the ivy, my palms to the wall, pinning her in front of me. My pulse was racing, and the now-roaring fire in my veins demanded a release. I grabbed the back of her neck and pulled her to my lips and held her there just a breath short of kissing her again.

I closed my eyes and whispered against her skin, "I want to fuck you right now." I exhaled long and hard. Oh, god, that sounded so raw. She probably thinks I'm just a horny beast. "I mean, I want you Chelsea, I want to hold you and kiss you and make love to you right now, right here. With goddamn April and everyone in the back yard. I don't give a shit about what they think. I just want you…you…just you."

But I couldn't have her right now. Not the way I wanted to.

I crushed her lips with one last kiss to savor and let her go. She pushed her hair back behind her ears, straightening her skirt, cheeks wonderfully flushed. Then she looked at me and smiled, wiping the back of her hand across her lips like she'd just finished a satisfying dessert.

I leaned against the ivy next to her, both of us staring out straight in front of us for a moment, waiting for our bodies to calm. Well, mostly mine.

She cleared her throat and said, "Is Henry pulling the funding from your movie?"

I laughed. "Good question. Better than a cold shower."

Chelsea ducked her chin to her chest with a light laugh, and brushed the wrinkles out of her white shirt. "Is that what this meeting is about?"

"Yes…" I ran a hand through my hair and rubbed the back of my neck. "Henry's here to convince me to keep April."

She looked at me, eyes sharp and bright. "And are you?"

I turned and met her gaze, those eyes pulling me ever deeper, and realized there was another reason I needed

Chelsea. I needed her advice. When she asked me questions about the movie, it felt like I could finally see the project in focus. This was the first movie that really meant something to me. I wanted to pour my heart and soul into it, and it seemed like the only time I felt I still had a hold on the real vision of the movie was when I talked to Chelsea about it.

"I can't," I said, my eyes drifting to the sky. "She'll ruin it." I sighed. "But it's either her or the funding."

"What if you rewrote her part?" Chelsea asked. "I remember April had suggestions for a few scenes."

I snorted, "Yeah, she wants to make sure any real meaning is taken out so it doesn't distract from her close-ups."

"No, seriously. You should keep your funding and rewrite April's scenes."

I shot her a quizzical look, not understanding.

There was a sly smile on her face when she continued, "I get the feeling she's more of an actress that yells 'line' than one that studies the script."

I straightened and stepped away from the wall, Chelsea's words pulling my focus away from what my body wanted. "What sort of changes would you suggest?"

"There's no reason why April's character can't still be the main love interest in the beginning of the movie. Subtle things can point out that the relationship's been over for a long time and she's just in denial," Chelsea suggested. "Then you can shoot completely separate scenes with a new love interest. The new character can seem insignificant, a co-worker or something, and the love story kind of sneaks up on everyone. Including people who are too full of themselves to read anything but the pages they're on."

Well, shit. Chelsea was brilliant. "Hell, yeah. This could work."

She continued, "If you rearrange some of the scenes you've already got, then the love story can be unexpected. Audiences love that. They'll see it coming before the characters do."

"Unexpected," I repeated. There was no better word for it.

"Sweetheart, you're a genius…oh sorry, I mean…" I realized I was referring to my maid with a term of endearment. This was way too confusing, but this wasn't the time to figure it out. "Chelsea, you always surprise me."

Before I could continue, Jamison appeared on the front step and from the look on his face, it was obvious he knew exactly where to look for me. Chelsea smiled at me and stepped out from the shadows to head inside, arcing a wide circle around Jamison as she trotted off.

My eyes followed her as she left and I was sure I had a stupid grin on my face. "Just like her," I said to myself more than Jamison, "to leave me wanting more."

He huffed and said, "Just get inside. Someone has to handle April. She's been asking for you nonstop. That horrendous woman is getting on my last nerve."

Chapter 23

Chelsea

"I asked for extra ice," April said, holding her drink over her head as she lounged in the lawn chair in the backyard of the guest cottage.

I plucked the glass from her hand and headed inside to add more ice. Alex was upstairs in the guest bathroom showering, and April was taking advantage of his absence to make sure I knew my place.

"Honestly, Henry, don't you think Alex is too soft-hearted?" April asked. "I mean, the ancient butler is one thing, but that half-witted girl is another. How many charity cases does he need around his home?"

Her words floated in through the open kitchen window as I worked. I knew she knew I could hear, and that she was talking loud enough for her caustic remarks to reach me. I lingered near the kitchen door, peeking out just long enough to see how Henry would react.

Henry shrugged. "Alex always had a soft heart." I could see Henry peering into his drink glass, quiet for a moment before he said, "You should have seen how many times he tried to help his brother. It was a lost cause, but Alex just didn't have the heart to turn his back on him."

"Tragic," April said without any real emotion in her voice.

I walked back out to the patio area with April's ice-laden drink and wondered at their heartlessness. The same words in other people's mouths would have been complimentary, respectful, but in their tones it made Alex sound pitiful.

Then an idea for Alex's screenplay popped into my head. He could get back at April with the way he wrote her lines. I could come up with a few suggestions. A play on words could be wickedly funny coming out of April's mouth, especially since she'd misunderstand them and deliver the speech in the completely wrong tone. Still thinking about the clever scene, I smiled as I went back out to the patio and handed the drink to April. She narrowed her eyes and all but hissed at me. Apparently, I wasn't allowed to smile.

"Why don't you find something useful to do?" April snapped. "Change the linens on the bed…and the bathroom is completely out of towels."

I couldn't help but smile at her again as I said, "I'll head up there right away."

April sat bolt upright as soon as she realized her mistake. Alex was still in the bathroom showering. Unable to stop myself, I winked at her and turned to go. April was flustered into speechlessness, and I made it inside before she could call after me to come back.

As I entered the guest cottage, I was met by Jamison's scowl. "What does she have you doing now?"

"April said the upstairs bathroom is out of towels. I told her I'd take some up there right away," I said with an innocent smile.

"Quite a miscalculation on her part." Jamison's eyes twinkled. "There are fresh towels in the closet under the stairs."

We could both hear April complaining about her drink, and we looked out the kitchen window in time to see her get up from her lawn chair and fling the ice onto the lawn before she marched toward the house.

"You better get those towels upstairs." Jamison winked at me. He picked up a wide tray to run interference and met April in the doorway. "Ms. Temple, here are the refreshments you requested. Let me bring them out and make a plate for you."

I quickly found the closet under the stairs and pulled out a stack of fluffy white towels. I trotted up the stairs and made it past the landing before I realized what I was walking into.

Alex, naked in the shower.

The thought of it washed over me and I had to stop to lean against the wall for a moment. My blood sizzled with the possibilities.

Just minutes ago, I'd had my legs wrapped around his waist, pinned up against the ivy. I thought I'd convinced myself to just do my job and stop chasing after Alex, stop hoping for something that was a fantasy. Alex had given me an ultimatum and I made my choice. I thought I had it all figured out, and yet nothing felt decided, because the minute he got near me I fell to pieces.

This wasn't the time for some internal debate or time for me to make life-changing decisions. I had towels to deliver.

I slipped into the guest bedroom, and saw that the bathroom door was wide open. As I moved forward, I could see clouds of steam billowing up, partially obscuring my view of his magnificent body. His skin was slick and glistening. I could see the muscles of his wide shoulders ripple as he reached up and rinsed the shampoo out of his hair. My eyes followed the suds washing down his back and over the curve of his ass. I'd seen him naked before, but the sight of him still made me catch my breath. This time, when I licked my lips, it was for real.

A quick twist of his wrist, and the water stopped. The shower dripped for a moment before he reached for the door. I froze, waiting for the moment he'd open the shower door so I could see…all of him. Then it swung wide and Alex stepped out. I was so easy. Here he was trying to clean up for the meeting and I was sneaking around, gawking at his…oh, it hung so thick and heavily against his thigh. Suddenly, his head shot up, and I was busted.

"Um…there weren't any towels," I said when he caught

sight of me.

"You seem to be holding four," he grinned and stepped forward, reaching for one.

I held one out and he took it, not bothering to cover himself as he dried his hair with the towel. His eyes never left me, even as I ogled him. His broad chest narrowed to a tight stomach, and I couldn't help but follow the tawny trail of hair down from his belly button. He'd barely made two passes with the towel when he stopped and tossed it aside.

"Chelsea…" He stepped closer and lifted my chin with his fingers as I felt a blush heat my face. Damp locks of hair fell into his face and he said, "Just the feel of your eyes on me is enough."

His voice was rough and filled with desire and it made my pulse rush. I closed my eyes and gave in to the delicious taste of his kiss, the feel of his lips moving against mine. When he broke the kiss he pulled back slightly and I could feel the warmth of his breath when he spoke.

"No, not enough."

I'd completely forgotten about the meeting ,or that the others were waiting for us downstairs. I'd even forgotten about the towels, which were smashed to my chest with my arm still around them. I was so mesmerized, so engulfed in the whirl of heat building in my veins that I'd forgotten about…everything.

Alex scooped me up in his powerful arms and the extra towels dropped to the floor. He carried me into the next room and over to the bed. He smelled of fresh soap, and tasted of cool water. I welcomed the weight of him on top of me as he stretched out on me. Our lips found each other and the kiss continued from what we started outside as if there'd been no interruption at all. The heat was just as intense, the fire inside roaring to a flame in a heartbeat.

Being in his strong arms and feeling the passion in his kisses, I no longer worried about April. all my worries about the other women in Alex's life dissolved with each searing kiss. I highly doubted Alex had ever slept with April or anything like that, despite all her attempts and insinuations.

Maybe I'd been wrong about him after all.

I thought of Carrie, and her lovely daughter. I still didn't understand who they were to Alex, but I knew the embraces he gave her were nothing like this. This was the pull of something stronger, something undeniable, a force that didn't acknowledge ultimatums or obstacles of any sort. I'd have to know at some point, but for now, I was okay with letting it go.

Alex tore his lips from mine and said, "I'm sorry, this isn't what you wanted. You wanted to keep it professional but..." He shook his head and his eyes searched mine as he stumbled over his words. "I can't stay away from you. It's torture for me to know you're right here and I can't touch you." He stroked a finger down my cheek, then across my bottom lip. "You're so beautiful. Simply delicious. I want you all the time. You don't know how many times I thought about sneaking up the stairs to your room..."

My hands locked on his back, keeping him pressed to me as I looked up into his eyes. I needed to explain my choice, clear the way for more of this, but with his arousal pressing into me, and thinking of what he just said about wanting to sneak up to my room at night, I couldn't think straight. Despite my hands holding him in a vice grip, he must've seen hesitation in my eyes because he pulled back. I sat up just as there was a polite throat clearing from the doorway.

"Ms. Temple would like an apple instead of grapefruit," Jamison said. I stood up and smoothed down my damp shirt as Alex headed back into the bathroom. "She claims you never delivered the ones she ordered yesterday."

"Of course, I'll come right down," I said a little flustered that Jamison had walked in on...well what he'd walked in on.

"I bet they're in the trash," Alex said, coming back out of the bathroom with a towel around his waist.

"More likely some hiding spot in a cabinet we won't find until the smell helps us," Jamison said darkly as he left the doorway.

I brushed my hair out of my face and blew out a breath. "Oh god. That was embarrassing."

Alex smiled and said, "Don't worry about Jamison."

I turned to head for the stairs. "Still…I'd better run down to the main house and get some apples before…"

Alex grabbed my arm, his eyes piercing me with sincerity. "Please, tell me you know I've never been with April."

I nodded, unable to tell him how glad I was to hear him say it so plainly.

"I'm so sorry she treats you like this," he said. "She's such a..."

"Bitch?" I offered with a laugh.

"Yeah, she is one alright, and you don't deserve the crap she dishes out, but she'll be gone soon. I promise," he said.

"It's okay. I understand," I said, taking his hand. "I don't want you to lose your funding because of me." My fingers tightened around his. "I'm trying to be more self-confident, and I'm not going to let her push my buttons anymore. You know, when you meet someone like her, well, you just have to wonder what made them that way."

He looked at me with admiration on his face. "Has anyone ever told you that you're the most amazing woman?"

I poked a finger in his solid chest. "Just think about those rewrites I suggested earlier."

"I *have*." He grinned and grabbed my jabbing finger. He pulled my hand to his lips and kissed the back of it with a wink. "And I know just the screenwriter to help me."

I tried to ignore the soaring feeling in my chest, but knowing that Alex had never been with April, *and* that he admired my screenwriting, made me feel so light I almost floated down the stairs.

April was already sneering when she marched inside. "Honestly, how long does it take to get a decent breakfast? We're trying to have a meeting here."

Alex followed me down the stairs, and I watched the sour look wipe clean off April's face. She smiled and sidled over to slip her arm through his despite his attempt to sidestep her. She clung to him so she couldn't see when he rolled his eyes. But I did.

"You like apples, don't you, darling?" April asked him. "I seem to remember you like them sliced with a little honey drizzled over the top. I especially remember your ideas about other uses for the honey."

"I'm sure I can find some honey," I chirped.

April's bright pink lips formed a pout when her sexual innuendo failed to get a rise out of me. Knowing that Alex hadn't been able to keep his hands off me gave me the confidence to brush off her catty remarks. I'd already decided I wasn't going to waste another breath letting her snide remarks and snarky attitude bother me.

I skipped down the front steps of the guest cottage on my way to the main house. April's behavior was atrocious, but what she didn't realize was that she was just embarrassing herself the way she acted around Alex. It was actually sad to think that she equated self-worth with powerful men desiring her body. I was sure no man had ever turned down the chance to claim her as a lover, so she probably assumed that Alex's polite reserve was only temporary and he'd give in soon.

April's motivations were easy enough to figure out; however, what drove Alex was more difficult to discern. Yes, he wanted to get out from under his father's shadow, and make his own choices, yet he hesitated. I assumed it was because of his older brother David. Jamison had told me about David's drug problems, but it certainly was low of Henry to hold that over Alex's head every time he wanted to control him.

What I didn't understand was why had Alex kept me on in the very beginning. I knew getting hired was meant as a joke, or at least as a way to irritate his father, but once that had been accomplished Alex could've sent me home. Henry had disapproved of me from the first hint of my arrival, still, Alex had decided, on his own, that I should stay.

I walked into the main house, and before I had time to give it another thought, the phone rang. An office line had been connected to the kitchen so Alex could be available to take business calls no matter where he was.

I answered, "Hello, Alex Silverhaus residence."

"Well, hello, who is this?" a booming male voice asked.

"Chelsea, er, the maid. Mr. Silverhaus is in a meeting. May I take a message?" I asked.

"Chelsea the maid? I didn't know Alex had a maid."

"I'm new. I'm here for the summer." I winced as soon as I said it. Jamison was always crisp and professional on the phone and he never chatted. "May I take a message?"

"So Alex got himself a little extra help for the summer. Sounds like he finally took our friend's advice. Makes me think I'm missing out," the man said. "You do sound delicious. Please tell me you're wearing one of those French maid uniforms with the white ruffles."

I scowled at the receiver. "Sorry to disappoint. If there's no message, I'll be going now," I said.

"Oh, I like that. Don't tell me. Just let me imagine it."

I swallowed and pursed my lips hard to keep from saying the wrong thing. "Well…have a nice day."

"Wait…no, sorry. There *is* a message. Just let Alex know I found him a new love interest," the man said.

"I'm sorry?" I squeaked.

"I'm Thomas Quinn, his casting director. I found him a new love interest for the movie. Tell him she's exactly how he described her."

I knew I shouldn't ask, but the words just popped out. "Oh? How did he describe her?"

Suddenly his voice became low and seductive. "I'll tell you if you describe what you're wearing," he said.

Geez, were all the men in the movie industry like this? For a minute, I wondered what he was doing with the hand that wasn't holding the phone. I quickly shook my head to clear that disturbing visual, and decided, if I seriously ever wanted to work in this business I'd better become more thick skinned, or I'd be getting my feelings hurt all the time. Not unlike what'd already been happening with the people in the movie industry I'd met so far, but at least I had April to thank for toughening me up.

With my new attitude, I nearly laughed as I played along.

"Yeah…um…you were right about the French maid's uniform except my ruffles are black."

He groaned, "Thank you. I needed something to get me through this next casting call."

"So…his new love interest? You were about to tell me how Alex described her."

"Oh, yes. He said she needed to be slender, not too many curves, with long black hair," Thomas said, "Oh, and dark blue eyes. He was really into the eyes."

I could hardly keep the smile out of my voice as I said, "I'll give him the message. Have a nice casting call, Mr. Quinn."

Chapter 24

Chelsea

Jamison met me on the lane as I headed back to the guest cottage and said, "I've been sent to get Henry's cigars from his car."

I held up my basket of apples and asked, "Anything else we should bring, just in case?"

"I'd say an exorcist, but I think our blonde demon might be staying a while longer," Jamison said.

"She's not so bad," I told him, "as long as you don't believe a word that comes out of her mouth."

"I suppose she's forcing me to get more exercise," the butler said.

I shot him a sidelong glance and said, "Oh really? Is that why you use a golf cart to buzz around the property?"

He gave me a scowl, and I headed off to the garden stifling a laugh.

"About time," April snapped, "and it looks like you forgot the honey."

I placed the basket of apples on the garden table and said, "There's some in the cupboard above the stove. I'll get it right away."

But before I left, I took a moment to prepare the table with plates for the apples. I was purposely stalling so I could hear what Henry was about to say. From the look on his face,

April's outburst about my mistake must've interrupted him. Judging by their body language, it looked like he and Alex were in the middle of a heated conversation.

Henry turned to Alex and pitched his torso forward in the chair. "You know you're not going to be able to get another big-name actress. Not without losing nearly a month's work. Just think of how much money that is for an already stretched budget."

"Excuse me, Mr. Alex?" I interrupted. "When I was down at the house, you had a call from Thomas Quinn, your casting director. He said to tell you that he found who you were looking for."

Alex smiled at me and said, "Thank you, Chelsea. That's great news."

I saved my smile for after I turned my back to them to go find the honey. Both Henry and April pounced on the mysterious news, pitching questions like dirt clods at Alex.

"You think you can replace me that easily?" April squawked.

"He's not replacing you, are you, Alex? Quinn's just finished hiring extras, right?"

Henry's last remark floated in to me through the open window as I reached for the honey jar from the kitchen cupboard. It sounded more like a threat to Alex than a question, and I wondered if this was going to get ugly. I took a breath and scooped up a knife to cut the apples and returned to the garden patio just as the conversation began to heat up again.

Alex winked at me as I stepped onto the flagstones. Henry was in a full on lecture session and Alex was taking it all in stride. I couldn't deny the relief I felt at seeing him at ease.

"You have to realize the full scope of making a movie," Henry said. "It's not all on camera. Most of the work is done in marketing, and that's where all the hard work starts. April's name is gold for marketing. She's the driving force behind your sales." He turned to her with a smile, and brushed a hand down her bare arm. "And just imagine how great she's going to look on a poster."

April batted her lashes at Henry, then turned to Alex and said, "I don't even think you've seen my reel. I can act. Maybe you're just worried about having me too close."

Henry frowned as April tried to rub her hand up Alex's thigh, and said, "She's doing you a favor, Alex, considering the tight budget and the measly amount of pay you're offering her. The last film she made with me broke box office records."

April turned back to Henry at that reminder and gave him a dazzling smile. "You've never steered me wrong before."

"And I haven't this time either, my dear," Henry said. "Alex is going to realize this benefits all of us. He'll watch your reel and see what a magnificent actor you are." He turned to his son. "She just needs the right vehicle."

"That's exactly it," Alex said easily.

I purposely took my time cutting apple slices and drizzling them with honey. I didn't want to miss any of this. I kept my eyes down and focused on my work, wondering who would explode first, April or Henry?

"I'm not sure this is the right vehicle for April's talent at all."

"You're wrong," Henry said. "I'm sure it is."

"Ah, I don't know. It just doesn't feel right," Alex said. He gave me another brief glance, and I could see he was enjoying needling his father. "I'm sure you've got something better for her. Something up to her box office expectations?"

I turned and caught Henry frowning, clenching his mouth tight. I could tell he didn't like the position Alex put him in one bit, and it was obvious he wasn't used to it. He took a long, careful sip of his coffee, and that was when April finally exploded.

"How dare you two talk about me as if I wasn't even here. What's next? Treating me like some invisible maid?"

April sneered at me as I handed her a small dessert plate with honey covered apple slices. She waved it away, so I set it on the table in front of her. She leaned forward, narrowing her eyes and jabbing a manicured finger in the air as she spoke.

"Look, you two, here's the deal. This is the movie I want to be in. End of story. Now you make it happen."

"Well..." Alex scratched his chin, his eyes glinting. "Maybe we could figure out how to make it work. There might have to be a few script changes."

April tossed her hair and leaned back triumphantly in her chair. "Didn't I say that in the first place?" She dipped a finger into the pool of honey on the plate in front of her and licked it off, doing her best to make it look seductive. "Really, Alex, you should trust my instincts more. I've been acting since I was a little girl."

After all the fuss about the apples, she didn't even eat them. Not a surprise there. I continued my duties and served plates of eggs Benedict that Jamison brought out from the kitchen.

Alex smiled and said, "You're right. If you're okay with a few script changes, then I see no reason why we can't work together."

Henry seemed pleased with the arrangement, and beamed as if he'd made the deal himself. He ignored the plate I presented to him and held out a hand as Jamison arrived just in time to give him a celebratory cigar.

"That settles it," he boasted, waving his cigar. "A few changes to the script and everyone's happy."

Jamison leaned in to light the cigar, and I thought everything was settled. Then April caught the smile Alex gave me and narrowed her eyes. "Not so fast. I have a few demands of my own."

"Such as?" Henry asked, puffing away contentedly.

"I need a trailer, not just a little RV, but a real star trailer. I want my own hair and make-up artist. He's been with me through everything," April said.

Alex ate his breakfast, apparently lost in thought over something else and Henry nodded absently as he puffed his cigar.

Annoyed with the lack of attention, April continued, "And I want to redecorate the guest cottage. Honestly, it's so out of date. If I'm going to stay here during shooting then I need to be comfortable."

"Redecorating is fine. In fact you can knock down walls if you want," Alex said, and popped a bite of food in his mouth. "Though I doubt you'll want to stay here during construction. Perhaps you'd be more comfortable at Henry's while we update the guest cottage?"

April bit her lower lip and pouted. "No, here is fine. Though I'll need a driver at my disposal and my personal chef flown in from LA." She waved a hand around the table. "I can't believe you eat this…this crap. It's not weight conscious food. I have to maintain my figure. Hollandaise sauce is too rich, goes right to the hips..."

April's demands continued until even Henry started to look embarrassed. While he was busy trying to reason with her, I decided I'd had enough of her antics. I stifled the urge to shake my head as I poured Alex another glass of orange juice, and then headed back inside. As I opened the screen door I paused and looked back at the group around the table. Alex turned away from the two bickering co-workers and caught my eye. He smiled and mouthed *thank you*, and then winked. I smiled back and continued on into the kitchen.

Still, things weren't sitting right. I didn't trust April, or Henry for that matter. Alex may have won this time, but knowing April, this was just round one. It was difficult to manipulate a manipulator, and as I began to wash the dishes, I wondered what else she had up her Gucci-designed sleeves.

Chapter 25

Alex

I raked a hand through my hair and paced the set, suddenly doubting all of my choices. *Dammit*. Maybe the coffee shop scene wasn't unique enough. It was just supposed to show a connection before the main character and his love interest knew each other. The way people can be perfect for each other, but ricochet around the world, never crossing paths. I worried that it'd look like every other opening scene in every other movie that'd been shot a million times before.

I began to feel a cold sheen of sweat break out on my forehead, and I started to worry that I'd had too much of my own coffee that morning.

To add to my worries, the five minute scene was taking nearly two hours to set up, and my stomach was in knots. I had to stop this or I'd end up with a premature case of ulcers. As the lighting technicians finished adjusting the gels, I stepped back trying to get a new perspective, hoping that would calm my nerves. I crossed my arms over my chest and scanned the set. What would Chelsea think of it if she were here?

The coffee shop set was plain, but was it good enough? Was the clutter on the counter too random? Should it be more organized? Did it disrupt the audience's view?

I took a deep breath, and then let it out slowly. It was fine, and Chelsea would agree. Why was I so worried? The set looked realistic, and the scene would play out exactly the way things happen in real life. A quick, seemingly meaningless encounter at a coffee shop, then when the two characters talk about it later on, they would think there'd been a guiding hand nudging them toward their fates.

Like Chelsea and I meeting on the website. My cyber joke on my old man could've gone one of a hundred ways. I could've met another April, hell bent on a free ticket to Hollywood or a rich husband. Or both in April's case. Instead, I'd met Chelsea, and I thanked my lucky stars that Karma had smiled on me for once. Just thinking about Chelsea waiting at home was enough to make me feel calmer.

"We're ready," a production assistant told me as he rushed past me, heading to April's enormous star trailer. She wasn't actually in the coffee shop scene, just doing a voice-over narration. It'd been Chelsea's brilliant suggestion, and the thought of April not getting her way had me smiling even wider.

The actor playing the main character popped up next to me, rubbing his hands together with nervous excitement. He wasn't a big name, but definitely an up-and-comer. He had the acting chops to go with the looks and, unlike many actors of the same age, didn't seem to have any problems with substance abuse.

"I'm ready," he said. "The set looks good, and I like your choice for an opening scene. It feels like the right entry point."

"Entry point. I like that," I agreed as he found his mark and made himself comfortable.

It was time. I released the deep breath I was holding, anxious to get started. When the actress playing the true love interest walked out, I nearly laughed out loud. Her black hair was short and waved gently, different than Chelsea's, but she had the same wide blue eyes, details I'd decided I should keep from Chelsea for now.

The actress found her mark and a voice whispered from behind me. "Mr. Silverhaus, we have a problem."

I turned to face a terrified production assistant who continued in a whisper, "Ms. Temple refuses to come out of her trailer. I couldn't understand exactly what she was saying, but she was yelling…well, more like screaming."

What the fuck? I tried to remain calm on the outside.

"Hmm." I tapped my finger to my chin trying to keep from exploding. "Screaming? Kind of like a high-pitched shrieking?"

He nodded with a worried look on his face. "Yeah. Something about script approval…I guess?"

The poor guy was sweating bullets. Not a good sign.

I closed my eyes, my hands on the canvas director's chair in front of me strangling the fabric with clenched fists. It'd taken April all of five minutes before shooting began to realize she wasn't starring in the scene. I had to think of something fast before she read through more scenes and discovered she wasn't the center of attention anymore. When the hell had she decided to actually read everything?

I straightened and told the P.A., "Tell her we're just trying out something, and I have a second shoot of the scene planned." He just blinked at me and didn't say a word, as if I'd just sentenced him to a firing squad. "Sorry, man. I feel your pain, but don't worry. I'll be right behind you."

I clapped him on the shoulder and smiled. The young man nodded, but I could've sworn he gulped as he led the way off set to April's enormous star trailer. The hulking vehicle blocked one entire door of the sound stage and most of the crew muttered as they detoured around it during their workday. He shuffled around it and knocked softly on the screen door of the RV.

"Just wait until my agent hears about this!" April shrilled inside. "Better yet, wait until the head of the studio hears about this!"

"Ms…uh…Ms. Temple?" the P.A. squeaked. "Mr. Silverhaus said they're just trying something. There…uh…there's gonna be a second shoot later on."

"Mr. Silverhaus?" April shouted through the thin door.

"You mean the one in charge of the studio, or the one that's trying to ruin my career?"

A heavy object hit the door and the P.A. flinched as if he'd already been the target of April's projectiles. He looked at me and shrugged helplessly.

"Maybe you should talk to him yourself." He spoke to April through the door, but looked at me with begging eyes.

I heard shredding sounds and speculated that April was mauling the pages for today. I waved away the assistant and stepped closer to the screen door. I leaned a hand against the side of the RV and tried to peer inside. Only the top half of the flimsy aluminum door had a screen, but the screen was made of black mesh and it was difficult to see in. Although I couldn't see her, I could hear her just fine. Hell, everyone on the movie lot could hear her. Whenever April was upset and yelling like this, she made it a point to incorporate her famous ear-bleeding scream into her voice.

"April? What's going on?" I barked.

The door to the mammoth trailer flung open and I jumped back when it nearly knocked me in the nose. April posed in the door, as her eyes swept the lot to make sure there was an audience.

"You're ruining my career!" she yelled.

"Don't get your panties in a bunch. Nothing's on camera, yet," I said. "Can we just get this scene done before lunch?"

"What scene?" She scowled at me. "As far as I see, it's just me narrating a bunch of people in a cafe. I'm a star, not a spokesperson. People bring me coffee."

"Exactly," I said, stepping close to look up at her. "It's just a regular life scene in a coffee shop. It's only going to be five minutes, and that's why you're just narrating it."

"Then who's she?" April asked, stabbing a bright red nail into the wrinkled pages of the script she'd tried to shred earlier.

I peered at the script pretending like I hadn't seen it before.

"She has more lines than I do!" April said with another stab.

"She doesn't have any lines in this scene," I said, exasperated.

"Where's that P.A.?" April's head popped up. "He needs to fax a copy of the script to my agent. I'm not moving a muscle from this trailer until my agent has seen all of this."

The script she was holding was an old draft. Chelsea had brilliantly suggested giving the old one to April and then we'd pop the revised draft in on filming day, the one that had April as the past love interest and not the true love interest in the story. However, I'd underestimated April's cunning.

I sighed. "I'll send a copy of the scene to your agent." Hours of set-up had just been ruined, and now it looked like we were going to lose half a day on the first day of shooting.

I trudged back to set and felt the tension pulling on my shoulders. Producing was a new and exciting challenge, but the weight of it was exhausting, and I was getting frazzled. All of my decisions would set the tone for the entire shoot. If I lost control now, everything could unravel. I'd seen it happen before on my father's sets.

The director walked over to where I stood and said, "I just heard we're scrapping the narration. Are you sure you want to do that?" He threw a glance back at the actors still hovering around on the set. "They just rehearsed it and it moves the scene forward."

I pinched my thumb and finger to the bridge of my nose. "Have the script manager read it." I exhaled. "If we don't add it in post, then we'll spend a little money for a recognizable voice."

The director nodded. "Good thinking. Celebrity voice-over would be great for the trailers too."

I sank into a director's chair behind the monitors as the director took over, and the first of many takes started. I ran my hands over my face and relaxed back into my chair, ready to watch as the script manager read April's part. It all worked out in the end and she did a good job filling in for April. I had to smile when she even stuck out her hip, ala April Temple style as she read.

I looked around at the crew members' faces and everyone was smiling. I could tell it was a good scene. The director thought so too, but still, he called for eight takes. I wasn't going to sweat the load, though. Eight takes wasn't unusual in this business, especially so we could get all the angles. Once it was done, all eyes turned to me, and the heat was on again.

I sat up in my chair, invigorated by the way things were going now. I was beginning to get the hang of this. It was like being up to bat in the big game. Problems were being pitched at me a hundred miles an hour, and I had to make quick decisions that would whack the problem away and lead us to victory. It was a powerful feeling for sure. I could see why my father liked it. It'd be easy to let it go to my head.

I began to get my confidence back as I clicked off my orders with a crisp decisiveness. "Actors can finish up fittings with wardrobe and break early for lunch," I said. "Call up the extras and let's get our exteriors and crowd scenes started. We'll see where we are after that."

My happy hiatus from gray hairs and high blood pressure was short lived, however. A brief five minutes later, a make-up artist ran up to my seat like the back lot was on fire. My stomach sank when I saw the look on her face and she said, "They've got a problem in wardrobe and you need to get in there, fast."

I knew before I rounded the corner what I would find. *Fucking April.* There she stood, feet in a wide stance like a gunslinger, in the center aisle of the wardrobe room, her face contorted with an angry scowl. On the opposite end of the room stood the new actress and a shocked seamstress, trapped by her fitting. I could tell the new actress was trying to ignore April, but that was impossible. April was anything but ignorable. My head dropped back as I looked up to the heavens, cursing my father for putting me in this position. Again.

"Whose dick did you have to suck to get here?" April spat out the words at the Chelsea look-alike.

Extras and assistants were edging away as April stalked

toward her prey. The new actress just looked at April, determined to ignore the insults in a way that made me admire her.

"*I'm* supposed to be the star, now suddenly they've added you, at the last minute…jumping right into scenes with the hero. It had to be someone high up." April was on the poor woman now, shooting daggers from her eyes.

But the girl stood her ground. "I have a good agent. Want me to get you his card?" she asked.

April lunged for her, clawing at her dress and the seamstress who'd been altering her costume leapt back with pins still in her mouth.

The half-finished costume ripped as April spun the actress around. She pulled her close and barked in her face, "You're the one who sent the tabloids that story, aren't you? You're trying to ruin my chances." She looked to the others and said, "Don't be fooled, she's a snake. Now that she's slithered on set you all better watch out."

The young actress went pale and stammered out a few words of protest, but the damage was already done. The crew was confused and looked at the new actress with questioning eyes, as if April might be right. The poor girl had been humiliated. She recoiled, pulling her torn costume together and fled April's false accusations.

I threw my hands in the air as she tore past me in tears.

"Alright everyone," I called out. "Calm down. Let's just all…fuck it, just…go to lunch."

Now I understood why my father used to keep a flask of Scotch in his briefcase when he was on set. I spun on my heels and strode out of wardrobe, fighting the urge to go for a long lunch in a dark bar or choke the shit out of April. That woman drove me to want to do violent things. Instead, I retreated to sit in my car, clenching my teeth and feeling like I'd just struck out with a hundred mile an hour curve ball from April.

Neither Henry nor his Scotch would help now. I needed to talk to Chelsea. She'd understand. I fished my cell phone out of my pocket and called the house. When Chelsea answered, a wave of warmth washed over me and a smile replaced the tension in my jaw.

"Just calling in from hell," I quipped, sarcastically. "How's your day going?"

Chelsea laughed. "That doesn't sound very good. Rough start?"

"Let's just put it this way…please, tell Jamison to make sure the bar is fully stocked for when I get home."

"Ah, I see. Lots of problems?"

"No. Just one…one big, blonde one."

"April. I take it the rewrite didn't go well, then."

"Didn't go well? You might say that." I gave a short laugh. "It was more like a disaster. I suck at this. My dad made it all look so easy. Every time I felt like I really had things under control, you know, like I was a master conductor coordinating everything into a perfectly synchronized concerto, fucking April…I mean, freaking April threw a wrench in the works."

"Whoa. I see."

"I wish you were here, Chelsea." I settled back into my car seat and felt the tension easing out of my shoulders. "Talking to you makes me feel better. Anyway, April decided today was a good time to start practicing her lines and she read through the script."

"Oh, no."

"Yeah, she noticed the changes," I said.

"Darn, I thought for sure she wouldn't see it until she was on set," she said.

"One of our production assistants arrived just as she realized she was only narrating, and not starring," I told her. "Everything exploded and I think my blood pressure may have gone through the roof." I chuckled. "Being a producer isn't as easy as I thought. You handle stress better than I do. *You* should be a producer. Seriously. Where'd you learn to roll with the punches so well?"

"Oh, me? Well, foster kids learn to adapt, sort of a lifelong habit," she said.

176

"Foster care?" I asked, sitting up in my seat, suddenly distracted from my own crazy morning.

"Um, yeah, my brother and I were orphaned when I was eight," she said on a quick breath. "Anything else exciting happen on set?"

I wanted to reach through the phone and tip her chin up so I could look into her mysterious blue eyes. How'd I not known she was an orphan? And she had a brother? I swallowed hard, realizing what a dickhead I'd been, acting like a spoiled rich boy who expects life to rotate around him.

"I didn't know you have a brother. Older?" I asked.

"No, younger." There was a pause as I waited for her to explain, but she didn't.

"Well…is he in Portland?"

"Yes."

Something in her voice and her short answers told me she didn't want to chat about it over the phone.

"Sorry, I didn't mean to pry. And, yes, other exciting things happened on set," I said. "Did I tell you April made the new actress cry?"

Chelsea's voice returned to normal. "That's terrible! Not surprising, but terrible."

"April accused her of trying to sell false stories to tabloids in order to ruin her career. The poor girl had no idea what to say," I said.

"Well, your crew is intelligent. They'll figure out April's lies soon enough," she said. "I mean, she has a reputation already."

"Now tell me about your day. I really wish I could be by the pool right now. Or, better yet, swimming, with you, my little water nymph."

I imagined her blushing as she smiled.

To my amusement, she taunted me, "I might just have to go for a swim myself after I finish all my work today."

"Oh, you tease…please continue."

I leaned back on the headrest and let that mental image come into focus. Chelsea naked in the pool, the tips of her black hair drifting on the surface of the water, and clinging to the swell of her breasts. The feel of the water swirling between us as I pull her close.

Chelsea's voice was thick as she cleared her throat. "Well, you'd be bored here. Not enough drama."

I groaned, "Why'd I decide to be the producer? I should've just invested some money and bought an executive producer credit along with a screenwriter credit. I could be waiting for you in the water right now."

Now there was a thought that could keep me distracted and hard all day. *Damn.* I wanted her.

Chelsea finally broke the silence and said, "I better go. Jamison will be looking for me."

I sighed. "And I suppose the producer of this movie should stop hiding in his car."

"Besides a stocked bar, is there anything else we can do for you?" she asked.

"Yes, actually. Start thinking up a scene that explains how the hero and the new love interest actually meet. I've got a bunch of ideas, but they're all the kind of meet-cutes you've seen in at least fifty other movies."

"What makes you think I know the way people meet?"

"Come on," I teased. "You must've had dozens of college guys falling over themselves to meet you back in Oregon."

"Not really," Chelsea laughed. "I guess I'll have to get creative."

I said goodbye with a smile on my face. Chelsea probably never noticed all the heads she turned with that beautiful face and those fathomless eyes. She didn't even know how beautiful she was when everyone else could see it. I could tell by the way she'd give a little smile and look at the ground.

I got out of the car and swung the door shut as I jammed my thumb on the key fob to lock it. There was so much about Chelsea I didn't know and I really didn't like the possibility that there could be some young stallion of a college guy hot for her back in Oregon, or worse a boyfriend waiting for her return. She'd denied it when I'd suggested it before, but she'd never really given me an alternate explanation. Whatever she was reluctant to divulge over the phone, I wouldn't be able to find out until the end of the day. Then I'd have time to sit and talk, time to get to know her better. It was just going to be hard to face the long stretch of the afternoon dealing with pain-in-the-ass April when all I wanted to do was be with Chelsea.

I yanked open the door to the studio wondering about Chelsea's past and feeling a ping of jealousy. Maybe there was someone back home who knew her far better than I did. Someone she cared about for more than some summer fling.

Chapter 26

Chelsea

"Welcome back, Ms. Temple. Good day on set?" I asked.

The uniformed driver held out his hand and she took it as she got out of the car.

April gave me a dismissive look and said, "Did my packages arrive? I ordered a few things to make the guest cottage livable."

"No, Ms. Temple, nothing has arrived yet," I said.

Letting go of his hand, she waved him away like a fly. He looked at me questioningly and I shrugged. The driver was supposed to take April directly to the guest cottage, but it looked like she'd ordered a detour to the main house.

Fluffing out her curls, April swept past me and then waited for me to follow her to the center of the foyer. After she passed, I rolled my eyes at her back and walked inside.

"My first scene was a success, and I'm expecting Alex will want to celebrate."

I bit my lip and took the silk wrap she tossed at me. It was unbelievable how different her memory of the day was from what Alex had described. April's ability to edit her life to her own specifications was amazing. Unfortunately, the movie editors didn't seem to have the same magic. I'd heard Alex on the phone with them three times in the last hour since he'd arrived back at the house.

"I believe Mr. Alex is still working."

"Ridiculous. Am I going to have to find him myself?" April asked. "Honestly, you are a terrible servant, leaving a guest waiting like this."

I nodded and slipped into the narrow servants' hallway.

"Come in," Alex called out to me. "Good timing, Chelsea. I think I've finally wrapped things up for the night. Now all I have to do is wait to hear Henry's opinion on the dailies."

"That's great. Now for the bad news, April is waiting in the foyer," I said. "She said you'd want to...celebrate."

Instead of the panicked irritation I expected, Alex snorted a laugh, stood up and headed for the office door. My spirits sunk. It looked like I was in for another evening of running back and forth to do April's bidding. Alex must've noticed the dread on my face, because he laughed again and gave me a quick hug.

I stared at him. What the hell?

"I thought she might pull something so I came up with a plan," he said.

I raised a brow. "Looks like you're getting good at your job, Mr. Producer."

His eyes sparkled in the sun, and I was caught in his look. Alex's wide hands ran slowly down my arms and the soft friction sent crackles of electricity straight into my core. He started to lean in for a kiss, but I stepped back. No getting caught up this time.

"Ms. Temple is waiting," I said.

Although we talked like equals, I was still wearing the maid's uniform. As much as I thirsted for a taste of his lips, as much as my body wanted to answer the melting softness in his eyes, I really didn't like being flirted with behind closed doors. It reminded me of our situation. I was still his maid and he was my employer.

Alex gave me a small frown and opened the office door. "Don't worry, like I said, I have a plan."

"She's your guest and I'm your maid. You don't need to

reassure me," I said, not able to meet his eyes. I knew it'd come out too harsh, and I regretted it as soon as I said it, but it was too late.

Alex straightened up and rolled his shoulders. I felt a kick in my chest as I recognized the move. He often did the same thing when Jamison dropped big hints, as if a weight dropped on his shoulders and he wished he could get it off.

My chest hurt again. I was tired of all this. Of putting up this charade of being the maid in front of guests then clawing and kissing each other in secret. I needed to be honest with Alex, and he needed to know that pursuing our feelings in our current roles was taking its toll on me. What I regretted more, however, was what I felt as he rolled those wide, strong shoulders. It wasn't guilt that was hitting me, but the realization that I was starting to know him well enough to know his gestures, an intimacy more unsettling than the press of his lips against mine. I hadn't planned on that, and I didn't know how to handle it, so I'd pushed him away.

"After you," he said.

We took the short walk down the main hall to the foyer, and the entire time, I felt like I was falling. The desire I felt for Alex pulled me forward, but my balance deserted me. I paused in the hallway overwhelmed by a helpless kind of vertigo. I hadn't felt this way since my father had passed, when he didn't come home. That bottomless drop had opened daily for years, and now I realized what it was. Longing.

I longed for Alex. I missed him when he was out of the room. I wanted to reach for him though he was just a couple of steps away and waiting for me to catch up.

"Chelsea, are you alright?" he whispered.

I nodded and forced my feet to move. The flirtations, the sexual tension, the hot flares of our kisses, even the memory of our bodies melding together, were things I could learn to handle. But now I felt like the bottom was dropping out from under me again and I could fall.

Alex put on a bright smile as he stepped into the foyer to face April. "You're here!"

"Where else would I be?" April asked stiffly.

"The guest cottage, of course. How am I supposed to surprise you if you don't let the driver follow the instructions I gave him," Alex said, waggling a finger at her.

"A surprise?" Her face brightened. "What surprise?"

"You want me to ruin it by telling you?"

April tossed her hair. "I want to know I'm not just being thrown out into the cold night."

I hung back, listening and patiently waiting for them to finish their conversation, but as usual April reacted as if her life was made up of movie scenes that she had to act out. I wondered why she couldn't just be herself. Why did everything in her life need to be so dramatic? If only she was that good on screen.

"I hired you a spa team. You're supposed to be sipping champagne right now while getting a foot massage and pedicure. There's a hot tub filled with scented oils and a Swedish masseuse waiting to ease any tension from your first day on the set," Alex said.

"Oh, darling, you're so thoughtful," April said and sprung into his arms for a hug.

She wrapped herself around him and I tried not to gag. Alex finally extracted himself, and turned away in an effort to escape, but April clutched his hand and drew it to her low neckline as she kissed his knuckles.

She purred, "You'll be joining me later?"

"You know I can't," he said. "A producer's work is never finished. Especially when half the crew is in the U.S." He rubbed the back of his neck. "The time difference is hell on my sleep. But, anyway, you go enjoy your pampering and get a good night's sleep. See you on set tomorrow."

Alex disappeared down the hallway and missed seeing April's face change from her usual simpering to disdain sharpened by her failed proposition. She held out her hand and snatched the silk wrap I handed her. Then she swept out the door and barked at the driver to take her to the guest cottage. As the heavy wooden door swung shut behind her, I shook my head and breathed in the returning peace.

"Chelsea?"

I jumped a mile as I realized Alex had come back into the foyer. He stood under the chandelier, unaware of how the light turned his hair to gold. He looked like a movie star himself, and I thought how furious April would be if she knew that he didn't rebuff my touch.

The thought added warmth to my cheeks and it must've come out in my smile because Alex relaxed. He plucked a rosebud out of the large arrangement Jamison kept fresh on the center table of the foyer. Toying with the flower, he swept his gaze over me, and the heat spread from my checks to my entire body.

Whenever Alex looked at me, I felt like he saw the real me. His eyes pierced through the shell of my exterior, the front I put up in my role as his maid, the mask I'd had to wear to survive my years as a foster child. I believed he could sense what was in my heart, in a way no one else had ever done. Next to the curvy bombshell beauty of April, I felt like I didn't compare. But as he stood here in front of me holding the rose, I could see a special look deep in his eyes, something meant only for me.

At least, I hoped it was.

"Your guest is gone. Well done," I managed to say.

"Then it's official," Alex said.

"What is?"

"You have the night off," he said, and handed me the rose. "What're you going to do with your free time?"

I smiled and waved the fragrant, crimson petals under my nose. "Well, I know this movie producer who needs a few scenes written. I might spend some time thinking about how two people meet."

"You're going to take your night off and work?" Alex asked, raising his eyebrow.

I shrugged, eyeing the deep, velvet texture of the curled petals. "What else would I do?"

"I was hoping you'd have dinner with me," he said. He

reached out and touched his fingers to my arm, sending a shiver up my skin.

"Alex, I…I'm not sure that's a good idea," I said.

"Jamison will be there." His fingers trailed gently down my arm until my hand rested in his palm. "I just want to make sure you understand. I want you there as my guest. You won't have to work. The three of us can cook together and I'll clear the dishes."

"Well…" I tried to protest, but in my heart, I just wanted to agree.

"I'd really love to have you join me," Alex said, "I mean, unless of course you have a hot date or something."

I laughed, not wanting to let go of his hand. "Alright. Dinner in the kitchen sounds like the perfect way to spend my free time. I'll just go change."

Alex squeezed my hand, and I nearly had to pry it lose from his grip in order to leave. He stood there a sensual smile curving his lips, his eyes half hooded as if already dreaming about how things would go after dinner. I headed for the stairs to the servants' quarters feeling giddy, but reminded myself not to get too excited. It was just dinner, and besides, we wouldn't be alone, Jamison would be there.

I skipped up the stairs just in time to hear a call coming on the Facetime app on my laptop where I'd left it open on my writing desk. When I reached it, I was surprised to see it was Clara calling from Oregon. I clicked on the call and the screen popped open to Clara's smiling face.

"Hey girlie. What's up?" she chirped.

I almost shushed my best friend, but then I realized there was no way anyone could hear her. "Clara, what're you doing up at this hour? Isn't it crazy early in the Oregon?"

"Nice to hear from you too. What's going on? And, yeah, I'm still up. You know this summer job is a night job. I just got home. Anyway, what're you doing? I can't see you. Stand in front of the camera."

"I have to get ready for dinner. I don't have a lot of time, so talk fast while I change."

Although my back was turned to the camera I could hear the excitement in Clara's voice when she said, "Oooo, so you're going on a date with him?"

I spun back from my search through my drawers for something nice to wear and hissed, "It's not a date. It's just dinner with him. And Jamison will be there too."

"Why are you whispering? He's not there in the room with you, is he?"

I stood in front of the camera long enough for her to see my deadpan stare and said, "Clara…get real."

"Your butler buddy won't get in the way and you know it. Give him half a chance, and I'll bet he'll be planning your wedding. In fact, give me Jamison's number because we have a lot of things to coordinate," Clara said.

"This isn't a date and we're not getting married. We're not even seeing each other," I whispered in front of the laptop screen. "Not really."

"But you've got the hots for him. I bet when he's gone, you think about him day and night." Clara giggled. "Well, night, anyway. I bet you dream about him too, don't you? Hot dreams with hot sex."

"What I'm doing is wishing I hadn't told you any of that," I said.

"You're in love," Clara said with a sing-song tone to her voice.

I groaned, "This is exactly why I should have kept my mouth shut. That's ridiculous."

Clara laughed. "What's ridiculous is Chelsea Carerra thinking she can have an easy fling with any guy. I know you. You're not a one-night-stand kind of girl."

"But you've never met Alex. I could be delusional for all

you know," I said.

"Oh, please. Chelsea, you have the most brutal ability to read people I've ever seen. If you're getting all aflutter over him, and it appears you are, because you haven't stood still one second while we've been trying to talk…can't you sit down in front of the screen?" Clara didn't wait for my response. She just made a face and went on, "Yup, that means you've seen it in him to."

I dashed out into the hall to get my dress from the tiny wardrobe at the top of the stairs and left her calling my name. "Chelsea? Where'd you go? I didn't stay up this long to talk to the air, you know."

She was right. I was a good judge of people, and if I wasn't getting clear signs of affection from a guy there's no way I'd open up. With Alex, I felt like a field laid open to the sky.

I stepped in front of the computer screen holding up the nicest dress I'd brought with me. It was also the only dress.

"Ooo, yes. Wear that," Clara said, her eyes widening as I spun around in front of the desk. "I say dare Mr. Silverhaus to gaze upon you in that dress without getting a stiffy," she teased.

"Stop it, you perv!" I laughed. "Oh, Clara, I wish you were here. I miss you," I said.

"I miss you too, but trust me, hon, as soon as Alex gets a look at you in that dress, you two will want to be alone," Clara said.

I said goodbye to Clara and slipped on the dress. The fabric fluttered over me and the feeling went straight to my stomach. No longer in a uniform, I was excited to see Alex. I reminded myself I wasn't his date, but tonight I wasn't his maid, either, and that thought made me smile.

Chapter 27

Alex

The silverware I was holding clattered to the table when Chelsea walked into the kitchen. Jamison gave me a sharp look, but then I saw his eyes get caught too. Chelsea was stunning. It was the same white dress she'd worn for her birthday dinner, and it was having the same effect on me now.

I imagined running my hands up that short skirt, yanking off her panties...

"Ah, Chelsea. You're just in time to get the bread out of the oven. I don't trust him not to drop it." Jamison's words jogged me out of my thoughts, and although I knew they were spoken to Chelsea, I knew he wanted to remind me of his presence.

She smiled, proving Jamison right as I fumbled for another fork.

"The bread smells delicious. Is it the honey-wheat one you make?" she asked Jamison as she went to the drawer to remove oven mitts.

From where I was placing the silverware, I watched the two of them working together smoothly, chatting freely. The two of them moved so naturally together. I envied Jamison. He seemed to know Chelsea better than I did.

Still engrossed in her conversation with Jamison, Chelsea turned the baking pan over and popped the loaf of bread onto a wire rack. "Karl would love this bread. It was his favorite when we were little."

I stepped a little closer to the large kitchen island trying to get in on the conversation. I really wanted to know more about Chelsea, but it seemed like I was failing on my own. Maybe I needed Jamison's help.

"Is Karl your brother?" I asked.

Chelsea looked up and nodded, then went to help Jamison dress the salads. I'd already finished setting the kitchen table, and tapped my fingers on the granite countertop, feeling like I was watching a movie of two people making dinner. Like I was the audience and not actually there.

Jamison waved for me to go sit at the table so that he and Chelsea could serve our dinner. I wanted to help, to make sure Chelsea felt like it was her night off, but I went the wrong way around the kitchen island and caused a traffic jam. Finally, I extricated myself and escaped to the table. They joined me and the conversation continued, but I still felt awkward. This wasn't going the way I'd planned.

It felt like I was in some strange competition for Chelsea's attention, like I had to say something to prove my position and be part of the group. I knew Jamison like a father. He'd seen me through diapers and toilet training. So in an effort to show how close we were, I said, "Jamison's an excellent baker too." I nodded like I was some kind of expert about Jamison's past, but my remark just came out sounding stupid and Chelsea barely acknowledged it. "He even makes a roast that's baked in a flaky crust."

"Beef Wellington," Chelsea replied. "Yes, he told me all about it." Then she turned her attention back to Jamison. "I want to learn how to make the pastry leaves and decorations for it. Can you show me, Jamison?"

"Beef Wellington is a winter dish, dear," Jamison said, serving a slice of pork on Chelsea's plate. "Do you want us to cook like Dotty?"

They laughed as if they were sharing some kind of private joke. I tried not to frown and asked, "Who's Dotty?"

"Mrs. Carerra. That's my mom's name, Dotty. The foster family that adopted me. It was such a big house, and the kitchen was always in total chaos. She's such an angel, though. She always cooked whatever we voted on, and believe me, there were a lot of us to cook for."

"Pot roast in the summer, gazpacho in the winter. Total chaos." Jamison said it with such authority that it confirmed what I'd thought earlier. He really did know Chelsea much better than I did.

They laughed again, and I started on my salad. I raked through the fresh greens from Jamison's garden, and felt my emotional pendulum swing. On the one hand, I was glad Chelsea felt so comfortable here in my house. She seemed genuinely happy. Plus, Jamison was happier than I'd seen him in years. Everyone was so damn happy.

Except me.

I was jealous. I felt left out in my own house, but I wasn't giving up.

"So you were adopted by the Carerras, but you mentioned you were in foster care for a few years before that. How old were you when they adopted you?" I asked.

"I was in high school, sixteen years-old."

"And how old was your brother? He's younger than you, right?" I asked, determined to learn more about my beautiful guest.

"Karl?" Chelsea asked, sharing a glance with Jamison. "No, the Carerras didn't adopt him."

"That's strange. Don't they try to keep families together?" I asked.

She let her fork rest on her plate and said, "He wasn't available for adoption at that point."

I looked at her, confused, hoping she would continue. Chelsea's eyes were stormy, the blue tumbling with emotions I couldn't read, but I felt the same hesitation I'd sensed on the phone with her before. Had I hit a nerve?

"It's...complicated," she said, "and I seem to recall you don't like people complicating your life." She gave me a tight smile. "Unfortunately, not everyone gets to have a simple, straightforward life like you."

Damn, I'd done it again. I'd hit a nerve without even really knowing how I kept doing it. Chelsea looked pissed at me. Like I'd just sat on her favorite Chihuahua dog or something. But she was right. Despite divorced parents, my life had been easy. Jamison was always there for me, and I'd had everything I ever needed. Chelsea was also right about what I'd said. I remembered exploding at her about things complicating my life.

Funny thing was, I tried to explain how meeting her had upset everything in my life, but in a good way. She lit up my life like nobody else, and she just didn't know how amazing she really was. But, of course, I'd fumbled it. Instead of telling her how I felt, I'd given her the ultimatum that had created this distance between us. I wanted to get closer to Chelsea, but watching her and Jamison, it seemed as if I knew nothing at all about her.

I sat back and looked to Jamison for help. He gave me a polite sniff and changed the subject. "I hate to mention her name for fear she'll appear, but how did our actress do today?" he asked.

I launched into the story of April and the multiple takes and soon had them both laughing. Finally, it felt like my house again and the tension in my shoulders relaxed.

"Well, while you were on set we had our own excitement here," Chelsea said.

"Really? What happened?" I asked.

Jamison said, "Nothing. Alex isn't interested in dusting schedules and household chores."

"Come on, Jamison," I said, finally confessing, "You two are making me feel left out in my own home."

Chelsea's ocean blue eyes caught mine. When she smiled, I felt my heart jump. That had been a real smile.

She explained, "The dining hall chandelier was on the dusting schedule for today, and Jamison decided it was easier to stand on the dining table than get the ladder."

"Oh, no. Did you fall? Are you alright?" I asked.

"Well, I care about the chandelier," Jamison sniffed.

"You should've seen him," she said with a smile. "He was an acrobat. The duster got caught in the lower tiers, and he had to get a chair to stand on. When I came in it was like one of those balancing acts out of a circus."

Her eyes danced with laughter, and I smiled back at her. Finally, it felt like we were connecting. "And I bet he didn't ask for help. He's stubborn like that."

"*He* only pulled a muscle in his back," Jamison said snidely, making reference to the fact that we were talking about him when he was right in front of us.

"A pulled muscle?" Oh, I was going to use that. "All the more reason for you to go relax. I told Chelsea earlier, I'm doing the dishes tonight."

Jamison gave his precious china a glance, then sighed. "Keep an eye on him, please, Chelsea."

As he left, wincing when he thought I wasn't looking, I refilled Chelsea's wine glass and with a smile and said, "You should relax too. It's your night off."

I stacked all the dishes and carried them to the sink. I knew Jamison hand-washed the china, and I figured I could wrangle a plate or two with a soapy sponge.

"Here, let me help," Chelsea said. She brought her wine glass over to the counter and then pulled a bottle of dish soap from the cupboard below the sink.

My eyes followed her graceful moves as she worked, my gaze trailing down the enticing curve of her ass when she bent over and down her long seductive legs.

"You know you make things easier, right? I never meant to say you complicate my life."

"Then what did you mean?" She straightened and turned to face me.

"I don't know how to say it," I said tipping her chin so her eyes met mine.

All I could do was touch my lips to hers and hope the kiss said more than my words. She opened to it, her mouth parting on a sigh, and she rose up on her tiptoes to taste the wine on my lips. I leaned back against the counter, and she pressed against me, licking flames of desire following the path of her tongue.

Her hands reached up to tangle in my hair, leaving her body draped across mine. I ran my hands down her back from the bare skin of her shoulders to the soft flowing dress. She shifted against me, pulling a moan deep from inside me. My fingers twitched at the hem of her dress, desperate to touch her. When I felt no hesitation from her, I slipped my hands underneath it.

I trailed my fingers up the backs of her thighs to the thin border of her panties. The caress caused her to shiver and smile, her lips curving before opening deeper into our kiss. I wanted to lift her, but I felt woozy, my mind deliciously scrambled by the circles of her hungry tongue. When she dragged one bare leg up my pants and wrapped it around me, a lightning fast adrenaline rush fired through my veins, and my cock jerked with pleasure.

I swept my hand up her exposed leg to the knee at my waist and then traveled slowly along the silky skin of her thigh. When I reached the border of her panties again, I remembered how, in the pool, she'd begged me to rip them off. I yanked the narrow lace aside and thrust my finger inside. She was wet and ready for me, just the way I'd always pictured her in my dreams.

Her hands left my hair and raked down my chest to my belt. I nipped at her bottom lip as she yanked my pants open and shoved her hand down to find me heavy and hard. When she wrapped her fingers around me, I nearly lost control.

I pulled back from our melding kiss to look into the ocean of her eyes again. I wanted my cock in her pretty mouth, her eyes watching my face so she could see how much she pleased me. So she could see the power that she had over me. Then I wanted to open her up, tease her soft clit until she begged to feel the girth of my cock filling her, stretching her.

It was complicated, the surging, pounding need I had for

her. Yeah, she was right about that. She spun my head around like crazy, but it was a wonderful kind of crazy when I was with her like this, heart pounding, pulse racing, and only one thing on my mind. Having Chelsea as mine. Knowing that the torrent of desire in her eyes was all for me.

I needed her down on her knees in front of me. She hadn't tasted my cock yet, and there was something inside of me that ignited like fire every time I pictured her that way. I cupped her face with my hands and locked eyes with hers. Gently I pushed her down. It was a simple signal, and she didn't resist as she acknowledged it with a smile. She looked up at me through her thick lashes as she licked her lips, and I made a sound in the back of my throat. I threw my head back when I felt the warm wetness of her lips around my shaft, then snapped my eyes back to her face and watched as she took me deeper into her mouth.

My hand instinctively went to her hair, and I tangled a fist into those long silky locks as she sucked me. I groaned and whispered, "That's my girl, suck it."

She grabbed the base of my cock with one hand and sucked harder, each pull of her mouth sending a bolt of nearly painful pleasure through me.

"Look at me," I said, my voice husky and low. "Look at me, Chelsea. See what you do to me? You make me crazy for you."

Her eyes flicked open and she looked up. I tugged her hair, tipping her head back slightly to get a better look at the hot desire in her eyes. Seeing her lips stretched wide around my shaft made my hand tighten in her hair. I needed her to see me, to understand all of the things I couldn't say.

"See that?" I hissed through clenched teeth. "My naughty little temptress. See what you do to me? Running around my house, tempting me every day. You make me so hard."

I moaned again as she stroked my base harder, covering with her hand what she couldn't take into her mouth. The swirling ecstasy of seeing her sucking my cock, of thinking about how I wanted to fuck her in every room of my house, was bringing me to orgasm too quickly. I wanted to make it last, relish every beautiful sight of her in the throes of pleasure.

I tightened my grip on her hair and stopped her movement. "Wait…" I panted. I moved her head until she released me, lifted her to her feet and pulled her into my arms. I kissed her lips, tasting myself on her lips. "I want to be inside of you…"

She shimmied out of her panties, dropping them to the floor in a move that made my mouth go dry.

"We should go to my bedroom. I don't have a condom here."

She gave me a soft smile, one full of promise and heat. "It's okay. I trust you and I'm on the pill."

Well damn. No way was I going to pass up the opportunity to go into her bare.

In one swift move, I lifted her to the smooth granite of the kitchen island. I couldn't wait for the bedroom. I wanted her now. As I stepped into the open spread of her legs, the sensual sapphire of her gaze drilled into me, and I was lost. Yeah, I wanted to fuck her, but I also wanted to crawl up inside of her and be one with her. The thought blew my mind, and I thrust into her. She wrapped her legs around me and pulled me deep, the wet throbbing draw of her making me clench hard. I loved being in her, feeling her hot, wanting body clutching at mine, panting, and clinging to me like there was no tomorrow.

Without her, there wasn't one. Wasn't a future, wasn't a reason for existence. She'd walked into my life and consumed me so completely that I didn't know who I was without her.

I licked and bit my way down her neck, knowing I was leaving marks on her soft skin and not caring. I was so close to the edge and I needed her to be there with me. I rolled my hips and felt her body tighten.

"With me, sweetheart," I murmured.

I took her mouth again, devouring her even as the first ripples of orgasm rolled over us both. When the wave finally broke, and we rode each other to completion, I knew there was much more between us than a simple complication.

Chapter 28

Chelsea

The scorching heat of Alex's lips still burned across mine the next morning when I woke. The bright morning sunlight of my small attic room did nothing to expel the leftover memories of the previous night. I reveled in the blaze of tingles racing across my skin, not wanting the sensation to end. When he'd pressed into me, it'd felt like coming home.

I licked my lips. I was wet again, wanting Alex, and when the phone rang I hoped it'd be him. A quick flash of fantasy had him taking the attic stairs two at a time to find me there in bed aching and ready for him.

I rolled to my side and grabbed the phone. I was met by April's icy voice grating in my ear.

"You're still in your room." Her voice was edged with the usual disapproval. "I tried the house, but no one was around. I need you to come to the guest cottage as soon as possible."

I sighed, mumbled an apology I didn't really mean, and hung up the phone. The joy of last night still throbbed through me, and all I wanted to do was lie back and explore the memory again. April would have to wait one more minute.

My fingers trailed down my stomach to the waistband of my panties. I closed my eyes, remembering the strength of his arms, holding me, guiding me to where he wanted me. And even before he'd lifted me onto the counter, when I'd gone down on him, *oh my*, just the memory of it gave me shivers. I'd loved the way he'd grabbed my hair. I'd never had a man do that before, be so confident and commanding, in control yet giving me everything for my pleasure as much as for his. It had been a delicate balance of control and vulnerability that had awakened a feral reaction from deep inside of me that I'd never even known existed. He touched parts of me no other man had reached, a man compared to the boys I'd been with in college.

A few light strokes of my fingers, and I was panting again, wishing his hard body was right here on top of me. One last thought of his hungry mouth on mine, devouring me, thrusting his tongue deeper as he fucked me deeper with his cock was enough to cause a shuddering orgasm to course through me.

I fell back in my bed and enjoyed the hot blush on my skin. I blew out a breath and smiled. I'd have to tell Alex what just the thought of him had done to me and see how his body reacted to my confession. I indulged myself a moment longer and imagined his hardening erection, but then stopped before it could get out of hand. Slick with another wave of arousal, I shook my head and forced myself out of bed. I had work to do.

It wasn't so bad to head up to the guest cottage one last time, knowing that April was leaving. I even managed a smile when she yanked open the door and pulled a disgusted face.

"You're late," she said, stalking inside.

"How can I help?" I asked.

April bit her lip and looked around. The guest cottage was spotless, she'd already started the coffee pot, and it appeared all her bags were packed.

"I suppose you could put away all these candles," April said, indicating the hearth of the fireplace. "Alex gave me quite the surprise last night with a romantic massage, the full pampering package."

"I'm sure it was very relaxing," I said. I doubted it'd been quite as relaxing as my own night, but I kept that thought to myself.

April smirked, "I always find pampering very

invigorating. I kept the masseuse here late, and we burned out almost all of the candles."

I said nothing as I gathered up the candle stubs and tossed them in a garbage bag. April was trying to make me jealous of her night and it was all I could do not to think of mine. The thought of what she'd do if she knew about Alex and me was enough to turn my face to stone. April still believed Alex was her conquest despite his protests, and she'd retaliate in a heartbeat if she thought I was getting what she wanted. April was unpredictable with one exception: she would destroy anyone who got in the way of what she wanted.

The fact that I was the maid just made it worse. I rolled the knowledge over in my mind as I thought about my decision. I'd been rehashing it for the last two days. I could've stopped working for Alex when he asked, and then instead of cleaning up the guest cottage under April's spiteful eyes, I would've been curled up in bed with Alex, safe in his strong arms.

My mind started to drift and I jumped again when April cleared her throat.

"I need you to…um…check all the drawers in the bedroom and make sure I haven't forgotten to pack anything."

I shot her a look and watched as her cat-eye lined lashes batted around nervously. What in the world was wrong with her? I didn't say anything though, only nodded and went upstairs.

Everything was packed and the dresser drawers had been left open. The only personal item in the room was her jewelry box. I shook my head as I looked inside at the oversized baubles and flashy earrings. There was a gaudy gold star necklace heavy with sparkles on the pendant. It appeared April's taste was just as questionable as her acting skills.

Just as I was reaching out to see if she really had a cubic zirconium pin in the shape of a cougar, she appeared in the door. I jumped back and scowled at her catty smile.

"I was just coming to grab my rings," April said. "I suppose you can't wear rings in your line of work, scrubbing toilets and all."

"Do you need me to clean the bathroom again?" I asked.

"No, no, I'm sure you have a schedule to keep." She looked down her nose at me. "If I haven't left anything in the drawers you can just head back down to the big house."

I felt the hairs on the back of my neck bristle. April was up to something, and I knew from experience I needed a witness and quick. I moved toward the door, but when April refused to move I had to awkwardly squeeze past her, protruding breasts and all. Being so close to her I caught a whiff of her sickeningly sweet perfume.

I trotted down the stairs and continued along the driveway at a brisk pace. This wasn't the way I wanted to greet Alex this morning, but it seemed April had one more scheme for causing trouble, whatever that would be, and he needed to know right away.

From the curve of the steep driveway I could see the rear view of the main house. The glint of sunlight on water pulled my attention and there was Alex swimming laps in the pool. I stopped and caught my breath in awe at the sight of him. Pulled out of my worries for a moment, I remembered the first time I'd seen him swimming.

Even from the hill I could see the sheen of the water on his skin as he stopped at the end of a lap and looked around. My heart leapt at the thought that he was looking for me. If only I'd made the other choice, I would've been in the water with him. I dropped my chin to my chest and stared at the dirt on my work shoes. Instead of being with Alex, I was getting dusty in my rush to get away from April and her latest jealous scheme.

I reminded myself that this wasn't about me. I had Karl to think of. He was my responsibility and I couldn't risk his future, not even for something I wanted so badly.

I started down the driveway again, devising a plan in my head. Once April was gone, I'd talk to Alex and tell him why I'd made the choice I had. I'd simply explain that I needed the money and I wanted to work for it, but I also wanted him. I didn't expect that we'd still be able to make it work, but I hoped knowing the truth would be enough for him. Maybe then after the summer, after Karl was set up at Rainbow Roads, maybe he could visit…

Too many maybes, I thought and shook my head. Last night was enough, more than enough, for me. It had to be. I couldn't expect anything else.

Suddenly, I heard sirens. The sirens were so different than American squad cars that it didn't really register that they were police at first. It was like watching a movie scene. They sped up the main drive and skidded to a stop in the circular driveway. Four police officers headed up the steps just as Jamison walked out the door.

I ran the rest of the distance, worried about whatever had prompted the invasion. When I trotted onto the gravel of the circular drive, I saw Jamison look up and I stopped. He waved me away with the slightest nod of his head. I frowned. Unsure of what to do, I slipped into the side garden. I headed straight for the pool, but April had beaten me to it. Still not knowing what was going on, I hung back near the climbing roses. Alex had already wrapped a towel around his waist and was comforting April who was crying carefully choreographed tears.

"I just never thought someone would hate me that much. My father gave it to me. Who would do that?"

"The police are here. Let's go talk to them," Alex said. "I'll just run upstairs and get dressed."

"No! Send Jamison, don't leave me." April burst into fresh tears.

Alex frowned, but nodded as he led April toward the house. I peeked out from behind the trellis. Neither one seemed to notice me as they passed. From the expression on his face, he looked perturbed, and every once in a while he'd flinch, but he didn't push her away. April was dramatically sniffling and he was struggling to keep his towel up as she clung to him in her desperate performance.

At a loss for what to do, I went into the kitchen and filled a carafe with coffee. I took my time, preparing a tray with cups, cream, and sugar, hoping Jamison would come through the kitchen. I was dying to know why the police were here.

When I heard someone coming down the back stairs, I stepped closer to the doorway. It was Jamison carrying a pair of jeans for Alex. I was about to step into the hallway to ask Jamison what on earth was going on when Alex darted into the hallway. I ducked back into the kitchen and leaned against the wall, with my ear turned to the open doorway so I could listen. Hopefully, I'd figure out what happened and how I could help.

"She's saying it was stolen." Alex's voice was even, not betraying what he was thinking.

Jamison responded with a sigh of exasperation. "She's overreacting, as usual. I'll call the set. It's probably there."

"She says she never wore it to set, that it's too precious to her. But the police asked for the number for her make-up artist anyway, the one that handles all her jewelry," Alex said.

"Do you think it was the make-up girl?"

"Doubt it. They've worked together forever, remember? April made me fire that other poor girl and hire her instead," Alex said.

Jamison pitched his voice low when he spoke again, "You know what she's trying to do, don't you?"

"I do. What the fuck, man? Why is she so goddamn...so fucking wicked all the time?"

I could hear the anger this time and I couldn't take it anymore. I grabbed the tray and stepped into the hallway. Alex looked like he was about ready to punch the wall.

Our eyes locked and his gaze drilled into me. I wasn't sure what to make of the look he was giving me. A tumble of confused thoughts and feelings assailed me as the same sweep of nerves I'd felt earlier in the guest cottage assaulted me again. Before I could say a word, he turned and headed back into the front parlor where April was sobbing to the police.

I felt like an idiot standing there holding a stupid tray of coffee. I turned to Jamison and in a weak voice said, "I made coffee."

Jamison gave me a sympathetic look and gestured with a sweep of his hand for me to precede him down the hallway. I wanted to riddle him with questions as I squeezed past with the tray, but I had the sinking feeling I knew the answers. April had found a way to cause trouble, and it centered on me.

"Coffee?" I asked as I entered the parlor. I tried to keep my voice cheerful. All four officers turned toward me, and I could tell by the expressions on their faces that this wasn't going to go well.

"Are you Ms. Carerra? Chelsea Carerra?" the officer with a notepad asked.

"Yes," I gulped, unable to help being intimidated by their four stern faces.

April shot a self-righteous look to the officer standing next to her.

"And have you worked for Mr. Silverhaus for long?" the first officer continued.

"Um…just this summer," I stammered, my mouth going dry. I reminded myself that I hadn't done anything wrong.

"Is this your first job as a live-in maid?"

"Yes," I said.

"So you don't have many references? Any previous employers who can vouch for you?" the officer asked.

April quickly cut in, "References aren't what people are interested in on *that* website."

The officer scribbling in his notepad shot a knowing glance to his partner and then at Alex. Apparently the officers were familiar with the reputation of the site where Alex had found me.

Under their accusing stares, Alex shifted his weight and cleared his throat sharply. "Chelsea has no criminal record, and her work has been excellent."

"Jealousy can be a strong motivation," the larger officer near the door said.

"What's going on?" I asked, wishing my voice was more than a squeak.

Alex looked at me. "April's tennis bracelet is missing."

He shifted his jaw as if he were grinding his teeth. "Instead of doing a thorough search for it, she called the police."

"It was stolen!" April cried. "I was wearing it last night. In fact, you can ask the masseuse you hired, or the manicurist. She commented on how elegant it was."

April's face crumpled in practiced despair again, and the police officer standing next to her patted her awkwardly on the back.

"So you had it last night?" the taller officer asked.

"Yes," April snuffled.

"If the manicurist commented on it, then it's possible she took it," Alex said, crossing his arms over his chest.

"But I had it on when she left," April insisted. "I wore it to bed. I remember, because when I woke up it was imprinted in my skin."

She rubbed her arm and gave the taller officer a forlorn look. He furrowed his brows and asked, "Did you remove it at all this morning?"

"When I showered," April said.

"And was anyone else up to the guest cottage this morning?" he asked.

"Yes, Chelsea," April said.

Shit.

Suddenly all eyes were on me when the taller officer asked, "Is that true?"

"Uh…" I bit my lip, my heart pounding. "Yes."

He turned to Jamison and asked, "Is that part of the normal schedule?"

Jamison's face flushed, but he finally had to say, "Well…um…not exactly. That's much earlier than normal."

"So you knew Ms. Temple was leaving today and if you were going to steal anything it would have to be early this morning," the larger officer said.

"Why would I steal from her?" I asked.

"Jealousy," he said with a shrug.

"There was no need for Chelsea to be jealous of Ms. Temple," Alex said firmly.

The police officers considered this for a moment. It seemed to take the logic out of my potential motive, opening the field to the other potential culprits. I knew I was innocent, but something still wasn't sitting right with me. It was clear April had called me to the cottage this morning to give me opportunity, but that wouldn't be enough.

"Are you sure it wasn't the masseuse or manicurist?" the taller officer asked. "We should probably begin there."

"Or it could have been left on set," Alex interjected.

"It would be easy to organize a search of the house and grounds," Jamison joined in. "Besides, April, with all your packing it could easily have slipped inside a suitcase."

The four officers gathered around Jamison to discuss searching. I took my chance to pour them coffee, wanting to appear willing to help. Alex caught my glance, and nodded for me to look over at April. Instead of sobbing with rage or working herself into a tantrum at the loss of attention, she was sitting quietly examining her manicure. The calm assurance on her face, made my stomach do a sick flip. She wasn't finished yet.

April waited until the officers were preparing to follow Jamison, then stood, and proclaimed, "She hates me. Even Alex or the butler can't deny it. Ask them, they'll tell you. That's why she stole the bracelet."

"You don't know that…" Alex tried to derail her accusations, but she cut him off.

"I know how women like her think," April said. "She's jealous of the attention you give me. She's jealous that you want me over her, and it hurts her. So, she decided to hurt me. She found out my father gave me that tennis bracelet, she waited for the right opportunity, and then she stole it."

I stood still, my arms and legs too heavy to move. I'd been in this situation before. The first foster home I'd been in, one of the family's biological children had accused me of stealing something, and no matter how much I'd protested, I'd been sent to a group home the next day. People rarely gave the foster kid the benefit of the doubt. And now, all I could do was stand here and wait for what happened next.

Alex made a disgusted sound and stepped between the police officers and me, as if to deflect any more harmful remarks. "I'm sorry, but this is ridiculous. There *are* some issues here that need to be straightened out, but we certainly don't need to bother you anymore."

One of the officers cocked an eyebrow and leaned around Alex to address April. "Without proof, Ms. Temple, there isn't much we can do."

"Did you search her?" April spat the words like daggers.

Fuck.

Suddenly, I remembered April standing in the doorway, forcing me to squeeze past her on my way out. It all made sense now. I knew what she'd done, and knew what would happen next.

"Easy enough, Ms. Carerra," the larger officer said. "Just empty out your pockets."

I swallowed hard, lifted my chin. Slowly, I reached into my pocket and felt the cool metal I'd known I would find. I pulled the missing tennis bracelet from my uniform pocket, all eyes on it as it sparkled in the palm of my hand. No one saw the slow smile spread across April's face, except me. When they looked up she was dabbing a tear from the corner of her eye. Then in a grand, dramatic gesture she held out both hands to reclaim the precious bracelet.

I shot a glance to Alex. His jaw was clenched hard and he stared straight ahead as he said, "Now that it's been found, we can deal with this here. There's no need to press charges."

"Oh, no," April said, tossing her head with a cold, triumphant glare. "I definitely want to press charges. She's a thief, and I'm not about to let her take advantage of your good nature one moment longer."

"You will need to come with us," the larger police officer said to me.

"I didn't do it." I turned to Alex, wide-eyed. Why didn't he say something to stop all of this? I could explain to everyone how April tricked me and with Alex and Jamison's support, the story would make sense.

Suddenly, I wondered if Alex believed her story. My stomach twisted. Why had I taken this job? Why had I come here to Holland? I'd thought things would be different in a place where people didn't know my history, but all it had done was show me how I didn't belong in this world. All I wanted to do now was go home, and get away from these manipulative, spoiled, rich players.

Alex spoke quietly, "Chelsea, don't say anything else. Just go with them. I'll be right behind you."

April clasped the bracelet onto her wrist as if all was said and done. "You know, I have no idea how the justice system works here in Holland," April said with a smile. "All I know is that this looks better on me…and those seem to fit you best." She gestured to the handcuffs the officer held.

Seriously? Was it really necessary to handcuff a maid over a small piece of jewelry? My heart sank, but I nodded and held out my wrists. I stuck out my chin and straightened my shoulders. I wasn't about to let April think she'd gotten to me, although on the inside, I was devastated. I'd only wanted to give a better life to my brother, but that seemed like it was going to be as much a dream as everything else I'd ever wanted in my life.

The officer clamped the handcuffs on my wrists and gestured for me to head out the door. He took my arm, and on the way out, I threw a glance over my shoulder, not at April's smirking face, but at Alex. I'd expected this kind of treatment from her, but as I looked at Alex I felt crushed. He should've stopped this. He had the money and the influence to do whatever he wanted.

But maybe that was the thing. Maybe he didn't want to stop it.

Chapter 29

Alex

I was beyond pissed. My blood was boiling, and it felt like something rumbling in the pit of my stomach was about to explode. I couldn't believe April would go this far. Her heels clicked across the marble floor to the front door and she waved at the four police officers as they loaded Chelsea in the back of a squad car. Then she closed the door, leaned against it like the cat that just swallowed the canary and smiled at me.

"You're fucking fired," I seethed.

She simply rolled her eyes and peeled her back off the door, seemingly immune to my pending rage. "Oh, not this again."

I caught Jamison's glance as April tossed her curly blonde hair and slipped past me into the library. Jamison gave me an almost imperceptible nod.

"April, where do you think you're going?" I threw my hands out and followed her into the library. "You're no longer welcome here, and you're off the film."

She poured two drinks from a crystal decanter and waggled one at me.

"Relax, Alex, dear. I'm sure your little trollop will be fine in jail." Stepping closer, she offered me a drink. "I'll keep you company."

"You're a fucking piece of work, you know it?" I shook my head in disbelief. "She's on her way to jail because of you. And that's reason one on the list of reasons why you're fired."

I clenched my fists, and fought the urge to slap the drink from her hand. I stepped back to put some distance between us. She put down the rejected drink all the while sipping at hers.

"You still don't understand, do you, honey?" she asked.

"Oh, I understand alright. I understand exactly what happened and I'm not going to let you get away with it," I said.

"No," she said with another plump smile. "You don't understand. You can't fire me."

I leaned against the wide desk, frustration making me feel heavy and tired. Jamison hovered behind April, wiping up the droplets where her drink had spilled on the silver tray at the side table. She frowned at him, but he nodded politely and added a splash of tonic to her drink. She basked in the attention, and then ignored him as he stood behind her, awaiting her next request.

"Oh, yes, I can and I *am* firing you," I repeated.

April swirled her drink and moved a step closer. "How about you call Daddy and ask first?"

Of course, she thought Henry would defend her against me. My father had a weakness for starlets like April, and she'd spent the past year kissing his ass, flirting with him, and probably sucking his dick just to cement her spot in this movie. *Like I'd even want to stick my cock in that after my father had.*

"Good idea," I said, "Henry can pick you up and drive you to the airport."

April's smile slipped. "You know your father will do anything I ask. He wants me and that means he wants me to stay on the film."

I knew the smile that curved my lips was cruel, but I didn't care. "I have news for you, April. Henry only wanted you in this movie because your name has a certain draw on audiences, but when the studio hears about this, he won't think twice about backing me."

April forced a laugh and said, "Henry never liked

Chelsea. He won't care she's in jail. In fact, he'll be glad when I tell him how she stole from me."

She brushed a hand over the tennis bracelet and smiled, as if certain that Henry would soon buy her a bigger and better one to match.

"Except she didn't steal it from you, and I know it. You framed her," I snapped.

She shrugged. "Either way, she's in jail and I'm still on the film."

I crossed my arms over my chest and squeezed tight. April was so confident she'd get her way. In her mind, this was all a game and soon I'd give in and admit my attraction to her. She honestly thought she could play me off my father, as if jealousy would drive me to take what he clearly wanted, but she didn't know the half of it.

A sour feeling spread through my stomach. This woman was poison, and I needed her out of my life. Not only was she causing chaos on the movie set, she was driving a wedge between Chelsea and me. It killed me to see the hurt on Chelsea's beautiful face when they put the handcuffs on her.

I knew Henry would roll out the same old stale argument: the film's budget would suffer, April's star status was gold, we'd lose thousands. But I didn't care about that anymore. Yes, there'd be consequences for the film, and we'd be set back at least a month, but it'd be worth it. Star status or not; it would be a cold day in hell before I let that witch back into my house or back on my film.

My hand balled into a fist. I wanted to slam it on the desk. I wanted to snatch her drink and hurl it against the beautiful mahogany panels of the library. I hated this house. All the expensive décor, all the chandeliers, the pool, the gardens, none of it meant a thing when it came from Henry, when it always came with strings attached. Just like my film. None of it was worth a dime if it meant Chelsea had to look at me the way she did when she walked to the squad car, her eyes steeped with resignation and mistrust. She probably hated me right about now.

I wanted to call the cops, have April forcibly removed from the property. Call my father and tell him that I was done with all of it unless he caved about firing April. But, I reminded myself, April was crafty, and I had to make sure to play her right. I figured I'd better cool my jets before I lost it, and did something that'd get me in the headlines of the newspaper. That wouldn't be the best way to get what I wanted.

She thought she understood how my father thought, but she had no idea. I did. My father wouldn't do anything for me because I was his son, but I knew what buttons to push, and I was going to push them all. I just had to be smart about it.

I pursed my lips and narrowed my eyes at her. "Chelsea was right about you."

April's mouth puckered into a frown, and she took a long sip before managing to ask, "What did your little maid say about me?"

"She said you were jealous enough to try something stupid and now you've gone and proven her right," I said.

April's crimson manicure curled into claws before she caught herself and smoothed down her glossy dress.

"She's the one that's stupid," April, said.

Jamison shifted slightly. April's heavy eyelashes flicked up to him and she waved her drink glass at him. He poured another drink with one hand, and gave her a slight bow.

He was good.

She smiled and said, "It was so easy to get her up to the guest cottage this morning. She *is* good maid material. I'll admit that. Always ready to jump. Like a little puppy, really."

"How long did it take you to plan your little charade?"

April laughed, "I thought of it last night during your little relaxation gift. All I needed to do was get her there earlier than normal. Butler here..." She waved a dismissive hand at Jamison. "All he had to do was tell the police it was strange and that helped make the case."

"You figured they'd believe your terrible acting?" I asked, winding her up just enough to keep going.

"I didn't need them to believe me," she snapped. "Your little maid slut was stupid enough to let me slip the bracelet into her pocket. Then they caught her red-handed."

"And all because you were jealous of Chelsea," I said, shaking my head. Only half of it was acting. I'd always known April was petty and shallow. I'd just never realized how far she'd go.

"Not jealous, honey. Not willing to share," April said with a slow lick of her lips.

Jamison spoke up, and said, "I think that's enough, sir."

I nodded and turned to April. "You'd better call Henry for a ride, because I'm heading to the police station."

April sat up, craning her neck to give Jamison a withering look. "What? Why?"

"So they can hear what Jamison just recorded on his phone." I tilted my head at her widened eyes. "And to bring Chelsea home. Now, get the hell out," I said, striding toward the door. "You need to be gone when we get back, or you'll be going to jail for trespassing, and I sure as hell won't be there to get you out."

I didn't look back, but I felt April's narrowed gaze boring into me. A moment later, I heard her purr into her phone, "Henry, honey, I need someone to save me."

Whatever she told my father wasn't important. All that mattered now was getting Chelsea out of that humiliating place and back home with me.

Where she belonged.

Chapter 30

Alex

My phone rang as I parked the car outside the local police station. "Hello, Henry," I said, not needing to look at the caller ID.

"You fired April Temple." It was more of an accusation than anything. "What the hell's wrong with you?" His voice was laced with the usual criticism he always reserved for me.

"She's caused enough trouble," I said as I killed the engine.

"What happens in your personal life shouldn't affect the film," he said.

"My thoughts exactly," I retorted. I'd had enough.

I heard my father draw in an angry breath. "I don't know what this little drama with the thieving maid is all about, but set it aside and do what's best for the production. Losing April means losing investors, not to mention time, and money."

That was exactly what I'd predicted he'd say. *Same old shit, new day.* "Look Henry, April accused Chelsea of stealing, she went so far as to frame her," I said, slamming the car door shut with more force than needed.

"Some petty spat about a piece of jewelry isn't reason enough to fire an actor." He shot back. "She's part of the actor's union, for Christ's sake. Do you have any idea how much paperwork this'll create? Not to mention that firing her without just cause could bring on a lawsuit."

"Except for the fact that I have proof she framed Chelsea. I'm at the jail right now, picking Chelsea up. April's the one creating a hostile work environment, not Chelsea, and the police are going to have that on record once I give them the proof that April set up the whole thing." I paused outside the entrance, not wanting to have this conversation in the middle of a police station. "And I can't guarantee they won't want to press charges against her."

His voice changed from hostile to contemptuous. "Oh, Alex, don't be so dramatic. I'm sure your little fling is just fine," he said. "April, on the other hand, is inconsolable."

"I'm sure you'll find a way to console her. You seem to be really good at that," I said.

"No. *You* will. What exactly are you going to do to smooth all this over?" he asked.

"Don't worry. I called her agent on my way here, and I've sent an email to our casting head," I said. "I'll conference call with the investors later and explain everything."

"I meant with April," he snapped. "I've brought her to my house for the time being, but you need to fix this…and fast."

"Sounds like you finally have your starlet right where you want her, Henry. Well, don't worry, I'm not going to mess that up for you."

I pictured my father yanking at his collar, the ruddy color creeping up his neck. He had a habit of doing that that when he was frustrated, and I swore I heard April whining and purring at him in the background.

April, the starlet was a wonderful fantasy, but April Temple, the petulant houseguest, was something entirely different. I smiled and kicked at a rock on the pavement, anxious to end this conversation and get inside to take care of Chelsea.

"The least you can do is come over for dinner and try to work things out," Henry said. He actually sounded stressed.

"Sorry, Henry, I'm busy. Open a case of champagne and

have yourselves a good night," I said and clicked off the call.

The smile stayed with me as I took the first few steps, then I thought of Chelsea's morning and I felt a stab of remorse. My poor little water nymph must be worried to death. And she must be really angry with me for bringing April into her life to begin with. I could only imagine how horrible she must be feeling about the false accusation. I hoped she realized I didn't believe April for one second, but the idea that she'd sat in jail for the last couple hours probably thinking that I sided against her was enough to send me running up the last flight of steps.

The police station was bright and airy, with white gleaming floors, wide windows, and breathtaking views of The Hague. A few employees worked at white computers, while here and there people sat in interviews at small round tables.

Across the open office was a small sitting area with sofas and chairs. I saw Chelsea sitting comfortably on a light blue sofa under one of the wide windows, sipping a mug of tea. The uniformed officer seated across from her tipped back his white-blond head and laughed out loud, nearly making me stop in my tracks. I'd expected to find her wrought with worry, maybe even in tears and wearing an orange jumpsuit, not sipping tea and laughing. I didn't see what was so funny about being in custody. Not when I'd been so worried about her.

"So this is where they keep the hardcore criminals?" I quipped, hoping to make light of my surprise.

Chelsea looked up and smiled, but the officer frowned, and said, "She's not yet through processing."

Clearly, he was in no hurry to finish the paperwork spread on the coffee table between them. I caught the look he gave her, and knew he'd been stretching out the time on purpose. My stomach clenched and I couldn't decide what was worse, Chelsea being alone in a jail cell or here in the sunshine with this guy drooling over her. The way he clicked his pen made them both smile at some inside joke, and for a second I wished there were bars between the two of them instead of a coffee table and the damn sunshine.

"Ah. Well, I have a recording here that I think should be submitted along with…" I waved a hand over the massive paperwork. "All these forms." I pulled out Jamison's phone.

Chelsea hid her shining smile behind the mug of tea as I played April's confession for the officer.

When the recording finished, I addressed the officer. "My butler also heard the confession, and he would be willing to come in and give a statement if necessary."

"This is quite outside regulations." The officer sat with his pen still paused over a form as though thinking.

I shot him a steel glare. "Well, why don't you go find someone who can decide that before you go any farther here?"

He popped up out of his seat. "Wait right here."

After he left, I eased down onto the sofa next to Chelsea. "And here I was worried you'd be in a jumpsuit and working on your first tattoo."

"If it makes you feel any better, they made me wear the handcuffs all the way down the driveway," she said with a grin. "Oh, Alex, I was joking. Believe me, I'm fine."

I breathed a sigh of relief, glad that she wasn't upset and even gladder that she didn't seem to be angry with me for all of April's antics. "Hey, look Chelsea. I'm really sorry. This never should've happened. You'll be glad to know, I fired April. She's gone."

She frowned, which wasn't the reaction I'd been expecting.

"What? But what about your investors? The film?" she asked, setting the mug down hard. "Don't make everything harder on yourself just because of this."

I took her hand. "I had to do it," I said, "Should've done it a long time ago, but I was too...well, too much of a coward, I guess. But I couldn't let her hurt you like this. I don't want anyone to hurt you, ever."

Chelsea squeezed my hand and smiled. "April's really gone?"

I exhaled a deep breath and relaxed. "Well, she's at Henry's. Let him deal with the…we'll just let him deal with her."

Chelsea laughed. "Poor Henry."

I glanced up to see the officer scowling at me from across the room as a tall man in a dark suit listened to what he was saying. The man nodded, frowned, and then marched over toward us.

"Ms. Carerra," he said, holding out a large hand. "Captain Dollard. It seems you have strong character witnesses who vouches for your innocence."

"And a recorded confession," I added.

"Soft evidence," he said, dismissing me. "I have an officer talking with Ms. Temple at the moment."

It was impossible to tell what the man was thinking. His expression was as indifferent his whitewashed surroundings. I put an arm around Chelsea and scowled at him.

"Look Captain…I mean…Captain, sir, Ms. Temple is, well, she's an actress, and she can be very, um, convincing. What I'm trying to say is, she's already admitted to framing Chelsea. She even explained how she did it. I have it all right here recorded on this phone. That should be enough to let Chelsea go."

This definitely wasn't going like the white knight rescue I'd imagined.

The captain ignored me and addressed Chelsea again. "Ms. Carerra, you have a spotless record in the United States. That, plus the character witnesses and the fact the stolen property was recovered means you most likely will be leaving us with no more than a warning."

Chelsea thanked him and the corners of his mouth tipped up in the barest curve of a smile. The junior officer raced up, smiled at Chelsea, and leaned in to speak quietly with the captain. The Captain's eyes brightened and he turned to Chelsea. "In light of new information, you're free to go. It seems Ms. Temple has dropped the charges."

Apparently, April hadn't counted on my father wanting to avoid a scandal.

"I'll escort you out," the younger man offered with a

smile.

Chelsea noticed the hard set of my jaw and squeezed my knee before she got up and accepted the officer's arm. I didn't like this young guy's fawning over Chelsea, one bit. The tables were turned now, and Chelsea had someone flirting with her while I watched. I didn't like it one bit. Another man eyeing her, enjoying the touch of her arm or the lilt in her laughter as much as I did. I swallowed hard. It made me realize all the more how much I wanted Chelsea to be *my* girl and no one else's.

I forced myself to keep an even keel and politely follow them out. They stopped at the front counter for her to sign a few more papers, and it seemed like an eternity before I had her alone in the car. Finally.

I jammed the key in the ignition and turned to study her face. "Are you alright?" I asked, starting the engine.

"Yes, fine. Just a little tired," she said.

Before I shifted the car into reverse, I let the engine idle for a moment. I reached across and stroked a wisp of hair out of her face. I wanted to pull her into my arms and comfort her, tell her I'd protect her, and never let anything bad happen to her ever again. Instead, I held back, sure that she hated me for being so spineless, for not standing up to my father, not firing April sooner.

"You know Chelsea, I never believed April for a second," I said, meeting her eyes. "I'm sorry I've been acting like a dickhead half the time."

She shrugged as if throwing off my apology and said, "It's okay. But…thank you."

Searching her face, I wasn't sure how to read her right now. Was that a polite *thank you* or not? I didn't want to press my luck so I just said, "Why don't you rest a bit while I drive us home."

She nestled into the passenger seat while I put the car in reverse. The words echoed in my mind as I drove. *Drive us home*. It sounded good, and it'd felt even better when I'd said it. Chelsea may have thought of herself as merely my maid, but now I knew I wanted her to be more. I wanted her to be mine.

The question was, what did Chelsea want?

Chapter 31

Alex

Once home, I tried to give Chelsea some space, but barely thirty minutes had gone by when I found myself climbing the servants' cottage steps, needing to see her. Up in her attic room, I found her fresh out of the shower, wrapped in a thin robe and brushing her hair. She was sitting at her small desk and looking out the window.

I leaned against the doorframe and crossed my arms over my chest, admiring a magnificent view of my own, my eyes drifting down her long, wet hair and finding a spot to nestle on the exposed curve of her perfect breast. Her robe was barely tied. "Got rid of the prison stench?"

Chelsea stopped brushing and chuckled as she turned to look at me. "Having a few cups of tea and answering some politely-worded questions doesn't really count as hard time."

She placed her hairbrush aside on the desk and turned further in her chair.

"Don't stop on my account." I nodded to the brush. It was the movement of her arm that was working the robe open in the front, but now that she faced me it gaped open enough for an eyeful.

She must've suspected something from the goofy grin on my face and the way I was eyeing her, because she glanced down at her robe, and then back at me with a smile. But she made no effort to pull it shut.

"Well, anyway, sorry I slept the whole way home," she said. "I never got a chance to ask you how you feel."

"Like an ass," I said honestly. "I never should've let April anywhere near you."

"No," she said, "I meant about the film. You finally took control of things. That's…"

Her words faded into the background. I was mesmerized when she stood and her long hair flowed around her shoulders. Talking about the film was the last thing on my mind as her loose robe fell open again.

Her eyes dipped down to follow my gaze, and when they returned to my face I saw a heated passion that sent my blood rocketing.

I was across the room in two strides, and then her body was flush against mine. The robe parted completely before our lips touched, and when I realized it was Chelsea who held open the ties, the rush of desire sent my happy cock into overdrive. I grabbed her ass and pressed my hips against her naked skin.

The groan I swallowed escaped as a low growl. I slipped my hands inside the robe, and across the curve of her lower back. The robe created an alluring effect, but I wanted her naked so I could relish every inch of her. I practically tore it off her shoulders, and in one toss, it was cast aside. I continued my exquisite torture, running my hands up and down her soft flesh, panting hard against her lips as our kiss deepened. Her tongue slid along mine, twisted around it.

She wrapped her arms around my neck and lifted against me. I dragged my hands down her tight ass to her silken thighs and pulled her legs up around my waist. Holding her, I managed the three steps to the bed and lowered us together, lost in the ecstasy of her indescribable spell.

When I stood up to peel off my shirt and pants, my heart was pounding and my head was spinning with the sight of her. This happened every time I was close to her. I was totally enraptured, like I was falling, uncontrollably falling, into some wonderful warm place, like I was falling right into her.

She lay on the bed, her arms flung over her head, a smile playing around her kiss-swollen lips. I froze, breathless from the sight of her. She was so beautiful. I felt her burn away every silly worry, absolutely everything that had ever seemed important. In this moment, there was no one else but her.

My cock throbbed harder and my mouth was dry with anticipation. I wanted to taste her, bury my face between her legs and pleasure her until she screamed my name. Her lush mouth widened as I lowered myself to the bed and pressed my aching cock against the softness of her thighs. Lost in a steamy cloud of desire, I locked my gaze on her eyes. Reaching for her hand I guided it to her wet pussy. Without breaking my gaze I pushed her finger against her clit and made her touch herself, then pushed her finger deeper into the fold. Wet with her arousal, I drew her finger back to her lips and made her taste it.

"This is what I live for," I said huskily. "See how wet you are for me?"

I rubbed her fingers around her full, red lips and pressed one finger inside her mouth.

"Now suck on it." She complied, her plush lips closing around her own finger, cheeks hollowing out as she sucked.

The sight of it was so hard-core, so seductive, I had to part my lips for a breath of air. It made me think of when I'd watched her lips around my cock as she'd sucked me off in the kitchen. *Damn.*

"Does it taste sweet? I bet it does. I can't wait to taste you." I panted the words, barely able to concentrate on anything except the fire racing through my veins, and the endorphins showering my brain.

She released her finger with a gasp as my hand found its way to her hot core. I caressed her, fingers sliding over and between her folds, and she arched, her head rolling to the side, an airy moan escaping her parted lips.

Damn, I loved that sound.

I shimmied down her twisting torso, my hands trailing over her breasts to catch her hardened nipples for a tweak before raking across the flat expanse of her stomach.

I kissed her bare mound as I pushed her legs open. She was so beautiful. Every inch of her. I spread her pussy open with one hand and slid a finger inside. She felt so good as I stroked in and out, fucking her with my finger, teasing her, knowing she wanted more pressure on her clit, wanted more of me.

I loved the way she arched and wiggled when I fingered her, when I touched her. I loved how she responded to me. I exhaled a raspy sound and quickly added another finger and stroked her again, curling my fingers to rub against the top of her. *Ah, she's so tight…and wet…*

She moaned again and wiggled more, making those little high-pitched sounds that made blood rush to my already-hard cock. The noises spurred me on, and I splayed my left palm out on her abdomen, pulling her skin tight and spreading her pussy lips even more to make that hard little nub pop out even farther.

Then finally, I was ready to taste her, I continued stroking her with two fingers as I buried my face in her wet flesh like I was devouring the most luscious dessert. I licked. I flicked. I swirled my tongue, and she gasped and writhed. I pressed harder with my left palm, trying to hold her rocking hips in place, reminding her who was in control. She didn't get to rise up to meet my tongue. She had to take my direction and wait for it as I decided. It would make her orgasm more explosive.

She clawed at the sheets, desperate for what I had to give her. Desperate for me. Not because I had money or because she wanted something from me. Just me.

"That's my little nymph." I stopped my tongue long enough to talk, but kept my fingers stroking. "You like that don't you?"

She let out a long exhale that was almost answer enough. I still needed her to say it though.

"Say it."

"Yes," she breathed. "Yes…"

"Tell me how you like it. Like this?" I flicked my tongue across her swollen clit.

"Oh, god, yes, like that."

"Yes, who?"

"Yes, Alex. I like it."

I gave her a couple of reward licks, loving the way my name sounded on her tongue. But I wanted more.

"No, tell me how you like it. Talk dirty to me. It'll make my cock so hard for you." It was true. The thought of sweet, shy little Chelsea saying anything even the least bit dirty was already turning me on.

She smiled, a sensual smile that was pure sex. "Lick me, Alex. I want your tongue on me…on my clit. I want you to lick it harder while you fuck me with your fingers."

The words all came out in a hot, wet gush and although I'd thought this would be kind of hot, the effect on me was more than I'd anticipated. I had to fuck her *now*. My cock was about to explode. I swallowed hard and buried my face between her legs again, wanting to bring her right to the edge before I slid inside her and made her come.

Just as she was arching and twisting against my face, I rose up on my knees and grabbed my cock ready to drive it in and push her over the edge. I'd never wanted anyone as much as I wanted Chelsea. And as I thrust inside her, I let everything go. I closed my eyes and drove in deep, hunched over her heaving chest, falling and falling into a state of sheer bliss, falling into my Chelsea. I heard her gasp, and she clawed at my shoulders when she came, but I was too lost in pleasure to acknowledge the pain. She clenched around me, and I called out her name as I exploded inside her.

I had to tell her. I rolled to her side and pulled her into my arms, cuddling her close in the narrow little bed. I traced a finger along her chin and she smiled up at me, her head nestled on my shoulder.

I kissed the top of her head and said it the only way I knew how. "You're mine, beautiful. No one else but you."

Chapter 32

Alex

The mind-blowing sex with Chelsea stayed in my mind like a lucky charm the rest of the night. That was the kind of "welcome home" I could live with forever. I held tightly to the memory of her kisses and her body as investors yelled at me over the phone, but numbed by the pleasure of our night together, their heated remarks simply bounced off me.

At first.

My post-sex high cushioned me from taking to heart any of what they had to say at the beginning, but with each hour that passed, and each added phone call, my positive outlook melted away like a snowman in July.

My production team estimated how much time we'd lose to reshoots, even after I'd cut down April's part, and I added up how much firing April would cost the film. It was an unfortunately high amount. Henry called three separate times, threatening, coercing, and bargaining. By the time I emerged from my office, I saw that it was two o'clock in the morning, and I was a fucking mess.

The next morning was no better as my phone started ringing at four, and by eight o'clock, I was using both hands to prop up my head. I stared at the spreadsheet of the film's budget on my computer screen, still not sure how to save my movie.

"It can't be that bad." The sound of a voice tore my eyes away from the computer screen. There was Chelsea, standing at my office door with a mug of coffee and a big smile.

"Well, four of our six major investors pulled out, and we stand to lose two months while we reshoot," I said, letting my head drop to the desk with a solid thunk. I kept it there until Chelsea set the coffee down. Only then did I sit up and look into her beautiful face.

I reached for her hand and said, "But on a lighter note, it's always a pleasure to see your smile first thing in the morning." I pressed my lips to the back of her hand and she looked down at me with a grin that lit up my day. "You must be psychic. I was in desperate need of coffee." Then I glanced at the computer screen and said, "Or maybe a gun to shoot my brains out. This budget is killing me."

Chelsea leaned down and gave me a light kiss and whispered, "Don't tell the boss I just did that." Then she straightened and turned to the budget showing on the computer screen. "Well let's see…" She propped a hand on one hip and studied the spreadsheet for a minute. "How about you trim the budget and cut a few corners?"

"I could hack off entire limbs of the project and these two figures would never meet," I said, pointing to the spreadsheet.

Chelsea plopped down on the corner of the desk and swung her foot back and forth as she thought. She had a thoughtful expression on her face. "What if you condensed the story into one night and shot it in one house?"

I slouched in my chair and took a sip of the strong coffee, hoping it'd clear my brain fog. "What do you mean?"

"A lot of April's scenes were backstory, right? If you adjust the timeline of the script down to one night, it would cut out the flashbacks completely. Just have the information come out in dialogue, conversation between characters, something like that," she said.

I thought for a moment. "Mmm, I don't know. Will the audience get it? I mean, what about character development? How'd that work? I need to show what the character is like."

"People understand inferences, especially about other people's baggage. Don't underestimate your audience," she said. "You don't have to beat them over the head with details about a character for them to get it."

I sat up and took another long sip before I said, "Tell me what you said about the house again?"

Chelsea smiled and stood up. "If the movie takes place in one night the characters don't even need to leave the house. Maybe it could be like a dinner party or something. It's the relationship that's your story. The rest is just superfluous."

"If we did that, we could cut back the set budget, the location permits, and all the extra set dressing," I said, feeling the caffeine hit my blood at the same time her ideas took hold. I sat up straight. "That just might work."

"Good luck," she said.

I caught her flat look and felt a wave of guilt. I should've paid more attention to her instead of just talking so much business. Especially since she looked especially delectable this morning. Her hair was down today and it moved seductively as she walked to the door.

"Hey, wait. Come back," I said.

She shook her head and her hair spilled over her shoulder. Was she wearing it down on my account? I hoped so.

"Your hair, you look…beautiful today," I said.

Chelsea tipped her head and said, "I didn't come in here to distract you. I just wanted to deliver your coffee. It's what I do. Don't feel bad about working."

She didn't sound angry, but...

"Thanks. It's just…I mean…last night was wonderful. And before that," I said, my mouth going dry. *Shit*. This was harder than it should've been. "Do we need to talk?"

"Not right now." She paused, and then added, "Not unless you think we do?"

I ran a hand through my hair, my head buzzing with half-finished thoughts. I knew Chelsea had concerns about her being my employee, but I looked at her and thought that maybe it didn't have to be complicated. What we had going seemed to be working fine for us.

"How about later?" I asked. "I mean, it would be nice to spend a little more time with you just to relax."

She gave me a shy smile and said, "Okay. Maybe a nightcap?"

"It's a date," I said.

I felt a wild flight of hope that maybe we could make this work. If we saw each other during our free time, it would be more like a relationship than an affair between employer and employee.

At least, I hoped Chelsea would see it that way.

Chelsea

Alex's eyes lit up and followed me as I entered the dining room with a loaded tray. As I took the sandwiches to the buffet, I realized he was watching me with a silly grin on his face. Just staring, as if he wasn't even listening to what the production team was saying. They were in the middle of a lunch meeting, and Alex had been in the middle of explaining the changes when he'd suddenly stopped talking so he could watch me carry in this dumb tray of sandwiches.

He snapped his attention back to the group, cleared his throat, and said, "So, in the hopes of saving the production, and further off-screen drama, I fired April Temple." He held up a hand, palm out as if anticipating moans and groans from the group. "Yes, I know, it has a direct effect on the budget and unfortunately, the majority of investors have left, but I believe we can still create a quality film. One that will be much better for the absence of Ms. Temple."

I glanced around the table at their faces, expecting to see

shock and astonishment, but there was none. Maybe, secretly, they were as relieved as I was to see April go. It was nice to know that there were some men with decent taste out there after all.

From the corner of my eye I saw Alex watching me again as I worked, fetching drinks for the group. It was unnerving, and I couldn't read his expression. He frowned for a moment, and I quickly flicked my glance away. I didn't want him to think that I was being nosy. As I turned to hand someone a fresh water glass, I reminded myself that this was work. No flirting now. I had to keep a distance.

"Alex," the director continued. "I think the crew is willing to stay if you have a solid plan."

Suddenly, Alex's eyes were beaming at me again, this time blasting a hole in my resolution. He smiled slowly, and there was something in that smile that froze me in my tracks.

Oh, shit.

"As a matter of fact, I do," he said, and stood. "Thanks to the creative thinking of our newest team member." Alex turned to me for some reason I didn't understand. "Everyone, I'd like you to meet Chelsea Carerra."

I shot him a horrified look, but forced it into a smile as everyone turned to consider me. I wiped my hands on my apron and gave a weak wave.

"Chelsea is a student here to work for the summer, but she's also a talented writer. If you look at the synopsis I gave you, you'll see her ideas for the script will save us enough time and money to keep going, while still maintaining the integrity of the storyline."

Everyone's heads swiveled back to the table, and I took a few deep breaths, glad the spotlight wasn't on me anymore. Alex smiled at me over the long table and it felt like a warm embrace, giving me enough courage to stay where I was and not run out of the room.

He gestured to an empty chair and then sat down. "When you're done, Chelsea, grab a plate and a seat. We've got lots to talk about." He turned his attention back to the script laying open next to his plate.

When I'd walked into the room, I'd been nothing but another faceless worker, but now I was going to be sitting down with Hollywood big-wigs to discuss a script.

While I was still wearing my uniform.

Awkward, to say the least. Why hadn't Alex just invited me to the meeting ahead of time and let Jamison handle the lunch duties? Well, it was what it was, and it'd just look worse if I ran out to change my clothes. I grabbed a sandwich and sat down at the table. There wasn't anything wrong with being a hard worker.

"So you're suggesting we take out all the flashbacks?" the director of photography asked me. "You do realize that film is a visual medium and not everything can be conveyed in dialogue, right?"

Okay, hadn't been expecting a direct question so soon.

"Yes," I said, swallowing hard, "but I think the essence of the flashbacks, the emotional ties and complications, can be shown through cutaways to the characters. How they look at each other, avoid certain topics, body language, and that sort of thing."

The two writers nodded in understanding, and Alex said, "If we all agree this structure works, then we can go ahead with the investors we have, and not stretch the budget beyond what's already working."

This was a whole new side of Alex, and I was definitely liking it.

Within the hour, he had every possible problem broken into categories and assigned to sections of the team. As we broke into brainstorming groups, I stood and wondered where to go. Just as I was moving toward the writers, the set designer stopped me.

I thought he was going to make a remark about the film so I asked, "What do you think of filming it in one house?" Will that work?"

He simply shrugged and said, "Any chance I could get another ham sandwich? Extra mustard, please."

I stepped back and nodded, my cheeks flooding with heat as he went back to his conversation. Alex had given me a chance to step out of my maid's duties and prove that I belonged. But I still had to help Jamison with lunch. It was my responsibility as his employee, and yet I really wanted to enjoy my new status as production team member.

I took a deep breath and told myself it didn't matter. I'd grab the man's sandwich and be back after the brainstorming session when they regrouped. I headed toward the door, forcing my chin up and straightening my shoulders. I could do this.

Before I took two steps I heard the director ask Alex, "Who is she exactly?" I slowed my pace, dawdling at the buffet to collect some dirtied glasses so I could hear how he answered.

"My maid, but I'm not going to let that stop us from using good ideas, right?" Alex asked. "What do you think? Will the changes work?"

"Well, yeah but..." The director lingered over the words. "Hey look, I'm not one to judge, but isn't that the maid you hired as a joke? The one from that website?"

"Why? Does she seem like one of those girls?" Alex asked, clearly avoiding having to answer the question.

I started moving again. I didn't want to hear the director's response. Was that how everyone perceived me? As a gold-digger in a maid's disguise, fawning over Alex and waiting for my chance to jump out of uniform and get into the movie industry?

My heart stumbled as I wondered if Alex had the same thoughts as me. Yes, I wanted to work in movies, and I wanted to write screenplays. The last hour had shown me how much I enjoyed it, but if I continued, would Alex start to wonder if I was using him? Had been using him all along?

He hadn't actually defended me, had referred to me as nothing more than his maid. So maybe he was thinking that already.

I made it out the door and leaned against the wall in the

hallway. I felt as if I were barreling down a narrow stretch of road. There was a crossroads coming soon and the chances of me crashing were very high. Nothing about this summer job was going like I'd imagined it would.

"It's a thin line, isn't it?" Jamison asked, appearing in the kitchen door.

"Am I that obvious?" I pushed past him and set the tray on the kitchen island.

"Between working with people and working for them," he said.

I turned and said, "Is it even possible? I mean, you do it, but you've been with Alex since he was a kid. You're family."

"And what are you?" Jamison asked.

I could feel the fiery blush go to the roots of my hair. I knew there weren't any real secrets between Jamison and Alex. He knew everything that went on in the house, but I wasn't ready to admit I'd given in to temptation again.

"I don't know." I pushed my hand through my hair and bit my lip. "What does he want me to be?"

Jamison shook his head. "That's not it, Chelsea. You have to be yourself. Even as everything is changing."

"But what if I don't want everything to change?" I asked.

He looked at me, his expression kind. "It already has, my dear."

Chapter 33

Chelsea

I didn't count on waking up early since I'd been up most of the night worrying. Jamison was right. Everything had already changed, and all I could do now was decide how to handle it.

I'd managed to fit in with the production team for a little while during the meeting. They'd been happy to have me help with brainstorming, but I could tell they weren't ready to share their scenes. I needed to make sure they knew I wanted nothing but experience. I wasn't looking for my name to be listed in the credits of the movie, and I certainly wasn't looking for money from any of this. I just wanted to know what screenwriting was really like, and that meant I'd also need to find a way to balance my maid duties with the film. After all, I couldn't let Jamison down.

My worries spun like a tornado in my head as I went to the kitchen to make myself an espresso – extra strong – so I could go to work on Jamison's list before the sun came up. When it was finally a decent hour, I grabbed another cup of coffee and checked to see if Alex was in his office.

"Good morning?" It was more of a question from the way Alex was slumped over his desk.

"Wow, you're up early," he said with a tired smile.

"Double duty," I said. "Actually, I was wondering if I

could run something by you about working with the writers? See, I don't want them to think I'm looking for money or credit. I just want to learn the ropes, you know?"

Alex was eyeing the mug in my hand and only half-listening. "Coffee?"

"Oh, yes! Here, I brought you some," I said, rushing over to his desk.

"Slow down." He laughed and sat up, running his hand over his face. "It's too early for that much energy. How many gallons have you already had this morning?"

"Sorry," I said with a sheepish smile as I handed him his coffee. I glanced away, trying to compose myself before looking back.

When I did, I saw that Alex was leaning back in his desk chair, a wide smile warming his eyes, which were now twinkling. Suddenly, he didn't appear so tired, although his shirt was mostly unbuttoned, as if he'd come down to answer a phone call before he'd finished dressing.

"I'm sorry. I'm interrupting you and you're busy." I turned to leave. "I'll just go."

Alex caught my wrist and said, "No, I need a break. Plus, I have to tell you how excited everyone is about your ideas."

"Really?" My eyebrows flew up. "I felt like I was stepping on everyone's toes yesterday."

"Not at all," he said with a dismissive gesture. "Films are always taking on new people and switching roles. They're used to it."

"But I'm your maid, and now suddenly I'm working on your film. Doesn't that bother people?" I remembered how the set designer hadn't looked very happy in the meeting.

"Well, I don't give a rat's ass if they're bothered or not." He shrugged. "Sorry, I mean, it just doesn't matter. They're big boys. They know how this business works. Besides, you have great ideas."

More than anything I wanted to help Alex. He'd fired April because of me, and I felt like I needed to fix the damage that grand gesture had created. It was my fault. If I weren't here, things would've never gone so haywire. I just didn't want him to feel like he needed to do this because he felt guilty for everything April had put me through.

"Alex, are you sure? I mean, what about April? She talks and stirs up a lot of trouble. Besides, I don't think I can be both your maid, and work on the film. It wouldn't look good."

"Who gives a shit about how it looks? I mean, who cares?" he asked and trailed a finger lightly across the back of my hand. "I'm telling you, the only thing people care about right now is salvaging the film, and your ideas have made that possible. Everyone's inspired, and it's all coming together again."

"That's great, I guess." Self-doubt crept up on me. He had to be just trying to reassure me, right?

"You don't believe me? Here, take a look at these," he said, and tugged on my hand. He pulled me around the desk to look at the computer screen. "These are all the emails from everyone on the team this morning. They're really running with your ideas."

I leaned over, peering at the subject lines.

"See that one? The director has a new shot list. And there're several more right there about dialogue changes." He leaned back in his chair. "It's great. I think the production will be back on its feet in no time."

"That's wonderful!" I said.

"It sure is," Alex said, his voice thick.

I glanced back to catch his gaze roving up my legs to the hem of my black skirt. He looked at me and slipped his hand up the trail his dancing eyes had blazed. Tingles of pleasure shot up my legs as he caressed them. The two sensations crashed together at the apex, and a flood of desire washed over me. I'd bent over with my elbows on the desk to better see the screen, and I smiled as I realized how suggestive it must've looked from his vantage point. The look on his face said it all.

I shifted slightly, both taunting him and egging him on. I knew I shouldn't, but I couldn't control myself. The nano-second I got near him, the heat between us raged and it was pointless to resist. Now I knew the meaning of the phrase *putty in his hands*, because every time I looked in Alex's eyes, or breathed in his scent, I became completely submissive to him. He could do whatever he wanted to me. His presence was like a drug, and I just wanted more of him every time we were together.

As my legs shifted, and his hand slid a little higher, his lips parted. His chest, bare between the open buttons, rose and fell faster as I let his fingers explore.

"I don't want to get between you and your work," I teased.

"No?" he drawled. "I think you're doing a pretty good job of distracting me from it right now." His pulled his hands out from under my skirt and smiled. "And I love it."

In a flash his strong hands jumped to my hips and he guided me down until I was sitting on his lap facing the computer. He loosened my black hair from the tight bun I was wearing and let it fall over him.

"How about you read the emails while I…uh…work on something else?" His voice was low and heavy with lust.

Heat pooled in my stomach. "Team work?"

I felt his chuckle as he pulled me back against his powerful chest. I could feel the heat of him through my white cotton shirt, and suddenly, I was a hot ball of fire wiggling in his lap. His fingers pulled at my shirt, yanking it out of my waistband, then undoing the buttons one at a time. I shifted, fidgeted in anticipation, and finally, the cool air rushed over me as he opened my shirt wide.

He swept my hair to one side, exposing my neck, and nuzzled his mouth to my ear as I leaned my head back on his shoulder. A puff of air escaped my lips as I felt the warmth of his breath. I closed my eyes and breathed deep, absorbing the sensation of his feathering kisses, alternating with gentle suction and scrapes of his teeth. It was maddening.

With my shirt out of the way, Alex reached around and cupped his hands over the satin and lace of my pink bra. The hot friction made my nipples pucker, and he slid his hands inside to pinch my nipples between his thumbs and forefingers. The light, rolling squeeze was enough to send reverberating jolts of pleasure between my legs. I arched my back to push my breasts into his hands, and when the squeezing caresses of those hands pulled me back against him, I could feel his erection, hard as steel against my ass.

I rubbed against the swelling pressure and heard Alex's breath go ragged in my ear. His hands left my breasts, and swept down my bare stomach, over the waistband of my skirt to circle my knees. His mouth found mine as he teased me with the tickling circles, matching it to the swirling licks of his tongue. Then he pulled my legs gently apart and I opened for him, eager to ease the sticky heat between my thighs. He put his knees inside mine and spread me open wide before he dragged his hands upwards, pushing my skirt to my waist.

One hand returned to my breast as the other slipped down inside my panties and rubbed across my now throbbing clit. I gasped over the waves of pleasure, crying out when he finally slipped a finger deep inside me. His teasing strokes took me higher and higher, my feet pushing against the legs of the chair as I pushed against his probing finger.

"Oh, god, Chelsea," he groaned.

Suddenly, he lifted me off his lap and leaned me over the desk. I heard him fumble with his pants, then he was leaning over me, kissing my neck, his mouth searching for mine as our hips aligned. Our lips found each other as I reached between my legs to guide his nudging erection, feeling him heavy and throbbing against my wetness. I welcomed his first thrust with a deep moan, breaking our kiss. Alex pressed one hand on top of mine, our fingers intertwining as he started a pounding rhythm. This was no languid love-making. This was fucking, pure and simple.

His other hand cupped my breast, his fingers rolling my taut nipple again and sending shudders of pleasure through the core of me. I braced my legs and pushed back against his hips, matching his rhythm and clenching tighter. I arched my back, taking him further inside, wanting him deeper. He answered by slowing the tempo, but increasing the pressure, building it until I couldn't breathe for wanting him.

Then, with a roll of his hips and a rough press of his fingers, I came. The release was sudden and so powerful I collapsed on the desk. Alex reared up with a satisfied growl rolling out of his throat, and I felt him explode inside me, cock pulsing against my own still-quivering walls.

Alex fell back into his desk chair, pulling me with him even as he slid out of me. Aftershocks trembled through both of us as he held me close. His lips lingered against mine, and I felt his tongue trace around them. As he tasted me, the kiss deepened, and his hands came to hold my face as he tangled his tongue with mine. Curled onto his lap, I felt his cock jerk again.

"You're right," he said with a sigh. "We should stop before the whole morning is gone."

I flushed. "Sorry, I didn't…I mean, seriously, I just came in to bring you coffee."

Alex stopped me with another melting kiss. "Wasn't complaining."

I finally pulled away and said, "I didn't mean to confuse my house duties with working on the film."

"I'd rather think of it as nothing to do with either of those things. Like a coffee break. The hottest, sweetest coffee break I've ever had." He grinned and nuzzled my neck again.

I wished it could be as simple as that. Was it possible to keep everything separate? I came into the room as his employee, bringing him coffee, and here I was in his lap, half-naked bodies still entangled, the inside of my thighs sticky with the evidence of our love-making.

Alex pulled me back into another kiss and all my thoughts went blurry again. All I could do was feel the swirling circles of his tongue, his hands slipping down my back to curve around my rear. He pulled, wanting me to shift, encouraging me to straddle him, to take him inside me again. As always, the temptation of him was too much to resist. and I moved, slipping my legs through the arms of the chair to sit astride him.

His eyes pierced deep into mine. "I can't get enough of you, Chelsea."

He wrapped his wide hands around my waist and rocked me against him. My already quivering center melted into waves of pleasure, and I felt him harden beneath my wetness. I clutched at his shirt collar, pulling myself up, and then letting him guide my hips down until he was fully seated inside me.

This time we hardly separated. He stayed deep, and I rocked against him, my already sensitive flesh pulsing around him. We rubbed and throbbed, lost in each other until our bodies crested together. Alex wrapped his arms all the way around me, keeping me locked against him until the last aftershock passed through him, to me, and back again.

Spent and happy, he dropped his head back and laughed. I tried to clear my head enough to stand, but all I could think was how on earth had this happened on a simple coffee break?

My eyes traveled lazily around the room and landed on the clock on the wall. *Oh crap, I'm late*. I should've been helping Jamison in the garden by now.

"I have to go," I said, at a loss for how to switch out of post-coital mode and back into my housemaid role. This was just getting more complicated with each passing day.

The phone rang and Alex swore out loud, just as annoyed at reality interrupting us as I was.

"Fuck." The word came out with a breath of exasperated air. He didn't unwrap his arms from me, but I saw him glance at the caller I.D. It was business.

"Go ahead, get it," I said. "I have to go back to work, too."

I grabbed at my clothes and pulled myself together as he answered the phone. It was a quick exchange with the set caterer wondering about whether or not to provide April's specialty orders. A conversation that barely took as long as it did me to clean up.

That was the call he had to take? I buttoned my shirt and willed the burning blush off my cheeks.

He hung up the phone, smiled at me, and said, "When you see Jamison will you tell him I'd like a Waldorf salad for lunch?"

"Yeah, no problem," I said, finishing up the last of the buttons.

"I've been thinking about it," Alex said, "and it's like a fairytale. It'll make a great movie, maybe our next project."

"What are you talking about?" That came out of the blue. "What fairytale?" I asked.

"Us. You know, the maid who's also a muse," he said with a wide, satisfied smile.

"You might want to work on your Prince Charming," I muttered.

"What?" He was already tapping on his computer keyboard and was clearly only half paying attention.

"Nothing," I said, turning to go.

"Oh, Chelsea? Tell Jamison we should all eat together in the garden. A celebration," Alex said.

I nodded and restrained myself from slamming the door behind me. The maid and the muse. I balled one hand into a fist. That's all I was, and I had a feeling it's all I would ever be.

When I reached the garden, the look on Jamison's face didn't help. It was as if he knew what had just happened, and he probably did. I delivered the messages about lunch feeling lower than the dirt I turned over in the garden beds.

Jamison opened his mouth to say something, but his phone beeped, signaling that someone had pushed the front doorbell.

"Don't worry, I'll get it," I said, standing up.

On my way through the servants' hallway to the front door I hoped it wouldn't be one of the production team members from the film. Being seen covered in dirt would be worse than me carrying in lunch. When I opened the door, however, all thoughts of that worry were blown away.

"Hey, Sissy." It was Zach. He dropped his backpack and opened his arms.

I stared, my brain refusing to accept what I was seeing.

"Zach? What? How…"

My foster brother laughed and pulled me into a hug. I was so shocked I let him hold me a few extra seconds, and only pulled back when I felt his hand sweep gently over my hair in a decidedly *not* brotherly move.

"What're you doing here in Holland?"

"You didn't think you could send out a distress signal and not get a response, did you?" He was grinning broadly as he picked up his backpack and slung it over his shoulder, waiting for me to invite him in.

My jaw dropped as I remembered what I'd said to him last. I'd been upset, thinking about going home...shit. I'd never told him that things were better.

"So when do I get to meet that playboy scum of a boss of yours?" Zach asked, stepping around me and walking into the foyer.

"Well, I'm still not sure. But…"

"I bet he thinks he can take advantage of you," Zach said, eyeing the rich furnishings with a look of disgust. "A life of money makes people think they deserve things. Think other people should just give it to them."

I wanted to tell Zach how Alex wasn't like that, but suddenly that sounded so lame, so naïve. "We can't talk here. Let's go into the kitchen."

Zach tossed his backpack on the wide kitchen island and opened the massive built-in refrigerator. He grabbed a soda, cracked it open, and took half a dozen gulps.

"Wow. That was a long flight," he said. "But it was worth it."

He smiled at me, and I had to smile back. Zach's hair was rumpled, and there was a rough shadow of stubble across his face, but his eyes were bright. Zach was always smiling. That was one of the traits I loved about him the most, but now it felt too warm. Too little like a brother. I'd forgotten how persistent he'd been about his less-than-brother-like feelings for me.

"I missed you," he said.

"You didn't need to come," I said with a sigh. "I was

being silly, everything's fine. In fact, I'm working on a film project now, helping with rewrites. Alex and I are…"

"Working together?" Zach asked, raising a brow. "Hmm. Sounds like he's making you do more than housework. Is he paying you for the writing? Or is that just another one of the bonuses he expects from you?"

"Well, it's my first time writing a screenplay. I wouldn't expect to get paid and this is good experience. I love the writing. I think it could be a career for me," I said. "And in this business, getting a foot in the door is really important."

"Good." He placed his soda can on the counter. "After you're done with this summer maid gig, I'll introduce you to that producer I met."

"Alex is a producer."

"He's a spoiled rich guy. You can do better than that," Zach said, and plopped onto a stool at the kitchen island. "Karl can't wait for you to get home."

I leaned on the counter. "How is he?"

Zach scratched the back of his neck and his eyes darted down.

Crap. That wasn't good.

"Neglected. It's so crowded there, I don't think he's had more than three therapy sessions this month," Zach said, squeezing my hand.

It was hard to hear, but I had to know. I was flooded with guilt. Seeing Zach, sitting here and talking to him made it all so clear. I'd been living in a bubble. I needed to get my priorities straight. I needed to start thinking about home.

Chapter 34

Alex

"We have a guest joining us for lunch," Jamison said, startling me out of a rather pleasant daydream of Chelsea in a slinky black dress as we walked the red carpet for the film premiere.

I'd just been imagining unzipping it, running my fingers down her spine, when Jamison had interrupted.

"What the…please, tell me it's not April or my father." I said, sitting up straight in my chair. I didn't need that headache right now, not when things seemed to be going so well.

"It's Chelsea's foster brother. His name is Zach."

"Foster brother? Here? In Holland?" What was he doing here? I gave myself a mental shake. "That's right, she said she was adopted." My stomach tightened. I wasn't ready to meet her family. "What the hell, Jamison? You could've told me he was coming."

I was snapping at him, but I was pissed at myself. Once again, Jamison had the scoop on Chelsea's life and I didn't. I hadn't even known she'd had a foster brother in addition to Karl. Jamison pursed his lips and cocked an eyebrow at me without saying anything.

There were probably hundreds of things he could tell me about Chelsea, but the point was that he knew and I didn't. For all our intimacy, Chelsea hadn't opened up to me yet, but I knew most of it was my fault. The more I thought about it, the more I realized that most of our conversations revolved around me. Maybe I was an egotistical rich kid after all.

"I guess it's my own fault. I never gave her a chance to tell me," I said.

Jamison relaxed a notch and said, "I'll make sure she knows he's welcome to stay."

"I'm excited to meet him." Okay, so maybe that wasn't the exact right word, but it was better than telling Jamison about the knot in my stomach.

Jamison's lips quirked up at the corners. "I believe the feeling is mutual."

His tone made my shoulders stiffen. "Oh, shit, is he some protective big brother? He probably knows about the website where we met. He wants to kill me, doesn't he?" I ran my hand through my hair. I was so used to people kissing my ass that I hadn't considered any alternatives.

Jamison gave me a strange look. "I think he's more interested in saving her from you and sweeping her off her feet."

I stared. I had to have heard him wrong. "Her brother?"

"Her *foster* brother. I'm sure he'll make the distinction for you." For some reason, this seemed to amuse Jamison.

I frowned and followed him out to the garden patio. Through the window, I saw Chelsea in the kitchen, loading our lunch onto a tray. Her eyes met mine, but dropped quickly. Apparently, she was keeping busy inside, leaving me to meet Zach alone.

"Alex Silverhaus, nice to meet you," Zach said, holding out his hand.

I smiled and shook his hand, trying to measure him up the way guys do during a handshake. He was an inch or two taller than me, lean and hard-muscled. His brown hair was wild and sun-streaked, reminding me of a typical all-American extreme sports fanatic. Not rich, but not someone I could easily dismiss either.

"Zach, right?" Probably raced dirt bikes or something

dangerous like that. The sort of thing that got girls all wet in their panties. "So, you're Chelsea's brother?"

"Well, I'm one them. We had a big family. You're probably thinking of Karl," Zach said, his bright green eyes measuring me.

"Karl?" I asked. He waited for me to let go of the handshake first, then stood his ground, crossing his arms across his chest.

"Yeah, her younger brother," he said arching an eyebrow. "But you're just her employer so I don't suppose there's any reason for you to know that, other than Karl is the *only* reason she's here."

"And you're her other brother?" I asked, ignoring the sting his words prompted.

"I'm her foster brother, not blood. We met when we were both adopted as teenagers so it wasn't like we grew up as siblings. We've always been more friends and confidantes than brother and sister."

Fuck me. This guy was laying it on thick, implying some kind of claim to Chelsea because of their family ties, but I got the impression he liked her, and not in the friendly kind of way. I didn't know much about the dynamics of foster families, but it was clear he didn't see any problem with having the hots for his foster sister.

Zach glanced around the patio area and at the pool. There was no envy in his eyes, but the appreciation there was tinged with something else. "I'm glad she found this gig. Short, and the money's right. Just enough for what Karl needs. Chelsea can't wait to get home and get him moved into his new program."

I jammed my hands in my pockets. So there was even more that I didn't know. "He doesn't live with Chelsea?"

Zach snorted. "How would that work? She's still working her way through school. Not everyone was born into *this*."

He stepped back and gestured to the manicured lawn, the carefully tended garden, and the patio table set for lunch with a white tablecloth and my monogrammed silverware. Jamison finished uncorking a bottle of white wine and filled the crystal glasses at each place.

"She goes to Oregon State for writing?" I asked, reaching into my memory for the details, something to prove that I, too, knew Chelsea.

"Chelsea's a lot more practical than that," he said, pushing his wild hair out of his face as he laughed. "Yeah, she's talented at writing, but she takes business classes so she'll be able to support Karl with a *real* job after she graduates."

This guy was beginning to annoy me. Another jab at me. This time at my career. The film industry did have a – well, a certain reputation that could be a little sleazy at times, but I wasn't like that. He didn't know me. And he also clearly didn't know just how talented his sister was.

"Yes, she does have a gift for writing. Did she tell you she's doing the rewrites for my latest film?" I asked.

"Sure," Zach shrugged. "Like I said, Chelsea's practical. Keep the boss happy and all that. You're paying her for it, right?"

"Actually..." *Shit.* "We haven't discussed that yet," I said, scratching my head. "The experience is good for her, and she'll be able to leverage it later on."

"Leverage isn't really what she needs," he said, giving me a tight smile.

"And I suppose you know what she needs?" I asked, striding over to the table. I was doing my best to keep my temper, but he wasn't making it easy.

"And what she wants," Zach said, picking up a wineglass for a quick sip. He never stopped smiling, but now I saw sharp edges. "She doesn't really like a lot of complications, people trying to take her focus off what's important."

"Her brother," I said, sliding out the chair and motioning for him to sit at the table.

"His name is Karl," Zach said, still standing.

"Well," I said, forcing my fingers to stay light on the wineglass. "Things aren't very complicated here. Chelsea likes her job, and I support her writing." I couldn't resist a little jab of my own. "Something, I guess, she wasn't getting at home."

Zach put down his glass and crossed his arms. "Chelsea's not big on people supporting her. She's very independent. The last thing she wants is another person putting demands on her. Best to let her go her own way."

Home to you? I thought. *No way, asshole.* I gripped the stem of the glass, wondering what this guy's angle was? Why was he really here? Was he just playing the role of protective big brother–foster brother? Or had I read him right and he wanted her too? Was he warning me off without knowing how I couldn't keep my hands off of her? *Shit*. Unless she'd told him.

Chelsea stepped onto the patio carrying the lunch tray, her long hair tied into a braid. With a jolt, a wave of apprehension washed over me and I watched helplessly, as Zach jogged over to help her, leaving me waiting at the table. *Fucker's smile heated up twenty degrees when he looked at her.* Not that I blamed him, but when Chelsea returned it with an easy laugh of her own, that burned.

At the end of the summer, would she tell him I'd been just an easy fling, a quick, fun affair she was easily able to leave behind when she returned to real life? Or would she even think about me at all? The thought made the white wine bitter in my mouth.

"Waldorf salad, tuna steaks, and those whole wheat rolls you like so much," Chelsea said to me as she and Zach reached the table. Jamison followed behind. Oh, look at that. Zach was carrying the tray for her. Jamison could have carried it. Zach was trying to score points with her. No, he was trying to show me up. I rubbed my hand across my mouth, stifling the urge to blurt out the wrong thing.

Zach eyed the food as they placed it on the table. "Fancy eats. Can you imagine ordering up whatever you want for lunch?" He said it like I didn't exist and he was only talking to Chelsea.

Chelsea chuckled. "Yeah, but we can't get Zach's famous

Serrano pepper quesadillas here in Holland. Remember those, Zach?"

Zach laughed as if remembering something fondly from their shared past, and that just pissed me off even more.

"I'm sure you can't get that here. I always keep a jar of Serrano peppers in my fridge, just in case you want one," Zach said, flipping Chelsea's swinging braid over her shoulder with a familiarity that irked me.

Chelsea pushed his shoulder, then rolled her eyes as he pulled out her chair with a flourish. She sat down, the smile still bright on her lips. After he pushed her chair in he spun to his own spot at the table. I half-expected someone that long and tall to be gawky, but he had the tight grace of an athlete. Chelsea watched him too, and my first bite of salad felt like gravel.

Suddenly, I felt like I was locked in some stupid testosterone-laden competition over Chelsea. Brotherly love? *Fuck that*. His love for her was carnal, pure and simple. He was no brother, foster or otherwise. He was a man and Chelsea was a beautiful woman. And if I didn't do something, I was going to lose before we even started playing.

I cleared my throat, and said, "Did Chelsea tell you how many of her ideas we're using in my movie?"

Soft wisps of black silk escaped her braid and Chelsea brushed them aside, as if she was surprised that I was back in the conversation. "Oh, yes, they decided some of my ideas worked really well on the re-write."

"Re-write? Wasn't going well, huh?" Zach asked, leaning back in his chair.

"One of the actresses was disrupting the set and everything," Chelsea said, sitting forward. "It'll be all over the tabloids soon, if she has anything to say about it. Can I tell him?"

I nodded, feeling hollow as her eyes bounced off me and back to Zach. Clearly, he was the one who had her attention.

"April Temple," she said as if delivering a punch line.

Zach erupted from his relaxed lean and smacked his hands

on the table. "You've got to be kidding me! Queen Wiggle-Scream?"

Chelsea clapped two hands over her mouth, but couldn't muffle her shriek of laughter. She glanced at Jamison and me. "I'd forgotten about that. We saw her in *Fanged Fog* at the drive-in that summer."

"Chelsea does the best impression of April Temple," Zach said without taking his eyes off of her.

"Really? You never told me that," I said, folding my arms on the table in front of me. I tried not to sound like a petulant child.

"It's silly," she said and waved a hand in the air. "No reason to mention it."

I watched her as I rested my chin in my hand. There was a light in her eyes I hadn't seen before. She could be herself in front of Zach, silly and nostalgic. He made her feel comfortable, and the result was luminous. Her eyes sparkled. She was playful and reached out easily to grab his arm, touch him, even in jest, to swat at him, anything to make a connection. It seemed his teasing made her lively...and more attractive than ever.

I wanted to jam my chair between them, or better yet, knock Zach all the way back to the drive. The jealousy ate me up, and I started comparing myself to him, running down a mental list of pros and cons. Our physical appearances. Finances. Education...

What the hell was I doing? I was letting this guy get to me. My glowering made Chelsea do a double-take, so I quickly cleared my expression and said, "Oh, this I have to see. Go ahead, give it a shot."

"We called her Queen Wiggle-Scream because every time she screams her whole body does this goofy move," Chelsea said.

"Come on, stand up, really throw yourself into it. Remember?" Zach said, pulling her up. "You have to commit. I'll be your monster."

I was the one who wanted to scream, but instead, I sat

back and kept a smile in place.

I watched as they acted it out. Zach stalked her across the patio and lunged for her waist. Chelsea threw her hands up to her face, screamed, and sent a jiggle from her shoulders to her hips. I had to laugh because they were right. It was April's overacting done exactly right. But my mood changed, and my chuckle stuck in my chest when Zach picked up Chelsea and whirled her around, turning her faux scream into a real shriek of laughter.

His hands were on her hips, her arms clung to his shoulders, and suddenly I was jealous again. I yanked my hands under the table to hide my clenched fists.

"Chelsea was just in my office this morning, helping me celebrate firing April Temple," I said.

Zach put her down. He hadn't missed the red-cheeked look she gave me. My fingers relaxed a little when I caught Chelsea's eyes and saw that she didn't look angry.

I couldn't resist getting in another dig, so in a selfish move, I continued, "Working with Chelsea is really great. Feels like a good fit. I hope to have her there more often."

They returned to the table and sat down, Chelsea holding a hand low on her stomach, the way people did when they'd been laughing, but the heat in her eyes was all for me. I knew she remembered our morning, and how it had felt with me inside her. In my periphery, Zach's eyes darted between the two of us and it was my turn to lean back in my chair and suppress a smug smile. He may have had his hands on her hips, and his eyes all over her, but I'd had the real thing.

"Will that be before or after her maid duties?" Zach asked, stabbing his salad.

"Come on, Zach," Chelsea said.

"No, I'm curious how it works for you. I've had plenty of jobs where the duties changed. At first, it feels great because you're taking on more, it's interesting and fun. Then you realize you're putting in extra hours without pay, expected to do way more than time allows, and bam! You're being taken advantage of." He finished his last sentence looking at his plate.

Coward. Look me in the eye and talk to me like a man.

Chelsea fidgeted in her chair, clearly ill at ease with how the conversation was going. Her fork stopped in mid-air and her brows furrowed.

"Well…see, it's not like that," she started. "Writing is more like my hobby, right now anyway."

I took another sip of wine and reconsidered what I wanted to do with lover boy, Zach. I didn't like his insinuations, but I needed to back off and give Chelsea a break. I could see that it was getting awkward for her, and her happiness was more important than what I wanted. What I really wanted to do was bitch slap the cock sucker every time he eye-fucked her, which was about every two seconds. But instead of causing a scene, I took the high ground.

"No, he's right," I said, nodding. "And it's easy to fix. We can choose specific times to work on the film, and ask Jamison to make sure the schedule works. There's no reason for it to be complicated."

Chelsea's eyes crashed into mine and I swallowed hard. I wished her brother would disappear. There were other complications, other things I wanted to talk about with Chelsea. Things I wanted to say to her that I should've said before, but at least I was offering a start to make things right.

"So I suppose you won't have any time to show me around?" Zach asked, pulling her gaze back to him.

"I…I wouldn't know what to show you anyway," she said, "I've only been through The Hague once on my way here and once when I…"

She fumbled with her fork and ended up grabbing her glass of wine and taking a large gulp. I cringed. She'd almost said *when I went to jail*. I certainly didn't want Zach to know about that.

I smiled and tried to brush it off, but Zach noticed the chasm in the conversation and squeezed her hand.

"I don't care, I came here to see you. I wouldn't care if all I saw was the kitchen, and your room."

My stomach clenched at the thought of him in her room. The room where the two of us had...

"Hell, I'll even dust something if you want me to," he said.

I watched the change come over her again, as if the sun burst through high cloud cover. She relaxed, her shoulders straightening, her braid swinging as her conversation became animated. Her delicate hands took flight, punctuating her laughter with graceful dives and swooping over to Zach's open hand on the table.

She turned to him, laughing, and I felt her shoulder cut me from the conversation. The bleeding ebb of feelings dropped my heart to the ground. If this was how I felt now, how would I feel when the summer was over?

My eyes traveled over the wide expanse of manicured lawn as I faded from their conversation. I'd come to the house in Holland especially for of its beauty and silence. It gave me room to work, and quiet to think. Except being here without Chelsea...the fast approaching autumn was going to hurt like hell.

Soon, she'd head back to the uproar of college life, the busy pace of a regular job, and college courses. And where would that leave me? Standing back here with my heart in my hand. The best I could do for her was to make sure she got the paycheck she needed.

I picked at the corner of the expensive cloth napkin and said, "You have paid time off, if you want to take it."

Chelsea's shoulders shook with laughter as she turned back to me. "Paid time off?"

"Yes, Jamison will tell you it's our standard practice," I said, tossing my napkin over my unfinished plate. "You earn two days off per month. You should take them now and go enjoy The Hague."

"I rented a car," Zach said, as he beamed at her.

"I'm here to work, Zach," she said, holding a palm up. "Remember? This isn't a sight-seeing trip, I'm here to earn the deposit for Karl's program."

If I thought she wouldn't go because of our dinners in the kitchen, our run-ins by the pool, I was wrong. All morning I assumed she'd be in my bed that night, but the thought was gone now. I wondered if it'd even entered her mind at all.

Zach was here now, reminding her of why she'd taken the job in the first place. He'd brought her back to herself, and I'd be a selfish son of a bitch to stand in her way. The Chelsea I saw now was luminous, confident and driven. *Fuck*. It wasn't me who brought any of that out in her. I hardly recognized the vivacious woman at this table in front of me, but she was a better version of the one I'd know.

I had to do it. I had to let her go.

"Don't worry about the money, Chelsea. I'm serious about the paid time off. You have it, and you should use it. Take Zach and go enjoy yourself," I said.

She didn't ask about what I'd do. She didn't protest and ask about the film. Instead, she clasped her hands together and smiled. "Thank you, Alex!"

My heart dropped. The blue eyes I wanted as my own didn't even look my way as she turned to Zach. He grabbed her hand and squeezed. She may as well have taken that delicate hand and shoved the table knife right into my heart. Okay, there were only butter knives on the table today, but still, it hurt. More than I wanted it to.

"First, let's check with Jamison. He'll have tons of great suggestions for places to go," she said, jumping up and pulling Zach to his feet. "We can talk while we clean off the table."

"No, just go," I said, "It's officially your day off, staring right now."

"*Paid* day off," Zach reminded me, like I'd be such a jackass that I'd forget and stiff her for it.

Chelsea thanked me again and headed toward the house without a backward look. I tossed back the rest of my wine and started to call for Jamison to bring something stronger. Then I remembered that Zach and Chelsea were talking to him, and I didn't want to be a total dick.

Zach's surprise visit had revealed the real Chelsea, and

she was spectacular, even more beautiful and amazing than I'd known. *Fucking, Zach*. Why'd he have to come and piss on my bonfire? Clearly, this had been a rude awakening of the worst kind that showed me where I stood.

Alone with the checkbook.

Chapter 35

Alex

The best way to get Chelsea off my mind was to work. Or at least that's what I thought would help, but the mind had a way of fucking with you when you were down. It dredges up all the thoughts you want to avoid and won't let them go. In this case, it was Chelsea's beautiful face and her light-hearted laughter. It echoed in my mind as I headed to my office, and the images only stopped when I heard voices on the front steps.

"Nice to meet you, Carrie and Emily."

I snarled as I recognized Zach's voice. He hadn't left yet, but I was relieved Carrie was here because I needed someone to talk to. I stepped back from the narrow glass that flanked the front door, hoping my visitors hadn't spotted me. I needed a moment to compose myself. I definitely didn't want Zach to know he'd gotten to me.

I took another peek and saw my niece bound up the steps in answer to her name. She stopped in front of Zach and said, "You're too tall. Do you fall over a lot?"

"Actually, no, I surf a lot, skateboard too, so I have good balance," Zach said with a charming grin.

"He used to be really klutzy when he was little," Chelsea said.

"Childhood sweethearts?" Carrie asked lightly.

I smiled behind the door as my sister-in-law tipped her

naturally platinum blonde head and waited for a reply.

"No, no, no, this is Zach," I heard Chelsea say. "We grew up together, fostered, and then adopted in the same family. He's my brother."

"Foster brother, not blood," Zach made sure to clarify.

"Nice to meet you, Zach. How long are in you in Holland?"

"Not long," he said. "Just making sure Chelsea is doing alright."

"I'm sure you've discovered Alex is more a team leader than an employer," Carrie said. "Everyone's on equal footing in his house. I know he never thinks of Chelsea as a maid."

Thank you, Carrie. Finally, someone was rooting for me. Now I'd gone from waiting to calm down to being too curious to interrupt. I couldn't see exactly what they were doing out there, so I leaned close to the door, but it was too close and Emily caught me peeking. She gave me an impish grin.

"Chelsea is a princess. Like Cinderella. She lives in the attic room, right?"

Chelsea's cheeks turned rosy. "I do live in the attic of the servants' cottage."

"I used to play there. I was Cinderella, but I guess you can be her now," Emily said.

"Does that make me Prince Charming?" Zach asked.

"Wrong fairy tale," Emily said and turned to see if I was still watching.

Chelsea's eyes followed her gaze, and I was busted. I had to join them on the front steps or admit to eavesdropping by skulking away. I straightened up and walked through the door.

"Carrie! Emily! Always the best surprise. Do you want lunch? These two ran off before finishing so I have plenty," I said.

As soon as Carrie's eyes met mine, Chelsea's shied away. She must've seen me spying too. I was relieved when Emily lunged at me for a hug to cover my embarrassment. She threw her arms around my neck, and I pulled her up into a bear hug. She always made me feel better, no matter what happened.

Chelsea smiled at us even though Zach tapped her arm and took another step toward his rented car, trying to coax her away.

"Can Chelsea stay and play?" Emily asked.

"No, sweetheart, she has the day off and she's taking Zach to do some sightseeing," I said. *And I'm okay with that. Not. Go fuck yourself Zach.* "Have a nice time," I called out as they headed to the rental car.

"Maybe next time," Chelsea said, and then waved as she ran down the steps to join Zach.

Carrie smiled at her retreating back. "Next time we can all spend the day together and really get to know her."

I swung Emily into the foyer and said, "Good luck with that. She's been living her for months and I don't even know much about her."

Carrie followed us inside and tossed her purse on a side table. "I find that hard to believe." She gave me a sideways look. "What exactly have you been doing?"

I put Emily down and let her run ahead to the garden terrace. Jamison was in the kitchen, already putting together fresh lunch plates for us. Carrie blew him a kiss before she followed me down the hallway and caught my arm.

"Emily can't hear and Jamison's busy. Just tell me," Carrie said, tugging on my arm. She had that tone in her voice like women get when they want to hear relationship gossip.

"Tell you what? That I slept with her, but I still don't know anything about her?"

"Is that what's bothering you?" She raised her brows, a knowing smirk on her face. "Or could it be a strapping young lad named, Zach?"

I grabbed the doorframe to keep from punching a wall. "You think this is funny? He's probably filling her head with ideas of the evil employer taking advantage of his innocent maid."

Even I could hear the bitterness in my words.

"Come on, Alex. Lighten up. Chelsea knows it's not like that." She tilted her head. "Doesn't she?"

"I think so...I thought so." I exhaled a long breath and shook my head. "I don't know. Maybe I have it backwards, and I'm the one being taken advantage of here. Zach's reminded her of why she took the job. I'm just a fringe benefit."

Carrie gave me a sympathetic frown. "Poor baby."

Emily ran up to meet us at the door and tugged on my hand. "Come on. Let's go to the garden."

Carrie followed as Emily towed me out into the sunshine, where I offered Carrie a chair. Happy that we were outside to watch her, Emily ran off to explore the garden, and I took the chair next to Carrie.

I could understand Chelsea's motivation a bit better now. Karl was her brother and she had to take care of him. I mean, I got that. My brother had depended on me when he'd been in the dark pit of his addiction. It was a bitch to carry that heavy weight, but I didn't mind, he was my brother. It was kind of the same for Chelsea. She felt that weight, too. It's what balanced her and what drove her. How could I be jealous of that?

"So, tell me about Chelsea," Carrie said, relaxing back into her chair.

I took a deep breath and tried to explain. "I hired her to make Henry mad."

"Oh, I know. Your father told me all about it."

"Well, the joke's on me, because instead of some easy-to-dismiss bimbo looking for a summer of fun, I got Chelsea." I leaned forward and put my head in my hands. "And she's different, Carrie. She took the job because she needs the money to help her brother, her real brother, not that surfer dude brother."

"And you can't dismiss her?" Carrie asked.

"Dismiss her? I can't get her out of my head," I said.

"She's definitely not like the women you've dated before," she said. "Lord knows, you've paraded a few of those around like show ponies."

"Exactly," I flung myself back in my chair. Show ponies?

Really? Was I that bad? "I've never been this…I don't know how to explain it…this magnetized by a woman before." I threw my hands up in the air.

"So what's wrong with that? I have news for you, Sherlock, that's usually a good thing." Carrie leaned forward. "She's obviously attracted to you. I mean, you said the two of you slept together, right?"

"Yeah, and then it was awkward because she's working for me," I said, running my hand over my face.. "I didn't want her to think I thought of her like one of those girls from the website, so I gave her a choice. I told her she could quit the job and stay here as my guest. Then we could really see what was going on between us. She chose the job over me."

"Well, that was unfair of you." Carrie chuckled at my idiocy.

I glared at her. "For being family, you're being awfully hard on me. Where's the love? Anyway, at the time, I thought it was a good idea, but now..." I shook my head and blew out a breath. "I just wanted her to know she was more than a fling, that I was more than some creep who slept with the help. I wanted us to give it a real shot. I haven't wanted something like that in years."

"I know," Carrie said, reaching out to catch my hand and squeeze it. "But you said it yourself. She took the job because she needed the money to help her brother. That didn't change when you two got involved. How could you, of all people, expect her to choose a new relationship that might not be anything, over a brother who clearly needs her?"

I shook free of her hand and raked both hands through my hair. "You're right. I know that now."

"Hindsight is twenty-twenty. So why the long face?" Carrie asked.

"You mean besides stalker *foster* brother Zach with his surfer dude hair? Seriously? Do women really fall for that look?" I frowned. "And I don't buy his, 'I just traveled thousands of miles to drop in and check on you' explanation."

Carrie laughed. "He's quite attractive, but don't get your

tail in a knot. Chelsea doesn't think of him in that way at all."

"See, even you noticed it too. What's really up with him? He shouldn't be eyeing his sister, even if they're 'foster.' He's in some serious denial there for sure. I get the feeling he's here to save her from the sleazy rich playboy who doesn't deserve her," I said.

"I really don't think you have to worry about Zach and you know it. So, what's really bothering you?"

"I'm screwing it up, Carrie," I confessed. "I don't know how to get close to her. Every time we talk, it's about my movie or work or something else."

"And you want to get closer." It wasn't a question.

"It feels more like I have to."

"Oh, Alex, that's wonderful! Sounds like you're in love." Carrie beamed at me.

"Is that what this torturous feeling is all about?"

Carrie rocked back in her chair laughing at my misery.

I glowered at her. "You women always know this stuff better than guys, but what if Chelsea doesn't feel the same way?" *Then I'm screwed.*

Jamison joined us with our salads. He swallowed a chuckle and had to clear his throat. He set down the lunch tray and winked at Carrie. "Should I open a bottle of wine, or perhaps something stronger?"

"What do you think he needs, Jamison?" Carrie asked.

Jamison looked down at me and tapped a finger against his chin. "I don't know what he needs, but I keep telling him what he doesn't need is a maid. I can run the house just fine on my own."

"But what about the money?" I argued. "You know she needs it."

"You mean you're finally asking me my advice?" Jamison asked, crossing his arms over his chest.

Carrie laughed and cocked an eyebrow at me.

"I know, I know, I should've mentioned all of this sooner. Now that I've completely screwed everything up, just tell me what to do," I said impatiently.

Jamison took his time smoothing down his crisp shirt before he said, "I do have quite a lot of contacts in the area. There're a few households looking for help as they close up for the season."

"There," Carrie said, "problem solved. Chelsea finds another job for the rest of the summer, and during her time off you can work on your relationship with her."

"Are you in love with Chelsea?" Emily asked, bouncing into her chair. "I told you she's a princess."

"Like Cinderella?" I asked.

"Yup," my niece said. "You should tell her you love her at the ball."

From a child's perspective, life was so simple. If only it were that easy for adults.

Chapter 36

Chelsea

Why had I brought Zach to see The Hague? It was entirely too romantic. I'd hoped the sightseeing would keep the appropriate distance between us, but my plan backfired. The baroque architecture, the wide tree-lined avenues, and the sidewalk cafes only encouraged Zach to take my hand as we strolled. Even after I shook my fingers free and pointed out the old palace, minutes later, he clasped my hand again.

"I'm not a child," I said. "I'm not going to wander out into the road."

"Have you been keeping in touch with everyone back home?" Zach asked, refusing to let go. "I mean, besides me and Karl."

"Yeah, Clara mostly. We email every day," I said, tugging my fingers loose. Again.

I smiled at the thought of my college roommate and how she'd sneaked my lacy underwear into my suitcase. I'd been so convinced I wouldn't need something like that.

So wrong.

I bit my lip and said, "Speaking of Clara, have the two of you been hanging out?"

Clara wasn't the least bit subtle about how she felt about my foster brother. Somehow, though, Zach had missed all her heavy hints. I'd hoped being out of the country would've given her a chance to be even more bold.

"She texts me and checks in, wants to go for coffee or a drink or something. I just haven't had the time," Zach said with a shrug.

"Za-ach," I groaned, turning his name into two syllables. "You were supposed to be taking care of her while I was gone. Call her as soon as you get back. The two of you need to go out."

Zach frowned down at me and said, "We'll all go out for drinks when you get back. Maybe you can leave early. You should ask boss man for a big project or something. I can help. Put in the extra hours and get sprung early. We could even travel a little before we head back. What about Italy? I hear they make a great cappuccino there."

"Leave early and go with you to Italy?" I asked as the air squeezed out of my lungs. That sounded even more romantic than Holland and The Hague. *Crap.*

"Or anywhere you want. Paris?" His question stopped me dead in my tracks on the sidewalk. Paris. The City of Love. Yikes, that'd be even worse than Italy.

"I can't leave early, Zach. It'd be rude," I said, stepping around him. "Besides, I need to make enough for Karl's program."

Zach put his hands on my shoulders and forced me to stop. He looked me straight in my eyes and said, "I keep telling you not to worry about the money. I can help with the deposit. You know I'd do anything to help Karl."

"You don't have to, he's not your brother," I said.

"And you're not really my sister," Zach said, his fingers tightening on my shoulders. "You're more than that to me."

The traffic poured past us and church bells resonated from the center of the city. I tried to back away, but Zach wouldn't let me go. My eyes locked with his and I couldn't look away.

"Chelsea, you have to let me say it." His voice was soft and loose curls of hair fell into his eyes. He looked so sincere and my heart was pounding. I didn't want to hear it, but I knew I couldn't stop him. "Zach, you shouldn't do this," I said, putting my hands on his chest to push.

"There's nothing wrong with it. There's nothing saying we can't," he said. "It's just a piece of paper. I've looked into it. All I have to do is have my adoption undone. We've never been siblings. Not really."

"Zach, please…" I was too close now to be able to push him back, he'd pulled me in tighter as he spoke.

"I know what you're going to say, Chelsea, and it's okay. We can take things slow."

Before I knew it, he swooped down and caught my next comment in a kiss. I didn't pull back, too shocked from the fact that he'd actually done it. His chest was solid and strong under my hands. The wild waves of his hair brushed against my face, and his firm mouth warmed against mine.

It wasn't awful, but still, I was kissing my brother. Or was I just kissing Zach? My thoughts were jackknifing like crazy, and conflicting emotions crashed over me in waves. Through it all, only one clear thought stood out.

He wasn't Alex.

It hit me like a freight train and I broke free of Zach and pushed out of his hold. I almost laughed, but I covered my mouth with the back of my hand because I didn't want Zach to think I was laughing at him. I loved Zach as a brother, as a friend, but not with the same rush of longing and desire that flooded through me each time I thought of Alex.

"I love you, Chelsea. I always have. I know you don't feel the same about me, yet. Just say 'not yet' and I'll be happy. We'll go home and see what happens," Zach said.

The pleading on his face broke my heart.

"Zach, you know I love you as a brother," I said, trying to catch my breath. I had to make sure he was clear about how I felt. "You were always there for me, and I hope you'll always be there for me in the future. Please, think about that. I don't want this to ruin what we already have, I can't let this ruin us."

His green eyes filled up, but he didn't look away. "We won't ruin anything. We can't. I love you."

My heart was pounding. I was hurting him. I could see it

in his eyes. I was breaking his heart, and that was the last thing in the world I'd ever wanted to do, but I had to be honest. "Zach, please, it just isn't that way between us. There's someone out there for you, but it isn't me." I reached for his hand.

He stepped back. "No. You really mean there's someone *else* for you, and it isn't me," he said, curling his fingers into a fist. "You think that Alex loves you?"

"No…I don't know…I mean, I'm talking about you."

"You don't see it, Chelsea, but I do," Zach said, leaning against a stone wall. "Everyone in our lives has come and gone, but we're still together. You'll see when you come home. Maybe then you'll give me a chance."

"It's not about giving you a chance, Zach. It's about knowing what kind of love we really have. Family."

"You're just saying that because you think it's inappropriate. We aren't blood, Chelsea. We only lived together for a few years. We're only brother and sister on a slip of paper that I can take care of," Zach said. "What's really inappropriate is you thinking your boss loves you. You know how wrong that is, don't you?"

"You don't know anything about Alex," I shot back. I spun on my heels and started to head back toward the car.

"But I'm right, aren't I?" Zach accused as he caught up with me. "You've already slept together, and now you're trying to tell yourself there's more to it than just sex. You're trying to convince yourself that you're in love so you won't feel bad for having slept with your boss."

"When it's really love you don't have to convince yourself or the other person," I snapped.

"Chelsea, wait, I'm sorry," Zach said, grabbing hold of my elbow. Suddenly, his voice changed, and the expression on his face mellowed. "I don't want you to get hurt. You need to know where you stand with him, and you're not thinking clearly."

"I think we should head back now." I jerked my arm free, and strode the rest of the way to the car.

Zach got in the car and we drove in silence, the tension between us thick. Finally, after twenty minutes, Zach admitted to being completely lost. It took another ten minutes for him to reprogram the GPS on his phone with a new destination, and by the time we wove our way out of The Hague we were laughing again.

"Can we please pretend like that whole conversation never happened?" I asked.

Zach shook his head as he concentrated on his new directions, a familiar, stubborn set to his jaw.

"I'm not asking you to take it back, and I'm not saying I didn't hear you," I said. "I just don't want things to be awkward. I need you the same way I always have."

Zach bit his lip and kept driving, our prior laughter forgotten. With each turn, my stomach slid as if on a big block of ice. Zach had been the biggest constant in my life for the past few years. I'd been adopted, but he was the only one in the family I'd ever really kept in touch with. I needed him because he was a part of me. Maybe I shouldn't have leaned on him so much in the past.

As the silence grew, so did my confusion. Had I made a mistake? I did love Zach, but was I in love with him? Maybe if I allowed it to blossom the love we had between us would change. It was awkward because of our adoption papers, but it was just a technicality, a piece of paper. And he said he'd get a court order to undo his. I even knew our adoptive parents would understand. They already knew how he felt about me. They saw it before I ever had. Everything fit. Even Karl. Zach loved him too. It would be so easy. Our lives would just slip into place. No complications.

Except one, and it was a big one. The kiss. When Zach had kissed me, my entire being had cried out for Alex. I knew I couldn't possibly be in love with Zach, because I'd never felt with him like I did when I was with Alex. No matter how easy it would be, it wouldn't be the same.

"I can't pretend it didn't happen," Zach said as he parked the car. "You've known how I felt for a while, but we never said anything about it, and I couldn't let it just hang there anymore."

"I know, Zach. I just don't want it to change things."

"That's the problem, Chelsea. I wanted it to change everything. And I think it did, for you," he said, turning off the car and handing me the keys.

"What do you mean?" I asked.

"I still love you the same, and I still want us to be together, but you've decided on something else. That's why I can't go back with you. I'm going to get out here."

Zach laid his hand on the door handle ready to pop it. What was going on?

"And go where? What are you doing?" I asked, clutching his jacket.

"I'll head to the airport early and call you as soon as I get back to the States," he said. "I told Karl I'd see him on Tuesday."

"Stop it. Don't be silly," I pleaded. "You need the car. Just come back with me."

"Return it to the rental place for me, will ya?" He kicked open his door and stepped out. In his confusion, he'd driven us around in a circle, and we were back in the center of town near the train station. Or maybe he'd meant to do it.

This was awful. This couldn't be happening. I jumped out and ran around the car to stop him.

"You can't do this, Zach!" Guilt, loss, and an emotion I didn't quite understand were all raining down, twisting inside my stomach.

By the time I reached him his familiar smile was back in place. "I'll be fine. You're the one who's never traveled out of the country before. Remember? Just do me a favor, please?"

"Zach, get back in the car…"

He continued as if he didn't hear me, "Just make sure you know where you stand so you can decide if it's a good enough place for you." His eyes darkened. "But if I hear he's taking advantage of you, then I'll come right back here and make you let me save you."

I wrapped my arms around his waist and hugged him, my face pressed to his chest. Zach smelled like home, a mix of Portland rain and fresh air. He was familiar, solid, and I knew how much he loved me. I held on tight and wished I felt the same way. I squeezed my eyes tight, and hoped when I looked up that I would feel a flood of love for him, no matter how weird it would be.

"See you soon, Chelsea," he said, with a soft smile as he pulled himself free.

I looked up at him, and tried to will myself to go with him. We could run off together that night. I knew Zach would help me pay the rest of what I needed for Karl's program. All I had to do was call Alex and quit the job.

But that wasn't going to happen. Just thinking of Alex and how sweet his voice would sound over the phone was enough to stop me. I stood on the sidewalk and watched Zach walk away. When he finally disappeared from view, I rushed back to the car with one destination in mind.

The long drive gave me enough time to go over what I wanted to say to Alex. In my mind, it was a conversation of ground rules and schedules. If I knew when I was a maid, and when a screenwriter, when an employee and when a guest, then it wouldn't be so complicated. Or so I hoped.

By the time I drove up the long driveway I'd convinced myself that it would work, but the minute Alex's house came into view, my stomach burst into butterflies. I blinked hard trying to park the car before a blind panic took over. Who was I kidding? I was just a quick summer fling to him, and I was being an enormous fool.

I got out of the car and blinked again. A sleek Mercedes blocked the front steps, and there was Henry leaning against the driver's side door.

"Hello, Mr. Silverhaus," I said. "I believe Alex is home. I'll go find him for you."

"I'll talk to my son in a bit. There's no hurry," Henry said, holding out his arm to me.

I stopped and pulled back, sure that he was tricking me

somehow. Henry softened his eyes and gave me an encouraging smile, so I took his arm and let him escort me up the front steps.

"Actually, I came to see you," he said before we reached the top.

I pulled back and he turned to smile at me again. "Why me?" I asked, trying to keep the suspicion from my voice.

"Henry," Jamison called from the front door, "why don't you wait in the library, and I'll find Alex for you."

Henry tightened his arm around my hand and we continued up the steps together. "No need to bother my son, but I think a drink is just the thing."

"Chelsea, why don't you get some fresh ice?" Jamison said as Henry walked me into the foyer.

Jamison kept a straight face, but I knew his request was his way of trying to keep me from Henry's devious clutches. Jamison always knew when something fishy was up, but his efforts failed, and Henry continued without letting me go.

"You know I prefer my whiskey straight."

"How is Ms. Temple settling in at your house?" Jamison asked.

The light and polite question set off alarm bells in my head. If April was living with Henry, she'd probably sent him over with some manipulative plan in mind involving me.

"Like a moth in a closet full of silk," Henry said.

I tried to pull my arm free without appearing impolite and said, "Please excuse me."

"Nonsense, Ms. Carerra...or may I call you Chelsea?" Henry asked, putting a hand on my waist to guide me toward the library. "I came to discuss something with Chelsea, Jamison. I'll speak with Alex later."

Jamison shot a glance at the hallway leading to Alex's office. I really hoped he would go get Alex. I didn't trust Henry as far as I could throw him, and something told me I should have Alex in the room to hear whatever Henry had to say. Before I could see if Jamison went to get him, Henry led me into the library and closed the doors. I smoothed down my skirt and tried to remain calm.

"So, Alex tells me you're considering other work for the duration of the summer," Henry said, pouring a glass of whiskey from a crystal decanter.

"He did?" I asked, completely thrown. "I mean, that was considerate of him."

My head spun, and although I was relieved this wasn't about April, why was Alex trying to find me another position? Was I just a complication he needed to sort out? Then I brightened. Maybe this was so I could quit working for him so we could see each other. I let myself feel a flicker of hope.

Henry handed me a crystal glass and poured me a whiskey. I thanked him and sipped it, trying to settle my nerves.

"Well, it just so happens, a friend of mine is looking for a maid. The housework is light. It's mostly about entertaining. Benjamin loves to host and he needs live-in staff ready to serve his guests," Henry said.

"Benjamin?" I asked.

"Talbot," a smooth voice finished from the doorway. "My name is Benjamin Talbot, but my staff all call me Mr. B."

I turned and tightened my grip on the expensive crystal glass, hoping not to drop it. Benjamin Talbot could've stepped out of a portrait, his good looks were so polished and regal. Black hair was carefully slicked back, showing off the glint of silver at the temples that only made him look more distinguished. He was tall and exuded an air of complete confidence. I looked at his square jaw and sharp nose, and could easily picture him at ease in the royal palace. I couldn't quite place his accent, but it was something exotic.

His eyes caught mine, and I felt a flash of heat before I realized they were midnight blue. Wow, talk about charisma. It oozed from every pore in his body, but still I felt like some kind of specimen under his microscope. I didn't know whether I should be flattered, or creeped out by it.

"So Henry already told you about the job opening?" Benjamin asked.

"I...I guess?"

Benjamin Talbot smiled, his dark eyes running up and down the length of me. "You were right, Henry, she might be just what I need to finish the season. And if everything you told me is true, then it will be a wonderful way to end the summer."

What the hell did that mean? I bristled under his scrutiny, and yet my reaction was to give in to his piercing inspection. "What did he tell you?"

"Benji?" Alex asked, striding into the library. "Jamison said we had guests, but I never would've guessed it was you and my father. And Chelsea?"

Alex tipped his head, catching sight of me with the glass of whiskey I clutched. *Thank you, Jamison.* I knew he'd get Alex in here to witness this.

"Alex! How great to see you," Benjamin said. "I understand you've been busy, and I don't blame you, but you could have at least accepted one of my invitations to come out to the house."

"I know, I'm sorry. The movie really is taking up all my time," Alex said.

"Ah, yes. The movie." Benjamin smiled at Henry. "Sure. Well, I hear you're making big changes, clearing the way to get some real work done. From what Henry told me, I couldn't resist stopping by for a visit."

Alex smiled, and I couldn't tell if it was real or not. "You always did like a good story. How about you stay for dinner?"

Benjamin gave me a midnight blue wink and said, "Wonderful. Normally, dinner with two bachelors is not my idea of fun, but now that I've met Chelsea, how can I resist?"

I didn't know whether I should stand or sit, be complimented or offended. Were we all going to stand here like I was some kind of animal being haggled over at the auction block, making veiled remarks about the real reason Benji wanted me to work for him? Seriously? Would Alex throw me to this wolf? Or was he simply thinking of freeing me from working as his maid to uncomplicate things? And what, exactly, did that mean?

Despite its bitter bite, I took another sip of the whiskey and resigned myself to the fact that I'd taken this job to be a servant, not to be some esteemed professional in a cutting edge career job. What had I expected? If this kind of behavior was what was involved, then I'd have to handle it.

Just until the end of summer.

Chapter 37

Chelsea

Alex poured another drink for his father and Benjamin. When he got to me, however, I covered my glass with my hand and said, "I should see if Jamison needs help in the kitchen."

"Okay," Alex said, then dropped his voice. "And then maybe we can talk after?"

I nodded and smiled, still not entirely sure what was going on here. "Excuse me, gentlemen."

Benjamin gave me a shallow bow and right before I closed the library door behind me I heard him say, "Beautiful girl. A man could get lost in those eyes."

The compliment made me smile, although I was still a little leery of Mr. Talbot and what he wanted. The events of the day had my head spinning, to say the least.

When I walked into the kitchen, Jamison took one look at me and said, "So you met Mr. B?"

"I take it you know him."

"Of course," Jamison said, motioning for me to finish the sauce he was stirring. "Benjamin Talbot is old money, the kind of family fortune that's so old no one really even remembers where the money came from."

"He seems like a very nice gentleman," I said, stirring the sauce slowly. Jamison and I got along well, and I didn't want to spoil that by saying something I might regret.

"He is if you like that kind of man," Jamison said.

"Who doesn't like tall, dark, handsome, and rich?"

"Mr. B is a widower, a jet-setter, and used to getting his way," Jamison said with a sniff. "Not the easiest man to work for, if you have your own ideas."

"Did you ever work for him?" I asked, following Jamison's impatient gesture and spooning the sauce into an elegant, gold-rimmed serving dish.

"No, and I'm sure I would never like to," he said. His voice was polite, but stiff.

I accidentally sloshed a little sauce, remembering the way Henry had talked about me earlier like I might be eye-candy instead of just a maid. "Well, it sounds like Alex thinks I should go work for him."

"For Mr. B?" Jamison asked, tossing me a cloth to wipe the dish. "I knew he was planning to find you another position, but I don't think Mr. B is the man he had in mind."

I felt a clutch at my heart. Henry had been right. Alex wanted me to go somewhere else. All my worries from earlier came back. Maybe Alex had been biding his time until he could get me out of his hair. Maybe I really was just too much of a complication. Bringing Zach in had clearly been the last straw.

Jamison snapped his fingers in front of my face. "In the good way, my dear."

Crap. I hadn't been listening. "Oh, sorry. What did you say?" I asked as I loaded the savory roast dinner onto a large tray.

"It's not my place to say," he said, adding a flourish of spices to the top of the sauce.

"But you think I should avoid working for the sinfully handsome and rich Mr. B?" I asked, teasing.

"For those exact reasons." His mouth pursed. "He is well-known for lavishing gifts on his mistresses, though no one talks about how many different women he's seen with in any given month."

"So he's a rich playboy," I said.

Jamison shook his head. "I only mention it because he can be very persuasive."

"Alex didn't seem to have a problem with him, and he didn't tell me that he didn't want me working for Mr. Talbot." I didn't look at Jamison. "If Alex wants me somewhere else, this seems like good timing."

I didn't mention that I'd had to find out about Alex wanting me to leave from Henry, or that I still had no idea what Alex's real reasoning was, since Jamison seemed to think it wasn't as bad as I thought. Unless he told me otherwise, I thought it a good idea to make the break quickly and cleanly.

As if reading my mind, Jamison said, "You don't need to jump at the first offer that comes along. I'm looking into decent positions for you myself. Someone must need a maid for the last four weeks before summer ends."

I smiled. At least I knew I could trust Jamison to have my back. "Can't wait to get rid of me?" I asked, lifting the silver tray and waiting for him to open the door.

"You know that's not true," he said. He put his hand on my arm. "Please, Chelsea, just be careful. Things that seem too good to be true often are."

I followed him down the narrow servants' hall, and through the side door into the dining room. Benjamin applauded the dinner as I laid it on the table, and once again, his rakish eyes were dancing with delight. He was so transparent. It was obvious that it wasn't Jamison's presentation of the food that met with his exuberant approval. It was me.

"Absolutely delicious," he said, not even bothering to hide his true meaning.

I nearly rolled my eyes. The man was a ruthless flirt.

"Now don't be getting any ideas, Benji," Alex said with a grin. "You're here for dinner, not to poach my staff."

"Well, my *staff* has needs too," Benjamin said.

Wow. Absolutely no subtly at all. Making sexual innuendoes about the maid? I stifled my sigh as I finished refilling the water goblets and stepped over to the china buffet to return the pitcher of water. My opinion of Mr. Talbot lowered.

The fact that Alex didn't say anything made my stomach twist. How could any man let someone talk that way about a woman he cared about? And even if what we had was just a summer fling, shouldn't he have at least said something because he was my employer?

"I told Benji that Chelsea may be looking for employment elsewhere before she returns to the States," Henry said, and stabbed a piece of meat with his fork.

Alex didn't even look at me as he responded, "Well, Chelsea hasn't made any decisions yet, but I hope she'll take all the time she needs."

Henry stopped chewing long enough to say, "Oh, don't be silly. Benji is offering an absurd amount. She'd be a fool not to jump at the chance."

I was tired of them talking about me like I wasn't there. "Well, he did mention it earlier, but we didn't discuss the money."

Alex finally glanced my way, his gaze hard to discern. "I suppose if it's all about the money, and Benji is offering more, then you should definitely consider it."

I guess Jamison had been wrong after all. Alex didn't care if I went to work for Mr. Talbot.

Jamison cleared his throat, and Alex shook himself free of my gaze. "Come on, gentlemen, we know better than to talk business over dinner. I'm sure my father has a lot of good stories about his houseguest he can tell us. Don't you Henry?"

I didn't really care much about Henry and his stories, so I rounded the table to exit through the side door when Benjamin grabbed my wrist.

"Just something to think about," he said quietly, and kissed the back of my hand. I felt him press a slip of paper into my palm as he smiled at me.

I tucked it into my pocket and darted out the door. If Jamison had seen it, he said nothing. In the kitchen, he went right to scrubbing dishes, his chosen activity when he wanted to avoid conversation. I moved to help him, but he waved me away.

His set shoulders and vehement scrubbing spoke his disapproval. It stung. Did he think I was being disloyal, entertaining another job offer? But I wasn't the one who'd set the whole thing in motion.

Or was it something else. Did Jamison think I would forget about Alex and jump into Benjamin's bed? The thought burned in my chest. Did they all assume that? How could they all think of me that way?

Well, it didn't matter because I wouldn't be taking the job. I slumped onto a stool at the kitchen island and took out the slip of paper. One look, and a short laugh tore from my throat. Alex's father was right, the amount Benjamin Talbot was offering for a maid's salary was absurd.

Too good to be true.

I wasn't an idiot, and I wasn't the sort of person who could be bought.

The dining room bell rang and I said, "That's probably Alex asking for the wine."

Jamison tugged at his rubber gloves, but I jumped off my stool and grabbed the bottle of red wine on the counter. Jamison turned back to his scrubbing, though I could feel his frown follow me as I went out the door.

I peeked through the side door to the dining room and saw Benjamin Talbot laughing. At ease in the splendid dining room, he looked even more handsome than before. I estimated his age to fall somewhere in between Alex and Henry so he wasn't entirely unappealing, far from it, actually, but as tempting as he was, my eyes drifted to Alex.

Alex was laughing too, and when he did, the hint of a dimple appeared on his right cheek. He was telling a story, though what about, I couldn't tell. He punctuated details with his hands, hands that I could almost feel on me.

He caught my stare from where I stood, and the longing look in his eyes melted my heart. Its molten heat seared through my body. When he looked at me like that, everything else vanished. I had to pause for what seemed like a full minute before I could continue into the room. When I did, Alex's smile widened, and he stopped telling his story.

"The wine you rang for?" I asked, holding out the bottle.

"Yes…I mean, no." Alex popped up out of his chair and pushed it back. He had a strange look on his face, one that I couldn't place. "We were just talking about Sonoma, and I wanted to grab a different bottle from the cellar." He addressed the others at the table and said, "We'll just be a minute."

With that, he took my by the arm and ushered me through the main dining room door.

"Sorry, I just grabbed the bottle Jamison put out," I said, confused about what was going on.

Alex snatched the bottle, but I didn't let go, clinging to it as he swept his other arm around me and pulled me close. His dimple appeared as he leaned down and crushed his mouth to mine, lips tasting and giving, tongues touching with delicious friction.

My entire body lit up as I ran my free hand up into his hair and pulled him deeper into the kiss. Any doubts I had fled. Alex was what I wanted. I didn't want to leave this house and work for Mr. Talbot or anyone else. Right now, all I wanted was Alex, whatever way I could have him, for however long he'd have me.

Finally, he pulled back. "I've been waiting to do that all day." He leaned his forehead against mine.

Suddenly aware of the hard glass of the bottle poking into my chest, I asked, "What about the wine?"

"If I take you down into the cellar," Alex said, leaning close to talk against my lips, "we won't make it back upstairs before midnight, much less dessert."

The kiss that followed was dessert itself. Perfectly sweet.

"Mmm. That sounds nice, but you're right. Can we talk after dessert?" I asked, trying to keep my thoughts from dissolving. I needed answers.

"After," he said, his breath hot against my wet lips, his

body hard against mine.

"We need to talk about you helping me find another position," I said, tugging the wine bottle out of his hand and pulling back.

Alex's eyes were glazed over with desire, and it took him a moment to focus on what kind of position I meant. Then he blinked and said, "I heard Benji offer you a job. Jamison and I were thinking you'd want to work nearby."

"Why?" Suddenly, doubts filled my mind again, and I snapped back to reality. Why'd he want me out of his house? "Why would I want to switch jobs now? It's practically the end of summer."

Alex pulled me back and smiled as he said, "So there's no confusion."

"Well, I *am* confused," I said honestly. "Mr. Talbot offered me a great salary, but I don't know anything about him or why I would want to stop working for you."

"Benji is a great guy," he said. "A little lonely, which is why he entertains all the time, but he's a good guy."

"That's not what Jamison said." And Jamison wouldn't have kept his opinions to himself, which made me wonder why Alex would say otherwise.

He sighed and ran his hand through his hair. "Yeah, maybe not him. It was just too damn convenient."

I took another step back. I needed some distance to clear my thoughts. With him so close, and smelling so good, it was difficult to keep my head straight. "I need to know, is all of this job-switching so you and I can...date?"

He stepped forward, caught in the heat still flaring between us. "Now I'm thinking maybe it's not a good idea. There are definitely advantages to having you under the same roof."

His hand slid down my back, and I shivered. The hot desire between us was melting my resolve again, and my body pressed the length of his before another clear thought cooled me. It was nearly impossible for me to tell how Alex really felt when moments like this one happened all over the house at any time of day. It had to be just as hard for him to think straight. As long as I was so readily available to him, his true feelings would get lost in the haze of pure lust.

"No, you're right," I said, wrenching myself free before I could second-guess what I was doing. This needed to happen. "I should go."

I turned back towards the kitchen, but Alex caught my hand. "Chelsea, what's wrong? I want you. I want you here as my guest, as my date, not my maid." His thumb moved back and forth across my knuckles. "But I know you need the money for Karl, and I know you wouldn't let me just give it to you, or that's what I'd do. I want you to have another job so we can be together."

I wanted to believe him. A chance to make more money, as well as see Alex on an equal footing outside of his house and my maid's position.

"Please, Chelsea, don't think it'd because I'm trying to push you away. I want you here, you know I do." There was a note of desperation in his voice.

"I know," I said softly. "Go back to the dinner, and I'll grab that pinot noir from Sonoma."

When I walked back into the dining room with the new bottle of wine several minutes later, and saw Benjamin Talbot's bright smile, my decision was easy. He was a family friend, and the offer he made was to help Alex as much as me. He might've been a bit...overly familiar, but it wasn't anything I couldn't handle for four weeks.

I uncorked the wine, allowed Alex to taste it, then poured three glasses.

"May I suggest a toast?" I asked.

"Please," Alex said, quirking an eyebrow.

"A toast to Benjamin Talbot. I'm happy to accept your offer of employment, Mr. Talbot," I said.

Mr. Talbot and Henry grinned, but Alex's smile slipped as he watched them raise their glasses to celebrate. I almost questioned my decision, but then I remembered Karl, and the money I needed, and I knew this was the only way to have that and maybe have Alex too.

Chapter 38

Alex

Jamison caught me standing in the pool, arms draped over the stone edge, my mind drifting away from the laps I intended to swim. He placed a mug of coffee on the patio table and threw a towel down on the deck in front of me.

"Good morning?" he asked.

"Not particularly," I said, as I grabbed the towel and walked up the pool steps.

"I thought you had a date with Chelsea last night?"

I glared at him. Jamison knew full well I'd been in my office all night drinking, pacing, and doing anything but working. He knew I was pissed at myself. He didn't even blink at my scowl, just waited for me to unload my frustrations. I could be a pain in the ass like that, and he took it well. He knew me even better than my father did. Henry talked. Jamison listened, and I always counted on him for that.

"Her boss couldn't spare her," I sneered. "Something about a big party coming up. What has Henry gotten her into?"

Jamison handed me the mug, and we sat down at the patio table. I sipped the hot coffee and ground my teeth. I'd barely tasted the steaming liquid when I set the mug back on the table and pushed it away with disgust. "That tastes awful. What happened? Did our fancy coffee maker break?"

Jamison just looked at me without a word.

"What? Why are you looking at me like that?"

Calmly, he said, "I know how you get. You're like a petulant child when things aren't going your way."

I sighed. "Sorry, you're right. I shouldn't take it out on you."

"So what's new, my dear boy?" There was a hint of a smile on his lips.

I ran my hand through my hair and then reached for the coffee again. *Fuck.* I wanted to say it out loud, but I needed to stop acting like a spoiled brat and show Jamison a little more respect. I ran my finger over the rim of the smooth white porcelain coffee mug and finally said what was really bothering me, "I haven't seen Chelsea in four days."

Jamison crossed his arms over his chest and took a deep breath, saying nothing, just watching as my fingers traced around the handle of the mug. It was his signature stance. The one that said, "go on," without saying a word.

So I continued, "The whole email thing is working for her rewrites of the movie script, but it's not the same, around here, I mean…"

"You miss her. Isn't that a good thing?" he asked.

I gave a short snort. "About as good as a hole in the head."

Jamison sat back folding his hands in his lap.

"It's hard to concentrate and get any work done, because, you're right. I miss her."

Jamison's eyes softened.

"And don't think I just mean I miss our…personal time." I leaned forward, resting my elbows on my knees and shook my head. "Chelsea was more than a maid from the get go."

I straightened in my chair and looked at Jamison smiling at me from across the table.

"You saw it didn't you? The first day she came and you brought her in my office to meet me…" I gave a short laugh. "Damn. When I saw her face…I could've swore I heard bells."

Jamison shook his head, smiling. "Yes, yes, I remember."

"Was my jaw on the floor?"

"Well, you did look rather surprised."

I shook my head. "Man, it felt like I'd been hit with a wooden mallet. I was seeing stars and hearing bells...what the hell?"

"I believe it's called being love struck," he said with a chuckle. "So, did you make another date?"

"Sort of, sometime after this big bash Benji is throwing," I said, slumping back in the chair. "I don't know, Jamison. It's still all kind of strange. Don't you think that if she really liked me she would've stayed and worked for me and not taken Benji's offer?"

"Oh, I'm not sure about that."

"I mean, she took the job for the money, I get that, but..." I shrugged my shoulders, doubts creeping into my mind. "I don't know, maybe that's all I was, a stepping stone to a bigger salary?"

Jamison folded his hands again and fixed me with a cool look. Clearly, I'd disappointed him. "Chelsea's not like that."

I picked at the design on the patio table, lost in thought. She'd already chosen a paycheck over me once before. Why not Benji's money this time? It'd almost made me sick that night, when she'd said she'd take the job. Benji wasn't really a bad guy, but I didn't like the idea of him ogling her. Plus, there was still something off in the way he and my father had behaved around her that night at dinner. At the time, I'd chalked it up to Henry trying to control my life the way he always did. It didn't matter if he knew it was my love life or not.

I snorted. What love life? I could sum it up in about two words right now. *Love stinks*. All I wanted was to see her and talk to her. *Shit*. My whole body was aching to be with her. I needed to see her face, to hold her in my arms, and kiss her. When we'd talked on the phone last night, it'd been all I could do to keep myself from getting in the car and driving over to Benji's to say to hell with this. But she'd said she was too busy to talk, although she really wanted to have dinner with me, but her new, freaking job got in the way.

I told her I didn't care if we ate late, I just wanted her to come over. I begged her. I should've just understood and let it go. Instead, I felt rejected, like maybe she was making an excuse. Like she'd gotten what she'd wanted, and now she was trying to blow me off.

Our short phone conversation circled in my head all night, playing on my doubts, and now I was hurting. I gulped the rest of the coffee despite my initial opinion. Jamison's coffee was fine, as always. It'd only tasted bad because I was pissed. And moping. I still had a long list of phone calls to make this morning, but first, I had to make real plans to see Chelsea. I needed to know how she felt about me. What if she wasn't missing me like I missed her?

"You know it was Henry's idea for Chelsea to work for Mr. B," Jamison said.

"Yeah, that's strange that he'd do something helpful for once," I said. "Though I suppose living with April is making him do all kinds of strange things. Like come over here for dinner."

"Why do you suppose Henry suggested Mr. B. as an employer?" Jamison asked.

I rolled it over in my mind. My father and Benji were friends, but then he knew all of our neighbors. He could've asked any one of them to hire Chelsea. And yet, the one possible employer he brought to dinner just happened to be single, handsome, and was notorious for changing mistresses like other men changed shirts.

Shit.

"Do you think April has plans to get between Chelsea and me?" I asked.

Jamison was good at getting me to come to my own conclusions without actually putting forward his own opinions, usually by just steering me in the right direction. He refolded his hands.

I continued, "April would throw me over for Benji in a heart beat. Hell, she'll probably eat up Henry and spit him out soon enough. I guess she thinks Chelsea would do the same. But why would she give Chelsea a run at him first? April's not like that." I frowned.

"It's not in her nature to be generous, that's for sure," Jamison agreed.

It didn't make sense. April wanted revenge, she wanted to hurt Chelsea, not throw her in the path of a richer man. April's feelings for me weren't real enough to want to get Chelsea out of the way like that.

"Maybe April's already met Benji and she wants to use him to get at Chelsea. You don't think Benji would be influenced by April and make life hell for Chelsea, do you?" It was the only thing I could think of.

"No, Mr. B.'s not mean hearted." He cocked his head and added, "Though we do know how he is."

"He does have fangs. You did warn Chelsea, right? You know, about his womanizing?"

Jamison nodded. "Of course, I did."

I smiled, imagining Chelsea's reaction when Jamison had told her. She wouldn't have appreciated the suggestion that she couldn't handle her new employer's advances. Then the next thought burned me. Benji was an old family friend, but if the old bastard so much as looked at Chelsea...I wanted to wrap my hands around his throat.

My mind jumped back to the dinner and the way he kept eyeing her, and smiling at her. Yeah, he had a reputation for flirting with any woman he admired, regardless of age, status, or relationship, but there'd been something different in the way he'd looked at Chelsea.

I clenched my fists.

There'd been something in my father's eyes too, a look I knew well. These two were in on something together. No doubt, Henry was up to his old tricks. I could smell it from a mile away. I just didn't know what it was–yet.

I rolled it over in my mind. Chelsea was April's rival, that's for sure, and if Henry *was* helping her get revenge it'd be done in a devious way. I jumped up out of my chair at the realization. *Fucking Dad! Fucking Benji!* I knew what they were planning now, and I knew exactly which vulnerability they'd use.

I pulled the knot on my towel tighter around my waist. "It's all my fault, Jamison," I said, and started for the kitchen door.

"What do you mean? How could any of this be your fault? Nothing's happened," Jamison said, following me inside.

"Nothing happened *yet*," I said. "I'm the one that found Chelsea. I'm the one that hired her. Remember?"

Jamison stopped me in the hallway. "You did it as a lark. You didn't spend more than five minutes scouring the website. You shouldn't feel guilty for hiring Chelsea. In fact, it was lucky for both of you."

"Exactly."

"A silly prank that could have backfired on you, if Chelsea wasn't who she is," Jamison said.

"Yes, *we* know that, but *Benji* doesn't," I said.

Jamison let go of my arm as the realization sunk in. "Oh bloody hell, what do you think Henry told him about Chelsea?"

"Hell if I know, but I bet April had a shit load of juicy info to tell him about that website. God, why did I ever go on it?" I spun toward my office to call my father. I had to find out how much damage he'd done and figure out a way to fix this cluster fuck.

Jamison scrubbed his cheeks with both hands. "That could explain why he offered so much money. But on the other hand, Mr. B is successful enough. Why would he need to do that?"

I clutched my phone in a stranglehold as the last pieces fell into place. "He was complaining about his last mistress. She broke it off with him. My father told him to swear off society ladies for a while and have a little fun. Shit. Maybe Benji wants to make his ex jealous."

Jamison stepped over to my desk and fished an ivory colored envelope out of my un-opened mail pile. He held it up in the air and then handed it to me. "And what do you bet the ex-mistress has been given *this* same invitation."

I let go of the phone and sliced open the envelope. The Talbot family crest clued me in that he was definitely up to something. Sure enough, it was an invitation to Benji's big party. The same party that Chelsea would be working, and the very reason I hadn't been able to see her.

"Get out my tux, Jamison. I'm going to Benji's party. He's going to try to make Chelsea the other woman," I said. "And there's no way in hell I'm going to let that happen."

Chapter 39

Chelsea

As I struggled to pull the zipper to the top, I remembered the first day I'd met Alex, and how Jamison had purposely gave me the wrong size uniform. Jamison and Alex too, for that matter, had thought I'd taken the job for ulterior motives. I supposed Jamison was messing with me at first, giving me a hard time due to the nature of that awful website, but *this* uniform was worlds apart from that one, at least in looks. It was much more–how should I describe it? Elegant? No, sexy was more like it. And maybe the wrong size–yet again. I made a mental note to talk to the head housekeeper beforehand the next time I started a new job. Oh, wait. There wouldn't be a next time. *Thank god!* I was never taking a maid job again. Ever. Way too complicated and too full of handsome men and surprises…

I stopped and thought for a moment. It seemed like forever since I'd seen Alex, and I missed him terribly…along with his naked swim sessions at the pool.

I'd moved to Mr. B's palatial home just a day after he'd made the the offer. The whole purpose had been to work for someone else so Alex and I could pursue our relationship, so I'd wanted to get started as quickly as possible. The only problem was, my new employer kept me too busy to see Alex at all. I frowned and tugged at the zipper again. Jamison had given me a uniform too big, now this one seemed too small.

If I could just get this zipper up… A light knock on the door startled me out my thoughts.

"Yes?" I called out.

Mr. B walked into my room and immediately came over to help me with the stubborn zipper, his dark blue eyes twinkling at me in the mirror. I was relieved to see him. I'd expected the housekeeper, a pinched-mouth woman who gave me nothing but sour looks. The other women on staff followed her lead and were far from friendly. It didn't matter. I was here to work, not make friends, but it was nice to see Mr. B's warm smile.

"What do you think of the uniform?" he asked, smoothing the wrinkles from the satin down my back.

"Well, it's a little tight," I said. "But the scoop neck is cute."

"I agree," Mr. B said, smoothing more wrinkles from my hips as he glanced over my shoulder at the plunging neckline. "I hope my guests don't spill the drinks you give them."

For a moment I held my breath as his hands slipped around my waist. What was he doing? Then I laughed at myself as he reached for the black lace apron that completed the outfit, on the chair next to me. Mr. B was a consummate flirt. Jamison had warned me, but I hadn't heard any rumors at all about him consorting with the hired help.

I stifled the urge to shake my head as he wrapped the apron around my waist and tied it. He reached around me again to pull up the bib portion of the apron and his hands brushed over the curve of my breasts. Okay, that was toeing the line between flirty and inappropriate. He caught my blushing gaze in the mirror and shook a finger at me.

"No bra, Ms. Chelsea? Are you trying to get my guests to spill more than drinks?"

Mr. B lowered the bib of the apron again to show me what he'd noticed. I followed his dark eyes to my protruding nipples. *Oh, crap.* They could be seen through the fabric. I grabbed the ties, quickly pulled the ruffled bib of the apron up, and tied the ribbons behind my neck.

"Well, the darn dress is too tight to wear one. There…" I'd finished tying the bow and smoothed the bib with my hand. "The apron covers it...them…" I blew out a breath in exasperation, flustered by his attention to detail. *Shit*.

Mr. B stepped back and waggled his eyebrows before he turned to go. "Too tight looks just right to me."

I laughed, recovering my senses. Mr. B was a womanizer, but he had no real interest in me. If he had, he would've been all over me right now. He certainly had the opportunity more than once since I'd been here. No, he was just a blatant flirt, I decided, and he probably acted that way around all women. Besides, with a palace like this and an overflowing guest list of elegant ladies, he probably wouldn't notice me again tonight.

I peered in the mirror and poked at my hair one last time, then turned to leave. If I wanted to keep this job, I'd better get downstairs.

As I stepped into the hallway the housekeeper, stopped me with one of her usual sour looks. "That's your new uniform?"

"Yes," I said, "Mr. B just approved it."

She snorted, slicking her brown hair into a tight bun. "I'm sure he did. Well, I certainly hope you can work in that outfit, because I'm not going to be shorthanded, tonight of all nights."

I followed her, stifling the urge to make rude gestures behind her back as she marched me to the kitchen. Four weeks. I'd spent years in the foster care system. I could put up with obnoxious people for four weeks.

Once there, the cook glared at me over a steaming dish of clams and shot a glance at the housekeeper. "A *lace* apron?"

"Apparently, Mr. B *approves*," the housekeeper said with another snort.

"Dress for the job you want, huh?" The cook said, throwing me another nasty look.

I looked down at my uniform. The black dress was tight, shiny satin, with a low scooping neckline, but the capped sleeves and knee-length hemline made it elegant. Okay, so, the black lace apron wasn't very practical, but I thought it added class to the ensemble. It was sexy, sure, but respectable: exactly the image Mr. B wanted to project, and he was the boss, after all. So whatever he wanted he'd get. I was just here to do a good job. Plus, from the looks of the staff, I was the only one in good enough shape to wear something like this anyway, so it made sense that I was the one who'd gotten it.

"I'm serving drinks and appetizers. And Mr. B wants to make sure I look…" I noticed the housekeeper's severe black dress with long sleeves, and the cuffs pulled tight with buttons. "Um…modern and elegant."

The housekeeper pursed her lips, handing me a tray of champagne glasses and lead the way to the foyer.

Mr. B's home was more than a palace, it was a showcase. The marbled foyer was the size of an amphitheater with a chandelier the size of a small car glittering overheard. I positioned myself, tray in hand, in the foyer where dark blue rugs, the color of Mr. B's eyes, softened the echo as guests began to file in with sparkling smiles and blinding jewelry.

A short and stocky man noticed me and called out as he strode in through the front door, unaccompanied, "What's this? A new maid, old man?"

Mr. B smiled and winked from across the foyer. He came forward to greet a beautiful couple, speaking perfect French as they entered the foyer after the man. I still hadn't figured out what his nationality was.

The short, stocky man took a glass of champagne from my tray, eyeing my new uniform. "I like what the old man's done with the place."

I could hear a knot of young woman start a hissing conversation behind him as they glanced at me. Obviously, his remark brought had brought me to their attention. My eyes darted to the women, and then quickly back to the tray I was holding. It was just a job.

"Don't worry," the man said to me, "a little jealousy never hurt anyone. Besides, at least half the guests here will be more than happy to see you."

Before I could consider what the man meant, Mr. B beckoned for me to join him. I nodded to the short, stocky man and stepped over to Mr. B.

"Mr. Allister has requested a whiskey. Do you think you could go to the study and fill a few glasses?" Mr. B asked.

"Yes, sir," I said, with a nod.

Mr. B smiled and put both hands on my waist to turn me in the right direction, as if I didn't know where the study was. "The study is that way. Third door on the left." He gave me a joking pat on the bottom and said, "Off you go. Thank you."

I took a deep breath hoping to keep the blush from warming my cheeks. I knew he was showing off to his friends, but I'd hoped no one else saw the pat on the butt. No such luck. I noticed the two women directly in front of me raise their noses as I walked past.

"What is Mr. B playing at?" one asked.

"She's not even remotely attractive. Honestly, black hair and thin? Electra will laugh when she gets here," the other said.

Their rude remarks were countered when a man leaning against the stairs next to them chimed in, "She's beautiful. Her hair's as shiny as her dress. I bet it feels like silk."

I wished his compliments made me feel better, but all it did was make me feel like running from the foyer. Grateful for a chance to escape, I hurried to the study, wondering who the hell was Electra, and why these women were so jealous of me. I wasn't here to take anyone away from them. I was just here to work.

Once inside the library, I shut the door behind me, and took as deep of a breath as the dress would allow. Suddenly the reality of playing the sexy maid was beginning to feel too real. I knew I had to brush it off and not let these people get to me, but it was hard.

Mr. B's guests were used to servants and considered them as a piece of property to be judged. Since I was a servant too, I realized I shouldn't expect anything different. Luckily, all I needed to do was make it to the end of the summer, and then I could go back to Oregon, and forget all about what I was starting to think had been a giant mistake.

I let that thought steady my hands before I poured a few glasses of whiskey and placed them on my tray with the remaining champagne glasses. There was no reason I had to listen to any of the guests beyond their drink requests. I shouldn't take anything they said to heart.

I resolved to be politely deaf and let my selective hearing be my shield for the rest of the evening. I didn't know anyone at the party, and the only thing that mattered was pleasing my boss by doing a good job. And if he wanted to watch me do it in a sexy uniform, so what? There were plenty of waitresses in the States who had to wear hideous uniforms.

And then there was Alex. Would he be coming to the party? Or staying away because of me? What would he think of me in this dress, being paraded around as the new, sexy maid? I assumed he'd been invited, considering his friendship with Mr. B, although, I hadn't seen him yet. I was struck with a sudden sharp longing. Everything would be better if I could just see Alex. This stupid tight dress, the mean-spirited remarks, none of it would matter if only Alex would show up soon. If I could just see him again.

Chapter 40

Alex

I expected to see Chelsea in the monstrous foyer, but I didn't see her beautiful face among the milling guests. I made my way to the servants' entrance near the bottom of the stairs, but only ran into a tight-lipped housekeeper.

"Mr. Alex, how nice to see you again," she said, holding out a tray of canapés.

I nodded and took one. "Have you seen Chelsea around?"

The housekeeper pursed her lips even tighter, and said, "I've seen her all around, showing off her new uniform."

Considering how the woman prided herself on a traditional black, buttoned dress, I tried not to laugh at her jealous tone. Anything new probably set the woman off. But one phrase made me curious.

"All around?" I asked. What the hell was she talking about?

Leaning across the canapé tray, she whispered, "He made her go clear to the study to get whiskey, then upstairs to fetch his cigarettes."

"Chelsea, the new maid, right? Isn't that what she's supposed to do?" I asked.

"He told her to go up the *main* staircase." She said it as if the act of walking up stairs was somehow scandalous.

I chewed on the canapé to hide another smile. A simple

thing like a maid using the main staircase in front of guests was the kind of thing that filled the old-fashioned housekeeper with horror. Maybe Benji had just wanted someone a bit less uptight around the house. Then I caught a glimpse of Chelsea and felt a wave of my own horror.

Her new uniform was a black satin dress, just one size too tight. As she moved through the guests with her silver drink tray, more than one head followed her. I held my canapé in mid-bite and watched as Benji eyed her from the front door, accepting the appreciative nods of the men around him.

I threw the remainder of my canapé onto the housekeeper's tray to her startled surprise. *Damn him*. He wasn't just appreciating her good looks. He was fucking showing her off. A hot fog of anger enveloped me.

She wasn't a toy, and as sure as hell wasn't his. The sight of Chelsea in that dress, her long athletic legs flexing as she trotted up the stairs, must have thrilled the group of men now ogling her.

In the instant I looked to catch her again, she was gone. I strode across the foyer, and headed toward the terrace. As I parted the crowd, a young female server in a crisp white shirt stopped to ask if I'd like a glass of champagne.

"Is that your uniform?" I asked, flustering the pretty redhead.

"Yes, sir. The catering company requires a white shirt," she said, then she wetted her pink lips before asking, "Do you like it?"

"I thought Benji, I mean, Mr. B had his serving staff wear black satin now."

The redhead stuck her lower lip out and pouted. "No, there's just the one. Mr. B's new maid."

"Why do you say it like that?"

"Have you seen her? I mean, she's pretty, but I don't see what all the fuss is about." She threw a glance over her shoulder. "Anyway, all the men around here are just drooling over her."

My stomach knotted. Chelsea was beautiful, that was a

given, but most of these rich old coots wouldn't spare more than a glance at the most seductive of servants. So why the sudden interest?

"Bunch of old men, all hot and bothered because she's available," the redhead said.

Shit. "Available? What do you mean?"

She took the advantage to slip her arm through mine and pull me close. With her accent, I knew she was native. "Well, from what I heard from the cook, she's been hired for more than housecleaning. For providing *different* kinds of services, if you get my drift. And Mr. B's been suggesting the others might want to have a go at her and hire her after he's finished with her."

Through the haze of anger I felt the redhead squeeze my arm as she licked her pink lips again. "Not that you'd have to worry about that. I bet all you have to do is smile at a girl to get a date."

I didn't return her bright smile even when she batted her eyelashes. Instead, I looked around for Chelsea again. When I spotted her at the foot of the main staircase, I pulled free. The redhead recoiled.

"Seriously? You too? Disgusting," she said and marched away.

By the time I got from the terrace doors to the center of the foyer, Benji had joined Chelsea at the foot of the stairs. He slipped an arm around her waist and steered her over to a cluster of his friends. They took glasses of whiskey as well as admiring looks up and down her lithe body. I ground down on my teeth to suppress my rage. Chelsea was so innocent. She stood there taking all of their leering, shoulders straight and seemingly oblivious to their gawking. From the way she reacted, I didn't think she was even aware of exactly what was happening.

And it was all my fault.

I pushed through the crowd to join them. Benji saw me coming and frowned at the murderous look on my face. He leaned down, whispered something in Chelsea's ear, and sent her on another errand with a squeeze of her satin-covered bottom. I just about jumped over the tuxedoed body blocking the path in front of me to choke him. Lucky for ol' Benji, there was a group of men in my way. But the list of who I wanted to choke next just got longer as more leering men crowded around Chelsea. They were all chuckling and the men watched her ass as she walked away.

I stepped up to the group around Benji and heard a short, stocky man with a big grin say, "Honestly, Benji, I didn't take you as someone to hire out for such things. Must be a tasty way to get your breakfast in bed."

"Doesn't seem your style," I said, joining in the conversation.

Catching my heated look and the matching tone in my voice, the other men wisely drifted away.

"And why not?" Benji asked, tipping his head to watch someone across the foyer. "Other people enjoy intimate relationships with the people they pay, don't they?"

I cringed. He was talking about me, I knew, thanks to April's big mouth. He didn't know that it was different between Chelsea and me. Except I knew how it looked on the outside, and if I said it out loud it'd sound so cliché, so naïve of me.

At a loss for what to say next, I followed Benji's gaze. There was Electra, his last fling, draped over the arm of a muscular blond man.

"Her yoga instructor," Benji said with a tight voice.

I narrowed my eyes at Benji and said, "You're doing this to make her jealous, right? You hired Chelsea so you could parade her around here like a toy just to make your ex jealous?"

I looked again, and Electra had the yoga guy locked in a long kiss. With his eyes still on his ex, Benji said, "Oh, I plan to do more than just parade her around."

"Over my dead body," I ground out. My blood rushed as I grabbed a handful of his expensive tuxedo lapel. I wanted to deck the fucker even if he was a family friend.

"Now, Alex, don't be a fool." My father's voice chimed

in from behind, managing to take the edge off my anger.

Benji shoved me off with a confused look on his face. "Alex! What has gotten into you?" Then he looked at Henry and straightened his crumpled jacket. "Henry, get your son under control, will you?" he said. With a last brush of his jacket sleeve he strode off through the guests in the direction of Chelsea.

I reached after him, but my father caught my arm. "Let him go, Alex. She's not worth it. And besides, Benji has just agreed to fund your movie, so don't look a gift horse in the mouth, son."

My father kept a grip on my arm as I lost sight of Benji in the sea of guests. He was wrong. She *was* worth it. She was worth more than anyone here.

Chelsea

"Chelsea?" A soft voice stopped me at the terrace doors. I'd just come from the kitchen with a newly refilled tray of champagne glasses for the guests.

"Carrie, how are you?" I glanced down at my lacy apron top. I hoped Carrie wouldn't comment on my uniform. Her face was a sympathetic one in this crowd of sly looks.

"I'm fine, but how are you doing?"

"Oh, things are good," I said, noticing another woman giving me a snide look. "Just settling into the new job."

"Do you like it?" she asked.

Loyalty won out. "Yes, Mr. B is charming and very generous."

The woman behind Carrie snorted into her champagne glass, and my heart sank. This was all wrong. Everyone here had the wrong idea about me, and I was afraid Carrie would think the same. And I didn't know how to fix it.

"Don't worry about rumors," she said, patting my arm. "Just remember the truth."

I blinked back sudden tears as I said, "Thanks, Carrie. I don't know what's going on, but I'm getting all sorts of weird looks from people."

"Like that?" Carrie asked, nodding towards a gaunt man who was giving my dress an open-mouthed leer.

"Oh, god help me," I said, suppressing a shiver. "Yes."

Carrie laughed and took a sip of her champagne. She was the only woman who hadn't given me a catty look or a disgusted dismissal, which struck me as odd. I still couldn't figure out if she and Alex were divorced, separated or what, but whatever she was, she made me feel better.

"Look Chelsea, Benji can be quite persuasive when he wants something," she said. "Don't let him or any of these snoots get to you."

I nodded and caught the housekeeper glaring at me.

"Oh, sorry, Carrie. The housekeeper just gave me the evil eye. I'd better get back to work, but thanks for the advice."

Carrie smiled and I gave her a little wave as I stepped away to return to the kitchen.

Before I'd even had time to lower my hand, Benji appeared, took the tray of glasses from me and placed it on a side table. He took my hand and said, "Chelsea, dear. You look very lovely tonight. Have I told you that?"

I looked over my shoulder while he was still holding my wrist, but Carrie was gone. I remembered her advice, but I would've appreciated her presence.

"Um, yes, I believe you did. Thank you."

"I must speak with you for a moment in private, if you don't mind."

"Well, actually, the housekeeper…"

Without waiting to hear my answer, he pulled me along the edge of the party. It felt like all eyes were on us. I tried to pull my hand away, but he wouldn't let go. I glanced over at the crowd, smiling and trying to appear nonchalant when I caught sight of Alex.

At first my heart soared. I'd hoped he'd put in an appearance at the party. He looked devastatingly handsome in his slim-fitting tuxedo, but no sooner had I spotted him than I caught the look on his face. His eyes were hard, icy steel. A slice of cold shot down my spine. My stomach twisted. Alex wouldn't believe the gossip, would he? Surely he'd think like Carrie, right?

"Don't worry, Chelsea," Mr. B said, pulling me close as he opened the library door. "I just want a quick word."

I looked again and saw Alex scowl. Was it because of how closely we stood? I tried again to pull back, but Mr. B only held me tighter. He ducked into the library, pulling me after him, hard enough that I bounced against his chest. My cheeks flamed. I could imagine how that must've looked to the guests outside, and especially to Alex. So this was it? He pulled me in here to do what? Leer at me? Fondle me? Have whatever the hell he wants because he's rich?

I felt a spark of anger.

Mr. B shut the door and released me, smoothing the salt and pepper hair at his temples. "I apologize, Chelsea. I just wanted to make sure you were doing alright."

I exhaled. Here, I was worried that he called me in here for some hanky-panky, but he'd really only wanted to check on me. I shouldn't have believed the worst.

But still, better to get back before I gave others more to gossip about.

"Oh. Well, I'm doing just fine. Thank you for asking," I said turning back to the door. "I should get back…"

"No, no, please, don't be angry," he said, putting a flat hand on the door to keep it shut.

"But I'm not angry, Mr. B." I was confused. "I just want to make sure I do my job properly, that's all. So like I said…"

He chuckled and leaned down to kiss my shoulder. "You're doing just fine."

Oh shit.

"What's going on?" I asked, trying to dart under his arm.

Mr. B caught me around the waist and said, "Oh, a feisty one. I like that. Henry told me all about how you came to work for Alex. He said his son hadn't taken advantage of all that your company offered. So, I thought perhaps you would be happier here."

"All that my company offered?" I asked, not really wanting to acknowledge what he was hinting at. If I played innocent, maybe it'd be less embarrassing.

He wasn't as old as Henry, and he was ten times more handsome than most men. It wasn't that his advances were gross. I just wasn't interested, and I didn't want him to get angry and fire me. All I wanted to do was extricate myself from his embrace and open the damn door.

"Yes, Henry told me all about the website. I know it's completely consensual, and I believe you find me attractive. Don't you? I know you found the money I offered you attractive." He leaned in closer holding his arms tightly around me.

"Mr. B, I think you have the wrong idea," I said, as I wiggled to get free.

How had I gotten myself in this situation?

He shrugged, and his grip loosened a little. "Ah, well, if so, I apologize. But perhaps you just need to get to know me a little better."

Mr. B let me slip from his grip just enough for me to reach the door handle with one hand, while one of his arms still gripped me around my waist. I pulled on the handle and swung the door outward. It was heavy and didn't move easily, but he gave it a tap with his foot and it opened wide. Just as we were in full view of the party and all the guests, Mr. B slipped his arm back around my waist and pulled me into a helpless kiss.

I was off balance. I grabbed on to his lapels, praying we didn't fall to the ground. It registered one second later that he was kissing me, passionately, and in full view of everyone. And with my luck, Alex was probably standing right at the front of the group. How the hell was I going to explain this? I'd thought working here would help us define whatever this was between us, but now it seemed things were even more complicated than before.

I'm so screwed.

Chapter 41

Alex

Get the fuck out of my way. I yanked my arm out of my dad's grip and left him standing there with his mouth hanging open. Half a dozen people tried to stop me to chat as I struck out to cross the foyer. Now, wasn't a good time. I had to find Chelsea. I looked out the terrace windows where the party spilled over into the gardens, but still, no Chelsea. She'd disappeared into the crowd before I could talk to her. My heart sank.

It was all my fault for hiring her as a joke in the first place. Chelsea had taken the website at face value, never assuming it was a casual hook-up site for gold diggers and rich men. At least in my house it hadn't matter. It was just Jamison and me, and we understood Chelsea's motivation. But here, among the wolves, the rumors were flying, expanding, and building like cumulus clouds.

Before I had a chance to breathe, a voice purred in my ear, "Hello, handsome."

Fuck. Not now. I drummed up my best poker face and turned around.

"April…" I was about to tell her this wasn't a good time. I had to take a call. I was on my way out. Any excuse so long as I didn't have to talk to April right now. I needed to find Chelsea.

"I'm doing well, you sweet man," April said, tittering for the benefit of the guests around us. "You were right about me leaving your little movie to find something better."

No surprise there. In her mind, she'd quit my movie to pursue bigger opportunities, and she wanted to make sure everyone around us heard.

"Glad it's working out," I said, trying to tug my arm out of her grip.

"How can I *ever* repay you?" she fawned, pressing her prominently displayed breasts against my captured arm.

"I'm sure you'll find a way. Now could you just…just leave me in peace to mourn your loss," I said, yanking my arm back. "Go take a shot at one of these other rich guys, okay?" I didn't mean for it come out sounding so harsh, but I was getting pretty damn tired of tiptoeing around April.

Her eyes narrowed as my loud tone caught the attention of the guests. She flounced back a step, making sure to curve a hip out in a practiced pose.

"Well, your father's more of a gentleman than you. In fact, he's found me a starring role in a new movie," April said. "He's done advising you, now that your finances are a mess, and has focused all his attention on me."

The way she smoothed her hands down her electric blue dress drew the attention of others. April smiled.

"Well, that's just dandy then. Everything's worked out great," I said. Except for Chelsea. I turned again to scan for her in the crowd.

Out of the corner of my eye, I saw April's bright smile slip. She wasn't used to losing the attention of men near her.

I couldn't help myself. "You know Chelsea is working on the film now. We're almost done with rewrites and getting ready to start shooting again."

"Oh, yes, that's right," April said, slinking closer again to pat my arm. "I know it can't be easy, using cheap labor like that. Sorry, I couldn't stick around to fill out your marquee."

"No problem," I muttered, trying to move away. She noticed my lack of interest and frowned.

Thankfully, April stopped pressing against me when my father joined us. Like a chameleon changing colors, April immediately stepped up to my father's arm and wrapped herself around him.

"Henry dear, tells me I won't have to settle for second best again."

"Good evening, Alex," he said. "Hasn't Benji done a great job with the place? Perfect for entertaining." He seemed nervous and wouldn't look me in the eye. Besides, we'd already talked earlier. Why was acting like we just met?

"A little flashy, but I hear good taste weakens with age," I said.

Henry frowned over the crowd as April petted his lapels admiring her gaudy jewelry. "Speaking of flashy," she said, "have you seen what your little maid is wearing? Black satin and lace, not your standard maid's uniform, but I hear Benji isn't paying her for the standard services."

Although April's smile was small and secretive, she was about as subtle as a cat with canary feathers sticking out of its mouth.

"Yes, *Father*, don't you think it's time you cleared up this whole misunderstanding?" I asked, "It's only fair to Chelsea, and I'm sure Benji would appreciate hearing it from you before he's embarrassed."

Henry's eyes flicked over to me. "I only told him the truth about how you found Chelsea and the website."

"From the sounds of it, Chelsea jumped at the chance," April said. "Henry says all Benji had to do was hand her a note, and she accepted the position within minutes. I wonder what was in that note?"

I felt the burn in my chest. April was a self-serving bitch. She'd say anything to create a divide between Chelsea and me. My logic told me I was right, but that damn little seed of doubt burrowed in like a tick on a dog. April mentioned the one thing that bothered me. Why had Chelsea accepted the position so quickly that night at dinner?

One moment we'd been kissing, and the next she'd been

standing in the doorway announcing her job change like I was some kind of ghost in the room. At the time, I thought it'd be a good thing for her to take the job. We could see each other, no complications. But once she'd moved in here at Benji's house, she'd put me off and we hadn't seen each other for days. It killed me to doubt her, but my emotions were messing with my head.

"You know," April said, turning to Henry, "I think you were right about Chelsea all along. A few minutes ago, I saw Benji take her into the library. They looked quite cozy when he closed the door." She turned back to me with a sly, sidelong glance.

I started toward the library, but Henry caught my arm. "Really, son, stop acting like a fool. She took the job of her own free will, and you haven't seen her since. Take the hint for god's sake."

April reached out and patted my arm again. "It can't be easy, baby. Getting rejected by two women in one week. But you'll get over it."

I pulled away as I turned and damn near ran over the redheaded server. I steadied her silver tray and apologized. In return she gave me a venomous look and spun off without offering me a canapé.

April cooed, "It's just not your week, baby. Maybe what you need is a rabbit's foot or something else to rub for luck."

She shimmied her low neckline at me until Henry pulled her back. My father cleared his throat, and put his hand on her back to get her to leave. As she turned to go, she gave me a wink as well as one last up and down gaze before my embarrassed father managed to steer her away.

Just when I thought I'd finally have a chance to go look for Chelsea, I recognized the warm voice of an old friend behind me. "You Silverhaus boys have never been lucky in love."

"Dirk, ah…" *Shit*. I was trapped.

If one more person stopped to talk to me, I was going to explode, but there was nothing I could do. He was a long time friend, a close buddy of my brother's. I had to say hello and be polite. I couldn't brush him off, but what April just said about Chelsea and Benji in the library had my head spinning. Part of me said that it was April up to her old tricks and Chelsea was probably washing dishes in the kitchen, but the other part of me was fuming.

"Good to see you, man," I said, clapping him on the back.

"Look at you all dressed up. You Silverhaus boys have all the good looks. Still miss your brother. A day doesn't go by when I don't think of him," Dirk said, raising a glass to Carrie across the room.

My sister-in-law caught his gesture and smiled back. She tipped her head for me to go join her. I shook my head and nodded toward the library doors. I had to think of a way to get rid of Dirk and get into that library. Carrie pursed her lips and started across the room with a look on her face like she had something to tell me, but I just smiled. In my mind I was already planning to pawn her off on ol' Dirk so that I could go find Chelsea.

My attention was drawn back to the conversation as Dirk said, "Maybe that's your problem, you're too handsome to catch a decent girl. There're rumors flying tonight, buddy. Something about you tangling with a maid, and that she jilted you for a better paycheck with Benji. You should hear Electra. She's about to start breathing fire."

"Uh…yeah. I've heard the rumors." And they were getting to me. "I haven't seen her in days though and…" I was about to go off on Dirk and give him an earful. The longer I stood here listening to everyone gossip about Chelsea and speculate about who was going to 'tap that ass' next, the more infuriated I became.

I glanced at Carrie, who was tearing herself away from a cluster of women and then I shot a look at the dreaded library door. "Ah, Dirk. Why don't you do some catching up with Carrie. Here she is now. I'll talk to you later…" I mumbled the last part as I pushed past a bewildered-looking Carrie.

I drifted off, lost in thought as I headed for the library. I'd never once made my attention seem like part of Chelsea's job. Or at least, I'd never thought I had. Maybe she'd really thought I was using her.

Then again, maybe she *was* using me. If I thought about it, she'd only had light duties and plenty of time off, and she also had her first screenwriting gig because of me. From the outside looking in, Chelsea got everything she wanted from me, and then moved on to a bigger paycheck.

The burning in my chest was sharper, and I rubbed a palm against my white dress shirt as if that would calm the pain. I'd hightailed it to the party just for a glimpse of Chelsea. Both times, when I saw her, she was smiling under Benji's eternal ogling, apparently not at all uncomfortable or embarrassed, even in that ridiculous outfit. *What the hell was up with that?* Either she didn't know what he expected, or she didn't mind.

I snagged a whiskey off a passing tray and threw it back in one gulp.

If she was aware of Benji's motives and she enjoyed it, I mean if she was flirting back with him and wanted it, then that stung more than this whiskey burning down my throat.

Dammit! I was falling for her. Like barreling down a hill a hundred miles an hour with no helmet and a brick wall at the bottom kinda falling. It was fast, and it felt euphoric, but the brick wall at the bottom was gonna hurt like a motherfucker.

That was why I couldn't bring myself to doubt her even as my head turned over the grim possibilities. I was blinded by my heart, and I longed to sweep her off her feet.

I had to face her. I had to try. I needed to know what Chelsea really felt for me now that work didn't stand in the way.

I turned toward the library and wiped the whiskey from my mouth with the back of my hand. Before I took one step, the heavy wooden library door flung open wide and there was Chelsea. Arched back, black hair spilling loose, she clung to Benji's lapels as his lips devoured hers. The ripple of shock turned to a wave of laughter as the two secret lovers were exposed to the entire party.

When Benji's ex saw the couple, she slammed her crystal glass to the marble floor, spraying Carrie's dress with red wine even as the glass shattered. Carrie jumped back with an open-mouthed gasp. No one noticed the blood dripping from Electra's cut hand, but me. It was like a crazy, wild scene from a movie.

A fucking horrible movie.

My heart fell to the floor. I looked around but all eyes were on Benji as he pulled Chelsea back to her feet. Her eyes caught mine, and all my hopes were drowned.

Chapter 42

Chelsea

I tried to tell him to stop, but I was off balance. If I pulled away I would've fallen flat on my ass, and thanks to this dress, I would've given everyone an even better show than they'd bargained for, so I hung on and kept my lips shut tight.

There was no denying his skill or the feel of his strong arms around my back and waist. Mr. B was handsome and well-muscled. He'd clearly kissed many women, and being kissed by him wasn't entirely unpleasant.

But Alex's lips were always hot, searing against mine and…why was I even thinking about how this kiss felt? I was kissing my boss! I groaned at the realization. No, no! *He* was kissing me. I wasn't kissing back, but the moment I felt him smile against my lips I knew that he misunderstood my throaty exhale as a sign of pleasure. Aghast, I tried to get my feet under me and end the kiss.

Then I heard the gasps and the nervous laughter echoing back from the hall. Tipping my head for a look, I saw that the library door was standing wide open, and a semi-circle of guests were watching our embrace. *Oh crap!* I could just imagine how this must look to them.

Mr. B smiled against my lips again, this time at the sound of a crystal glass smashing. Then he was lifting me up to my feet, only hanging on to steady me. He faced our audience, all of his guests, with his arm around my waist, and tucked me in close to his body before I could protest.

Then with a theatrical flourish, he gave a bow and announced with a wry smile, "Dinner will be served shortly," as if this were all some kind of show or a joke to entertain his guests. How nice of him to amuse his guests at my expense. My face burned. He reached out to pull the library door shut and I heard chuckles and laughter, but it didn't erase the crease in my brow.

I moved with Mr. B as he stepped back from the door, too shocked to know what to do. Just as Mr. B reached for the door handle to shut it, I caught a glimpse of Alex's face in the small crowd. His eyes were colder than before, his jaw clenched tight. Right before the door closed and cut off my view, for a split second, our gazes met, and I saw his face harden. He was furious, and I was to blame.

I only hoped that once I could get away, he'd be calm enough to listen to me, and I could explain what had really happened. Then his face shifted, and my heart froze in my chest. I saw him step back, turning his body away as if he didn't care, but it was clear in the slope of his shoulders that I was nothing more than a disappointment.

The heavy library door latched shut, and I ripped myself from Mr. B's embrace. He let me go this time, but I turned after two steps, everything I had bottled up inside me exploded out. I swung back at him, pounding my open palm against his shoulder.

"What were you thinking? What were you doing?" The words came gushing out, choked on a rising sob.

"Now wait a minute." Mr. B said. He caught my wrists and crinkled his brow. "I can't kiss you?"

"No. I'm sorry if I gave you the wrong impression, but *no*, you cannot kiss me," I said, wrenching my hands free.

"Ah, I see. I'd heard that was sometimes the way these things worked, everything else but kissing. Too intimate, right?" he asked.

My mouth dropped open. "Excuse me? What do you think I am, a prostitute?"

"That was the impression I was given."

Mr. B adjusted his dinner coat and smoothed his shirtfront. He looked completely confused, which was the only thing that kept me from slapping him.

"Not by me!" I said, my breath giving out as the implications hit me. "Who suggested that?"

Mr. B's hard expression softened as he said, "Henry implied it when he told me how Alex hired you." He glanced away and his breath caught in his throat in surprise. "Oh, I see. What a fool I have been. It's not true, is it? Maybe for other girls, but not for you. Right?"

"Exactly," I said, sinking onto a low, red sofa. My hands were shaking, but at least I knew now that Mr. B had simply misunderstood. He wasn't a bad guy. A bit of a lech, but not someone who would've forced himself on someone he knew didn't want it.

Mr. B sat down next to me and brushed a strand of hair back from my face. I flinched away from his touch, blinking back another wave of tears.

He tilted his head to the side and spoke softly. "It was only a kiss, my dear."

I raked my hair back and twisted it into a bun. "But Alex saw and now he thinks what you think...he thinks all I care about is the money."

Mr. B nodded and then gave a sad smile. "Alex. No wonder he wanted to knock my block off back there in the foyer." He paused for a moment, and then asked, "Are you in love with Alex?"

"It doesn't matter now. I saw his face." I wiped at an escaping tear even as my heart broke from the truth of what I'd said.

His eyebrows shot up. Then he rubbed his chin with his hand. "Well, sometimes jealousy is good for a relationship, like a tonic."

I blinked and noticed his thoughtful glance at the door. "Is that why you made sure the door opened? You wanted someone to see us kissing? To make someone jealous?"

"And I believe it worked, though I do not know what good it will do," he said. He slapped the palms of his hands on his knees as if ready to stand. "Love makes people do foolish things."

Before he could say another word, I popped up from the sofa. "I have to go and stop Alex. Please, I can't have him thinking the wrong thing."

Mr. B joined me and said, "I'll go with you and vouch for you. I'll explain everything. Alex is my friend, I didn't do this to hurt him or you. I didn't know."

I nodded, but before we could take a step, a sharp knock on the door startled us both. Mr. B called, "Come in."

The housekeeper who entered could barely speak; her lips were pursed so tightly. "Your guests are waiting, sir. You must lead them in to dinner."

Mr. B turned to me. "I'm sorry, Chelsea, I must be a good host. Do what you must, but remember that you are still most welcome here," he said, and strode off to join his guests.

The housekeeper stayed behind a beat to glare at me, and it took all of my willpower not to let loose on her and tell her to mind her own business. I was angry at Mr. B too. He'd abandoned me to go to his dinner guests, and would most likely to be congratulated by his friends while I'd have to take the walk of shame through a firing squad of dirty looks and nasty assumptions. He might correct them, but he might not either. Alex was his friend, but I had the feeling the woman Mr. B wanted meant more to him than his friendship with Alex.

I bit my tongue as I sidestepped the housekeeper. I hadn't done anything wrong, and I didn't need to defend my actions to anyone except Alex. I couldn't waste another minute. I had to find him and explain.

"You're supposed to be helping me serve," the housekeeper said as I stepped through the door.

The idea of facing tables full of speculating guests made

me dizzy, but I refused to stop. "I have something I need to do first. Mr. B said it was okay." Let her make of that whatever she wanted.

I knew there was no way in hell Alex would be joining the guests for dinner. The look on his face told me he wouldn't be fit for polite company so, I headed outside. I darted out of the kitchen, across the marble foyer and skipped down the front steps of Mr. B's palatial home. Far up the driveway, I spotted Alex's long stride. I broke into a run to try to catch him before he reached his car.

"Alex, please, wait!" I called.

He spun on the driveway and glared at the small knots of guests that lingered over cigarettes. My heart fell. He wouldn't even look at me.

When I reached him he said, "Please, don't embarrass me any more than you already have. I know all of these people, and they've known my family for years."

The look on his face crushed me. I stared at the ground, the lump in my throat making it difficult to breathe, and too ashamed to look him in the eye.

"You know Chelsea, I had you wrong from the start. I guess you're not the woman I thought you were."

"That's not true," I said, too afraid, even for tears to start flowing. How was I going to make him understand what had happened?

Alex turned and kept walking. I trotted along beside him trying to keep up, my spinning brain trying to find the words to fix this.

"I'm not judging you, Chelsea. I get it. I sacrificed a lot for my brother. I'm just pissed at myself for making up a goddamn fairytale about us. It was right in front of my face, but I didn't want to see what was really happening."

I stopped cold, my spine stiff with shock. "What do you think was really happening?"

"You played a great part, so I guess some of it must be true, because when it came down to it you went with the money," Alex said. He shrugged his shoulders, as if he didn't care. "We had fun and I took it too seriously. I'll get over it."

"Wha. . .what?" My heart was pounding. This wasn't happening. He said it so casually, his voice flat, devoid of any emotion, and that hurt more than if he'd just yell at me, cuss at me, call me a bitch or something. At least then I'd know he felt *something* for me.

"I'm not into complications. You know that," he said. "Look, Chelsea, I'm glad you found a better job for better pay. Good luck."

I stopped walking and watched Alex disappear down the driveway. I choked on all the things I wanted to tell him, but I still kept my mouth closed. He'd said it again. He didn't like complications. He'd edited our entire relationship together to come up with a simple explanation that made it easy for him to walk away. What could I possibly say to change it?

Sucking in quick, shallow breaths, I walked back to the house. My feet felt like cement as I dragged them up the steps. The only thing Alex had right, was that I would do anything for my brother.

I slipped into the servants' hallway and leaned on the wall outside of the dining room. The spinning in my head didn't slow, but I managed to pull in a few deep, shuddering breaths and pull myself together. As I listened to my own ragged breathing, Mr. B appeared in the doorframe. He was smiling and holding a glass of wine in one hand, the other shoved into his pocket. I stood up, peeling my back off the wall and straightened my uniform.

"Sorry, I was just coming in…"

Mr. B gave a jerk of his head, and signaled for me to enter the dining room filled with all the dinner guests. As soon as I stepped inside, Henry joined us at Mr. B's elbow, with a huge grin on his face.

"So I have to call out my friend, here, on the little prank he pulled this evening." He tipped his head at Henry. "You would think we'd be past these things now that boarding school is ancient history for us, but a little fun is hard to resist." Mr. B's voice carried across the dining room and the guests hushed to a whisper, to listen.

Henry leaned toward me with a drink in hand and teased, "You did fall for it pretty easily, Chelsea. Good show." He chuckled.

I blinked and looked at the smiling faces up and down the elegant dinner table, not sure what to make of all this. Was this some game? Another way to humiliate me? I'd put up with a lot of shit for being a foster kid, and I was getting pretty sick of getting more as an adult.

A wave of homesickness swept through me, and all I wanted at the moment was to see Zach and Clara again.

Mr. B was still talking. "And thanks to your naughty implications, everyone here can stand witness to my weakness for beautiful women. So, on behalf of my wayward friend and his awful sense of humor, we'd like to wipe away the gossip you, no doubt, heard earlier."

Henry turned to the guests and held his glass high. "A toast then," he said. "To the best kiss I've seen off-screen in a long time."

"And to Chelsea," Mr. B added with a smile. "May her name be *un*-besmirched."

Henry extended the joke and said, "Even if her lipstick is smudged," getting a wave of light laughter from the guests before they all raised a glass.

It was a miracle. I'd expected to face a group of sour scolding faces, but Mr. B turned it all around, and made the whole thing into a party joke. A stupid party joke, but thankfully, I was out of the limelight and off the hook.

Except for one thing. The most important thing. Alex hadn't thought the joke was funny. He wasn't even in the room to hear the explanation. All he knew was that I'd been wearing a sexy uniform and he'd seen me kissing Mr. B.

Moments later, it was all forgotten, and once again, I was the invisible maid, just going about doing my duties. The problem was, now I was invisible to Alex too.

Alex

It was the ass-crack of dawn when Jamison came into my office and found me crashed on my couch. He pulled on the cord, and the blinds snapped open.

"Ah, what a beautiful morning."

Throwing a bent arm up over my eyes, I groaned, "What the hell, Jamison? Are you trying to blind me?"

There was nothing cheery about the bright sunshine cutting in through the wooden slats. I hadn't really been sleeping when he came in to check phone messages for me. My mind had successfully sabotaged any attempt at sleep since I'd left Benji's shitty party.

He tugged on the cord again, brightening the room even more.

"Oh, that's just great. You *are* trying to blind me. But that's a slow torture. Just kill me now. Put me out of my misery, Jamison."

I lifted my arm enough to squint up at him. He was hovering over me now, my wrinkled tux jacket in hand. Apparently, he'd found it where I'd dropped it on the floor last night. Well, more like ripped it off and thrown it, stomped on it until it was a crumpled pile, along with my shoes, tie, cufflinks, and all the other crap I didn't give a fuck about right now, which was pretty much everything.

"The party went that well?" he asked.

"Like I said, do me a favor, put me out of my misery. There's an ice pick over there by the whiskey glasses. It'll make a nice clean wound. Aim for the heart. Everyone else has."

Jamison frowned and made a face at me. He wasn't buying my pity party.

I heaved myself up, swinging my feet to the floor, and sat with my head in my hands. "It was a fucking train wreck. A *debacle*, in your terminology."

"Mr. B always did like a show. Last time he hired a topless trapeze artist, a beautiful girl, who danced while hanging from a chandelier. After her choreography she hung upside down, while pouring the guests flutes of champagne. What was it this time?"

"This time it was him kissing Chelsea in front of all the guests."

Jamison stopped his quick dusting of my desk and tipped his head in thought. "You suspected Henry gave him the wrong impression of Chelsea."

"Well, I don't know. Now I think maybe I'm the one who got the wrong impression," I said.

My butler and closest confidante slapped down his duster on the desk and turned on me with an angry expression. "Chelsea is not like that. What's gotten into you?"

I caught my fingers in my hair and pulled. "I don't *know*. But it was so fucked up. You should've heard the rumors."

"I did," Jamison said.

I looked up. "How?"

"Honestly, you should know by now that people in service jobs all talk to each other. Mr. B's housekeeper called me this morning."

"Yeah? What'd she say?" I asked, standing up.

Jamison sniffed, "She said there were nasty rumors circulating about Chelsea, most likely started by Henry and April. But later at dinner, after the 'show,' Mr. B and Henry played it off as if the whole thing had been a practical joke."

"They did? What about Chelsea? What'd she say about Chelsea?" I hated myself for asking it, but I couldn't stop myself.

"Chelsea helped serve dinner and continued to work the rest of the evening despite any lingering doubts in her character. Do you have any idea how difficult that must have been?"

"Or maybe it proves Chelsea is just after the money," I countered.

Jamison raised his finger, ready for a full lecture like he used to give me when I was a kid, when suddenly Carrie appeared in the door.

With a smile, she walked in the room, glancing at my wrinkled jacket, now lying neatly over the back of the couch where Jamison had put it. "Or it sounds like you're just scared," she said. "Rough night? You look terrible."

My sister-in-law looked fresh and flawless in a striped sundress as she kissed Jamison on the cheek. The two of them joined forces and proceeded to present a united front against me. Well shit.

"Scared of what?" I threw my hands in the air.

"Scared that you actually care about Chelsea. Scared that she has the power to hurt you." She stood next to Jamison with her hand on her hip. "So, you've decided this is an easy way out, and you're taking it?"

"She could've stopped the rumors. She could've cleared things up with Benji. But no. She let him kiss her!" I snapped. "And it sure looked like she was enjoying it."

They both crossed their arms and sighed at me.

"You're the one who wanted her to stop working for you so that you two could date," Jamison said.

"She wanted the money," I said.

It was Carrie's turn now to throw her hands up. "Geez, Alex, she wanted to be with you *outside* of work. It's what you wanted her to choose in the first place, and it was the only way she could get the money she *needed* and be with you too."

I flopped back down on the couch feeling cornered by the two people I considered my real family. I raked my fingers through my hair and scowled. They were right. I needed to pull my head out of my ass. I needed to stop acting like a bitchy, little girl and get Chelsea back.

Chapter 43

Chelsea

I wanted to run, just get the hell out of this place, but as soon as Mr. B's housekeeper appeared at the bottom of the stairs, I forced myself to calmly walk the rest of the way.

"Your ride's here," she said with a smile. "But honestly, dear, you don't have to leave."

I took a breath, relieved that she wasn't spitting fire at me after the horrible spectacle I'd made of myself at the party. After all the sour looks shed given me last night, I'd almost expected a public hanging would be in order.

Jamison appeared in the threshold of the open door behind her, and I ran to hug him.

"Oh, Jamison. I'm so glad you came. I didn't know where to go. I just knew I couldn't stay here."

He gave a quick nod to the housekeeper and steered me toward the car.

"What about her," I glanced back at the housekeeper. "And Mr. B? Will they be angry that I left?"

"They'll get over it," he said, putting my small suitcase in the trunk of the car. Pausing, he said, "You did the right thing calling me, Chelsea." He slammed the trunk shut and smiled at me. "And besides, it just so happens my employer gave me permission to hire a head housekeeper of my own choosing," Jamison said, "and I choose you."

Jamison's words warmed my heart, but all I could manage was a feeble smile. I'd been such an idiot. I should've known better. Better about all of this. I should've done this, I should've done that. That kind of thinking always got me into trouble, and I usually thought of what I should have done when it was too late. No more. I was going to be smart now.

Once I figured out what that meant.

By the time Jamison parked his car, an impossibly small compact, next to Carrie's in the driveway, I'd gotten myself under control. Yet, the thought of the gorgeous blonde visiting Alex was enough to squeeze my heart. She'd been nice to me at the party, but probably because at that point in time, she thought I was out of the way. I bet he didn't call her a complication.

I stepped out of the car and turned to Jamison. "Are you sure this a good idea?"

"This way you can finish what you started and be with friends," Jamison said with a sniff.

"Isn't Alex going to be upset when he finds out you hired me?"

Jamison ignored my question and pulled my suitcase from the trunk. "The summer's almost over."

I took my suitcase and climbed the steps of the servants' cottage, back to my attic room. It was relief to be in my temporary home, hidden away. I dropped my suitcase and flopped on the bed. I blew out a long breath and stared at the dancing shadows of leaves on the ceiling as I rolled over my options in my mind.

I could leave Holland early, and hope Zach was serious about helping me pay for Karl's new program. Or, I could stay and work, making sure to avoid Alex every day. Or, I could march into Alex's office and tell him I was falling in love with him.

Yeah, like *that* was going to happen.

I kicked up off the bed and found a printout of the new job description Jamison had left for me on my little writing desk. I pulled up a chair and looked it over.

Head Housekeeper. My eyes ran down the page of duties. *Wow.* This was more work than I'd expected. I smiled. Jamison was generous, but from the long list of duties, I could see that this new job certainly wasn't charity. I was in charge of all the shopping, the meal planning, the linens, and Alex's schedule. It would keep me busy and keep my mind off the complications with Alex, though it didn't keep me away from him, unfortunately.

I rested my chin in my hand and looked out the window. It didn't leave much time for writing, but this was for the best. Working with Alex on the movie had been a dream come true, but I didn't feel like I'd earned my spot on his team. It seemed more like he just gave me the job as a favor, and that felt awkward because, in my mind, I hadn't deserved it.

Maybe once I was finished with this job, I could squeeze a screenwriting class into my fall schedule once I got home.

Home. Oh crap. I dug out my phone and punched in Zach's number, not sure exactly what I'd say considering how we left things the last time I saw him.

I started out trying to sound up beat and cheery. "Hey, Zach. It's Chelsea."

"I know," he said. His voice was flat, and I pulled back in confusion. "Sorry, but I don't have a lot of time to talk right now."

"Oh. Did I get the time change wrong again? Sorry, I'm so bad at that," I said.

Normally, Zach would've launched into a good-humored tirade of all the times my faulty math got us in trouble, but this time he sounded disinterested. "What do you need?"

"Need? Um…I can't just call to talk? To catch up?" I asked.

"No, that's not normally why you call."

I plopped down on the edge of my bed. "Sorry. It's just been crazy around here, and I wanted to hear a friendly voice." Something wasn't right. I could hear it in his voice. "Is everything okay? How's Karl?"

"I saw him about a week and a half ago. He's good, but he

misses you."

"A week and a half?" That was odd. Zach usually visited Karl every couple of days. He'd never stayed away this long.

"Look, Chelsea, I've been busy trying to do my own stuff," Zach said.

"I understand. It's just that Karl loves when you visit." I didn't know what to say. A knot in my throat was making it difficult to say anything. I felt like the floor was falling out from under me.

"He needs *you*. He needs his real family," Zach said, then I heard his voice catch.

"You're not real family anymore?" I asked, holding the phone with both hands. What was happening?

"No, Chelsea. I'm just a guy who lived in the same house as you for a few years. I'm not your brother. I love you and Karl, but I've got to take care of myself for a while."

"Zach, please, let's just talk about this," I started, but he cut me off.

"Maybe when you get back. Good luck, Chelsea. See you around," he said, and hung up the phone.

I dropped my phone on the bed. Without Zach to visit him, Karl would be lost in that large state-run program. *Shit*. Karl needed to be moved to Rainbow Roads as soon as possible, and there was no longer the option of asking Zach to help me.

Tears burned in my eyes, but I refused to give in to them. I needed to figure out what I was going to do.

I calculated the rate of pay Jamison had given me. If I worked weekends on top of my usual schedule, I could earn enough money to leave two weeks early. I had no choice. I would quit the screenwriting and do nothing but housework.

How was that for uncomplicated?

I stood up and changed into my white work uniform. As I buttoned up my shirt, I heard laughter and splashing in the pool. I peeked out the window and saw Alex tossing Emily up in the air and letting her splash down. I leaned to look farther and saw Carrie gracefully posed on a patio chair near the edge, smiling as she watched their water play.

It all seemed like a dream now, everything between Alex and me. All the searing, breathless kisses, all the heat of the moment tangling of fingers in each other's hair, all just a fantasy.

Alex was with his family, and soon I'd be with mine. Maybe this summer with Alex had been just a fling after all. Karl was the only important thing now, and if I worked hard, I could see him sooner than planned.

The thought of seeing my brother again, and seeing him happy in a better program, sent a flutter of hope across my chest, but it was short-lived. I wanted to forget Alex, but as I looked down at the pool again, I couldn't take my eyes off him. He was smiling, all golden and bright. I felt a stab in my heart. I still wanted him, and it hurt to know that in a couple short weeks I'd be on a plane, heading back to Oregon. Despite everything that'd happened, what I felt for him was still there. It hurt to know I'd probably leave Holland without ever telling him, always wondering if he felt the same. But it was what I had to do, and I always did what was necessary for my family.

Alex

I frowned as I saw Carrie and Jamison exchange a cryptic glance. I knew something was up. Emily swam off and I put my hands on my hips, trying to look stern, although standing in a pool, with Emily's inflatable dolphin inner tube around the waistband of my swim shorts didn't exactly stir up images of great confidence. I looked more like a freaking circus clown, but that was okay. Anything for that little girl.

Emily had insisted I try out her new pool toy, and I was

humoring her with it right before she swam off laughing and left me standing here looking like an idiot. I was pretty sure she'd planned it that way. I scowled at the stupid grinning face of the inflatable dolphin, tore off the inner tube and tossed it out of the pool.

"Jamison, is there something you want to tell me?" I asked.

Jamison feigned deafness, a habit I knew well. Carrie, on the other hand, just smiled and raised her eyebrows as the dolphin bounced on the concrete.

"Let me guess," I said. "You hired a new head housekeeper."

"You gave me full permission to do so, sir, and I thank you for letting me divide my work load," Jamison said with a sniff.

"So you hired Chelsea, didn't you," I said, wading to the edge of the pool.

Again, Jamison pretended not to hear me and handed me a towel. I snatched it from his hands with a snap. His attitude was ticking me off, and Carrie wasn't helping.

I hoisted myself out of the water from the edge of the pool, forgoing the steps, and confronted Carrie trying to give her my best stern look. "And you were in on this idea?"

Carrie rolled her eyes at me. Obviously, I didn't intimidate her at all.

"Anyone could have told you Chelsea wouldn't stay at Benji's, not after last night. So, it only made sense..." She waved her hand in the air as if I were a dumbass for being so dense.

Why was I always left out of the loop? I knew they had my best interest at heart, but seriously? I turned to Jamison. "This *is* my house, you know. You could clue me in once in a while…wait, Chelsea's here already, isn't she?" I asked. Now I gave Jamison my stern look. "Jamison?"

I wasn't ready to see Chelsea and face up to what I'd said to her. I'd acted like a dick last night, and Carrie was right. I was falling in love with Chelsea. That's why I'd acted the way

I had. I was hurt. Vulnerable. I wanted to push her away. Now, this morning, my actions came back to kick me in the ass, and I was embarrassed all over again. Would she even accept an apology? Chelsea was proud and independent, and I'd gone above and beyond in being an ass.

Just the idea that Chelsea was inside the house made my heart leap. *Shit*. I didn't want a clean break. I didn't want her out of my life. No, I wanted to hold her, kiss her. Tell her that I loved her. But first, I needed to apologize. No more talking about the movie or my life. I needed to be with her. For real.

I just hoped she wanted to be with me too.

I strode toward the house going over what to say to her. In all honesty, I didn't remember exactly what I'd said the night before. All I knew was that I'd doubted her. *Ouch*. I'd told her it was clear she cared for nothing but money. *Dumbass*. And then I'd walked away before she even had time to explain. The memory roiled in my stomach as I opened the kitchen door.

"Chelsea!" I said, surprised to find her at the kitchen island.

She looked up from the list she was writing, and then jumped off her stool. "Sorry, I'll get out of your way." She wouldn't look me in the eye.

As she darted around the large kitchen island, I cut her off, and she almost bumped against my bare chest. I saw her cheeks redden, but she still refused to look me in the eyes. I held out my arms, wanting nothing more than to wrap her in a hug, and tell her what an ass I was, but when she saw my movement she turned to flee.

"Wait, please. I hear you're our new head housekeeper." I blurted out. That sounded really stupid, but it at least stopped her.

Her eyes finally met mine, and I saw exactly what I expected: pride, determination. And now, a wall between us. What I didn't see was the shinning glow of excitement that she used to have when she'd looked at me. What we'd had was gone.

"Oh…well…yes. Jamison hired me," she said. "He said it

was okay with you."

"I hope it won't keep you too busy," I said, trying to move closer to her again.

She moved back, edging toward the door. "It's more responsibility, but don't worry, I plan to make it my complete focus."

"But you'll still have time to work on your screenwriting and the movie, right?" I asked, desperate for something that would give us a connection.

Her gaze hardened and she pulled her shoulders back. "No. I don't think so. I wasn't ready for it anyway, and I'm sure your team will appreciate not having to babysit a newbie like me while they work."

The wall was solid. She didn't want anything else from me. There were so many things I wanted to say, but it was too late, and I didn't blame her.

"Well, I know Jamison is glad you've decided to spend the rest of the summer here," I said, unable to say *we* because it hurt too much.

Despite her new attitude, I couldn't give up. I was going to fix things between us, I just didn't know how, yet. All I knew was I didn't have much time, and letting her go without a fight wasn't an option anymore.

Chapter 44

Chelsea

I tried my best to avoid Alex and it should've been easy once I decided to write out his schedule and make it available via email and in several rooms in the house. Many households were run by a butler, and the other servants rarely saw their employer.

Except Alex wouldn't let it go.

He demanded I be the one to bring him breakfast daily. He claimed it was because he wanted his head housekeeper to keep him in the loop, and he also wanted to review the menu choices. I started to suspect it was so he could torture me since we often met poolside, with him fresh out of the water, naked as a jaybird.

At least this time, he'd put on a pair of shorts before reviewing the schedule and planning the week's meals. But still, it wasn't easy staring at him shirtless, his powerful chest and ripped abs still glistening with water.

After the party at Mr. B's, Alex had seemed genuinely sorry for the things he said to me, but I refused to let myself think about what that meant. I didn't want to go down that path again. I tried to stay on task, but every time I did he pulled the conversation over to my personal life.

A life I needed to get back to.

"Good morning, Chelsea. Have a seat."

It was one of my last days at work, and I just wanted to go over the schedule and get on with my duties. We barely got past the pleasantries when he jumped right into my personal life, as usual.

"Summer's almost over." He leaned forward in his chair smiling. "I'm going to miss our morning meetings."

I nearly went weak in the knees when he smiled at me, but I had to remember, that in the past, wishful thinking had gotten me nothing but heartache. I'd lost Zach because of that wishful thinking.

"Yes, it is beautiful out here by the pool. The gardens, the roses…" I waved a hand around the patio area. "I'm going to miss this too." I couldn't look at him. "Oregon's nothing like this."

He glanced down at the patio table, then back up to me and said, "I suppose your brother, Karl, and your boyfriend will be glad that you're coming home soon."

"My boyfriend?"

"Yeah, what's his name, Zach?" Alex asked.

"He's definitely *not* my boyfriend, remember?"

"Bullshit." The word came out flat, but not cruel.

I gaped at him with wide eyes. "He's my adopted brother…though he's decided he doesn't even want to be that anymore." My throat tightened as I leaned back in the chair.

"Because he wants to be your boyfriend." Alex mirrored my position. "Get a clue, Chelsea. He made it abundantly clear when he visited. You'd have to be blind not to see it. You mean to tell me it didn't come up while you were touring The Hague?"

"It did, but I told him, I told him...it's none of your business," I said as I stood up. I didn't want to talk about Zach.

"I bet he didn't like hearing that," Alex said, smiling up at me.

"Not him. *You*. It's none of *your* business." I folded my arms. "Zach is not my boyfriend. I don't have one."

"You had me," Alex said softly. He stood up and came toward me.

"What I had was an employer who took advantage," I said, balling my hands into fists.

He recoiled and said, "Is that how you saw it?"

"How else was I supposed to see it?" My voice went up in pitch as heat rushed to my face. Why did he still want to do this? Sure, I was here, easily available, but it wasn't like he didn't have other options. Carrie was here all the time.

"I asked you to quit being my employee and stay here as my guest. I wanted you…" Alex said, reaching out a hand.

I snatched my arm away and hissed, "You knew I needed the money. It was an easy out for you!"

I wiped angrily at the hot tear that rolled down my cheek. I didn't want our last days together to be like this, me a crying heartbroken mess. I just wanted to go home and try to piece together some sort of a life.

"I didn't want an out. I wanted you," Alex pleaded, raising his voice.

"Yeah, and when I took the job with Mr. B so we could be together, you wanted nothing to do with me," I said. "You suspected the worst of me. Now that I'm here under your roof again, now you're suddenly interested in me again. Am I just an object for you to play with?" My voice cracked.

"That's what you think?" Alex asked, his voice quiet again. "You think I only want you because you're here?"

"I don't know." I threw my hands in the air. "You keep telling me you hate complications, that I complicate things for you. So let's keep it simple. You're the boss. I'm your employee, and there's nothing else."

I swallowed hard. I couldn't catch my breath around all the unsaid things that were choking me.

Alex was silent.

I needed to stop talking before I made things worse. I looked down at the weekly planner I held in my hand and tapped my ink pen against its hard cover. How could I tell him that I loved him? How could I admit I was the foolish girl that tried to make a summer fling into a fairytale? How could I say any of it when it hadn't been real? Instead, I closed the planner notebook, turned, and walked away.

The next morning, I forced myself out to the pool for our regular breakfast meeting, planner in hand, but Alex wasn't there. I'd expected to see him sitting at the patio table looking handsome and enticing as ever, wrapped in his usual swimming towel. Jamison joined me after a few minutes, carrying what looked like a hand-written note on a white paper in his hand.

"He's gone," he announced.

I stood there squinting at him in the sun, at a loss for words. I couldn't believe what I was hearing. I guess he really was done with me.

"The filming licenses came through and he's gone to the U.S. to start the reshoots," Jamison said, sinking into the patio chair across from me. "He had to go. The reduced fees were contingent on him filming there on location."

"So he had to leave last night? Without telling anyone, not even you?" I asked, raising an eyebrow.

Jamison shrugged.

I slumped back into my chair and stared down at my lap. I felt awful. This was all my fault. Alex had fired April on my account, lost the financing for his movie, and then all the other shit had happened. I hadn't even had the guts to tell him how I'd felt. The funny thing was, I'd thought I would be the one leaving. And now I didn't even get to say good-bye.

Stupid. But who was I kidding? I knew a real love affair with him was impossible. I'd never be the woman he was looking for, even if things between him and Carrie were over.

I exhaled a deep breath. "I didn't see that one coming."

Jamison looked at me puzzled. "You what?"

I waved a hand at him and rubbed my hand across my

brow. "Oh, nothing."

Jamison brightened and said, "You'll be leaving soon, too. You're probably glad to return to your home after, well…that is…your help around here will be missed greatly."

My contract was up in a week, and I was due to start classes again in three weeks. Summer was almost over, but I couldn't help feeling like it was more than just the season that was ending. Everything had changed.

"And you'll be joining Alex in the States?" I asked, already missing my friend.

Jamison smiled and said, "Yes, but let's not talk about that. Instead, let's talk about the going away present I got you."

"No, don't be silly. I owe you," I said, but Jamison shook his head and handed me a folded letter. I thought it was just another sheet of Alex's note to him, but now I could see it was typed, and on company letterhead.

"You loved screenwriting, and I don't blame you for turning down Alex's writing tasks, but I didn't want you to drop it completely," Jamison said.

I opened the letter and read it. It was an acceptance form from an Oregon production company, outlining my position as a production assistant with additional scene rewrites and screenwriting opportunities. It was a ground floor position for very little money, but it was my own door into the film industry.

"Jamison, you dear man…" I was practically jumping up and down. "You sent them my resume?"

"Of course I did."

Then, with a wide smile, he added, "Along with some of the pages you wrote for Alex. And my wholehearted recommendation."

"You sly old fox. I love you," I squealed with joy and for a moment, I thought I actually saw the butler's pasty white cheeks blush with color. "Next Generation Cinema." I read the company name off the paper, already feeling waves of excitement. "I don't recognize this production company. I'll have to go look it up. This is great! Thank you, Jamison. I don't know how I can thank you enough."

"Just do me a favor one of these days," Jamison said.

"Anything." I asked.

He leaned forward and said, "Go home and take care of your brother, but also take care of yourself." He tapped a finger on the letter, now laying on the patio table and said, "This is just one thing you wanted. I'm asking you to figure out what else you really want, and then grab onto it. You deserve it."

I sat back down, my smile disappearing. "It's too late for that, I'm afraid. I've already let it slip through my fingers."

"Maybe not," he said, leaning forward. "Listen, Chelsea, dear, I just want you to make sure, if you ever have another opportunity, you don't let *anything* get in your way."

From the morning of that quiet breakfast, the summer unwound quickly. I helped Jamison close up that beautiful house, and when he drove me to the airport, all he needed to do was lock the doors, and hand the keys over to the maintenance company. I hugged Jamison goodbye, and laughed when his stiff formality melted for just long enough to hug me back.

"You know where I'll be…at college. I'll leave you my dorm address." I told Jamison. "Maybe we can meet up stateside. Where are you going to be?"

He smiled, but didn't answer my question. "Have a good flight, Chelsea. I'll miss you. I'll see you again some day, but until then, keep your chin up."

I left Jamison standing in the terminal of the airport as I headed to check in for my long flight home. I turned back for one last goodbye wave, but he was already gone, just like the rest of the summer.

I fell asleep on the plane, and when I woke up, it was hard

to convince myself that Holland hadn't been just one long, complicated dream.

Chapter 45

Alex

Portland, Oregon, was turning out to be the ideal place to produce a feature film. The state supported its own film industry, and because I'd chosen to film on location here, the local chapter of the film board helped round out my crew. They'd even found this comfortable Craftsman house for me to rent only a few blocks away from our production offices.

The rented house was nothing compared to my home in Holland, but it was cozy, all warm hardwood and cheerful corners. Outside, the rain pattered on a quiet neighborhood street, but two short blocks away was a great run of restaurants, coffee shops, and other interesting hotspots.

Jamison appeared in the door to the kitchen, still looking befuddled due to jet lag. After his long flight, I'd given him a couple days off to adjust to the new time zone, but he still struggled. There wasn't much for a butler to do around this small house; nonetheless, he was up early and ready to work.

"The only thing that helps jet lag is following the new schedule," he said, suppressing a yawn.

"You need some coffee my friend. That's the magic cure for jet lag. Come." I waved a hand at the empty chair next to me at the kitchen table. "Have a seat. I'll pour."

Jamison obliged with a small smile turning up the corners of his mouth. "Well, I suppose you're right. Though I prefer tea, I believe coffee is in order this morning." He gave a small laugh. "Who knows. I might grow accustomed to drinking coffee now that I'm in the States."

"When in Rome…" I smiled, glad to see him in a good mood and glad to have him with me for the duration of the movie shoot.

I brought the coffee pot to the table and poured him a cup, then placed the carafe back in the coffee maker. I slid into my chair eager to hear what news he had about Chelsea. I knew I could count on Jamison to fill me in, even if I didn't ask specifically.

"So, tell me everything that I missed, Jamison," I said. I picked up my cup and leaned back in my chair waiting to hear all the news. "And tell me *everything*. Don't leave anything out."

He lowered his white porcelain coffee cup to the table and opened his mouth to speak, then he stopped. His eyes darted to the window and back to me. "It certainly does rain here a lot."

I laughed. "I kinda like the rain. It makes it easier to be inside working."

Jamison continued sipping his coffee and said, "Luckily, you don't have many outdoor shots in your rewrite."

"Yes, Chelsea's idea about keeping the movie to one location was brilliant," I said. I tried dropping her name hoping he'd take the bait and spill it about Chelsea. She was what I really wanted to hear about, and I knew that he knew it.

"Speaking of brilliant choices," Jamison began. My heartbeat picked up. Finally. Now he'd tell me about Chelsea.

"Your father finally decided to break things off with April. Seems she was a bit clingy and demanding."

"No." I feigned shock. "Not April."

"Henry couldn't keep up with her."

Suddenly, an image of how that must've played out popped into my mind. "Ha! Serves the old dog right," I laughed. "Though I have to say, he has balls. That break-up must have been one epic scene."

Jamison nodded. "She tried to burn down his house. I

wouldn't be surprised if you hear from him soon. How many rooms does this house have?"

"What the hell? Wait a minute. Back up. She did what?" I shook my head. *Unbelievable.* "Never mind, don't tell me any more. I've had it up to here with that woman. I really don't need to hear any more about April Look-at-me-Temple."

"Well, anyway, I'm sure Henry will love this house. It's big enough for three."

"Oh, no. He is definitely not staying here. I'll bet you a hundred bucks that April will hound him across continents before she's done being a woman scorned. And I don't want her anywhere near me, or my movie. No, Henry is stuck with April. He can stay away. Even continents don't provide enough distance for my comfort."

Jamison smiled, and let the escapades of April drop to a silent lull in the conversation. I waited patiently, hoping he'd bring up Chelsea next. Her name practically hung in the air as we both sipped on our coffee. Finally, I couldn't stand it any longer. I had to say something, though I tried to sound nonchalant.

"So how was closing up the house? Did Chelsea stay to help?" I asked.

Jamison's nose tipped a little higher and he sniffed. "Our head housekeeper was indispensable. I was sad to see her go."

"So you sent her off safe? She's home?"

"You can find out for yourself. Portland State University is only a few miles from here," Jamison said.

"I can't do that. I don't want Chelsea to get the wrong idea," I said even though it killed me to do it.

"Yes, yes, it's much better leaving her to assume you used her and then left," Jamison said as he stood. "Excuse me, sir, but I have a new household to bring up to standards."

"Hey, wait, Jamison…wait," I jumped to my feet and reached out a hand, but he stalked out the door, clearly annoyed with me.

Jamison was rubbing it in to make a point. I'd been an ass and the thought that Chelsea was a stone's throw away was killing me. Just the thought of her proximity was enough to start my nerves buzzing. But I wasn't sure how to proceed without botching things up.

Again.

I wanted her to get back to her real life and put her summer maid work behind her. Maybe then, when we met again, we'd be on equal ground. I'd always seen her as an equal even though I'd acted like an entitled son of a bitch.

One thing I knew for sure. This time, I wouldn't hesitate. I'd find a way to tell her exactly how I feel about her.

My phone rang and I grabbed it. "Yeah, Matthew…"

"Mr. Silverhaus, it's Matthew, your secretary."

"Yes, Matthew, I know. Your name comes up on my screen when you call. You can call me Alex. Remember?" I asked, trying not to smile at his eager nerves. "Anyway, am I late?"

"No, but a few of the new team members are here early so you can meet them before the meeting starts."

"Sure thing. I'll be there in ten minutes," I said.

I poured the rest of my coffee into a travel mug, found an umbrella, and headed out the door. Half way down the block my heart stopped two steps before my feet. A woman with long black hair stood on the corner in front of me. I couldn't see her face under her red umbrella, but my heart started to pound anyway.

I swore I'd tell Chelsea that I loved her the minute I saw her. For a second, I imagined it really was her, that I'd be telling her right here on this street corner. Could it be a coincidence? Fate?

The crosswalk light changed and the woman tipped her umbrella back as she stepped off the curb. It wasn't Chelsea. I was so thrown off that I missed the walk light and had to wait in the pouring rain for the next one.

I looked at my watch and scowled. If I didn't have to meet the new team members, I could detour closer to campus. There I'd have a better chance of running into Chelsea. The light changed and I shook myself. So much for my idea of being patient and letting her get settled. I needed to stop this. I was acting like a crazed stalker, ready to jump out at her on the street and probably give her a horrible shock. I couldn't be sidetracked now. I had a meeting, but my mind was already buzzing with plans for a campus tour later.

I reached the office and rushed inside. Matthew leapt up to take my umbrella.

"I set up the new team members in the back conference room with coffee and a plate of bagels and Danish," he said, handing me a list. "Who would you like to see first?"

I nodded and said, "How about the production assistant?"

Matthew disappeared to call in the person for the first interview as I opened the door to my office. I walked around the wide desk checking my cell phone for any new messages. I settled into my leather chair. Just as I swiveled around to face the door, my eyes popped wide and my jaw dropped as Chelsea walked through the door.

Chelsea

I rubbed my sweaty palms down the fabric of my skirt and looked up to see Alex looking as shocked as I was.

"I had nothing to do with this!" he blurted out.

I quickly spun around to close the door. When I turned back around my head was spinning and my heart was leaping out of my chest. I leaned against the door unable to speak. What the hell was going on?

"Chelsea, seriously, I didn't have anything to do with this." Alex stood and pinched a finger and thumb to the bridge of his nose as if to clear his head. "Wait. That didn't sound right. It wasn't the first thing I wanted to say if I ever saw you again."

"Looks like Jamison set us up," I said, still with my back glued to the door. I tried to laugh it off, but I wasn't finding this funny at all.

Alex stepped out from behind his desk and took a tentative step in my direction, then apparently changed his mind and came to the center of the room. "If you knew Next Generation Cinema was my production company you probably never would've come, right?"

"Well…no, I wouldn't have. Let's just say, you and I don't have the best track record of working together," I said.

My cheeks heated as I thought of what we *did* do well together. Despite everything, my body still sizzled at the sight of Alex. I'd thought I'd never see him again, and here he was, like there'd been no time lapse between us.

Tearing my eyes away from him I looked around the room, desperate to find something, *anything* else to focus on. Then an enchanting photograph hanging on the wall behind his desk caught my eye. It'd been enlarged to the size of a painting. It was all soft greens and bright blue sky, just how I remembered the secret grove. The tall ring of trees, the long, soft grass, and the dome of sky above us. Without any preparation at all, I was facing a stunning photograph of the first place we ever made love.

I wondered if he thought about that as much as I did. When I'd been in in Holland, I'd been so worried about the way he viewed me, so worried that I was being naive, or letting myself be taken advantage of that I'd let it overshadow how good we were together. But after hours on the long plane ride with nothing to do but think, and Clara's unstoppable questions when I got home, now all the good things between us seemed so obvious, and the rest was unimportant.

Oh, god. I was still in love with him. The realization hit with a flutter in my stomach and another wave of dizziness.

I blinked and swallowed hard. "Um…what did you want to say to me?"

As if lost in a fog himself, Alex ran a hand through his

hair, and then turned to look at me. "What?" he asked.

"You said you had something you wanted to say when you saw me again, and you haven't said it yet."

Alex moved back and leaned against his desk, crossing his arms with a smile. His eyes didn't leave my face, and it seemed for a moment that he was lost in staring at me. Then he snapped out of it, and said, "Ah, yes. How's Karl?"

Yeah, I doubted that was the question. His deflection somehow made me feel steadier, and I made it across the office to stand behind one of the chairs facing his wide desk.

"Karl's fine. Actually he's great." I relaxed and smiled back.

"So he got into Rainbow Roads?" Alex asked. "I Googled it when I got to Portland. It looks like a great program, but wow, the price…pretty expensive."

I smiled. "Yes, it is but I got lucky."

Alex gave me a hopeful smile, one eyebrow quirked up suggestively.

"They helped me find a scholarship for Karl because of his interest in working with the National Parks. All the money I earned in Holland is now in a fund to pay for his future in the program."

"What do you know? So you didn't need the job after all," he said, the corners of his mouth curving into a smile. "But hey, I'm glad it worked out."

The job. Right. I stood there gripping the leather back of the chair. I remembered the first day of the job. Alex had ignited a spark when I'd stepped through the door, and now, it was happening all over again. One minute in the same room with him, and I was right back to where I'd been when we'd first met. His infectious smile turned the temperature higher and I had to look away to get control again. But when I did, I noticed a framed photograph of Carrie and Emily on his desk.

Right. Just the dose of reality I needed to cool me down. Why would their photograph be so prominent on his desk unless, Alex was back together with his family? If he and Carrie weren't together, wouldn't he have just had a picture of

Emily?

I pushed away from the chair and edged back toward the door. I tried to sound casual, but I stammered, "H...how's Carrie and Emily?"

"Good," Alex said with a wide smile. "They'll be coming to visit in a few weeks."

"That's good...I mean, great!" I said, waving a hand in the air. "I'm sure Emily's glad her parents are back together."

Alex's jaw dropped and he couldn't manage a sound for at least twenty seconds. "Parents? As in, me and Carrie?" He let out a short laugh. "You thought I was married?"

I glared at him. "Well I don't see what's so funny about that. But yeah, divorced, I assumed, and reconciled now." I hoped I didn't sound as stupid as I thought I did.

Alex let out a huge breath and said, "Carrie's my sister-in-law, Chelsea. She was married to my brother. Emily's my niece."

All the air went out of me. What?

"So you're not getting back together with your ex...a wife, a girlfriend or anything like that?" I asked, fumbling to grab the back of the chair again.

"Hell no, I've never been married," Alex said, standing up with a wide smile. He looked down at me. "You mean all this time you thought I was married to Carrie? What on earth made you think that?"

I bit my lip, then said, "Well, the way you two acted around each other, always hugging, and so glad to see each other...and Emily, she drew that picture of you guys, and you played with her so well, like a really good dad...oh, geez, a really good uncle."

It was all clear to me now. My preconceived notions had colored everything I'd seen. All the times Alex played with Emily in the pool, tossing her into the water, it looked like what a dad would do with his daughter. But it was nothing more than what a loving sibling would do for his deceased brother's family.

My heart was bursting. Alex was even more amazing than

I'd thought. He was the most wonderful man I'd ever met, and I'd blown it. I lowered my head, blinking hard to keep back the tears. I was such an idiot.

Alex stepped close, took my hands and tipped his head down to catch my eyes. His voice was soft as he spoke, "Can I tell you what I wanted to say to you now?"

Afraid to speak for fear of making an even bigger fool of myself, I just kept my eyes on his and nodded.

"I love you, Chelsea," he said. His fingers tightened around mine. "I love you."

My lips parted, my entire body warming as my heart melted. Finally, I managed to get the words out, "I love you too, Alex. I have right from the start."

Alex's grin widened as he beamed. "So do you still want the job?"

"Job?" I asked. I shook my head. "All I want is you."

I threw my arms around his neck as he pulled me into a deep kiss. If I hadn't known better, I would've thought my feet had left the ground. Being in Alex's arms was where I was supposed to be. My world was complete. My brother was living in Rainbow Roads. I was starting my last year of college, and I had a killer job lined up as a PA. Zach was being less of an asshole. But most importantly, Alex was mine.

Who'd have ever thought that one indecent encounter, arranged through a dubious website, would result in me finding love, happiness, and Alex Silverhaus, the man of my dreams. I couldn't have written a movie script about this if I'd tried. What Shakespeare had written years ago was still true today, "All the world's a stage, and all the men and women merely players…" Put in modern terminology, my life was like a movie...

A movie with a happy ending—for now.

- La Fin -

Note from the author: Many readers have asked me what happens next to Alex and Chelsea, so I've decided to write an exclusive free bonus novella for my subscribers, called "After Indecent Encounter". Be sure you are on my email list so I can send it to you as soon as I'm done.

Acknowledgement

First, I would like to thank all of my readers. Without you, my books would not exist. I truly appreciate each and every one of you.

A big "thanks" goes out to all the Facebook fans, street team, beta readers, and advanced reviewers. You are a HUGE part of the success of the series.

I have to thank my PA, Shannon Hunt. Without you my life would be a complete and utter mess. Also a big "thank you" goes out to my editor Lynette and my wonderful cover designer, Sinisa. You make my ideas and writing look so good.

About The Author

M. S. Parker is a USA Today Bestselling author and the author of the Erotic Romance series, Club Privè and Chasing Perfection.

Living in Las Vegas, she enjoys sitting by the pool with her laptop writing on her next spicy romance.

Growing up all she wanted to be was a dancer, actor or author. So far only the latter has come true but M. S. Parker hasn't retired her dancing shoes just yet. She is still waiting for the call for her to appear on Dancing With The Stars.

When M. S. isn't writing, she can usually be found reading– oops, scratch that! She is always writing.

Made in United States
North Haven, CT
10 October 2024